SEDUCING DARKNESS

Psychic Justice Book 4

ERIN RICHARDS

www.ErinRichards.com

SEDUCING DARKNESS
Erin Richards

Print ISBN: 978-1943800100
Digital ISBN: 978-1943800094

Cover Designer: Robin Harper @ Wicked by Design

Editor: Hot Tree Editing

Praise for
Chasing Shadows
Psychic Justice Book 1

"I loved this book and it never faltered from its action and suspense. The story line not only kept my attention but each chapter was suspenseful trying to find out what the kidnapper was going to do and how Juliana would deal with it." ~*Night Owl Reviews* (NOR 5-Star Top Pick)

"This story was masterfully written and illustrates just what a frightfully good imagination the author has to work with." ~*Fallen Angel Reviews* (5-Star Recommended Read)

"A whirlwind of emotions, twists, turns and rediscovered love will keep you breathless!" ~*Fresh Fiction*

"The suspense will keep you turning the pages... The characters are complex and well-developed and there is never a dull moment in the story. If you love your romance with suspense, this is one book you need to read! 5 stars all the way!" ~*The Romance Reviews*

BOOKS BY
ERIN RICHARDS

Psychic Justice Series
Chasing Shadows, Book 1
Twilight Rising, Book 2
Stealing Twilight, Book 3
Seducing Darkness, Book 4

Forbidden Legacy Series
Forbidden Thirteen, Book 1

Wicked Paradise

Young Adult
Vigilante Nights
Dragonfly Nightmare
Bittersweet Wreckage

SEDUCING DARKNESS

CHAPTER ONE

A very drought *intolerant* rain slashed the windows as the plane decelerated on the runway at San Jose International Airport.

"Are you kidding me?" Marisa Meadows muttered at the splattered window. *I may not be the wicked witch—or wicked psychic—of the west, but I seriously melt in rain. It's the reason I live in San Diego and why I refuse to own an umbrella.* Since when did wet stuff fall from the sky in San Jose in October anyway?

Since when did coming home to San Jose irritate her so much? And she used the term "home" loosely.

Marisa plucked the sleeve of her thin pullover sweater and grimaced. Maybe the rain promised to erase the sense of evil riding her back for the last few months, or the sense something had set up residence in her body. An alien lifeform otherwise known as her alter ego—Evil Eddie.

Rain, sunshine, or evil, San Jose promised a respite from the senseless malevolence while she stepped in as assistant counsel at depositions for her law firm's top client and also caught up with her best friend, Lily Falbrooke. Marisa had not spent nearly enough time consoling Lily after her father's recent death and the entire upheaval of Lily's life from San Diego to San Jose.

The sensation of eyes trailing her as she disembarked the plane and walked into the terminal sent ants scampering up her spine. *What the what is wrong with me?* As a telepath, she read minds. She wasn't an empath who sensed emotions and feelings. Was she gaining a shift in her psychic makeup, or did she possess awakening abilities? *No. No way in a frozen hell.*

Telepathy already topped the list of her undesirable traits from the men she dated. Once she discovered he'd never get past the fact that she was a self-dependent lawyer and made a crapton more money than he did, she kicked him to the curb. No matter what men *said*, they hated it when their wives or girlfriends surpassed them in the dollar department. At least that particular trait encompassed the bottom-feeding men still living in the 1950s she seemed to attract. Thank the psychic gods for her ability to read minds, both a blessing and an epic curse as a rare psychic with the ability to drill past blocked minds... when her curiosity killed the cat. If she had to feel their emotions *and* read them, she may as well join a convent and strap on a chastity belt.

Ignoring the external and internal cacophony galloping through her head, Marisa stepped out of the way of the horde of people pouring off the plane near a support beam. Careful not to touch anything, she fished hand sanitizer from her purse and rubbed a hefty dollop between her fingers and under her nails to kill the plane cooties. As she finagled the sanitizer back into her purse, the strap slipped off her arm. The overstuffed purse thunked onto the tile floor and a nudge from behind jostled her funny bone against the beam. *Oww.*

"Watch it," she growled out, hating airports and reckless people who invaded her personal bubble. She wheeled around in time to spy a midheight, slender man disappear into the crowd with her purse under his arm. "Hey!" she screamed. "He stole my purse!" Frantic, she grabbed her briefcase to give chase, and stumbled in her high heels, slamming her shoulder into the beam. "Son of a cursed psychic."

Evil vibes washed goose flesh across her arms, and the fleeing man earned her darkest glare as she lurched forward. Strong arms embraced her from behind, preventing her faceplant into a spiky palm probably weeping at the near miss to suck the blood from her face.

"Miss, are you all right?"

Without facing the source of the velvety baritone behind her, she said, "A man in a black windbreaker with thinning blond hair just filched my purse." She pointed in the direction the thief had taken down the concourse, still able to spy his distinctive pale hair among the throng of people.

The man propped her against the beam, dumped his shoulder bag beside her carry-on, and weaved down the concourse after the thief, leaving her admiring his tall, well-toned body encased in a navy pinstripe suit and his flawlessly layered deep-brown hair.

Marisa's mind refused to shut down and the random thoughts of passing people filtered in, creating an incomprehensible jumble. Telepathy had both pros and cons.

"Ma'am, do you need assistance?" An airport police officer approached, his mind going all caveman. He assessed her long, board-straight hair he wanted tickling his abdomen while her raspberry lips encircled his dick and he pinched the nipples of her "melons" into bullets.

Can't get a real job on the streets, rent-a-mall-cop? Trolling the airport for a blow-up doll? Marisa waggled her head, a catlike smile curving her lips. "Officer Radisson." She nodded at his name tag and covered her nose from the cheap cologne he marinated in. "Some jackass assaulted me and ran off with my purse." She flicked her hand in the direction the thief and his pursuer traveled. "Drag your mind out of the gutter and do your job," she murmured just loud enough for him to catch a word or two. *Like I said, pros and cons.*

Red-faced, Officer Radisson unhooked his radio off his shoulder, took her information, and radioed for backup. He licked his lips, his attention riveted on her boobs, AKA melons. "Miss Meadows, I'll stay with you until we've apprehended the thief. Do you want me to escort you to airport security?" *Man, I'd love to get me a piece of her ass.* His internal monologue killed the clutter in her head.

And I'd love to shove a stick up your ass and turn you into a lollipop. Marisa shrugged back her shoulders, her intangible claws poking out of her fingertips. When she opened her mouth to rip him a new one, she spied her savior jogging toward them, her black purse clenched against his heavenly flat abs accentuated under his designer dress shirt.

Panting, he halted in front of her, a wide smile stretching his full, sensuous lips into the broad-shouldered, slender model territory of high cheekbones and honey-tan skin, sporting a light dusting of beard and mustache. A tiny network of crow's feet fanned the corners of his piercing pale-green eyes. Strong and meticulous fingers gave testament to white-collar work, which seemed apt for his expensive suit fitting him to a divine T.

Marisa slurped up the metaphysical drool of desire cruising down her chin. His bare ring finger booted him squarely into her playpen. Kittens and puppies could rain down upon San Jose if it produced specimens of the male species like her knight in shining Armani armor. Although he appeared ten years older than her twenty-nine, much older than the twits she dated, she'd do him in a nanosecond. Time to dump the boys and date up in the real-man pool. To top off his growing list of attributes, his mind was so blank, permanent ink refused to stick, his walls so thick her mental crowbar was powerless to penetrate them. Unable to remember the last time she'd met a man with impenetrable walls, Marisa almost dripped into a puddle of bliss. *Having her purse stolen was so worth it.* Maybe he carried an umbrella too.

"You're my savior. My purse carries my entire life." The moment she touched her leather bag, more evil vibes jumped ship and skulked up her arm. Voices elevated, joining a dim melody playing in her mind, both trying to deafen her. Dizzy, her knees weakened and stars flirted with her vision. Her fingers lost their hold on her purse and she listed forward into her handsome savior's outstretched arms. The voices faded into the strange melody and darkness ate the flickering stars.

❦

Awakening, Marisa found herself lying on a row of plastic airport seats, her head and shoulders nestled on the strong thighs of a stranger in navy pinstriped pants. Her bleary eyes cleared on the handsome stranger's face from her dreams. *Dream? No. Freaking reality.*

"Oh. My. God." Blocking the weird elevator music repeating in her ears, she struggled to sit up. "Did I pass out?" The snatch-and-run theft hit her memory. The security guard rushed over with an airport medic. "How long was I out?" She avoided the whispers and stares, focused on the blood-red flowers fluttering in a breeze, the cascading waterfall, and lush rainforest hills surrounding the field of flowers in her mind's haven.

"Few moments," Mr. Handsome said in a silky, suave

voice. "Are you okay?"

"I... yes. The peanuts on the plane didn't do much for my blood sugar." What else caused her to conk out? She didn't pass out... ever. *What the hell?*

He helped her sit up, and the medic handed her a bottle of water and chalky sugar tablets. Once assured she wasn't going to die, the medic left and airport security took a report from the stranger. Feeling her blood sugar fluctuate, she wolfed down the tablets and a protein bar from her purse.

"The thief gave up, dropped the handbag, and took off. I lost him in the terminal." Mr. Handsome waved the security man off.

"I can't thank you enough." Marisa gripped his arm, stared at her purse plunked on the floor near her foot. She feared touching it. "I owe you big time."

His wide smile lit up gold flecks in his eyes. "It was my pleasure to help a beautiful damsel in distress."

The heebie-jeebies began a slow creep over her skin, stemming from the "damsel in distress" bit. Jeez, she hated men who treated women beneath them, and the idiotic damsel line sat at the top of her shit list. *Well, you were a stupid damsel in distress. That'll teach you to wear high heels when traveling.* "Well, I appreciate it, and for catching me when I fell. I should've just stayed in bed this morning." Avoiding his strange allure, she straightened her sweater. With his hand on her elbow, he stood with her.

"I feel fine now, really." She eased out of his uncomfortable grip.

He retrieved her bag. Hesitantly, she looped the strap over her shoulder. Nothing happened and she swallowed a prickle of panic.

Without another word, he snagged her briefcase and his own carry-on and said, "I'd like to escort you to your transport. By the way, my name's Kenneth. My friends call me Kenny."

"Am I a friend?" Marisa laughed, fighting an unnatural blush. She never blushed! *Stupid blood sugar levels.* She waited for a clearing in the crowd and stepped into the foot traffic.

"I'd like you to be." He grinned, his magnetism sucking her in again. "Only if you want, of course."

"Let's cut to the chase. What kind of friend?" Shyness wasn't a natural word in her personal dictionary.

He leaned toward her. "Whatever kind of friend you'd like." He swept his hand forward. "I have a driver waiting who'll take you wherever your heart desires. I know a great place if you're available to get better acquainted." He held up his hand and chuckled. "Totally public. Great steaks."

Shaken six ways to Sunday, Marisa practically trotted toward the escalator. Glad to relinquish the task, she let Kenny carry her briefcase. Heck, he already believed her damsel in distress act. "Thank you, but I have a car waiting. I'm here on business and visiting a friend. I really must get going. Raincheck?" Lily had no clue Marisa planned to surprise her. Lily was way more important than dallying with potential husband material, even if he seriously sported a rare empty mind, which remained to be seen and tested. Otherwise, she could only offer a causal fling while in town.

"By all means, Marisa Mae Meadows. We *will* meet again."

Marisa skipped a step. She hadn't told him her name. Wait, she gave her name to the security guard. No. Not her middle name. Disorder set up a table at her emotional fair. Warily, she scrutinized his chiseled face and touchable, silky hair. Genuine affection and warmth darkened his eyes, offering something she hadn't felt from a man in too many blue moons. Without a second thought, she whipped out her business card with her cell number scrawled on the back.

CHAPTER TWO

Ric McAllister slogged through the Psychic Guild main building toward the patio door on the first level. Another command performance from his oldest brother, Jake, and the new love of Jake's life, Lily Falbrooke. They met frequently now since the Cabal, the underground group using and abusing Guild psychics, had ratcheted up efforts to destroy the Guild, going so far as to kill Guild psychics who didn't toe the line and do their illegal and immoral bidding. At least he'd get some good grub if Jake planned to que up the grill. Not like he had anywhere else to go on a Friday night with no date, nor any woman on his radar at all. *Shit on a stick. How'd Jake snag a woman when he wasn't even looking, and I get stuck with flighty chicks only on the hook for a good time?* He didn't begrudge his older brother. Lily Falbrooke ranked as one of the finest women he'd ever met, not counting her powerful psychic abilities. He'd bag her if Jake hadn't already.

He flicked off his baseball cap and rammed it in his back pocket. Head bowed, he stomped onto the patio pavers; the white fairy lights and candles Jake installed a couple weeks ago provided a romantic ambiance. When he spied his bro about to lay one on Lily along the dark edge of the Santa Cruz forest bordering the yard, Ric became fifth wheel fodder.

A fire sizzled and crackled in the pit, flames shooting toward a cloudy sky hosting an indigo twilight. Dampness rode the air from the earlier downpour and he shivered, glad for his leather jacket.

"Dude, the rain's gonna put a damper on your little love fest." He elevated his voice to break apart the sickening lovebirds.

"Little bro, I think *you* just did with your bad 'tude." Jake nuzzled Lily's neck, released her, keeping her pinned to his side.

Wistfulness plunged through Ric. He held no jealousy toward his brother, but damn if Jake didn't get his pick of the beauties. "You invited me. Don't accuse me of infringing upon your make-out session." Shaking off his stupid, Ric trudged across the patio. "Hey, flower child."

"*Lily*, dork," she said with a teasing edge.

He grinned. Scuffing his boots over the pavers, his grin faltered and unease joined the dampness seeping under his skin.

Lily touched Ric's hand. "What's wrong?"

"Another creepy clairvoyant vision. Remember the night we celebrated the end of your ordeal—"

"You had a weird clairvoyant cling-on," Jake cut in, taking on a defensive stance, despite Ric's scowl at his overprotective older brother. "What did you see? Cabal BS?"

Cabal threats had increased exponentially over the last six months, and Guild investigators hadn't been able to pinpoint *any* particular Cabal member. They knew very little about the Cabal except for their more recent recruitments and killing spree targeted at Guild psychics. Cabal members charmed, manipulated, and blackmailed Guild psychics to join them, and they remained way under the radar. Taking them down was the Guild's number one priority before the Cabal decimated the Guild ranks one by one.

"Not Cabal," Ric replied. "A dark-haired woman, mid to late twenties. Weirdly innocent and evil at once. She's in trouble, about to waltz into trouble, or cause major-ass trouble. Totally trouble incarnate."

Lily squinted. "Did you see other features about her?"

"Board-straight hair, slash of blood-red lipstick, porcelain skin—"

The French doors slammed open and banged against the inner wall precariously rattling the panes of glass. As if conjured from the dregs of his mind, a woman sporting a long, silky sheath of black hair, eyes narrowed to slits, and a furious tight-lipped slash of red barreled through the doors. Ric and Jake's middle brother, Liam, followed hot on her heels, gun trained on her back.

Ric gasped. "Well, *dayam*. It's *her*." He drew his gun and hurtled in front of Lily next to Jake who'd thrust her behind him. Although, Jake was her assigned guard, as Guild Guardians, they protected any psychic in peril.

"Lily, seriously, what the hell?" the gorgeous woman lashed out. "Call these brutes off. This jackass," she whacked Liam's arm, forcing him to point his gun at the ground, "didn't believe I was Guild until I had to shove my credentials up his rear door and prove I could read his pea-brain."

"Guys, stand down." Lily tried to squeeze between Ric and Jake, but their barrier of muscle didn't budge. "*Hello*. It's my best friend, Marisa Meadows, from San Diego. You know, *the* western Guild lawyer, authorized to enter the compound twenty-four seven."

Lily pried her arms between Jake and Ric and relenting, they stepped aside. She hurried into Marisa's waiting arms and they hugged fiercely, squealing like teenagers.

"I can't believe I had to learn about your torture-fest from the Guild grapevine. Jeez, Lily, what am I, chopped liver?" Separating from her best friend, Marisa pinned a withering glare on each McAllister brother. "And come on, hooking up with a Guild member. You broke the Guild Girl Code: no dating Guild members, no dating psychics, and especially no dating Guardians. Did you have an aneurism or something when your psychic powers whacked you upside the head?"

Jake grumbled, "*She's* our lawyer?"

"Um, Marisa, have you beheld the gorgeous trio of testosterone?" Lily pinned her fake shock on Marisa in the twist of her lips and exaggerated round eyes. "Plus, I'm not Guild. The code doesn't apply to me."

"Girl, you were born Guild." Marisa perused each brother. "I might make an exception if I were you. If it were *him*." Her narrowed gaze rested on Jake. "You're Jake, huh? Thanks for keeping my best friend alive, since she kept me in the dark."

"My pleasure." Jake winked. "However, she's a force to be reckoned with all on her own."

"No doubt. I've been telling her the same for years." Marisa linked arms with Lily, landed another dick-deflating glare on Ric. "And you're one of *them?*"

Sexy spots of pink appeared on her cheeks, even as she glared down her nose at him, as if he were an epic annoyance in her world. Ric wanted to infuse her icy façade with his warmth. He wanted to run for the hills, or close the distance between them and kiss her until she regarded him as her lifeboat in her turbulent sea. *Damn, I've jumped on the crazy train.*

"Yep. A psychic, a Guild member, *and* a Guardian." Ric stepped back, scrubbed his hands on his pants. If he touched her, he might either wither up and die or skim his hands over every inch of her. "Ric McAllister, the youngest. The best," he felt compelled to add.

Before Marisa's renewed glare destroyed a little something within his chest, Lily rounded on him, practically jiggling in excitement. "You saw Marisa at my dad's funeral. I bet it's why you had the vision. You've seen her before."

Psychic Marisa Meadows? Totally worth the price of admission into my sad-sack dating life. Except for the undercurrent of evil infusing the air around her. Definitely not love at first sight on her part. Desire ignited Ric's nervous system, spun the synapses in his mind, wound down to his groin, and incited a dance of lust. "Don't remember. Too distracted from guarding you." Marisa Meadows was one woman he'd never forget in a million years.

"Me?" Marisa drew her fingers down her long, lustrous hair to the tips. "Seriously. You don't remember *this?*" She wanded her hand down her voluptuous front, her breasts practically bursting the seams of her black sweater. A short, black skirt and black, spike heels fit her long, bare legs to a T. Man, she was beautiful in black, like a prowling panther, all sleek and ready to pounce. Holy sex on a stick, he wanted his lips on hers, her body twisted around him. Had his dry spell lasted so long he'd jump at the first hot-as-sin woman to cross his path... in forever? Or was some freaky intangible thing going on between them?

"I remember you now." Liam's jaw hung open, no doubt riveted on the healthy dose of cleavage Marisa's low-cut sweater bared. Ric wanted to slug his brother.

"Yeah, me too, and I was on the other side of the cemetery." Jake snickered. Lily elbowed his ribs.

Suddenly, Marisa snaked out her hand and encircled Ric's wrist. The moment skin met skin, her eyes closed and she teetered toward him. Ric twined his other arm around her waist to steady her soft curves against him. As fast as her eyes shut, they opened, wide and filled with a terror the kind he'd never seen. She shuttered her face and released his wrist, wringing her hand. He dropped his arms and hugged them to his sides as if she harbored rabid fleas.

Marisa clutched her large purse against her torso. "Sorry, I felt a weird vibe. So sorry. I'm not myself right now." A crimson flush took a spin at her cheeks. "Lily has me running scared after hearing her horror story." As though she dreaded catching the plague, she backstepped, tromping on Lily's foot. "Lily, let's catch up. You need to bust a couple veins. And if you're planning on staying in San Jose for good, I might need to relocate here to keep my eye on you."

Joy replaced the weird ambiance as Lily lit up like a beacon. "Seriously? I need a new law firm partner. A *real* lawyer." She grinned at Jake. "My current non-lawyer partner, Jake, has a new job guarding me from killing any more creeps." She kissed Jake's cheek, brushed her fingertips over Ric's hand, winked at Liam. "Be good, you three." The two women practically skipped into the house, taking their excitement with them.

Ric paced around the fire pit, suffering a spray of embers onto his scuffed boots. "What the hell was that all about?" A spiral of smoke drifted toward him, and he held his breath, swatting the smoke away.

"Guess we'll find out, little bro." Jake smirked. "Appears she's got your number."

Ric slugged his brother's upper arm. Jake winced, and guilt immediately scorched the tips of his ears. "Sorry, man. I forgot about your wound."

"Wounds, plural," Liam groused, joining the Guardians Who Need a Life Club.

"Jesus. Will you two get a life?" Jake said as if he'd

read Ric's mind. Oh wait, he probably had. Jake tossed a log on the fire, and a shower of sparks danced and withered in the damp air.

"This is *our* life." Liam flailed his arms, careful not to touch his brothers. He had a weird empathic ability to read people's feelings and use it against them that got him in more trouble than it was worth. "And I've been banished from it, from helping my brothers when they needed me the most. Stupid Guild probation."

Guild membership was voluntary for anyone with psychic ability. Rules and bylaws existed for both general membership and Guardians. For the most part, the Guild provided an organization for psychics to enjoy a special camaraderie, training, protection, and aid. The Guild treated its members like family, and it was well respected in the community. Unlike the Cabal, they didn't hide from anyone.

Liam had several more weeks sitting on the beach from his Guardian duties after being played a fool by a high-ranking psychic wench. He'd taken no part in Jake's latest assignment guarding Lily and breaking her father's murder case. Ric had acted as Jake's second in guarding Lily. With the case over, he sat on the Guardian rolls for his next assignment in a Guild fracturing from both the inside and outside, stemming from Cabal danger. They all wanted to bust the mystery wide open and destroy the Cabal for good.

"The Cabal's been too quiet. Makes me twitchy." Ric sank onto a patio chair, elbows propped on his knees. "I got a weird feeling shit's about to splatter the fan big time."

"From Marisa?" Jake's radiating tension bowled Ric over. "Is Lily safe?"

"Marisa harbors evil. I can't explain. It's around her. I don't know if it *is* her. Know what I mean?"

"No. You're the clairvoyant, not me." Jake sauntered toward the door.

"Dude, she won't hurt your flower chick." Ric pulled his drumsticks out of his pocket and tossed them on the ground where they clanked against his chair leg. For once, he possessed no yearning to air drum away his jittery energy. Marisa zapped the energy right out of him in more ways than one. He didn't think he'd ever met a woman sexier than Marisa Meadows, with blood-red lips he wanted to kiss to infinity, chocolate-kiss eyes he wanted melting over every inch of him, mile-long legs he wanted wrapped around his waist, creamy luminous skin surrounded by tresses of hair so dark and shiny, he'd swear she was Morticia Addams reincarnated. The flaming amber flecks in her chocolate eyes deflated the heat he experienced for her... and instigated an epic mystery he needed to solve more than life.

Stiff-backed, Jake halted without turning. "How do you know?"

"Lily won't let her," Liam replied. "Her telekinesis and clairvoyance are emerging fast. Ric and I've been working with her. At least I can do something while sitting on my ass waiting for the Protectorate to unlock my shackles. She can hold her own."

"Not very comforting." Jake raked his hand through his shoulder-length hair and returned to the fire. He sat in a patio chair circling the pit. "Lay it all out."

"Like I told you, just an aura of creepiness. Witchy." Ric drummed his fingers on the wooden chair arm.

"Witch?" Liam chuckled. "You're losing it, kid."

Although the youngest McAllister brother, Ric was only a year younger than Liam and normally the jab didn't bother him. Not tonight, though, and he pinned a mad-dog look on Liam.

"Wouldn't Lily know if her best friend is evil?" Jake

asked. "They've lived together in San Diego for six months before Lily came home."

"Not necessarily." Liam sat opposite Ric. "She's been gone from San Diego for a month."

"What do we know about Marisa?" Ric eyeballed Jake as if willing Jake to fling answers out of his mind. The idea of Marisa and her darkness bugged him to hell and back. The image of her gorgeous body pressed to his nearly killed the evil surrounding her and made him want to forget the world existed except for them.

"Lily didn't tell me much." An uncharacteristic blush crawled up Jake's neck. "We haven't progressed to that level in our relationship."

"No duh, man." Liam chuckled. "Her body's a playground I'd want to spend a lifetime climbing." Jake threw a small pinecone at Liam, bouncing it off his knee.

"Didn't you spend time with Marisa during your Guild tribunal?" Ric stretched the word tribunal to piss Liam off, knowing how much Liam hated how the psychic he'd been assigned to guard set him up, used his weird coercion ability against him.

Liam kicked Ric's foot, missed. "No, asshole. I didn't commit any crimes. I didn't need a lawyer since they'd already railroaded my ass off the reservation."

Hiding a triumphant grin, Ric noticed Marisa's bags and purse dumped on a scrolled iron bench by the French doors. Adrenaline spiked in his blood, and he walked to the bench. Not one to snoop in handbags sacred to women, he wanted to see if he received any clairvoyant vibes from it. Most times his clairvoyance hit him randomly like a bulldozer dumping bricks on his head. His gift provided him the ability to gain information about an object, person, location, or physical event through extrasensory perception, like the perception of contemporary events happening outside the range of normal awareness. Like in the movie *The Sixth Sense* and "I see dead people" and all. Except Ric didn't see dead people. The clairvoyant events he experienced involved very much alive people and the future.

"Don't do it," Jake warned. "You know women and their purses. Taboo times ten."

"Don't be a numbskull. I'm not planning to ransack it." The faint floral and baby powder scent of Marisa surrounded the bulging bag and Ric wallowed in his brief memories of her luscious body.

The moment he touched the black leather bag a sledgehammer hit the back of his skull. He felt himself sliding to the pavers in the unrelenting grip of the vision, barely heard Jake and Liam's shouts. Paralysis claimed his body, and he lay in a heap, his eyes frozen open in shock.

CHAPTER THREE

Feeling like she was on the witness stand, Marisa sat spine straight on the loveseat in Lily's Guild suite. The opulent furnishings and décor all dressed in a springtime garden of green and mauves calmed her skittish nerves. "How'd you score such cush digs especially when you *aren't* a Guild member? Spill, missy."

"They're trying to buy my membership because I bring a lot to their warped table." Smirking, Lily nudged Marisa's leg off the loveseat and sat with her back against the pillowed arm. "Enough about me. I'm totally stoked you're here, but what's really up?"

"Are you okay? *Really* okay after your ordeal?" Marisa hated her absence in Lily's life when she'd needed her the most. She had been knee-deep in an important trial with no backup and only scored time off to attend Michael Falbrooke's funeral.

Lily's eyes misted. "Every day gets a little better. Jake has been a godsend."

"I'm sorry. My job and part-time Guild job keep me swamped. I can barely spare a morsel for yoga anymore. Technically, I'm here on business."

Lily grinned. "I *knew* it. Only business drags you out of San Diego."

"Well, when I encountered rain *here*, I about high-tailed it back."

"How do you feel being home?"

"San Jose isn't home. I was born here. Big whoop." Too many influences she'd rather forget remained in San Jose. Part of her wanted to embrace the circumstances of her early years, the other part wanted to run screaming toward a drowning pool. "Tucson and San Diego are more home to me."

Lamplight dispelled twilight's dark skies, and the leaden overcast threatened to dump more rain as ominous as Marisa's strange mood.

Lily knew her history and didn't question her further. "Spit it out, or do I have to read your mind?" she asked.

Happy to leave the topic of her fractured family behind, she teased, "Leave the telepathy to the professionals." Settling in for the long haul, Marisa kicked off her heels and they clattered to the floor. "How about vino, vodka, or vino *and* vodka. Please. I need a drink *pronto*."

Lily crossed the room to a mini bar. Marisa focused on her familiar mental landscape, not wanting to "hear" her girlfriend's thoughts, their unwritten rule. Lily knew about Marisa's knack of breaking down impenetrable walls in people's heads. Marisa had never met another telepath who harbored such ability outside her family. Few people knew about her unique talent, or else she'd have the Cabal and every other criminal in the world riding her back like an eight-hundred-pound gorilla. *Nope. Not gonna be the newest freak to join the circus like Lily and her emerging double whammy psychic talents.*

"Riley assigned me with local counsel for a case involving his biggest client. Massive intellectual property embezzlement and infringement. Corporate headquarters are in Silicon Valley. Depositions start in two days."

"Wow. That's huge if the boss man didn't take the

case himself." Lily handed her a lemon drop martini, dry and lemony, the way she loved it.

"Thank you." She took a sip and the tart warmth slid down her throat. "Divine. I've missed you, Martini Master. Keep 'em coming." She enjoyed another large swig. "Riley planned on handling the case himself, but the client insisted I join the team. Kind of weird. Riley didn't give any big excuse when he assigned me. But if all goes well, the case will vault me into partnership territory."

"I take it you're defending the corporation?" Lily asked.

"Yeah. Stupid employees planned a coup, stole trade secrets, set up a start-up, got venture capital funding, the whole shebang. They got busted and the corp sued." She winked. "I know I'm good and I've been busting my butt for a case like this, but I still can't believe Riley handed it to me on a silver platter. I'll be working with local and corporate counsel. I'm fired up though."

"Maybe his wife talked him into letting go. Didn't she want him to reduce his traveling?" Lily reclaimed her spot on the loveseat, their knees bumping in a friendly reminder of their closeness. "Whatever. I'm just glad you're here. You're staying with me, right? How long?"

Marisa preened inside, scrutinized the majestic room. "Thought you'd never ask. Do I get a suite like this?"

Lily smacked her leg. "Not here. At my house. By the way, how'd you find me here?"

"Went to your house first. Took a wild guess and came here. Plus, I was required to check in at the Guild. Guess they're keeping close tabs on all members while the Cabal kills us off one by one."

"Ugh, don't remind me." Lily drew her legs up to her chest and rested her chin on her knee.

Marisa searched for Lily's lucky shamrock and spied one hanging on a gold chain around her neck. "Did your shamrock luck help you out?"

"I'm sure I'd be dead otherwise."

"Or did Jake McAllister, Guild Guardian god, give you incentive to stay alive?" Marisa fake scowled. "Girl, we follow a code. Why?" After feasting her senses on the three gorgeous McAllister brothers, she really didn't need to ask. Ric's rock-hard abs, chiseled chest beneath his tight Oakland Raiders T-shirt, his chaotic spikey hair and lagoon-blue eyes left an imprint she'd never shake. Something mysterious and alluring connected with her, so confusing, exciting, and taboo. Why did he have to be a Guild Guardian?

Lily pressed the back of her hand against Marisa's forehead. "I don't feel a fever. Did you get a gander at Jake? Who'd pass him up, code or not?"

A sudden freeze attacked Marisa. A new sense of foreboding chased the cold front. *Ugh. I should've just stayed in bed and never left San Diego.* She polished off her martini, grabbed the shaker off the coffee table, and settled in for an evening of campfire stories.

Lily regaled her with everything that had transpired since her father's funeral and solving his murder. After Lily took a breather from sharing her escapades, they hugged, wiping tears of horror and happiness.

"I'll kiss Jake for keeping you alive, code or not."

"I'll allow it just this once." Lily winked. "Your turn now. You going to tell me what bug crawled up your cute little hiney?"

Marisa refilled their glasses, and it was her turn to regale Lily with her airport adventure.

Lily straightened out her legs, set her glass down. "You fainted, as in out cold?" Marisa didn't need to read her to know Lily was equally freaked out.

"I don't know what happened. Seriously, it wasn't low blood sugar. I'd never felt such a weird sense of evil. It's been going on for a month. Like someone's watching my every move, a puppet master yanking my strings or something. It just got freakier at the airport."

Lily gripped her shamrock. "And you didn't tell me?"

Marisa waved off Lily's ire. "I didn't think much about it at first. A couple times I seemed to lose minutes, like lost memories. Heck, maybe I'm Sybil incarnate and have an alternate personality."

"Do you think the thief did something to you, you know, mentally, psychically? Rode shotgun from San Diego?"

"Doesn't make sense if all he wanted was my purse. In that case, he could've taken anything he wanted from my townhouse." Marisa rubbed her hands on her slacks. "He didn't touch me. I never looked him in the eyes. I didn't feel a mental intrusion. But the airport terminal was deafening and anything's possible."

"What about Mr. Gorgeous?"

Marisa shook her head emphatically. "Are you kidding? He was all concern and sincerity."

Lily shot her a quick grin. "I thought you hated intruding upon a potential *boyfriend.*"

The crux of many matters. Marisa winced. "I'm human. Anyway, he was shuttered to me. Refreshing, huh?"

"Then what was all that about with Ric downstairs? Isn't he as hot?"

"He's a Guardian." Marisa gave Lily her half-slit witch-eye, which worked well to intimidate men in court. Didn't work so well on Lily. "Remember, Guild Girl Code. Not going there." The idea of Ric's fingers sliding over her bare flesh caused a flush to skitter across her breasts.

"Okay, okay." Lily fluttered her fingers in the air. "But he had a weird, clairvoyant vibe earlier and recognized the evil surrounding you. He went so far as to say *you* might be the source."

Shocked, Marisa's mouth hung open. "Then he better go back to clairvoyant school."

"Did you get a reading off him?"

"My walls were up." Marisa contemplated long and hard about the tension she'd gleaned from Ric. She wasn't an empath and didn't feel things other people felt due to her mental walls. But something was going on with him. Par for her course that her evening turned out as screwed up as her day. "I think he was projecting what he felt from me, whether real or perceived."

"Whoa. But—"

"No buts. Do I look evil?" Marisa leaped up, scanned the room for her purse. "Crud. I left my *evil* purse downstairs."

Lily chomped on her bottom lip as if it were an appetizer. "Sure you want to touch it? As for the evil question, well, did you break all your mirrors, Morticia?"

"You're just a barrel of monkey laughs. How I've missed the insults and barbs. I have my work cut out for me to lob them back atcha." She returned Lily's teasing grin. "I need to take my blood sugar pill and eat before I hunt down a blood host. You know, my evil self and me."

Lily hopped off the loveseat and hugged her quickly. "I'm sorry. Jake's barbequing steaks. We meet here to go over Guild matters. I don't like Guild business going on at my house. I need the separation. Plus, they have a killer stocked pantry and fridge here. You game for an awesome porterhouse?"

"I'm ready for the whole cow, girlfriend." Marisa dropped the subject of her day from Evil Island, and they left Lily's suite behind.

The moment she hit the bottom step on the curved marble and wrought iron stairway, she knew something had gone backassward. Anxious voices deluged her mind.

"Lily?" Her panicked tone barely rose above a whisper.

"Mar, what's wrong?" Lily asked, her presence comforting and solid amid Marisa's mental tangle.

Legs rubbery, she sank to the stairs. Excruciating screams of pain hit her.

"Help us! Fire! We're trapped." A woman choked on a blanket of smoke practically visible to Marisa. Fists pounding on a door thundered through her skull. A red haze pulsed at the edges of her vision. The roar of fire spreading, sizzling, and popping clouded the jumble of sound. Who was she? She had to be near if Marisa was reading her thoughts.

Frantic, Marisa tried to stand and her knees gave out again, depositing her back on the hard stair, jarring her butt and spine. "There's a fire. A woman's trapped. She's nearby."

"Who? Where's the fire?"

Chilling screams shattered her skull, a tempest overriding the terror. "She's here!" Marisa's nails dug into the skin of her palm. She sprang up, her eyes darting from every nook and cranny of the compound's large reception room. Bypassing a guard, she raced into another room, searched for fire, an amber glow, anything to prove the revelation was merely telepathy and not her going batshit.

She tripped on the corner of a thick rug, caught her fall against a cushioned easy chair. Blood pulsed in her ears as she became hyperaware of myriad mental voices. Suddenly, her mind shut down, not a thought left in the ashes, no song of a fire, as if she'd dreamed the incident. Spent, Marisa sank into the chair, panting and fighting an epic bout of nausea.

The door to the rear patio sprang open, slamming against the wall so violently, a glass pane cracked and the sound echoed up to the vaulted ceiling. Jake McAllister raced toward her, gun trained on her. Menacingly, he hovered above her, blocking Lily behind him. His protection of Lily radiated off him in waves.

"Get up," he demanded. "Who the hell are you?" *What did you do to my brother?* His silent words filtered into her razed mind.

Bleary-eyed, she took him in from scalp to boots, gauged her escape route around his wide-muscled body, and wished she didn't have to check her gun in her luggage, sitting in the foyer.

"Answer me." Jake's shout pummeled her ears.

"Jake! Knock it off." Lily slugged his arm. "What's going on? Marisa? Jake?"

Marisa swallowed, regained her devil-may-care footing. "Screw you, McAllister. I didn't do anything to your brother. Put your gun down."

A dense fog enveloped her mental field of crimson flowers, muted the tinkling splash of the waterfall, and obscured the verdant landscape of her sanctuary. An image hit her. As she stared past the gun barrel, Ric McAllister stiffened in a huddle on the patio, lost in a blistering fire eating the flesh off two bodies.

CHAPTER FOUR

The clairvoyant vision struck Ric, clearer than any foresight in his twenty-eight years, or since he'd experienced his sixth sense for the first time at four years old.

The slender woman with long dark hair pulled into a ponytail headed through a gate to the large verdant backyard. Hunched over to block her movements, she unlatched the gate. Shadows hid her, not even a moon or exterior lights gave her away. Night drew onward, midnight in the near past, yet dawn remained distant. She exuded confidence in her trepidation, as if she knew exactly what to do yet worried about taking the first step and adding it to the misdeeds piling up on her moral compass. Excitement rolled off her. Strangely, it wasn't her *excitement. Nothing about her seemed to belong to her, not her thoughts, not her actions, not her at all. She was a puppet dangling from marionette strings.*

Uncertainty bogged Ric down. Did she have free will? The scene wavered in and out of his mind.

With a loose backpack strapped to her back, she slipped through the rear door of the mysterious dark and silent house, careful not to bang the walls. One dim nightlight lit the shadowy interior. In her quiet sneakers, she tiptoed up the stairs and down a hallway to the partly open door of what appeared to be the master bedroom. A man and woman lay on the king-sized bed, their backs to each other.

The woman twisted the backpack off and slipped her gloved hand inside. A plastic bottle of lighter fluid clinked against an engraved, silver lighter as she pulled them out. Actions stiff and mechanical, she moved by rote. Devoid of any emotion, thought, or feeling, it was as if another commanded her limbs, controlled her thoughts.

Shoes silent on the tile floor, she splashed accelerant around the doorway and up to the foot of the bed. The man stirred, and she stepped into a dark corner out of the revealing amber pool of a nightlight. He coughed and rolled over on his side. His gentle snores filled the room, hid the sound of her movements.

She continued to sprinkle accelerant around the room's perimeter walls. Lighter fluid fumes tickled her nose, and she pressed her face into her shoulder, stifling a sneeze against her jacket. Satisfied with her job, she returned the bottle to her backpack and flipped the top on the lighter. Remorseless and efficient, she struck the first spark, set it to a stream of accelerant. Amber and crimson flames undulated up a foot, and then fed on the liquid trails, not too quick to alert the slumbering couple. Backing out of the room, she lit another stream of lighter fluid on the other side of the door, ensuring the fire snaked to the window. The dangerous snake offered no chance of escape, no chance for life. Death became the only way out.

No longer caring about noise, she replaced the items in her pack, took out a long screw and a battery-operated screwdriver, and screwed the door into the jamb. She refused to confront the consequences of failure. Failure meant death. A bark of laughter loomed even as a sob climbed up her throat. Her mind stomped her emotions down into barren crevices.

Screams erupted from the bed, spurring her to hasten. She scanned her path to ensure she hadn't left anything behind. All clear, she raced out of the house the way she'd entered. If the couple lived, if she failed in her task, there was no telling her fate. Death might even meet her. Maybe she deserved it.

Death promised to make it all disappear.

The claw of her turmoil relented, and she became aware of the waiting car at the bottom of a wooded hill behind the house. A slight plume of air drifted from her mouth, the house's heat expelling from her body. The bands cinching her mind loosened another notch as she climbed into the passenger seat. A soft song played on the stereo, and she rested her head on the headrest.

"Go." Flames shot out the back of the house toward the night sky.

"We'll go when I say." A cloudy haze dissolved her partner's features.

The fire licked the rear corner of the house, spreading its taint to the roof. A mixed bag of agitation pulsated in her ears. What am I doing here? This is where I belong. *She glanced at her partner's profile, and her puzzlement blossomed. When he swiveled to her, she shifted her gaze, curled her hands.*

The tie around her mind stretched another notch, this time allowing emotions to spill back into her brain. Remorse, terror, horror, and a strange satisfaction tangled them all.

He flicked on the interior lights. "Look at me."

She shook her head.

"Look. At. Me."

Slowly, she turned and locked eyes. Screams filled her head. Smoke filtered into her mouth. She gagged on the thickening cloud. The stench of charred flesh became her undoing, and she passed out, falling over the center console.

The screams deafened Ric. Smoke stung his nose as if he were present in the burning room or felt the fire starter's emotions, experienced her actions and thoughts, her unholy dilemma of right versus wrong. His heart thundered like an eagle charging through his ribcage, trying to break the shackles holding it inside the cage of bones. Blood drained from him like an out-of-body experience, or a soulless body evolving into a ghost, dissipating into infinite darkness.

"Ric! Come back to us, bro," Liam shouted, shaking a life out of him.

The hold on Ric's limbs lessened. Was the prediction real? Did he have time to investigate to prevent it from happening? Who was the fire starter? He felt as if he knew her and the man who controlled her in the car, or did he only know the man through her eyes? The remnants of the horrifying scene and his perplexity pulsed behind his eyes.

The same evil vibes he'd experienced in his previous vision invaded his gut, twined around hollow threads linking his mind to Marisa. How had he connected to her? He searched the blackness inside her and couldn't even find her consciousness. Gently, he erected a wall of static to force Marisa out of his head.

He stretched out his right arm, flexed his hand, his fingers stiff from curling into a fist. "How long was I out?"

"About fifteen minutes," Liam said. "Dude, I've never seen you go so deep."

His eyelids fluttered open, and he was thankful for the night, despite the myriad candles and white Christmas lights peppering the patio. His knees and arms ached. "Did I hit the pavers?"

"Like a dead-asleep puppy. One minute you were standing, then next, bam, face kissing the ground." Liam injected a ribbing into his words Ric knew he didn't feel. The three McAllister brothers were too connected in the good old-fashioned sense of brotherhood to know when one suffered. Ric and Jake, almost twins despite their four years' age difference, wore their feelings and emotions on their faces. Liam wore his on his body in the way he moved, or didn't move.

Ric massaged his aching head, hoping to provoke his brain cells to return to the game table. "I touched the wench's handbag. Then it hit me." Sitting up with his back against the French doors, he unfurled his limbs slowly and stretched out his stiff legs.

"Yeah. The lay of the land." Liam stood stock still and ramrod straight.

He'd never fallen so deep into a clairvoyant event that he became shipwrecked, lost all his senses, and let the vision encompass his entire world. And he'd never connected to a strange darkness that shot a heated arrow of lust southward, a darkness named Marisa Meadows. Ric hadn't counted on the seductive nature of his mental link to Marisa, and part of him didn't want to terminate it. Instead of his usual electrical charge during a clairvoyant event, her darkness surrounded him with all of her and left him reeling with an imminent online trip to Wikipedia to name his feelings. She held no defenses as if she'd invited him in and didn't ever want to let him go.

"Where's Jake?" he asked.

"Taking care of that psychic—" Liam kicked Marisa's handbag out of Ric's reach. A notebook, compact, and her smartphone tumbled onto the pavers. A tube of lipstick pinged down the step to the next patio level toward the fire pit.

"Whoa, don't let your *chonies* twist you in a pretzel," Ric replied. "She's not the devil." *Maybe the devil's sidekick.* "Jake's not going *loco* on her, is he?"

"With his gun." Liam smirked.

"Give me a break. She won't hurt Lily." *I hope.* Ric stood, wobbled on his feet, and listed toward the side of the building. "Screw me royal. I'm wasted." He propped himself against Liam as his brother guided him to a padded lawn chair near the fire.

"What did you see?" Liam stomped around the patio, kicked Marisa's handbag again, checking his annoyance.

"When Jake returns. I'm only gonna say this once," he slurred and dropped his head between his knees to stave off the bile rising up like a rocket ship. "Quit pacing. You're twisting my brain up."

Jake herded Marisa out onto the patio. The air changed as if a storm loomed, and Marisa's charged presence behind him fanned the tempest brewing inside her. Her vibrant electricity shot straight to his groin, inciting ill-timed movement in his pants.

"Jake, put the gun away." Lily's demanding voice scraped across Ric's muddled mind. Jake didn't take his sight or gun off Marisa, Guild lawyer, psychic enigma, and the subject of Ric's budding lust.

Marisa stood ten feet away, her beautiful face a deceptive mask of indifference. Empathy rolled off her in waves. Her lipstick had dulled as if she'd wiped it off, or someone had kissed it off. Jealousy flowered in Ric. He'd kill to have those lips on his and no one else. He wanted her dark exotic eyes gazing at only him with need. He'd kill to skim his hands over the curves of her hips, her flat middle, cupping her so perfect breasts.

Another round of nausea hit, and he batted down his insane thoughts regarding this mysterious stranger standing defiantly so near him. He wanted her to account for her whereabouts. Most of all, he wanted his mouth and tongue tasting her hot-as-sin body.

The images refreshed and he needed to spill now

before he lost the nuances. Despite the confounding scene, it remained too intense, too sick, and he needed to know Marisa Meadows hadn't killed two humans by a fiery death, or wasn't planning the gruesome crime.

"Ric?" Lily nudged ice-cold water into his hand. "You okay?"

He held the bottle against his forehead. The cool comfort of the plastic exorcised the heat of the fire. "Thanks, flower chick."

"Can we sit and *calmly* discuss what's happening?" Lily tapped the gun in Jake's steady hand. "Without the firearm brigade?"

"You tell me," Jake demanded before he stuck his gun into his ever-present shoulder harness. After all, he was still Lily's Guardian and would guard her forever, or for as long as she wanted him.

Would he ever find the one he'd guard and love forever? Ric took a long swig of water and recognized his next Guardian assignment in one second of fleeting apprehension in her dark-chocolate eyes before her insolence whipped it away.

"Some grand reception here." Marisa flung out her arms. "I can bring all three of you up on tribunal charges for what you've done to me tonight. Are you willing to forfeit your Guardian lives for this freaking insane joke? Do you know who I am?" She inclined forward as if to pummel her words into Jake.

Jake snorted. "You tell us. One touch of your purse and Ric goes down. He senses evil around you, in you. So what's *your* insane joke, Marisa Meadows, Guild *lawyer?*"

"Is the Guild testing us?" The veins running up the side of Liam's neck throbbed. "I'd say we passed with flying freaking colors."

"You're all batshit. I came for an outside case and to visit Lily. Nothing more." Marisa tossed up her hands in a gesture Ric found maddeningly exciting, the golden flecks in her eyes shooting fireworks, her cheeks cotton candy pink. "Shall we call Guild bigwigs? I'm game. I'm all over that." She spied the contents of her purse strewn on the brick pavers. "What'd you do to my stuff?"

"What's wrong with you guys?" Lily knocked her forehead against Jake's upper arm. "Go harass Cabal minions and leave Marisa and her belongings alone!"

Marisa stomped over to her purse. Gingerly, she picked up the tiny remnants of her daily life and stuffed them inside the open top. When she rose, she held her phone and the purse strap dangled off her arm.

Finally, Ric raised a hand, quieting the level-five crapstorm blustering around him. "A foresight knocked me on my ass. The evil I felt earlier barreled over me when Marisa first arrived and exploded when I touched her bag."

Marisa dumped the subject of their speculation on the bench. "Okay. Whatever." She cursed unintelligible words. "Something happened to me at the airport. If you call off the dogs, I'll explain. First, I want to know what Ric saw." She pinned a funny look of part commiseration and part disgust on him. "You're ready to burst."

"And you're like a panther eyeing its prey." Ric settled into a more comfortable padded chair, and set his water bottle on the table, fighting the urge to hunt down his cathartic drumsticks.

Lily squeezed his shoulder. "A thief snatched her purse at the airport. A knight in shining armor rescued it, but neither he nor airport security were able to apprehend the thief."

Jake sat down in a chair between Ric and Lily, protectively taking her hand in his. Marisa and Liam sat across from them. Liam scooted his chair away from Marisa as if she carried the plague. Heck, maybe she did.

"If you're so innocent, then maybe whoever took the bag dumped a spell on it," Jake said.

"Really, Jake? A spell? Like what, a witch or wizard?" Lily did a cuckoo finger circle next to her ear. "Hello. We're not living on the corner of Witch Lane and Hobbit Road."

"No. I think he's right." Marisa repeatedly wiped her hands on her skirt as if they were dirty. "Despite the weird sense of evil hounding me in San Diego, it worsened at the airport." Like old vinyl stuck under the needle, she again explained what'd happened.

Ric wanted to comfort her and kick the ass of the man who'd aided her. Why did she stir up his senses? She was nothing to him. Or was she? The mysteries she symbolized excited him, handed him the opportunity to solve them... to solve her.

"What did *you* see?" Marisa sat up straight, braced for his reply.

She couldn't possibly be the fire starter. Or she did a stellar persuasion job. He also trusted Lily's faith in her friend, the lawyer who represented Lily's former corporate employer in San Diego and the western Guild.

"Every day is a gift. That's why they call it the future." Ric joked to defray the mounting tension.

"You mean present?" Marisa quirked an eyebrow.

"Nope." With rapt attention from the peanut gallery, Ric relayed his clairvoyant vision. Nose stinging from the illusion of smoke, the scene became real again.

His visions didn't always make sense. Sometimes, they weren't discernable or were impressions of events. Rarely did they occur in the past. Some occurred in the present, but most portrayed future events. Not all his foresights came true. They might be manifestations of things he'd read or dreamed or stories he'd heard. Too many variables layered his clairvoyance. Yet, this recent event was the most intense he'd ever experienced exercising all his senses. Even though he didn't recognize the woman, the man in the car, the house, or the couple on the bed, the scene was too vivid, about to happen. And telepathic Marisa Meadows saw it all unfold. "I guess I see dead people now."

Marisa's face paled, and a light sheen of sweat dotted her smooth forehead. "I smelled smoke earlier. Your vision sucked me in and caused me to fall on the stairs."

"Then it was you!" Liam bounded up, leaving her sitting in a void alone that Ric had a burning desire to fill.

"Oh. My. God! It wasn't me." She slammed her palms on the wide chair arms.

"Then someone's manipulating you," Ric suggested.

"Oh, for the love of Satan. You Guardians are nuts. I don't kill people. I don't set fires. No one's yanking my chains." She kicked off her heels and stomped over to the bench. Purse in hand, she practically seethed in rage. "I haven't been coerced!"

Ric had never seen a woman so steaming hot in so many ways. He adjusted the crotch of his pants to give room for the rise and swell of his lust.

"Maybe you projected your vision onto her." Jake scrubbed his jaw.

"I don't project," Ric lashed out, as stumped as the rest of them.

"Yes, you do. You projected on me in the SUV when we were rescuing Jake," Lily replied.

"Oh." Ric tugged on his short hair. "Son of a bitch. Maybe my clairvoyance is changing."

Marisa dumped the contents of her bulging purse into a pile on the table. Among the usual suspects in a woman's purse, two small notepads and ten million bits of paper cluttered the goods.

"What are you searching for?" Lily leaned forward to

examine the junk women deemed necessary to cart around with them twenty-four seven.

Marisa carried more than her fair share of womanly things, but Ric lost focus on them, her, and her reactions. Instead his eyes landed on a familiar silver, engraved lighter.

CHAPTER FIVE

Marisa's eyes bugged out. She reached for the lighter sitting between her coin purse and her hand sanitizer, and jerked her hand back. Had the airport thief slipped it in her purse?

"It's not mine," she said before the McAllister cavemen drew their weapons on her again.

"Don't touch it," Ric demanded in a rush. "Liam, grab a plastic bag." Liam heaved out a disgruntled sigh and jogged into the mansion.

"Anything missing?" Lily asked.

Marisa reached to shift things, checked herself, and clutched her hands to her middle.

"Use this pen." Jake offered her a ballpoint pen, surprisingly composed, when Marisa knew he was foaming for her head on a pike.

"Thank you." She used the pen to slide her wallet, notepads, and makeup into a pile and picked up her prescription bottle. She seized Ric's half-empty water bottle and downed one of her pills. They didn't need to know her blood sugar level had dipped into the pale.

Liam finagled the lighter into a plastic sandwich bag. After another minute of pushing the small slice of her life in circles like peas on a plate, she said, "Nothing's missing."

"Are you sure?" Ric asked. "I mean, you got the kitchen sink in there."

"Bite me, McAllister." Fire spiraled up her chest as she rounded on him. "You either believe my story or you don't. I didn't barbeque two people. I have no plans to turn anyone into a crispy critter. No one is pulling my strings. If you think so, then I've got a goldmine in my purse to sell you." She started to gather up her belongings, but Ric's large hand on her wrist thwarted her. Her skin sizzled beneath the touch of his skin on hers, and the heat from his nearness sent rivulets of fire across her breasts, very different than the fire of a second ago. *Get a life, Triple M.* The brut didn't deserve one iota of her untimely and ill-advised desire. Without a whole lot of oomph, she tried to wrench her wrist out of his grip, but his long fingers held strong as if he too felt the same desire.

"We'll run the bag for prints." He finally released her wrist, his fingertips tickling her palm as if he didn't want to lose her touch. She almost twined her traitorous fingers around his.

Eyeing her bottle of sanitizer, she massaged her wrist, hugged both hands against her middle again.

"Good idea. Hang tight." Lily dashed inside, returned with an empty reusable grocery bag. "Sorry. This is the first thing I found in the closet."

"Guess it's better than pissing off the Guardian taskforce," she griped as she crammed the mementos of her daily grind into the flimsy cloth bag.

"You need to understand our concern," Jake said quietly. "Lily just went through the ringer. The Cabal's more than on the prowl, killing psychics right and left. I think it best you stay here tonight. I don't want you at Lily's house. They have a room assigned to you here."

Lily rounded on him. "No. Jake! This is wrong and

you know it."

"Hey, if it helps you sleep at night, I'll stay here." Marisa slammed her wallet into the bag and snatched her shoes off the pavers. "Wouldn't want to hurt your tiny ape-men sensibilities."

"No, Marisa. You're staying with me. I have three perfectly good bedrooms you can use." Poking her finger into Jake's shoulder, Lily stood on her toes in front of him. "If you think she's a menace to Guild society, then have the Protectorate assign her a Guardian."

Marisa flicked her wrist. "I'd rather sleep in a jail cell than subject myself to a Guardian." The Protectorate was the Guild's version of police. They oversaw the Guardians, assigned them to cases and psychics in need, and mediated with and assisted local cops on their cases. Marisa's family had way too much history interacting with Guardians, none of it good. She shuddered.

Suffering a ration of cajoling, Jake agreed to "allow" Marisa to accompany Lily home as long as Lily slept with him in his loft apartment on the attic level of the Falbrooke house.

After their aborted dinner, they took a detour through the drive-thru for burgers on the way home. Marisa wolfed down her lettuce-wrapped protein burger and a decadent chocolate milkshake in the back seat of Lily's Mustang. Lily had just snagged her car from San Diego last weekend along with most of her belongings when Marisa was unfortunately out of town on a case. Even though they promised to visit each other as often as possible, she missed Lily so much. They had an epic cryfest before Lily drove off about the same time Marisa had returned home, and Marisa had practically eaten her way into a diabetic coma on milkshakes and ice cream afterwards.

Lily guided Marisa into a blue and cream guest room

with an *en suite* bathroom. "My mom decorated this suite. Matches Jake's loft upstairs with the blues and creams."

"Are you sleeping, *sleeping* with him?" Marisa slung her suitcases on the bed. Jake had carted her luggage into the room and grunted out a few curses before he took up a post in the hallway.

"Most nights." Lily flushed. "We didn't hit it off at first. I gave him a load of crap. But he worked me good, pushed all the right buttons, made it easy to fall for him."

"Good for you." She hugged her friend tight. "I'm so glad you found someone, even if he *is* a Guardian, a Guild member, and a psychic. And a McAllister to boot. Anyone is infinitely better than your asswipe ex-fiancé." She fake shivered and released Lily.

"No kidding." Lily sat on the bed covered in a rose and blue floral jacquard comforter. "Jake is as transparent as they come. All the McAllister brothers are, although I don't know Liam well. And Ric," she paused as if to gauge Marisa's reaction, "Ric's so sweet. He really came through when Jake hit trouble and I needed him. Since he's clairvoyant too, he's helping me cope with my new psychic powers."

Marisa stuck her tongue out at Lily. "Don't butter me up on *the* Ric McAllister. Remember the Code. I don't do Guardians."

"Maybe you should." Lily grinned.

"Maybe you should dump your Guardian and join the dark side. We have better cookies."

"Oh no. The light side cookies are delish." Lily spread out on her back on the bed, her expression soft and dreamy.

Prodding Lily over to lie down beside her, she pretended to gag. "Oh, girl, you have it bad."

"I know, right?" Lily elbowed Marisa's side. "You could have it bad with Ric or even Liam. But Ric... come on. There's something between you two already."

Marisa rolled over to confront her best friend. "Are you freaking crazy?" Blowing out a sigh, she said, "You know my family history."

"Ric's different."

"Not different enough. Eventually, he'll crap on me and break my heart."

Her older sister, Celeste, and their mother possessed the same telepathy, all three able to batter down walls people used to block telepathic intrusion. It didn't go well for them. Didn't bode well for her future relationships. It was the reason she only dated for fun... and sex.

Celeste overdosed five years ago after breaking under the pressure of her telepathy and the rampant thoughts she was unable to block. Their father had left their mother when Marisa was five once he'd gotten dead sick and tired of her mother mentally intruding upon him. His abandonment drove her mother into a depressive, alcoholic funk, leaving her unable to block out internal and external voices for a long time. Since Celeste's death, which did another number on her mother, her mother has lived in an institution near her family in Tucson, Arizona.

No way did Marisa plan to join the ranks of her mom and big sis. Fortunately, the men she dated never hit the level of "relationship" on her personal scale of justice. Either they bailed early or she kicked them to the curb when she couldn't cease her mental intrusions. Curiosity got the better of her, and her heart always forced her head to do the deed. She loathed herself for it, but she bore the self-loathing better than heartbreak. Avoiding the inevitable solved the problem.

"I don't want to hurt him," Marisa said. "It's best to leave it alone." *I don't want to hurt me.* "Besides, we just met, and he doesn't even like me. I'm the evil one." She did air quotes.

Notes of a familiar song repeated in her head, dim and nonintrusive. As if saying the word "evil" invited Evil Eddie to return for another helping of her sanity. A claw seemed to rake up and down her back with glacial tenterhooks, gouging her skin. Grimacing, she pressed into the mattress to quell the sensation.

"What's wrong?" Lily upped her grimace.

"This sense of something inside me, this evil, is driving me batty." The evil's temptation to let it immerse her refused to abate.

"When did it start?"

"A month or so ago." Marisa rubbed her forehead, working sense into her bedlam. "There's no rhyme or reason. It attacks me at all hours, or I go days without feeling it. Sometimes I lose time like I literally blackout. I haven't met anyone with Satan tendencies." A smile she didn't feel curved her lips. "No one malevolent if you know what I mean." The blackouts were like black holes in her time line of life, as if someone had plucked a page out of her life's book and tossed it in hell's best incinerator.

"Have you infringed barriers and searched telepathically?" Lily fingered her shamrock pendant, a sure sign of her agitation. She understood Marisa's hang-ups about intruding upon the privacy of people around her, including Marisa's unfortunate slippages.

The blistering claw drove another round of barbs into her churning gut. Bile rose. She bolted upright and sprinted to the bathroom, glad she'd kicked off her heels. She barely made it to the porcelain throne before upchucking her entire dinner. By the time the dry heaves settled in and Lily scuttled into the room with a cold compress, Marisa reached a dangerous conclusion.

No matter what it took, she'd hunt down this source of evil tormenting her. She'd break down every wall in every mind until she laid waste to the source. Instincts told her it had everything to do with the strange clairvoyant connection to Ric and the fiery deaths of the mysterious man and woman.

CHAPTER SIX

A persistent queasiness hauling an epic sense of *déjà vu* awoke Marisa from a fitful sleep on an unfamiliar bed. Her sneakers lay near the door along with her yoga jacket. Both of which she had *never* unpacked. The queasiness mushroomed.

"I'm losing it. I must've unpacked them." The thought flowed up the river of denial, even as blades of fresh mowed grass stuck on the bottom of one sneaker proved her wrong.

Suffering back twinges from sleeping curled in a ball, she stretched as she slogged into the bathroom and sipped the tepid ginger ale she'd left on the vanity the night before. The phantom scent of smoke clung to her nostrils, the fragments of Ric McAllister's nightmare fire etched in her memory.

"Argh. I'll never bounce the nightmare." Didn't appear she'd ever rid her memory of Ric's intense azure eyes drilling into her like he wanted to slice and dice her soul and then ravish her body until she surrendered... something. A hot flash skittered down her torso, traveling straight to her southern hemisphere, which wanted to fork out an invitation to Ric Off-Limits McAllister.

Her not-so-glorious inaugural day in San Jose had turned into a major bust. She'd hoped to spend quality time with Lily before facing a weeklong deposition-fest. Instead, she felt like the wicked witch of the west and a pariah all rolled into Satan's minion who needed to adopt an angel or two.

Marisa plucked at her knotted hair and glowered at her paler than pale reflection in the mirror. Mascara flakes clung beneath her eyes and lipstick smears decorated her cheek. She swirled her tongue in her dog turd-tasting mouth. "Mirror, mirror on the wall. Who are you and what did you do with Triple-M?" Grandma Mae should be turning over in her grave knowing her namesake had gone to bed without washing her face. "Thank goodness, the depo's don't start until Tuesday." A makeup artist couldn't fix her for public consumption today.

Her phone chirped from her grocery bag purse. Sometime that morning, Lily had tossed a large black purse onto the chair in the corner. Marisa fished her phone out and checked her messages. A text from her assistant in San Diego: "Delaney, CFO of Edison WebWorx, wants to meet you today, 10:00 a.m. You choose location."

Ugh. Just what she didn't need. Marisa held no yearning to breakfast with her client's CFO before the depositions tomorrow. She texted her assistant Lily's law office address. Now she had two hours to fix herself for the public.

A knock on the door startled her, and the door slid open to reveal the subject of the moment dressed to the nines in a drool-worthy black silk sheath cut four inches above her knees, a matching black blazer dangling over her arm.

"How's your stomach?" Lily asked. "Better still, how's your—"

"Evil twin?" Marisa flinched into a half wink. "Better.

For now. So… dressing like me these days?"

"Funeral wear actually." Lily smoothed her hand down her dress. "I meant to toss this outfit. I have client meetings today and well—"

"You look distinguished, hot, and sexy all at once in black?"

"Guess you'd know."

"I knew you'd trip the light fantastic into the dark side eventually." Marisa tossed a black G-string at Lily, who deflected it handily back into her open suitcase. "By the way, do you have an office or conference room I can borrow this morning?"

"Jake's out for the morning on PI business. You can use his office. Just don't tell."

"What? He doesn't guard your precious body twenty-four seven?"

"I refuse to be smothered, a compromise I made when I joined the Guild." She winked. "Yes. I'm really in the Guild now."

"Bad enough you live with the guy, work with him, *and* he guards you. And he's a telepath too." Marisa shuddered so fiercely her bones creaked. "How do you stand it? I couldn't work and live with a guy without going toons or killing him. I need my space." *I need my mind.*

"You can't live with a guy period."

"You have a point. I go through men like vibrators."

"You may as well date a vibrator, then."

"No drama that way." Marisa grinned. No heartache either. "Skedaddle. I need to get this hot mess," she waved her hand down her torso, "ready for prime time. See you at the office, boss lady."

CZSO

With twenty minutes to spare, a rideshare car dumped Marisa off at the Falbrooke & Associates office tower under a crisp blue sky. Night had driven the rain off, leaving a balmy autumn day behind. Maybe San Jose wasn't such a dreary place after all. Lily loved it. Her mother once loved it. She tugged down her short black skirt and buttoned one more button on her shimmery black blouse. With her borrowed black bag and spike heels, the panther in her was ready to strike the day, feral and hungry. *Thank my lucky black stars Evil Eddie has taken a hike.*

The moment Marisa entered the building, heads turned, voices hushed. The usual. Even without her black-as-death visage, she stunned. She didn't revel in it. It just was. More often than she cared to admit, she wanted to drill into their minds to prey upon their thoughts. Humbled by the genes she'd earned from her mother and deadbeat dad, she used them to her advantage when necessary. Most times, they were the bane of her existence, especially when male clients had a hard time lifting their pea-brains above her boobs to her steel-trap mind. Despite inauspicious beginnings, her clients respected her to the ends of the Earth once the firm sent them their final bill for a job well done. Most, if not all, requested her on all their future legal matters. And she usually didn't use her telepathy to get what *they* wanted. *Usually* being the key word.

Marisa entered Lily's spacious suite decorated in calming creams and greens including fake flora and fauna to bring the outdoors inside. The bubbly receptionist, Dawn, greeted her, already warned of her arrival.

"You're all set in Jake's office." Dawn led her down a wide hallway to a corner office. "Help yourself to the kitchen and dining room," she pointed out the rooms, "the library and conference rooms if you need. The conference room schedule is posted by the two rooms."

Marisa marveled at the expansive corner office with the floor-to-ceiling walled windows. "Nice digs for a PI."

Dawn hid a snicker Marisa didn't miss. "Partner."

"Yeah, I know all about how he wormed his way into Michael's life and practice." And into Lily's bed, head, and heart. Freaking Guild Guardian. How much of his telepathy helped him get what he wanted, AKA her vulnerable best friend? Did manipulating his telepathy shred his intestines the way it tattered hers?

"And he brought a boatload of wealthy clients with him." Lily walked toward her with two cups of steaming ambrosia.

Caramel latte in hand, Marisa about gelled on the spot. "You just hit my sweet spot."

"I haven't been gone that long." Lily clinked her mug against Marisa's mug halfway to her mouth. "Now about Jake and all his connections, we have enough business where I'll be hiring another lawyer and a paralegal. You in?"

Marisa licked a drop of heaven off her bottom lip. "Sorry, my paralegal days are over."

"Ha freaking ha." Lily play-slapped her arm. "There's nothing keeping you in San Diego since I'm gone."

"A good paying job." She returned the play-slap, losing her handbag and half her coffee to the impeccable slate tile floor. "Whoops."

"Jeez. Here less than a minute and you're already trashing my place." Lily jogged off for cleaning rags while Marisa blocked her mess to avoid snarling herself in a slip-and-fall lawsuit. Lily returned with a roll of paper towels, crouched down to mop up the mess. "Anyway. Think about it. It'll position you on the partner track too."

"I'm already on the partner track."

"But you aren't partner yet. You aren't *my* partner."

"I probably will be after I win this case." Marisa crowed. "Speaking of... I need to settle in before Delaney arrives."

"Delaney? As in Kenneth Delaney?" Wadding the sopping paper towels, Lily straightened. Dawn joined them with a spray bottle of cleanser.

"I think so. Why?"

"I have a meeting with him at ten too." Lily turned to Dawn. "Is he meeting both of us?"

"Seems so. I didn't know he's the one meeting Ms. Meadows."

Marisa sauntered toward her temporary corner digs. "Thanks for the cleanup, ladies. Sorry I'm such a klutz."

"Is this what we have to look forward to when you join the firm?" Dawn's eyebrows hiked to her blonde hairline.

"No." Marisa grinned. "First day jitters. Now we're done."

"Yes," Lily countered. "She'll need her own personal maid, assistant, and paralegal all rolled into one. She's very needy."

"Like an intern?" Dawn rose to her full height. "Jake's cousin is finishing up her paralegal degree and is interested."

"No! Argh. Well... maybe. Don't pressure me. Don't hire an intern unless you need the minion without me." Laughing, Marisa waved them off.

She settled in behind the desk, checked her face in her compact, and popped a mint. Since the events of yesterday had killed her free time, she made a grocery list. Dawn's voice drifted from the intercom and announced Kenneth Delaney, CFO of Edison WebWorx, Inc.

Marisa stood to greet the man who represented her law firm's top corporate client. If she screwed up this case, she could kiss her partnership goodbye. *No, you have no plans to screw up this case. You rock the lawyer thing.*

He sauntered into the room. Shock riddled her like a spray of bullets. In a good way. In a most curious way, before a tiny amount of dejection smothered it all. Why hadn't she pieced it together?

"Kenny? Do I still have the liberty of calling you Kenny?" she asked her familiar savior from the airport. "Were you stalking me at the airport?" She winked, but an ice cube bloomed into an iceberg in her middle.

Green eyes alighting, he advanced and clasped her hand in a strong handshake. "Marisa Meadows. Lovely to see you here and well." He perused her from her hair to her spike heels. "Very well, I see. I'm glad your airport altercation didn't traumatize you too badly."

She swished her left hand. "Purse thieves are dime a doz. No harm, no foul, especially with my knight in shining armor." No way did she plan to tell him about the harm that had truly nailed her and the backlash with Ric McAllister and his insane clairvoyant joke. Just contemplating last night again hurled her on another trip up crap creek. *Jeez, where's my paddle?* He'd think she was Marisa McCuckoo. And she had no intention of letting him think ill of her, not personally, not professionally. Even if she wanted sexy fun times with him while she was in town, she didn't date clients. That ship sailed the day she landed her first lawyer gig.

"As for stalking, I might be persuaded." Smile lines bracketed his full lips and extended to the light crinkles around his unforgettable, mesmerizing eyes.

"No, seriously. Were you and I on the same plane? Did you know my identity?" Disconcerted, Marisa returned to the Guardian-sized chair behind the desk.

Kenny sidled to the windows overlooking downtown San Jose before he returned and took a perch on a client chair. "I have to admit, it does appear I'm tailing you. I assure you, I'm not. I had no idea you were on the plane until I heard your name in the terminal. After you handed me your business card, I didn't get an opportunity to explain to your fleeing backside."

"I'm not running now. Explain away." Marisa poured a dab of antibacterial gel on her hands and rubbed it in.

"I visited WebWorx's San Diego offices and met with Riley on behalf of our CEO and Legal team. It was merely a coincidence we were on the same plane. If I'd known, I would've invited you to sit with me in first class."

His first-class arrogance didn't give her the thrill he probably expected. Men with money were simply men with money. She didn't need the strings attached. "Were you interrogating Riley about me and why he assigned me to attend local counsel?" The question had bugged her since her boss delegated her to his top client. "I'm not exactly a partner."

"Not yet." Kenny smiled his charming Cheshire cat smile. "Our CEO's pleased with your appointment. And I," he winked, "am doubly pleased with you on our team."

"Really?" Unable to hold back, her sarcasm stretched out the word. Did he know about her telepathy? No. Riley didn't disclose to clients that she was not only the California Guild attorney, but a high-functioning telepath. Not that he knew of her special breed of telepathy. Did Delaney know she had a way with interrogations that had nothing to do with telepathy and more to do with her ability to coerce with a look, a gesture, a smile, or a slight touch? How many *men* were they deposing? One day, she promised to fix her hair in a bun, wear a baggy turtleneck, stretchy beige pants, and glasses.

"Marisa... may I call you Marisa?" She nodded, and he continued. "Your prowess as a skilled attorney swung the pendulum in your favor. Riley crowed your skills to the nth degree, and we've seen you in action. Your legal skills will not go unrewarded if you play your cards right."

Saved by the bell, her cell phone rang. Lily. "Excuse me." She held up a finger and answered. "You joining us?"

"In a few. Ric sent you an article from the news this morning. Did you see it?"

"No." Annoyed, she white-knuckled her phone. "How'd he get my number?"

"I gave it to him. Check your email. I need to finish up with Jake, then I'll join you." Lily clicked off.

Marisa opened her email, read the headlines of the article Ric forwarded. *Couple perishes in bedroom blaze.* She skimmed onward. *The man and woman are believed to have links to the local Psychic Guild.* The pendulum on the decorative clock on Jake's bookcase struck the hour, striking the need to post an ad on Craigslist for another life.

CHAPTER SEVEN

After Ric learned about the local house fire on the morning's news, he drove to Jake's loft apartment. Using his key, he let himself into the Falbrooke house, through the kitchen, and up the back stairs to the loft apartment.

"Yo, Jakeman," he called from the landing. Jake let him in, citrus and steam wafting off his sopping hair and bare chest. At least he wore skivvies. "You primping for me? How'd I rate?"

Jake tipped up Ric's baseball cap. "Get your head in our biz, bro."

"Oh, shit. I forgot we were negotiating the security contract for the museum display." Even though Jake worked as a PI and partner in Michael Falbrooke's old law firm, which Lily had inherited after Michael died, the McAllister brothers owned a security and PI firm, which also provided security for antiquity shows. Most days, Ric and Liam did all the security work, while Jake tackled the legal and PI business end zone.

"We've got time to spare," Jake replied. "Saw the news. Does it track?"

"To the T." Ric slouched on the black leather sofa, set his drumsticks aside. "I got a better mind's eye view of the lighter and the woman."

"Let me guess. Marisa Meadows?"

Hesitantly, he nodded. "The lighter has her prints all over it, as well as the bag. I also picked up the airport security guard and two other sets of unidentified prints. Matches her story about the theft."

"Means neither the thief nor the dude who returned the handbag are in the system."

"No shit, Sherlock." Ric flipped off his baseball cap and scratched his scalp. "The lighter thing gets me. She said she never touched it."

Jake pulled on a charcoal dress shirt and tucked it into his black slacks, reminding Ric of his casual T-shirt and jeans, not quite fitting for hoity-toity clients. Marisa Meadows had definitely screwed him up in too many ways to count. "Lily's known Marisa since she moved to San Diego four years ago and believes Marisa would never do something so whacked. The woman's the western Guild lawyer, not that the lofty title means diddly in this world. Lawyers aren't above the law." The front doorbell rang in the loft hallway. Jake buckled his belt, arched his brows. "Niles?"

"Yep. Better safe than never." Ric hopped down the stairs, through Lily's living room to the front door, comfortable invading Lily's personal space since he'd spent a couple days housesitting when Lily and Jake were in Tahoe last month.

He greeted the distinguished older Guild director. Tall and wiry, Niles didn't have an ounce of fat on him, and he appeared ten years younger than his mid-fifties. He governed the Protectorate and sat on the Guild's ruling council. A big shot in the Guild, he handled matters discreetly whenever and wherever his Guardians needed him. The McAllisters were his top Guardians, and Jake was the only First Guardian in the western U.S. region, a spot reserved for the ultimate best. Since Jake was permanently assigned to Lily, he'd given up his spot on the top rung. He wouldn't lose his status as First Guardian, but having a permanent Guardian job shackled him. Ric had a shot at the best assignments now. His psychic and Guardian skills rivaled Jake's, and he'd be the youngest First Guardian in Guild history.

Ric led the way upstairs, felt compelled to say, "I swept the place for bugs yesterday."

"Leave it to you and Jake to keep the Falbrooke house pest free at all times."

"It's a daily grind, but someone's gotta do it." Ric pushed open the door to Jake's apartment.

Jake and Niles did a bromance hug. "Hadn't planned on seeing you for a while after my latest escapades." He rolled his arm, stretched his injured shoulder.

"It seems the Cabal's still running amuck." Niles sat at the dinette and placed his smartphone on the wood surface in front of him. Somberly, Ric and Jake joined him.

"Members of an avian species of identical plumage congregating?" Ric tossed out and met stone silence. "Jeez, dudes, get with the lingo. Birds of a feather flock together."

"I'll get with the lingo after you learn to speak English." A smile kicked up the corners of Jake's mouth.

Ric poked at a dent in the scarred table, traced the JRM initials their father had carved in the wood. Jake had nicked the table from the storage shed on their uncle's property where their family's furnishings had been stored since their parents died in a car accident. Ric and his brothers moved from New Orleans to San Jose to live with their aunt, uncle, and cousins when they were hitting their teens. Even though they all now lived in their own homes, the brothers hadn't divvied up the furnishings. Too many painful memories accompanied the chore.

"Ric?" Niles tapped the table.

Lost in nostalgia, he hadn't paid attention to the conversation. "Yo, sorry. When did you snag this table out of storage?"

"What? We're here to talk about a murder, and you're worried about household furnishings? Planting a picket fence anytime soon?" Jake asked.

For the first time ever, Ric saw such a future. He thumped the table. "We had a deal about the storage shed."

Jake held up his hand. "Sorry. You're right. We do. I needed a table. It was going to waste. The good table's still there."

"Boys," Niles admonished. "Set the squabbling aside. I'm putting you on assignment, Ric. Do well by this, and you're up for First Guardian status."

Ric's ears perked up and excitement sped up his heart. "I'm in." He didn't need to guess his assignment.

"You don't even know the assignment yet."

"First let's talk about the fire. You know I had a clairvoyant vision, right?"

"Jake told me. I've already contacted Alex MacKenzie. SJPD has officially assigned him detective liaison between the Guild and police. I've put him and his fiancée, Juliana Westwood, on notice of more psychics targeted by the Cabal."

"Do we know it was Cabal?" Jake asked. "Juliana's not Guild yet. There's no precedence for the Cabal targeting non-Guild members."

"She's close enough to Guild, especially close to Lily, and a significant catch for the Cabal, both as a psychic and a Wall Street wiz. There's no sense in taking chances," Ric replied. "Do we have an ID on the deceased couple, yet?"

Niles's clean-shaven face turned granite. "That's the

crux. They're not Guild, and we have credible evidence the Cabal may have instigated the fire."

"This mess just got realer. We need to stop those SOBs before they win this war." Ric nearly salivated at his drumsticks across the room; instead, he drummed his fingertips on the tabletop. He needed to deter his nervous energy, even if it pissed off everyone around him.

"Why's the Cabal targeting non-Guild?" Jake asked. "Were they psychics?"

A pained expression traversed the planes of Niles's face. "The woman, Celina Augusta, possessed minor telekinetic ability. The man, Mario Saldivar, held no abilities and appears to be an innocent."

"How does the Guild know about Celina?" Jake whacked at Ric's hands to end his drum solo.

"Better yet, how did the Cabal know about her?" Ric shoved his hands in his front pockets, preventing them from gouging more scars in the tabletop.

"Celina approached us a few weeks ago with interest in joining the Guild. I didn't tell her we'd placed a moratorium on new members," Niles explained. "She was fidgeting, eyes darting, the whole shebang. She demonstrated her telekinesis. Reasonably good abilities, and you know how we're trying to bring in more telekinetics since they're so far and few between. I knew something was wrong, though. I asked if she was being threatened or needed guarding. She said she wanted the camaraderie of a professional organization of like-minded individuals, basically word for word from our mission statement. I set up another meeting and had Juliana Westwood," he held up his hands as Jake and Ric both glowered at him, "under her *cop boyfriend's permission and guard,* sit behind closed doors to read her mind. Juliana captured her thoughts. The Cabal approached Celina with a future rank and generous monetary offer if she'd infiltrate the Guild and work the inside to do the Cabal's dirty work."

"What dirty work?" Ric asked.

Niles pursed his lips in deep thought. "It wasn't clear. She was too agitated and kept up a steady mental mantra of 'get in and get out. Do what the Cabal says and all your life dreams will come true.'"

"Motivated by money?" Jake tipped his chair back on its hind legs.

"She's in debt up to her eyeballs. Medical school loans," Niles answered.

"Who killed them?" Ric began pacing the apartment. "And why?"

Niles turned his chair around to set both Ric and Jake in his periphery. "The million-dollar question. It's possible because we put her on ice for admittance into the Guild, the Cabal took action against her, or she gave them the wrong answer." He lifted his hands, and then let them drop onto the table with a dull thud. "I think her boyfriend, Mario, was collateral damage. Bottom line is your prophecy came true, and quite possibly Marisa Meadows had a hand in it, the thief at the airport did, or someone's setting her up."

Stopping in front of the picture window overlooking the distant city under an innocuous blue sky, Ric let the words sink in. The Guild had put the kibosh on new members until they kicked the Cabal to the curb. On top of that, the Cabal had already reeled in a slew of Guild members to do their dirty work in the form of stealing, spying, blackmail, and other illegal activities. They'd told those Guild members the Cabal had plans to take over the Guild and either all psychics get on the right side or they'd get caught in the crossfire. Of course, the money aspect didn't hurt. The Cabal paid bank for their illegal services.

As for Marisa, he needed to tread lightly for Lily's sake, for all their sakes, especially for the sake of his traitorous heart. Every time he saw her, he wanted her in his arms, his lips on hers, her heart beating for him. Sunlight glittering off the windows of the downtown buildings quieted the electricity pulsing in his veins whenever he dwelled on the enigmatic woman. Was she a pyro? A killer? Did he even want to know?

"I vote for set up." Ric spun on his boot heels.

Jake grumbled unintelligible words with a bunch of four letters. "Maybe. Until we prove it, she's on my shit list. I don't like her around Lily."

Approaching the table, Ric nailed a black look on his brother. "Then why aren't you guarding Lily now? You let the woman spend the night here, and she's probably sitting in Lily's office. Do you really think she's a killer?"

Niles stood between the two hulking McAllister brothers. "And that's exactly where you both should be." He held up his hand to stop their justifiable rants. "I know I asked to meet you here in private, now it's time to get on with your jobs."

"What do you mean?" An inner excitement streamed adrenaline through his blood. "Did Marisa accept me as her Guardian?"

"I'm asking you to guard her from the shadows. I don't want her to know you're guarding her. I want you reporting everything she does and everywhere she goes without her knowing. You'll sleep here... somewhere, or Jake can guard her at night. Or we install her at the compound, whatever you think she'll buy. The minute she finds out you're tailing her, the jig is up, and you may position the Guild in greater peril if she's working for the Cabal and they catch wind."

Ric's fingers spasmed as if he held his drumsticks. "My assignment is to spy on her? We've never spied on a member. Do you really think she's a Cabal minion?"

Jake scuffed his bare feet on the hardwood floor, the soft brushing grating on Ric's last nerve. "It's insane," Jake said. "She's telepathic. She'll ID and rip him to shreds in seconds. I can erect walls, but Ric's susceptible to strong telepathy."

"Thanks for the vote, man," Ric groused. "I'm not that sketchy."

"Time's ticking." Niles stuck his phone in his pocket. "If I learn anything about the fire, I'll let you know. The police will issue the victims' names once the families have been notified. It'll be treated as a homicide investigation. MacKenzie's taking lead, and everything goes through me. We have enough sensitivities on our hands with this one."

Ric side kicked Jake's leather sofa. "I don't like it."

"You don't need to like all your assignments. Do your job or First Guardian status will become the unattainable dream. I figured you'd like a sexy single woman on your radar." Niles winked to defray his brusque authoritative words.

"Fine. I'll shadow her fine ass, until the fat lady sings at the end of the tunnel." He gave Niles a two-fingered wave as Jake escorted him downstairs. How was he supposed to shadow her when she could probably flay open his mind in nothing flat? He possessed only minor ability to block telepathic intrusions. Clairvoyants obtained their gifts of seeing past, present, or future by an open mind. His sixth sense always pried open his mind whether he liked it or not, and he had a tougher time blocking out psychics due to his vulnerability.

Jake reentered the loft and headed to his closet. "I gotta hit the road before we lose this client."

"How good is Marisa's telepathy?"

"Uncanny, according to Lily."

"As good as you?"

"We're in a league of our own." Jake's smirk slayed a little something inside him.

"Just kill me now." Ric slumped down on the leather sofa, the chill in the room seeping under his skin. "I may as well quit the Protectorate before they can my ass." Failure wasn't an option in his playbook. But this assignment may end his run in the good-luck department.

CHAPTER EIGHT

Marisa shoved her phone aside as if it had ignited the killing blaze. The fire had nothing to do with her, so why did she feel like she'd kicked off a murder spree brandishing flamethrowers?

Fingers trembling, she clamped onto the edge of the desk to still them. "Sorry for the interruption. Lily is on her way." Battling to keep her psychic walls from toppling, she wrung out her crimping fingers under the desk. "Can I ask why you wanted to meet Lily and me both? I thought you were here to discuss the depositions. Lily's not involved."

"Only because we haven't brought her on board yet. I'm hoping to change the tide today." Kenny steepled his fingers under his chin, like a cat ready to pounce on a broken cage full of canaries.

Marisa blinked back her surprise. The door opened and Lily walked through, smoothing down her wavy auburn hair.

"Kenneth Delaney, so nice to meet you. Please excuse my tardiness." Kenny stood and they shook hands.

"My deepest condolences on your father's passing. He was an astute lawyer." He gestured to the client chair beside his, and they both sat, leaving Marisa adrift and alone on the other side of Jake's massive desk, not a normal feeling for her.

Kenny continued. "I'm not sure if you knew, but Michael and I spoke about several legal matters. In fact," his gaze skipped from Marisa to Lily, "that's why I wanted to meet with you."

"I'm sorry, but I didn't see any case files with your name on them. Unless my partner, Jake McAllister, has taken them over." A flash of annoyance danced across Lily's naturally pale face.

Marisa hid a smile. Jake had temporarily concealed things from Lily after Michael's death in the guise of protecting the little missus and her frail sensibilities. *Idiot Guardian.*

"I had no dealings with McAllister," Kenny explained. "We were interested in working with Michael exclusively. We choose our legal teams with the utmost care, not that McAllister isn't an expert in his field."

"I get it. He's not a practicing lawyer," Lily added. "Then what can Marisa and I do for you and Edison WebWorx?"

Kenny grinned and flashed his mesmerizing orbs at Lily, carried her down into his lagoon of trust. Marisa squirmed in the leather chair as Lily seemed to fall into his charm, grinning like she'd won the Pulitzer for her lamest legal briefs.

"Well, I'd like to know the answer myself." Marisa and Lily never fought over men, but there was always a first time for everything. *Whoa. Wait? Did I just think that? Crap on a canoe up shit creek. What is wrong with me?*

"I'd like to woo Falbrooke & Associates to become my personal counsel and Edison's lead counsel for corporate legal matters." Kenny released his bombshell, his smugness sliding into a congratulatory smile, as if he'd bestowed said Pulitzer on Lily's firm.

"Seriously?" Lily practically preened. Scoring WebWorx could put her on the law firm map in Silicon Valley while she gained the new reins of her father's legacy.

Uncertainty whirled in Marisa's mind, and she sent out a tendril of telepathy toward Kenny. The wisp recoiled as it hit granite, and she internally berated herself for attempting to intrude upon his private motivations. "How does your offer include me?" she blurted out to hide her mild shock.

"My offer is contingent upon you joining the firm. Edison is pleased with the reputations you've both established. And, I'll admit, we're keen for more diversity in our outside partners. We believe you both fit the bill."

Lily leaned over the chair arm toward Kenny, and Marisa swore her best friend wanted to slobber Kenny with kisses.

"I'm sorry, but—" Marisa shut her mouth. Was the offer worth uprooting her life, relocating to San Jose, and leaving the familiar as well as an empty condo... an empty life? An empty heart and a head stuffed with voices? Not like the voices wouldn't follow her anywhere.

"Ladies, I know it's a big decision. I certainly recognize the changes this creates in your life, Marisa. We want you to relocate, of course, since our corporate offices are local. I'm sure Riley will be pleased at your success."

"Pleased?" Marisa snorted. "Are you kidding me? He'll be pissed. You're talking about poaching one of his best attorneys on the partnership track *and* his top client."

"Well, I'm not the one who'll be poaching you." He tossed his Cheshire cat grin at Lily. "However, we've contemplated all contingences." Kenny deliberately splayed his right hand on his thigh as though he fought the urge to ball it into a fist. A worm of unease chased goose flesh up Marisa's back. Kenny continued. "We'll throw him a few bones to keep his income up and honor our agreement. He'll continue to handle our current litigation until the case is resolved. As for losing his top talent, I'm afraid I win. He'll just have to suck it up." Kenny rose and buttoned his custom-made Italian suit over his sinful abs. "Duty calls. Think upon my offer."

Intrigued and harboring major doubts, Marisa stood to escort him to the reception room. He touched her hand, lingering proprietarily. One dip into his head could appease her doubts. But she refused to compromise their budding relationship by learning secrets belonging to him alone... even if he hadn't blocked her.

"I'm calling in my raincheck. Dinner tonight?" he asked.

Despite her grave misgivings, her walls dropped a skosh, and this time she easily slipped into his mind, gauged his sincerity, searched for anything to steer her toward or away from him. Her morals barely twitched as she did the deed. She'd hate herself later. His mind met hers, gentle and soothing as if he knew she'd slipped into his mind, but gave no outward sign, no flinch, no surprise. Quickly, she probed his welcoming mind, kicking her remorse to the wayside. No vacancy for guilt existed in her heart and head. Too many men preceding Kenny had slid by her tests and broken her heart. She refused to allow another. *Psychic Support Network, here I come.* His mind mirrored his words and demeanor and she learned nothing new. Walls ascended in both their minds, ending her moral dilemma. "Sounds lovely," she said.

"I'll text you."

Nodding, Marisa blew out a tiny puff of relief.

One final graze of his fingers on her cheek, and he departed the office. Rooted to the tile floor, Marisa rubbed the inflamed spot. The muted sounds of printers, people talking, and paper shuffling filed in.

"Marisa?" Lily joined the clamor in her head. "Shock got your tongue?"

"Shock, confusion, and the cat." She shook out of her strange fog. "You're loving this, aren't you?"

"You know it." Grinning, Lily curled her arm around Marisa's arm. "If my enticing offer didn't do it for you, his offer should seal the deal. Although I'll be a little miffed if you take my offer only because he seasoned it."

"Were you really serious?" she asked.

"Deadly. Jake's not a barred attorney, although he graduated law school. The clients he towed in have been demanding in the contracts law arena. I can't do it all. If we get Edison and Delany's work on retainer, I can probably increase your current salary."

Marisa needed to know more about what kind of legal services Delaney and Edison needed. She considered uprooting her life. No family tied her to San Diego any longer. A wistful crick of her heart gave tribute to her mother's decision to admit herself to an Arizona institution after Marisa's older sister had killed herself three years ago—for the same telepathy abilities Marisa battled. Her mother's internal walls had irretrievably crashed after Celeste died, and she'd never been able to rebuild them, leaving her vulnerable to psychic coercion. The voices nearly destroyed her mother. Celeste was gone and San Jose wasn't much farther from Tucson.

"Do it. Do it. Do it. You can stay in my house until you find your own place." Lily gilded the lily.

"All right. I'll think about it!" Marisa snorted out a laugh she didn't feel. "Geez, Louise, you're a nag."

"Only when I'm right." Lily squeezed her arm and let go. "Hey, you okay?"

"Thinking about Mom and admittedly how empty San Diego is with you gone now." Marisa gave her a wonky smile.

"How is she?"

"Same old, nothing new. She likes Tucson, and it's close to her family. A lot of quiet emptiness with others in the same boat. The caregivers and staff are wonderful."

"It's what she needs to quiet her head," Lily commiserated.

"I just wish someone knew how to teach her to reconstruct her walls." Marisa sank onto the thick-padded seat of Jake's chair behind the desk, the leather frigid against her bare legs, imparting a semblance of sense in her weird morning. She dragged her thoughts out of her dark dungeon before her pity party took a spin.

Lily sat in a client chair, kicked off her pumps. "At least she's not holding you back from making a decision to relocate here. Seriously, Marisa. This is as real as it gets." She bestowed a triumphant smile on Marisa. "And Delaney seems to like you, *like you,* if you know what I mean."

Marisa slouched back in the chair and rocked it side to side in a gentle lull. "Oh, I know what you mean. It's classic for a client to develop feelings for his lawyer when he's dependent, reliant, and impressed with said lawyer. Been there, done that. You know I don't get involved with clients. You know my issues with men." She blinked back her surprise. "Wait a hot minute. Two minutes ago, you were siccing Ric McAllister on me. Now Delaney. What's up with you? Did schizophrenia emerge from your repressed psychic abilities too?"

Lily giggled like a freaking schoolgirl. "Well, you didn't seem so keen on Ric. Just opening your senses to options. The man scene is far from dead here."

"Guardian. Client. Code. Looks dead to me."

"You agreed to dinner with Delaney." Lily swung her shamrock pin on its silver chain. She never left home without a shamrock on her body. Her good luck charm had saved her ass a million times, but had also carried a boatload of sorrow to Lily's life.

Marisa only had her black to bring her any luck. She hid behind it, in front of it, all over it. No wonder Ric McAllister sensed evil around her. Maybe she needed a new chapter in her life, which included a little color. Maybe a blue-topaz ring to match the color of Ric's eyes.

"Wheels are spinning," Lily prompted.

"Spinning into the ether. Back off, my precious. Let's just spin through one day at a time." Her mind revolved to the article Ric jammed down her throat in his red-flagged email earlier. "Why did Ric send me that article? Is he insinuating I set the fire and killed those two people?"

"No!" Lily defended. "He'd be here with the cops and cuffs in that case."

"Really? Would the Guild want to jeopardize a high-ranking member?" She swished an exaggerated hand up from her breasts to the top of her head.

The moment her words rolled out, the door opened and annoying-gnat McAllister waltzed in as if he owned the place. And her psychic morals hurriedly took a hike.

Marisa's blocks plummeted before she willed them to stay in place. Hell, she didn't think she could stop the sudden fall or the ease in which she slipped into Ric's mind. Or the hellish vision he dragged her mentally kicking and screaming into with a side order of lunacy.

CHAPTER NINE

Static buzzed in Ric's head, and the telltale exploding stars chased the noise. Reeling like a drunk at last call, he barely made it to the sofa near the door. The vision swallowed all his senses as it grabbed hold and took him for a ride, hitting speedbumps as Marisa slipped past his barriers and tromped into his head.

The woman's long hair reeked of smoke. She flicked the lid up and down on the engraved lighter, her short blood-red thumbnail contrasting with the paleness of her skin.

The faceless man led her into his home. The mansion's sleek modern lines cast jitters up her spine. The all-around perfect package had horrible taste in décor. Maybe she'd eventually change him, bring him to a more traditional style, or even a transitional one if he refused to slide to the left all the way to traditional.

"Brandy?" His cultured voice infiltrated her ridiculous thoughts.

"Sure. We have a lot to celebrate." She pressed her left breast against his arm, slithered around him, and painted her body over his backside. She slipped her hands past his hips, over his growing erection. Satisfaction chased her angst out the door, but seeds of guilt and sorrow lingered.

He turned, holding her against his chest, his hardness

pulsing into her soft middle. The overhead pendant light brought to her attention the windows to his soul and so much more, and on edge, she glanced away.

"Mmmm." He dropped a kiss on her forehead. "You did well tonight. Exactly as planned. I couldn't have hoped for a better outcome. Remember, reluctance has no place in life. Refusal will get you killed." He smiled, and she melted into his embrace. "You passed your initiation."

"Does that mean I'm in?" she whispered.

"You were in the moment I met you." Cupping her left breast, he gently kneaded it, his thumb flicking erotically over her hardening nipple.

His delectable ass earned her attention, and she dug her fingers into his butt cheeks and pulled him closer. "How in will you be tonight?"

"Deep." He nuzzled her neck.

"Nightcap first." She eased out of his arms. "I'm a little frazzled."

"It gets easier with time. You did the right thing. They were risky and in the way. They would have destroyed us and everything we've worked for."

"I know." To occupy her hands, she grabbed a bottle of apricot brandy from the bar shelf behind her. "Go get out of your suit."

"I was just about to suggest you get comfortable also."

"I will. In a few." Licking her lips enticingly, she prodded him toward the arched doorway.

She waited until his footsteps faded before she poured a healthy finger of brandy and gulped it down to quell her nerves. She waited for the warmth to quiet her turmoil. Why was she so jumpy? She poured more amber fuel in both glasses.

"Darling?" His voice sliced her awareness, quickening her pulse into stroke zone.

Glasses in hand, she swung around almost knocking

one into the faucet. Amber liquid sloshed up the inside of the glass and waterfalled back into the snifter. An eagle seemed to beat its wings against a cage inside her, attempting to escape the mess she'd made of her life, the death sentence awaiting her. It was inevitable, even if she had no clue why or what it meant.

She handed him a glass. "Just in time."

"Head in the clouds?" He cupped the snifter in his hand.

A cloud created by smoke and flames. *"Thinking of tonight and our first time together."* Fat fucking chance. *Startling her, the three words simmered below the surface. What the hell did they mean? She wanted to be with him. Didn't she? What was wrong with her?*

He approached her, held his glass up for a toast. "To tonight, to our future... togetherness."

She clinked her glass against his, swilled half the brandy. The liquid's velvet on her tongue was tasteless, and she ignored the renewed fire in her belly. He followed suit, savoring the expensive brandy on his tongue.

She took his glass, set both down with loud clinks on the marble counter. "Let's get cozy on the couch." As they strode down the hallway, she began a provocative striptease. First her jacket... then nothing. The doorbell rang as they passed through the foyer, delivering a dose of reluctance.

The man opened the door, his lover hanging onto his arm, to confront the backside of a woman on the porch. Long, dark hair streamed down her slender back. Fire blazed behind her. She turned slowly, hair obscuring her features. Flames engulfed her from the feet up, and she took on a smoky, ghostly visage, her hair blowing away from her face.

Ric bellowed, "No!" A knife stabbed his heart and chopped it into a million pieces as the ethereal and very much dead Lily Falbrooke met his mind's eye.

Flailing in panic, he awoke shouting Lily's name. He stumbled up from the sofa, head spinning as he searched the room. Lily floundered on the floor with a cold washcloth in her hand where he'd knocked her over.

"Sorry." He hoisted her into his arms and set her upright. "You're really here, right? Jake will kill me if anything happens to you on my watch."

"I'm fine." She slit her eyes. "What do you mean on *your* watch?"

"Nothing." He rushed to Marisa slumped in the chair behind Jake's desk, out like the dead. "What happened?"

"You both passed out at the same time," Lily responded.

Eyelids fluttering open, Marisa said between gritted teeth, "He wrenched me into another clairvoyant vision." She slammed the chair against the chair rail guarding the wall of windows behind her and gained her feet.

"*You* slipped into my head." Her fierce anger set off a new round of lust, contrary to his defensive words. He was sunk ten ways to Sunday.

"You two are freaking me out. Juliana Westwood is the only one I know who can mentally link to someone."

"It's not the same," Ric grumbled.

"You sure about that?" Marisa snapped. "Are *you* telepathic?"

"I see things about people that defy reason or normal. I don't read minds."

"What did you see?" She crossed her arms over her chest, straining the buttons of her blouse, offering an unintentional peep show at her lacy black bra and the creamy white skin of her breasts.

He salivated and penalized his brain's untimely desire to stoke his internal fire. "You tell me."

"Seriously? You're going to play this game?" Marisa

stomped her foot on the floor. "Un. Believable."

Lily held up a placating hand. "Let's sit and talk rationally." She waited until he'd plunked down onto the couch and Marisa sat board straight in Jake's chair before she turned a client chair sideways. "What did you see, Ric?"

"Dead people." *Damn it all to hell.* He refused to fess up. Why had he seen Lily on fire? Had Marisa seen the same thing? He scratched his skull, trying to scare up clues. "I don't see dead people. That's not my thing."

"Maybe it is now," Lily said with an empathetic tightening of her lips. "Psychic ability can change. Happened to me, others. Who did you see?"

"I don't know." He gauged Marisa's blank reaction. "Before the dead, I saw Marisa with a man. Getting naked."

She lunged up. "Again you think it was me? Are you freaking crazy?" She splayed her fingers on the desk and bent halfway over it, giving him another healthy dosage of her deep cleavage. Flecks of gold blazed in her eyes, searing into his soul, and he fought the jabs of fire in his groin.

"Crazy as batshit if it wasn't you." He pushed off the couch, stalked across the room, leaned on the desk, and met her face-to-face. "Who are you? Did you kill the couple? Who's the man you're playing house with?" Ric wanted to dip his tongue in the chocolate kiss of her eyes and never allow her to take her molten gaze off him.

"Look, McAllister. I'm telling you for the gazillionth time, you got the wrong fire starter. The bitch in your vision struck the match. The man called the shots. He's the one you need to hunt down. Didn't you get a *good* view of his face? In fact, did you get a look at the woman? Or do you blame everything involving a long-haired woman on me?" She flicked a hand toward Lily. "Hell, maybe it was

Lily. We have the same length hair. Red, black, you couldn't tell. Maybe it was your mother."

Lily waved her hand at Marisa. "Mar—"

"Let her get it out." Ric yanked on the hem of his T-shirt beneath his jacket, glanced at his boots, out the window, anywhere but at Marisa. "It wasn't Lily," he said softly. "Sure as hell wasn't my long-dead mother."

Marisa breathed in and out several times, her breasts heaving with each exhale, breasts he wanted moving against his naked chest. "Oh, Ric, I'm sorry. I didn't mean it." Unshed tears glittered. "I'm sick to death of all this. Lily, you know me. You know I'd never do something like this."

"Of course, Mar." Lily scurried to Marisa's side. "We need to get to the bottom of this before we all hit cuckoo town."

The two standing together, fiery red hair and long jet hair, creamy skin, gorgeous and hotter than hell started a double hum in Ric's veins. Jake was one lucky bro. Man, if he figured Marisa out, he might have a chance at the same kind of luck.

"I need to say something primed to hit your buttons." Ric hitched a hip on the desk. "It wasn't Lily. Because Lily was... the dead one."

"Whoa. What?" Lily clutched her neck.

"No." Marisa slammed back into the chair. "It wasn't her in the bed."

"Not what I said," he replied. "Did you see anything after you, sorry, after the fire starter stripped off her clothes in the foyer?"

"No." Marisa furiously began to type notes into her phone, and a heavy silence hovered over the room. "Sorry. I'm a note taker. Keeps my life sane. Go on."

Ric relayed what he'd envisioned after the man and woman opened the door. He had more to dish out, the reason he let Jake tackle their important new client meeting alone that morning. If his psychic abilities were changing, he needed to stay two steps ahead or he'd wind up in a river of denial, fighting the crazy barge. Once a psychic lost control, it didn't bode well for long-term mental wellbeing. Damned if he'd let a slip of a black-haired siren destroy him from the inside out, especially if he didn't at least get to taste her and discover all her wicked charms. He needed to solve the mysterious hot and glacial vibe she exuded. Never had he been so simultaneously attracted to a woman *and* repelled by her. It sounded bizarre, yet she turned him on in ways he'd never experienced. Furtively, he adjusted the crotch of his pants behind his leather jacket, trying to ease the pain of his surging erection.

"What does this mean?" Lily's voice wobbled. "Do your clairvoyant visions always come true?"

"Sometimes, I see things that've already happened. Other times, they're a sixth sense about a person manifesting in weird scenes that don't necessarily happen or involve that person or might happen another way. Let's say for the sake of this mystery, Marisa saw the fire happen, or I saw the fire in a movie or in real time. The event lingers and forms a lasting impression we can't shake. Then it manifests into these revelations, meaningless in the true sense, but displays our feelings about the event. They might be memory triggers of past life experiences, or fears, such as the fear of dying by fire. Or like this case, since the couple lay back-to-back on the bed, a fear of intimacy or problems with a significant other." He inhaled a deep breath of office tower air, wishing for coastal sea air to cleanse the leftover taint within him. "Other visions portray future events."

"If your visions can be anything in your overactive imagination, then why do you keep thinking it's me?"

"Mar, the vision came true, remember?"

"Oh. Right." Marisa rubbed her temples. "This is insane. I don't understand how your visions are reeling through my head. What did you do to me?"

"I didn't do anything." He fidgeted in his chair, trying to ease the pressure spiraling in his groin. "As soon as I entered the room, your walls fell, mine dropped, and bam."

"It's a rare phenomenon." Lily paled. "Happened to psychic Juliana Westwood during a kidnapping case and again with her and Jake last month."

Ric wanted desperately to ease both Lily and Marisa's concerns and serve up a dish of happiness. "When in Rome, the writing's on the wall." A muscle throbbed in his neck belying his lack of conviction.

"Huh?" Marisa's quizzical look slid to disdain. "I think you've mixed up your sayings."

"Do I need protection?" Lily reached for her phone, poised her finger over the screen. "Should I tell Jake?"

"I think you better," he replied. "Tonight, we'll all talk. Pizza's on me."

A tendril of hair clung to Marisa's brow. He wanted that tendril of silk coiled around his finger, then trailing his rock-hard erection. She rolled the chair away from the desk and stood, her stance wobbly.

"Agreed. I need fresh air." She produced a pair of sneakers from her handbag. Did she carry the kitchen sink in her bag now? Bending over to change her shoes, she asked, "What are you doing here in the first place? To tell us you see dead people? To scare the life out of my best friend? Thanks. You've succeeded in dashing our happy vibes into dust."

He recoiled at her acerbic tone, but her sarcasm refused to hide the lines of strain around her mouth. "To tell you there were no prints other than yours and the airport security dude on your handbag. One single print on the lighter." He paused for effect. "Yours."

Marisa's shoulders sagged forward. "I feel like a broken record. I never touched it. You saw me dump it onto the table." Her spine tensed as if she realized how ludicrous her defense sounded since she'd carried the lighter in her purse with multiple opportunities to use it for anything under the sun before she arrived at the Guild compound. But something inside Ric's intuition accepted her words as truth. "Someone's setting me up. How can the bag not have any prints? Both Kenneth Delaney and the thief manhandled it."

"Delaney?"

"My airport savior. Long story. Turns out he's a client of my firm." Marisa absently wiped her hands on her skirt as if culpable ashes coated them.

"We met him here today." Lily's excited gleam slashed the angst from her strained face. "Major client. Might sign with my firm."

"I'll check him out. There were prints on the bag, just didn't find a match in the system," he explained. He planned to spend every waking second clearing Marisa, discovering her angles, to drill deep into everything Marisa Meadows is and was, until she wound up in his bed.

His feelings barreled into him. He'd never fallen so hard and fast for a woman. Maybe she *had* invaded him and steered his thoughts and emotions around like a hot rod on the racetrack. Swift, furious, and expertly winding her way through his mind and setting course for his fickle heart. Worst of all, he may have fallen for a murderer.

CHAPTER TEN

Marisa joined the foot traffic in a typical downtown riddled with office towers of various heights and sizes. Deafening thoughts barraged her. She attempted to grow her field of red flowers, listened for the nonexistent breeze to flutter them on their stems. Instead, the tinkling waterfall dried up and wilted stick flowers met her, brown petals lying in heaps on the barren ground. The day's disturbances turned her safe harbor into zombie desolation.

She'd noticed Ric McAllister watching her leave Jake's office. Without granting her evil twin a moment to dip into his thoughts, a gut feeling told her he didn't want to let her out of his sight. He believed she'd either committed a heinous crime or landed in trouble with a capital T. At the moment, she didn't care, didn't want him near her. He was too distracting, his mind too enticing, his face too gorgeous, and his body too toned, all-around epically alluring. On one hand, she wanted to smack him; on the other, she wanted to wrap herself around him and take him for a spin into paradise. Unfortunately, taking him for a spin might be a permanent thing in his book and not a casual fling. For that reason, she needed to keep her distance. He was too important to Lily and the Guild to tease and screw with, or eventually disappoint and hurt.

Three four- or five-year-old girls with their nanny stepped in front of her, heading to the city park. Their anticipation of playtime on the jungle gym lent her a moment of joy. Playgrounds allowed her to drop her shields and let kids' happy chatter peanut butter over the adult tumult in her head. She willingly followed the cutie pies. The fresh-brewed scent of coffee drifted over from a sidewalk vendor, and she inhaled the airborne caffeine to feed her system. She stopped behind the excited girls at a crosswalk across the street from the park.

Maybe she needed to keep her walls down to figure out what lunacy she'd tripped into. She didn't make a habit of absorbing the thoughts around her, but she needed to eliminate this insidious evil from her life. It was time to settle the score, especially with Mr. Hard Body McAllister accusing her of murder. *Crazy times ten.* She couldn't even light an ant on fire, let alone a sleeping couple in bed. And why were her prints on the lighter? Had she inadvertently touched it in her purse while hunting for one of a million items? No way. Someone was jacking her. Who'd she tick off so badly they'd set her up for murder? Murder of all crimes! Not even invasion of privacy. What'd she do to deserve this? *Wait a hot minute. Why were my sneakers and sweat jacket dumped on the floor of my bedroom this morning as if I'd walked in my sleep? Where had I gone? What had I done?*

Squealing brakes, engines roaring, and honking horns competed with the converging voices crowding her new shop of horrors. As she passed a teenager, she "heard" the teen berate herself for screwing her best friend's boyfriend last night as she wondered how to keep their friendship intact. *Good luck with that.* A thirty-something man shouted out his mental glee at beating his wife in a game of drunken chess and winning a blow job.

TMI. TMI.

Another excited voice joined the fray. Angry and on the verge of losing it, a young man wanted to strike a young woman beside him, his girlfriend's best friend who'd talked his girlfriend into tossing out his stash of drugs and dumping him. He wanted a hit of cocaine to soothe his rough edges. *"What the fuck is karma doing in the park anyways?"* he mentally screamed. His thoughts bombarded Marisa. He planned to kick her—Karma's?—ass, and he couldn't wait to get home to show Leah who was the man and get her to dump her loser friend Karma. *Loser times ten.* Marisa barely made it across the street behind the kiddos before she hugged the traffic light pole to hold herself up and cease the torrent of inevitable negativity in her head.

Suddenly, she felt like a very big fish in a tiny bowl. *Well, duh, idiot. You're holding onto a pole like you want to dance it.* Steadying herself, she released the pole and followed the girls to the park as if she were a stalker.

The angry crackhead helicoptered over the young woman sitting on a bench at the park's perimeter as if to devour her in his rush of angry words. Afraid to get involved, surrounding people scattered.

Marisa held no such qualms. She stepped closer to them just out of his reach and said quietly to the frightened twentyish young woman, "Leave now before he hurts you. He's going to get your girlfriend Leah to crap on you." The pretty, dark blonde-haired woman beseeched her with wide hazel-green eyes.

Fuming, the loser rounded on Marisa, leaned forward as if to force his words upon her. "You don't know what you're talkin' 'bout. Get outta my business, bitch." His mental voice slammed into her. *"Leah and I need a nice fat doobie, and I'll smooth it over with her. She'll never know what hit her. Ha! She'll never know I hit her stupid ass for trying to leave me just 'cause Karma ratted me out. What kind of dumbass name is Karma, anyway?"*

His thoughts hailed upon her with a rabid intensity. Marisa bent double and whispered to the young woman, "You gals don't need to take his BS. Tell Leah she's better than this. There's more to life than weed and sex if that's all she's getting from him." Giving the druggie a wide berth, she left them behind, the woman's mouth hanging open. There was only so much she could do without jeopardizing herself and her abilities further. She'd gone too far past the red and her walls refused to rise.

Footsteps pounded behind her, and a hand clamped onto her shoulder. Expecting the dumbass abuser, she ducked and wheeled around in a protective stance she'd learned in self-defense class. Ric McAllister stood close, his face hidden behind sunglasses and a baseball cap. The knots in her shoulders unraveled down her arms, and she nearly hugged him.

"What happened back there?" he asked. "That dude's lost his chill."

"Are you stalking me?" She fought her yearning to take his glasses off and soothe her emotions in his blue warmth.

He shuffled his feet. "Maybe." He knocked off his cap and ruffled his hair, not caring that it stuck up in cute little chaotic spikes Marisa wanted to sift her fingers into.

The corners of her lips kicked up in a tiny smile before she set her mouth in a grim line. "I reiterated things the girl was already thinking."

"Do you make a habit of infringing upon people's thoughts?" He inclined toward her. "Are you reading me?"

Contemplating how much she cared to divulge, she turned and headed deeper into the park toward a bench near a tiered water fountain. She dropped onto the empty bench, and it sank a little as he sat next to her, less than a foot of space between them. She wished he'd scoot a little closer. His cologne, cedar with top notes of citrus and cardamom, infused her senses, leaving her dizzy with outlandish desire.

"I'm not reading you. I can systematically block people while listening in on others." She tried to erect partial walls to block him out, but her focusing field of flowers immediately withered into dry petals of discomfort. She rubbed her temples. "It hurts, though." Then she wiped her fingers on her skirt, wishing she'd brought her antibacterial gel after her altercation with the creepy druggie. He was still having an intense conversation with Karma. She tuned them out and concentrated on the action closer to the fountain.

"See the red-haired boy climbing the ladder to the slide? He's excited and wondering how fast he'll fly down." She subtly pointed to a woman rocking a baby carriage. "That woman's wondering if she'll get a raise for adding two kids to her daily nanny routine. She's pissed her employer foisted her sister's bratty kids on her without mentioning more money." The fountain's splashing became an elixir to her rattled mind, the tinkle a cool relief. "The teen girl on the other side of the fountain is frazzled with guilt for cutting class, but can't wait to meet her college-aged boyfriend so they can go screw each other's brains out."

"The rug rats have happy thoughts, but generally everyone else is a study in misery. Is that what you're telling me?" Ric's murmur thrummed across her senses, hitting her tranquil buttons. He got it, really got it.

"The little kids are mostly happy. It's why I like sitting near them. They let me drop my guard and clear my head."

"Do you ever read nice or happy thoughts from teens and adults?"

She took in the length of him, his too-sexy-for-words chiseled and cut cheekbones, his slightly square chin, blade nose, and his full pouty lips. Lips she wanted pressed to hers in a most desperate way. She flung off her intrusive hormonal imbalance. "Sure. The teen is stoked she's gonna have sex before her mom gets home from work. I'd call that semi-happy. How about you?"

Ten shades of scarlet painted Ric's clean-shaven face, his wide smile sending a stab of heat to her cranky lower regions. "Semi-happy?"

Tingles dancing over her breasts chased his hearty laugh. "If her mother finds out she's dating a college boy, she's toast."

"Sex is great," he said. "When you're with the right person." His fingers grazed her outer thigh, electrifying, zipping tiny currents to her toes.

His declaration hit an acrimonious soft and sore spot. So he wasn't the hit-and-run type, the type she usually bagged in her own hit-it-and-quit-it style.

All of a sudden, the maddening tingles evolved into deep prickles gouging her back. The junkie arrested her attention, his thoughts projecting so loud they yanked on her synapses.

"Oh no... he's totally strung out." She pointed the loser out to Ric. "He's got a gun. Call nine-one-one." She leaped up and began to jet down the walkway. "Hey!" She waved her arms, trying to get the young-woman-who-had-a-death-wish's attention. Why hadn't she left him? Maybe she feared for her friend Leah's life and was trying to buy time or reroute his attention elsewhere?

"Marisa!" Ric yelled, footsteps thumping behind her. "Let me handle it." He closed the distance between them. "Oh, hell. Karma!" he shouted, as if he suddenly realized he knew the young woman.

Before the name rolled out of Ric's mouth, the man

struck Karma on the side of her head. The blow sent her sprawling to the sidewalk. Cries and gasps of innocent bystanders escalated like a beacon of dread. Most of them dispersed and Marisa heard a call to nine-one-one. One man ran off to hunt down a cop, usually found on downtown beat patrol, Marisa read in his head. Other voices overshadowed the abuser's rage and glee at seeing Karma cowering on the walkway. Worst of all, he desperately wanted another hit to maintain his high, the drugs Leah had tossed at Karma's insistence, and the reason for his wrath.

Ric ground to a halt beside Marisa. "Don't touch her again, asshole. Karma, are you okay?" The young woman gave him a shaky thumb up.

"Get back," Mr. Abuser screamed, skin going apoplectic, spit flying into the ether. "Nobody move!" He brandished his weapon, a nine-millimeter. Marisa knew the type well, owning two, one tucked in her purse. The crowd froze, a few easing behind the sparse trees. Strung out gave the druggie a leg up on his little terrorism jig, but the drugs may inhibit his aim, which imperiled everyone in the vicinity, including the kids in the playground.

Marisa took another step forward. Ric practically tackled her from behind, pinned her in an arm lock and thrust her behind him. She struggled and kicked back at him. "Babe, calm down. Don't get involved," he ordered.

"Don't babe me," she said. "I can diffuse this situation before anyone else gets hurt."

"Really?" he said in a slight sneering voice, towing them behind a thick tree trunk. "Seems like you might have egged him on."

"Screw you, McAllister." She rounded on him. "He wants a fix. She turned his girlfriend against him, and the girlfriend tossed his stash. Do you know her? Who is she?" Too muddled to piece together a strand of information, the woman's thoughts refused to gel in Marisa's head.

"She's my cousin. She's like my sister. I grew up with her and her brothers." Ric drummed his fingers on the bill to his baseball cap. "I didn't see her face when I passed her earlier. Damn it. She's using her touch telepathy to read things. It always gets her in deep."

"You. Bitch. Get your ass over here." The madman's nasally voice wafted to Marisa. She didn't need to read him to know he was talking to her. *Son of a crackhead-junkie whore.*

"Now, before I blow a hole in your boyfriend."

Hands in the air, Ric stepped in front of her. "Dude, there's no need for guns here. Too many people. You don't want to hurt the kids."

"How do you know Karma?" he kicked the quivering woman's leg, and she cringed farther under the bench. "I want to know what game these two bitches are playing."

"Slide your hand inside my jacket and snag my gun out of my harness," Ric said in his head.

Completely obscured from the gunman's view, Marisa sidled closer to Ric's wide-shouldered back. She had to admit his body granted her an epic sense of security, but not at the expense of his life. Slipping her hand inside the back of his jacket, his spicy cologne wafted off him in waves, infusing her senses. The leather shoulder harness held his gun under his raised arm and she inched her fingers up to it. The snap proved her biggest battle since she didn't want to make an outward motion that might give the trigger-happy addict ideas. Like shooting Ric or any number of people frozen in their tracks.

"Fuck, fuck, fuck," the man repeated. His anger held a fearful edge as he realized his predicament. "You know what they say about karma, right?" he said aloud before

kicking at her again, missing by inches. *"I ought to kill the stupidass bitch. Then Leah won't listen to her bull any more. Maybe I'll take me a hostage. Like that black-haired troublemaker. Or maybe a kid on the jungle gym. Yeah, that's the ticket."*

Marisa forced all the other thoughts to the wayside to concentrate on him, but the cacophony in the still tableau filtered in. In slow motion, she unsnapped Ric's gun and worked it out of his harness.

"He's thinking of taking a kid from the jungle gym hostage to escape," she whispered. He nodded imperceptibly to show he'd heard her.

The gun filled her palm, warm from Ric's body and oh so comforting.

"Shove it in my back waistband," he said.

"I know how to use it."

"Please, Marisa," he pleaded. *"Do what I say and I'll keep everyone alive, including my cousin."*

Several cops circled the gunman from a discreet distance to avoid triggering a sudden move.

One lone man approached, hands up, his gun tucked into his holster, wearing plain clothes. "Set the gun on the ground and put your hands in the air," he demanded, cool and authoritative. "Let's talk. Just you and me. We'll let all the people leave, okay? Tell me what's going on here. Maybe I can help you sort it out."

Marisa had helped the police in San Diego in similar situations, breaching the minds of criminals and victims, trying to extrapolate their motives, next steps, and emotions. She never promoted her talent, but the police contacted her in extreme cases. She hated not being able to save the victim of her first case, and it killed her ability to lock out voices for weeks afterward. The trauma also temporarily killed her telepathy after she refused to allow herself a modicum of empathy for her inability to succeed in an impossible situation. The cops had called her too late in a bank heist. The gunman had already gone off the rails, no return ticket on the horizon. *Holy hell. I'm reaching the boiling point of a telepathic eruption and I digress into the mundane.* Marisa stuck the gun in Ric's waistband, her fingers lingering a few seconds longer than necessary, feeling the fire of his skin cloak her.

The gunman waived his arm, and then steadied his weapon on Ric's heart. "I want the woman behind pretty boy to talk to me. Only her."

"Let's not involve strangers. Just you and me. You don't want to hurt anyone, right?" the hostage negotiator said.

"Everyone can go, including pretty boy. Karma stays. This is all her fault. And I want the witch to stay."

Blood pulsing and hyperaware of myriad noises, Marisa tried to read him. A slew of emotions smothered her, and she had a difficult time picking him out of her mental haystack. Only a degree of guilt for interfering kissed her mind. However, from his earlier thoughts, it was only a matter of time before he pulled a stunt like this. *Don't let your guilt kick your can!*

A clear thought suddenly hit her. The gunman had wanted Karma to go with him earlier, to prove his worth for potential employment... with Cabala Incorporated. Paranoia ruled him on his downward spiral. Yet, his directions were distinctively clear: prove his ability to recruit for Cabala.

Cabala? The Cabal? Marisa's skin crawled.

"Okay. Good. Thank you." The negotiator interrupted Marisa's near short circuit.

Another hidden cop said, "Nice and slow, everyone leave the area and go about your business. That includes you in the leather jacket."

Ric didn't budge a muscle. People scattered, taking

their thoughts with them, and the gunman's mad notions floated to the surface.

"Damn it," he said. *"What am I doing? How am I gonna get out of this shit? Why'd she follow me here? Did she see me in the offices? They warned me to keep it on the down low. Recruiters 1310. Dumb name, calling themselves after their suite."* His thoughts wavered. *"Why'd Karma shit on me to Leah? It's all her fault."* His thoughts jammed up for a few seconds until his stream of consciousness rolled on down the track. *"I just want to talk to the black-haired witch. She's one of those mind benders. She can get me outta this mess and into that Cabala job they promised me. I bet he's one of those Guild Guardian dudes. Means, she's not on Cabala's payroll yet. Hell yeah. I can recruit with the best of 'em. Get outta the way, Guardian dude."*

"Move it, pretty boy," he said aloud. "You heard the copper."

Marisa's back went steel rod straight. "Please, Ric. Do you trust me? I'll do everything I can to keep Karma safe. Let me handle this." She met the gunman's wild gaze head-on. "You won't hurt me, right?"

"I'm staying with her," Ric said, low and lethal. "I won't interfere with your conversation. Okay, man?"

"Yeah, I know about them Guardian dicks and all their interfering ways. Maybe I outta score early points with Cabala and take him out now. Earn me the job. Yeah, that's the ticket."

The click of the gun hammer shattered the still tableau.

CHAPTER ELEVEN

Hands up, Marisa lunged around Ric, plopping herself in the gunman's visual range in front of Ric. "Ask me anything you want. Just let him stay." She flicked her thumb over her shoulder at Ric, who'd stepped beside her, furiously grumbling. "We can help you."

"Giving up the goods will land you dead." Holding one arm up, Ric snaked his other arm around her waist and towed her into his side. The heat of his body enveloped her in a wave of security. A whiff of cardamom fortified her.

"Tell us what you want," the negotiator said. "Let's talk rationally. No need for violence. We'll do our best to help you."

"Screw off. All you want is my ass on a platter. I want to talk to her. *Mano a mano.*"

"Only if you promise not to hurt her or Karma and talk right here," Ric replied. "With me by her side. I'll keep quiet, not interfere, not move."

The gunman's arm wavered, and he scratched his temple, tousling his shaggy brown hair. "Okay. Come closer." He straightened his arm and shifted his aim to Marisa's heart. "No one else moves. Got it?" His thoughts confirmed his words.

"We got it," the cop said. "I'm staying right here." He

signaled the other police personnel.

One slow foot at a time, Ric and Marisa stepped closer to the bench. Ric's solid warmth lent her comfort and confidence, a haven she'd derived from no other man.

Suddenly, a shout echoed on the street. "Stop!" A familiar man sprinted the same path Marisa followed earlier from the office building. Shock zoomed through her, and Ric's arm tightened as his body tensed fierce and lethal. "Marisa, are you okay? What's going on? What are you do—" He shut his trap as if he realized his mistake.

Kenneth Delaney. *Mr. Impeccable Timing. Who does that?*

A cop held Kenny back from advancing further. Had he not spied the goon waving a gun and the entire cop shop surrounding the park? Marisa mentally wobbled her head, allowing her walls to drop again. She'd erected them to stop the tempest of emotions snowing her own under while the park cleared.

The gunman hadn't flinched, but he again focused on the idea of killing someone before making a run for it.

"Can you tell me your name?" Marisa kept her tone level.

"Smith."

"Thanks, Smith. I'm Marisa. How can I help you?"

"Are you one of them?"

"Them?" Playing innocent, she concentrated on his mental minutia. The nearest cop projected a thought that if he had more time they'd set up a sting to capture Smith without injuring anyone.

"One of them mind readers," Smith replied.

"You mean a telepath?" She scooched closer into Ric's side, and his steely arm braced her from crumpling into a ball.

"Yeah, that."

"I am."

"Do you belong to that Guild org?"

"Yes. I belong to the Psychic Guild."

"Can you tell me what I'm thinking?"

"No. Your mind's blocked." Her lie easily rolled out.

"But you read Karma's mind."

"Her mind's an open cavern." The late morning sun hit her, and she squinted. She wished she'd worn her sunglasses, mostly to hide her expression from Smith.

"It's 'cause she ain't got shit between her ears, despite her college education." Karma uttered a loud sound between a snicker and a snipe. "Guess I got too much in my head for you to read, huh?" *I'm gonna snag this classy broad's ass for a big fat bounty. They promised if I snatched any psychic chick or dude even, and turn them in, a pay day awaited me.*

His gaze bounced to the building housing the Falbrooke law firm. Did the Cabal have offices open to the public? Had he visited suite 1310 in Lily's building? Surely, the Cabal wasn't that idiotic. Or had they suddenly turned hungry and desperate?

The Cabal had gone from luring Guild psychics with promises of greener pastures to outright killing the ones who refused them and now to bounty hunters and kidnapping? *How lucky did I get stumbling upon this jerk. Or are they following me? Are they the source of evil plaguing me? Not Smith, though. He projects his thoughts too much, has no walls, and, well, he's as dumb as a box of rocks. And how did he not know Karma's psychic?* Marisa recalled Lily telling her the entire McAllister clan belonged to the Guild.

"You're too smart for me to read." She stroked his ego, hoping to shift the playing field. "Smith, tell me what you want." Slowly, she lowered her arms, a bead of nervous sweat trickling between the valley of her breasts. He didn't stop her. "Can you put the gun down so we can talk one on one?"

"Think again."

"What are you doing?" Ric mumbled out the side of his mouth.

She nudged her elbow into his side and whispered, "Cabal."

Ric's muscles tensed hard against her. She desperately wanted to pacify his distress for his cousin. *"Does he know about Karma?"*

"No."

"Shut up." Smith stepped closer and leveled his weapon on Ric. "Or pretty boy here bites it." Ric didn't twitch. If she didn't contain Smith, they might all bite it.

"Whoa, Smith." The negotiator intervened. "No one here needs to get hurt. Why don't you tell us what you want?"

"Why bother? You're not letting me go. Or taking me alive. We all know it."

"What do you want us to do?" The cop inched closer. Several other SWAT members were realigning slowly to avoid sparking Smith's trigger finger.

"I want to talk to the dark-haired chick."

"Let Karma go first. Then we'll talk all you want." Marisa tried to push away from Ric, but his bracing arm refused to relent.

The gunman's gaze tore from the cop to her, to Ric and then down to Karma. "Fine, why the fuck not? She's useless. Already turned my girlfriend against me. She'll get what's coming. After all, her dumbass name's *Karma*." He stressed her name sarcastically. "Go. Tell Leah don't get her hopes up. I'll be back."

Without sparing him a morsel of time, Karma rolled out from under the bench and scrambled up. Marisa felt Ric's subtle nod, and then Karma zipped toward the police barricade near the main park walkway. Marisa watched her stop next to Kenny talking on his phone, and then a cop hustled her toward a waiting ambulance.

A strong psychic vibe stemmed from Karma, different from anything she'd ever sensed, and she'd met other touch telepaths before. *Whatever.* The gunman had no clue who he'd released. Several deep breaths slowed her rapid heartbeat.

"Move away from him." Smith waved his gun at Ric. "I won't hurt you. Just wanna talk."

"Let me do this," Marisa pleaded under her breath to Ric. "There're a million cops."

Ric growled. "I don't like this."

"This morning I was evil incarnate. Now you want to protect me. Can we say oxymoron?" One more push and Ric's arm dropped away. Attention locked onto the gunman, she took one step, two, and then three toward him. Ric followed, maintaining a two-foot distance, and it was two feet too much.

"That's close enough." Ric's thought hit her loud and clear.

Ignoring the sweat beading at her hairline, Marisa stopped five feet from the gunman. "Talk." The moment the word rolled off her tongue, the gunman lurched toward her. Ric lunged from behind, his arms outstretched to scoop her up, practically body slamming her. Smith bowled into her front and sandwiched her between them. Air whooshed out of her lungs. The gun's barrel jabbed into her forehead, and all Marisa comprehended was how dirty it might be and who else it had touched in his circle of drug addicts. Cries, shouts, and chaos deafened the roar of her pulse in her ears, the noise nearly blinding her.

"Back off!" Smith shouted at Ric. "She's mine now."

Inwardly cringing, hating the germs saturating her blouse, Marisa tried to heave in diminishing air. The acrid odor of fear and testosterone smacked her nostrils, forcing her to breathe through her mouth.

The gun cocked, terminated her cerebral tempest, leaving a splatter of the gunman's rabid, angry thoughts in incomprehensible consonants and syllables. She sagged against Ric as much as a body could sag sandwiched between Ric's tall hard body and Smith's shorter, lanky frame.

A dozen cops trained their guns on him, too close. Too many guns. Someone was going to die. Her? Ric? *Oh, hell in a Cabal handbasket. Why didn't I mind my own business?* Mental red flags flapped. The only thing keeping her coherent was Ric's body melded to hers, his heart thumping against her spine. He became her lodestone, her safety net, her refuge in the sea of madness. He rattled words in his head, and she focused on them, driving off the host of other voices threatening to unseat her.

"Stay with me, baby," Ric said. *"Breathe, breathe. I've got you. I won't let him hurt you."*

"All of you back off or she bites it," Smith screeched down her last active nerve.

Marisa built a foundation of blocks, and she erected her walls row by row, focusing on the wafting flowers in her springtime meadow. The noise subsided. It seemed like hours, but it only took seconds to find herself again. She lifted her left hand, since her right hand was crushed between the gunman and her breasts.

Cringing a little, she trailed her fingers up his ragged hoodie sleeve. "Kill me now and you won't ever discover what I can do for you. How I can help your chances of fitting in. The job you want."

Smith snapped back his head. "You said you couldn't read my mind," he accused. It was enough for Marisa to work with... until his rage discharged.

He waved his gun at Ric and almost smacked Ric's temple. "Get back. Or I'll start shooting. I just want to talk to her alone."

"Ric, do as he says," she croaked. "Please."

"Okay, Smith. We'll do this your way," a cop on her right said. "Ric, is it? Step aside, walk to the barricade. Is that okay, Smith?"

"Get him out of here." Smith vibrated against Marisa's arm over her breasts, a junkie's jitters missing a fix.

Ric freed her, his reluctance palpable. *"Don't antagonize him. Let the cops do their job."* He took a tentative step backward, and the mix of cool autumn air and fiery terror struck her backside in a wishy-washy wave.

"You aren't going to hurt me, right, Smith?" she asked, a balloon of hope floating up her spine. "I'm no use to you dead."

A mottled red tide swept his face, his five-day beard stubble absorbing the color except in bare patches bracketing his mouth. He kinked his head to the right, wrinkles lining his brow, curious and assessing, his response a frosty smile of deceit.

A new layer of sweat popped out. She hoped he wanted to hand her over to the Cabal. Alive. Dead didn't do it for her. Over her shoulder, she spied Ric behind the police barricade, toting her safety net with him.

"Let's go." Heaving on her, Smith positioned her in front of him like a shield. A silent but palpable alert ascended as the cops adjusted to the new dynamic.

"Smith, can we settle this here and now? Can you give me a better idea of what you want?" the negotiator asked, the only cop not wielding a gun on the perp. "Put your weapon down and let's end this peacefully. No one gets hurt. Okay?"

The gun muzzle pressed into the side of Marisa's neck. "Hell to the no. This chick here is my ticket." He jerked his head at Lily's building.

Marisa pressed forward, trying to snip the branches of his emotions to reach the root of his plan. But his thoughts remained scattered and chaotic. Random thoughts of bystanders peppered her, and she rebuilt her barriers, tried to shut out the conflicting voices. It worked just long enough to hear, *They'll protect me. Just need to get inside the building, dump her off.*

Shock sprayed holes in Marisa's belly. Did the Cabal seriously maintain offices in Lily's building? How long have they been under the Falbrooke's noses? Are they taunting the Guild? Surely, they weren't stupid enough to divulge their main location to this scumbag. Marisa peered at Ric who hadn't taken his sight off her. He nodded, gave her a wan supportive smile. His forehead crinkled as if he strained to speak telepathically. Her telepathy had some limits. And sometimes not enough.

"Toss your purse." Smith poked a knee in her rear, sending a jolt up her spine.

Marisa realized her bag was still looped around her shoulder, under her arm... with her gun nestled inside. "I'm not feeling well, and I'm overdue for my pill. I could go into diabetic shock if I don't take my meds." No sense in playing it straight. Only an idiot dope fiend would allow her to bring her purse without checking it first.

"Whatever. Go then." He kneed her rear again, and she took a few awkward steps forward, his arm still wrapped around her from behind.

Idiots 'R' Us. Her purse just became her Holy Grail. Moves from the self-defense class Lily forced her to take with her two years ago spun into her memory.

"We'll make a path for you, Smith," the negotiator said. "Slow and easy. We'll escort you wherever you want to go."

"You follow and I'll kill her." The gun stabbed her neck again. "Go."

At times her feet barely brushed the cement walkway as he half carried her. A breeze wafted fall leaves onto the sidewalk, crunching beneath their feet, balancing the static buzzing her mind. The cops remained in position behind her, and a line of them barricaded the street where Ric shifted closer to his young cousin near Kenny who wore a strange, angry mask. Or was it his veneer of concern?

As she finagled her purse over her middle like armor, Smith's thoughts echoed clear as day. He planned to take her to the Cabal offices to turn her in for a bounty and to seek asylum. She slipped her fingers inside her purse's main compartment and clasped her small handgun. How stupid did this guy have to be? One thing for sure, he offered plenty of fodder for the Guild's first real clues in locating Cabal members. If she survived to tell about it.

They continued their lopsided crawl toward the street, and Marisa prepared her body for a takedown. She contemplated stabbing her nail file into his arm or bending back his fingers, things she'd learned in the class. Gathering her strength, she slinked her arm forward, subtly moving it into position. The sound of a blue jay squawking in a tree to their right dissipated into the air of malice as they passed under the far-flung branches of the leafless maple.

Marisa deliberately tripped and lurched forward, dropping her weight. Smith grunted, lost his footing, and the gun hit her between her shoulder blades. As he hauled her upright, she slammed her elbow into his solar plexus with every ounce of strength she possessed. He roared like a charging lion. She managed to rotate out of his hold, and kicked the side of his knee, partially incapacitating him. His gun flew onto the lawn, and he doubled over, snarling bloody murder. A tremendous din from Smith, the cops, and bystanders deluged her.

Strength waning, Marisa stabbed her elbow into his temple. The brute power of her jab forced him down onto one knee, and she brought the muzzle of her gun to his temple.

"Don't move, asshole," she said on a breathless rasp.

Cops surrounded them, a million guns trained on Smith.

In a final show of defiance or ten pounds of stupid, Smith jolted upwards against her gun, shoving her off balance.

Her legs buckled and she lost her balance, falling backward. Arms pinwheeling, her head glanced off the side of a bench, barely missed ripping off her left ear. The last thing she remembered was the boom of one, two, three deafening close-range gunshots and her own weapon clattering onto the cement. A red haze shrouded her and her thoughts met a windswept landscape of blackened and crispy flowers.

CHAPTER TWELVE

Marisa absorbed the pain scorching her skull. Had a bullet struck her? Warm liquid trickled off the left side of her head pillowed on a soft, yet solid surface. Someone warm and solid.

"Marisa?" Ric's gentle voice wafted down and she realized he held her head and shoulders on his lap. "You're safe now. Paramedics are here."

She felt herself elevated and deposited on a gurney. The familiar and welcome feel of Ric's slightly rough hand clasped her right hand. Other than her brain bouncing angrily from side to side in her skull and her back twitching up a tempest, no searing bullet pain engulfed her. *That's good, right?*

"Ric?"

"I'm here."

"Don't leave me," she said through the thick muck in her throat. "Need to talk."

"I'm not leaving." He squeezed her fingers and not a small amount of gratitude ignited her frigid limbs, along with a tickling awareness down to the V of her legs. *Get real, hormones. I just got shot, and you're sending out invitations to Ric Off-Limits McAllister?*

"Marisa!" Lily's panicked screech joined her mental racket. The click-clack of heels on the sidewalk chased the screech down. "Mar? Are you okay? Jake and I saw the whole incident from the office; the cops had the buildings on lockdown." Ric liberated her hand as Lily squeezed closer and hovered over the gurney.

Lily swam in and out of focus. Two Jakes stood behind her as paramedics checked her vitals. Sound fell into a pocket of fuzz. Said fuzz seemed to fill her with nothingness, no walls, no voices, and no thoughts except her own. A stark hole burgeoned in her core as the implications of losing her telepathy whether temporarily or permanently hit her.

"Talk to me." Lily gripped her shamrock so tight Marisa thought she'd break the chain.

"I can't hear anyone. You know what I mean," she whispered for Lily's ears only. Ric stood beside Lily, the two Jakes now morphed into one behind the pair. Thank the psychic gods for small favors. She couldn't deal with *two* Jakes.

"Miss Meadows," a female paramedic said. "You're suffering from head trauma."

"Was I shot? I'm a little numb." Did her numbness stem internally or from outside sources?

"No, ma'am. You took a bad tumble and hit your head on a park bench. We're taking you to the hospital for a thorough workup."

The gurney swiveled and Marisa's head swung with it, shooting daggers into her empty skull. She winced, cried out. Within seconds, the pain dissipated into a sunshiny tropical island as pain meds took up residence. All she needed was a daiquiri and a gorgeous man to slather sunscreen on her fair skin. As the paramedics wheeled the gurney toward the ambulance, Ric grasped her hand again.

"We've given you something for the pain," the paramedic said.

"Thank you. It's hitting my buttons now."

"Can I ride with her?" Lily asked.

"No. Ric," Marisa replied. "Okay?"

"Whatever you want," Ric said. Another hand squeeze. Another wave of dumb and blind hormones marching southward.

"It's okay, sweetheart. We'll follow the ambulance." Jake contributed a crumb for the first time, and Marisa remembered who the McAllister brothers were. Triple G. Guild, Guardians, Gorgeous.

"Whoa, something's really, really wrong with her," Lily teased. "I'm her ride or die."

The paramedics hoisted the gurney into the ambulance. The sea of bodies outside the canary crime-scene tape reminded her she lay in a fish bowl at the moment. She hunted for Kenny among the million emergency personnel to no avail. Was Smith dead? Had her gun gone off? Had she shot somebody? Tremors attacked her so violently her bones prepared to splinter.

"Something's wrong with her!" Ric's manly voice vaulted above the ruckus, beeps, and blips inside the ambulance jammed with equipment and people.

"I'm okay. Just—" she stuttered. "Did I shoot anyone? Is Smith dead?" She tried to telepathically read the woman paramedic and met an empty galaxy. She tried the man paramedic. Black hole. Even Ric's mind remained blank. The respite from not hearing every thought around her started a mini freak-out. What if her telepathy never knocked on the door to her attic again?

"His real name's Johnny Wesley." Ric drew his thumb up and down her palm, sending more of those welcome tingly vibes across her skin, too relaxing, too much of everything good. "He's Karma's best friend's boyfriend, or was until Karma split them up."

"Is Karma okay?"

"Yeah. Thanks for helping her. I'd have killed the bastard myself if anything happened to her."

Marisa's bottom lip quaked. "So he's dead?"

Ric's thumb quit moving, but his fingers remained entwined with hers. "Yeah. Cops shot him. He pulled his gun on you when you went down."

Another bone-creaking shudder rent her in half. "Did my gun go off?"

"No."

"Thank God. I don't know what I'd do if I'd hurt anyone else."

"What do you mean anyone else?"

Marisa turned to the side, and his anxiety for her encased her in his intangible protective shelter. She could get used to this. *No. No. No. Idiot. Guild Girl Code!* She didn't need the protection of any man. Why did his presence comfort her though? Why did she want it? Or want him? "It was my fault. If I'd just left things alone—"

Ric's fingers caressed her lips. They smelled faintly of caramel, and she almost licked them. "You saved my cousin. Who knows what he would've done. He was strung out, searching for a scapegoat. Not your fault."

Marisa took a long moment to think, nodded. The ambulance hit a pothole, jouncing her in her restraints, thudding her head. She winced. "Lean in." Ric leaned forward and only a few inches separated her lips from his ear. "I need to tell you what game he was really playing. That's the reason I wanted you here." *Big fat half lie.*

An iron rod seemed to straighten Ric's back. "My good looks, smarts, and fun personality, or my overly protective Guardian genes didn't encourage the invite?" As he intended with his light-hearted tone, he brought a smile to her face. "Oh wait." He held up a hand to stop the words waiting to trip from her mouth. "I forgot the ubiquitous Guild Girl Code. Rule number one. Don't date

Guardians."

Marisa grinned. *Oh, hell on high water.* His grin lit her up inside more than any man's grin had a right to. Or was it the drugs forming a conga line in her blood? Man, had she whacked her noodle or what? *Focus, focus. Men have no long-term place in your life. And he just might be a long-term kind of guy.* "You're so full of yourself. And who said anything about dating."

"Rules are meant to be broken." Another heart-stopping grin rounded up a few more of her rogue hormones.

Resist. Resist. "Be serious."

The ambulance arrived at the hospital's emergency entrance, and the paramedics surrounded her, forcing Ric to drop her hand.

"Ric?"

His fingers returned to hers, where she wanted them like another drug. "I'm here. You can't get rid of me."

"Listen," she whispered. "I don't want Lily to know. We need to talk, just you and me. About Smith... Wesley."

Signifying his assent, Ric squeezed her hand again. The antiseptic odor hit her reality, kicked the worst time of her life to the forefront of her memories. The last time she'd entered a hospital was when her sister had taken a ride on her one-way ticket to the morgue.

Before they wheeled her into an examination room, Lily and Jake were by her side, along with two police officers wanting to take her statement. An ER nurse scooted them out of the way and told the cops they'd get their statement once the doctor released Marisa to talk. Ric let go of her hand and she smiled wanly as he exited stage left. She hated the loss of his touch. And she needed to touch him like she needed her telepathy back. The shock of her desperate craving boosted her resolve to regain her sensibilities, if she possessed any concerning

Ric McAllister, that is.

Left without her sidekicks, hospital staff poked, prodded, scanned, and stuck her with needles. A slew of questions and a pronouncement of head trauma and a concussion later, the ER staff allowed visitors for a few minutes before the official police interrogation.

Lily barreled into the room, Jake on her heels. "Oh, you poor thing. Are you okay?"

Marisa rubbed her bare arms against the assault of freezing hospital air. "I'll be fine. Can't hurt this thick skull." Would she regain her telepathy when she healed? What if she didn't? What if her gift changed?

"What's wrong?" Lily hugged her, whispered in her ear, "I'll kick them out if you want to talk alone."

Unable to muster a word, she nodded. When Jake and Ric reluctantly skedaddled, Lily perched on the bed and held her hand. She hadn't spent so much time holding hands with anyone in longer than she cared to admit. The erotic sensation of Ric sliding his thumb up and down her palm refused to flee. At least she hadn't destroyed her memories. Or her passion.

"What's with you and Ric?" Marisa knew Lily's smile meant to make her feel better.

"Nothing. He followed me from the building and we were just talking."

"He seemed awfully attached. And you *let* him." Lily's smile kicked into a full-fledged grin, the hint of pink lipstick residue hiding in the corners of her mouth as if she'd licked it off in her agitation. "I see a hookup in your future."

Marisa fake glowered. "So you're a clairvoyant all of a sudden?"

"Well, duh. My ESP abilities returned last month."

"You don't seriously see us together, do you?" She screwed up her face into a disgruntled scrunch she didn't feel. Not like she saw a future with Ric, at least nothing beyond a fun flirtation. If that. She might be better off dating a client if forced to make a choice. "Hey, what happened to Delaney? Did you speak to him outside the building? He waited behind the police barricade."

"Never saw him. He must've left before the police broke up the looky-loos. Anyway, I'm just teasing you about Ric. Tell me what's wrong?"

Marisa ignored the weird vibes Delaney's strange actions caused. "I really lost my telepathy." Lily's fingers clenched her hand so hard, her bones creaked. "Oww."

Lily didn't let up. "From the injury?"

"Yes."

"Can you read me?"

"Not a peep."

Lily let go of Marisa's hand, combed her auburn hair behind her ears. "I can talk to the Guild healer, Elizabeth. Do you want her to come down here?"

"No. Keep this between us. I don't want you to tell Jake either."

"Sure. But Elizabeth's discreet."

"It'll return in the morning. No big." A new round of pain attacked the base of Marisa's head, and her vision grew blurry. "Maybe tomorrow when you bail me out." Her eyelids grew heavy. "Please grab the cops before I fall asleep. Drugs are kicking my butt."

Marisa didn't breathe a word about the Cabal to the cops. It wasn't their business. She barely escaped her interrogation before a deep and trouble-free sleep claimed her.

⊗⊗

When Marisa awoke the next morning and stumbled out of the hospital bed to use the restroom, the door opened and Ric bolted into the room and clasped her elbow.

"You're back?" She eased her elbow out of his hand, needing an escape to a mirror more than she needed his guidance or the touch she hated to relinquish.

"I never left."

Disregarding her own potentially deadly appearance, she noticed his beyond five-o'clock shadow, the dark circles under his eyes, and his tousled hair didn't detract from his rugged handsomeness. Why tall, dark, and handsome Guild Guardian Ric McAllister who was so off-limits? She didn't need the distraction while in town for a job destined to set her up as a partner in Lily's law firm. *Whoa? What the what?* She hadn't thought about the offer since yesterday, let alone made a decision. With a conciliatory sniff, she patted his arm to appease his manhood. "Thanks for staying. You didn't need to."

"We took shifts. I sent Lily and Jake home. Besides, I wanted to be here when you woke up since you wanted to talk privately."

She glanced at the clock above the door. "Oh. My. God. I'm due for depositions in three hours."

"Lily handled it. Local counsel and Delaney are covering." He left her in the bathroom, allowing her to do her business in peace.

Only a skosh of relief skated down her arms at the free day on her horizon. The sensation of evil had also subsided with the loss of her telepathy. Neither had returned after a night's sleep. She quickly brushed her teeth, tried to comb down her crazy-witch hair, gave up, and patted water in the worst kinky spots. A faint red stain marked the last of her lipstick on her Sahara-dry lips. She slicked on the waxy hospital lip balm and hoped Ric didn't hunt down a paper bag to throw over her head.

She'd barely opened the door and he was by her side again. He guided her back to bed, bunched the covers around her, and sat in the bedside chair.

"When do my prison doors open?" More conscious of her external state of being, she smoothed down her hair again.

"After the doc examines you and decides you're ready to hit the road."

She mock pouted. "I barely have a headache." I barely have a head. "Can you hand me my bag, please?"

Ric reached for it, hesitated. The last two days came crashing down upon her otherwise hollow head. Zombies would reject her for lack of brainy dessert.

"It's not gonna bite."

He practically tossed the purse between her legs as if it contained cooties jumping ship bound for his delectable body. "Sorry. I'm still getting the creeps."

"It's not even the same purse." Exasperated, she lugged the handbag close, careful of the monitoring tubes sticking in her arm.

"Things don't add up." The corners of the room received his attention as he continued to speak. "You feel different."

"Same old me."

His roving gaze found a dock on her face. "You feel off."

Fire slithered up Marisa's chest. "Why can you sense anything about me? You're just clairvoyant, right? You see things happening to people they can't see, right? Past, present, or future?"

"Mostly future. Your telepathy kinda sucked me in. I usually read people's mental images and sometimes share their dreams and nightmares. Lately, it seems to transfer to other psychics, like Lily and now you."

"You saw the fire, the after scene in the house?"

He opened his mouth, shut it, and then asked, "Were those your thoughts?"

"Really? You think you saw such horror in *my* head? Sorry, dude, it was all *you*. You projected those images on me." The heart rate monitor gyrated.

Head cocked to the right, he held up his hand. "I had to ask. You'd ask the same."

"None of what you saw stemmed from me."

A long beat of silence engulfed them in the barbed air hissing from the ceiling vent. The blue lines of the heart rate monitor returned to normal. A nurse popped in the doorway and admonished Ric with a withering glare, then vanished.

"Let's call a truce. Tell me what you read from Wesley. Was he planning to hurt Karma or her friend?"

Marisa stilled, ready to confront him about the Cabal. "Why was Karma with him?"

"She ran into him on her way to Lily's office. She's finishing her paralegal degree, and Lily has an intern opening. Wesley accosted her in the park and blamed her for talking Leah into breaking up with him." Ric folded and unfolded the blanket between his thumb and index finger. "Karma is well... Karma, if you know what I mean. She has touch telepathy, and she helps her friends learn things about others. Not always good things. She reads history and emotions and uses what she learns against or to benefit the person she's reading. She's been doing it for money. Leah brought Karma an item belonging to Wesley, and she read he was still doing drugs, involved with a bad crowd after he promised Leah he was on the straight and narrow. Leah dumped him."

She smiled. "Karma's a bitch, so I hear."

"Exactly. That's my little cousin. She's a trip, but she's a good kid." He patted her leg, his hand heavy, lingering longer than necessary. And not long enough according to her obsessed libido. "Tell me what you read. Why you wanted to talk to me and not Lily."

Marisa glanced out the door window, back to Ric. "I don't want her to fret. She's been through so much." She gauged the trusting vibe radiating off him, the same trust she'd sensed from day one. Hell's unlikely bells, he did things to her insides, leaving her to feel like the sole wench on a pirate ship parading a slew of Captain Jack Sparrows. "Wesley was visiting the Cabal. In Lily's office tower."

Ric went bug-eyed and jerked back against the chair. "Seriously?"

"That's not the worst part. They're hiring bounty hunters to seize Guild members and bring them to the Cabal. Wesley planned to take me there, thought he'd score big points."

Spine rigid, Ric rose and paced to the foot of the bed, gliding his fingers over the footboard railing, as if he needed to keep contact with her without directly touching her. *Oh, right, Marisa Meadows. You just want him touching you. Shut the hell up.* The only voices who hadn't fled her roost continued their angel-versus-devil banter. "Why are they building a network of Cabal bounty hunters *and* Guild psychics? Sounds like they're expanding. Why didn't Wesley snag Karma?"

"Leah convinced him Karma was worthless as a psychic," Marisa replied.

"Good. She doesn't have much to do with the Guild either."

"The Cabal's now reaching its itchy fingers beyond Guild psychics."

Ric's heavy steps halted and a quiet lull competed with the hum of the machines. "And kidnapping psychics. They wheedle, bribe, threaten, and blackmail, but they've never resorted to outright kidnapping."

"And murder."

"And murder," he repeated and resumed his taut

pacing.

"They're building an empire." Marisa dragged the covers up to her chin as if to protect herself from the impending detonation of her Guild world. "The crap just hit the fan."

"You got that right." Ric propped his elbows on the footboard. "No one's safe now."

"Who's bankrolling this operation?"

"The billion-dollar question. As well as why. What's their end goal? We haven't figured it out or even gotten close to the top level."

"Well, I can bet the office Wesley planned to hit up in Lily's building is a shell and already cleared out." Marisa smoothed her hands down the covers, fighting the urge to touch Ric's strong arm. "They're probably bankrolling shell corporations to lease facilities and recruiting offices across the U.S. From what I've heard, they're rolling in dough from the illegal deeds they're forcing these psychics to do."

"And paying them well. The pay is a big lure."

"Maybe not so big if they're resorting to kidnapping." Her nails bit into her palms. Was the Cabal the source of evil tailgating her? Would it culminate in a battle against the Guild? What about the strange visions she shared with Ric? Too many questions and no answers made for a boatload of painful mysteries. Time to get to the bottom of it, even if she had to step down from the moral train and use her telepathy for the greater good of the Guild kind. If only she possessed her telepathy.

"Lily and Jake need to know." Ric interrupted her mental rant.

"Why?"

"We don't keep secrets from the top-level psychics we guard, especially when the intel has broad repercussions to every Guild member. You both need protection." He scuffed his boots on the floor, picked invisible lint off his shoulder.

Had the Protectorate assigned Ric as her Guardian? *Hell to the big fat no.* The Protectorate was under strict guidelines to cough up a contract between guard and guarded. They wouldn't dare foist a Guardian on her without her approval. "Pffft. The only protection I need is the little number in my purse that spits those little things called bullets."

"That little number sure helped you in the airport, didn't it?" Ric's sarcasm didn't go over her head.

"Well, duh. Guns aren't allowed in carry-on luggage. It's why I check my luggage." Well, that and because she tended to travel not so light. "Besides, the thief was a purse thief. Plain and simple." *Hello, denial.* Why then had he stolen two very benign objects from her purse, which she discovered yesterday morning when she'd stuffed all her items into her borrowed handbag? Missing items included her backup lipstick and a wad of gum in tissue she'd tossed in her purse after the plane landed. Both items contained her DNA. *Welcome to my shitshow.* All the more reason why she needed to break out the big guns. *Damn, telepathy, where the hell are you?* "This blows, Ric. Everything's turning into a Sherlock Holmes mystery of the *n*th degree."

"And you're at the core."

One part of her needed space from him for a few moments to gather her bearings. The other part didn't want to lose sight of his gorgeous, albeit, tired face.

"We need to scope out the office tower, find where the Cabal office is located. My guess, suite 1310."

"After watching Wesley head toward it with you, I got suspicious. Liam checked the building last night. He found one suspicious empty suite, number 1310. Appears they deserted it in a hurry. A desk and a few chairs left behind."

"Satellite office?"

"They probably have them everywhere."

"Prints?"

"Just Wesley's on the doorknob."

Marisa wanted out of the antiseptic stink so bad, she tasted freedom on her tongue, as well as a healthy dosage of ash and fire. She wanted to investigate the fire that'd caused no small amount of angst and finger pointing in her direction. She wanted to prove the McAllisters wrong, especially the hunk who'd started seeping into her every pore.

"Can you please find out when they're planning to spring me? Give me a few moments to think alone. I'll owe you."

"Can I get you anything? How's your head?"

She lifted her right fingers off the bed coverings in a wave. "I'll feel better when I get back to Lily's house. A little breakfast might rally the healing vibes." She bestowed her most charming smile on him, a smile that slurped up every ounce of her strength to achieve. "Thank you."

As Ric's footsteps faded off, Marisa closed her eyes and concentrated on two people passing down the hall. Their minds were blanker than two clean slates. She focused again on voices farther away, sometimes able to pierce minds at greater distances as long as she could hear them verbally. Nothing... maybe too far. Maybe too dead. She slammed her fist on the mattress. "Just lobotomize me already."

A faint rustling and a tiny squeak of a rubber sole on the floor alerted her to a presence in the room. The door shut with a quiet snick.

"Back so soon?" she asked without opening her eyes and breaking her concentration on drool-worthy Ric

McAllister.

A pillow landed on her face and a crushing weight smothered her last words.

CHAPTER THIRTEEN

Marisa tried to thrust the pillow off and met resistance and a muffle against her screech. Whoever held the pillow pressed harder, smashing her head into the mattress, cutting off her air supply. She scrabbled to find the nurse call button, but a heavy weight pinned her arm down.

"Listen up, Ms. Meadows." A man's gruff voice filtered into her left ear. "You're on the fast track to kicking it. But I'm your savior. Follow my instructions and your friends and mother will live to see tomorrow. You all might live to see next year too."

"What do you want?" Marisa's muted voice barely made a dent through the pillow.

A crumpled piece of paper hit the palm of her hand, and she fisted her fingers around it. "Tell anyone about this and Lily Falbrooke dies first. Don't remove the pillow for thirty seconds."

Before she counted to one, the pressure relented and a scuffle ensued. Gasping, Marisa tossed the pillow aside in time to spy Kenny Delaney race out of her private room.

Excruciating moments later, a flurry of footsteps charged back, depositing a panting Kenny beside her bed. "Are you all right? I lost him in the elevator."

Tears welled as she collected her wits and tried to

steady her galloping heart. She shoved the wad of paper beneath the covers. "He tried to scare me or something. I don't know. He didn't hurt me."

He moved a large vase of yellow roses on the bedside table. "A hospital security guard gave chase, and I rushed back here."

Heart rate decelerating to near normal, she squeezed his hand. "Thank you."

What new lunatic hell had she bumbled into? All she wanted was to do her job assisting local counsel with the depositions. She'd failed miserably, and WebWorx would probably can her law firm. *Riley will be pissed. He'll probably can me too.*

Kenny's gaze caught and held hers until a rush of heat pummeled the chills pervading her from the ventilation. "Thank you for the flowers." The fragrant scent of friendship masked the hovering maliciousness. She studied the twelve perfect long-stemmed buds nestled in fern fronds and baby's breath, the color for friendship and the promise of a new beginning. *Better than the red roses of love.*

"You're quite welcome." Perspiration dotted the light dusting of hair on his upper lip. "Are you recovering well?" He uncharacteristically tripped over his words.

Marisa drew up short. From the brief time she'd known the overly confident man, she never pictured him nervous. Too bizarre for words. *Heck, my whole life is too bizarre for words.* "Thank you for asking. Ric McAllister's checking on my release as we speak."

His demeanor chilled. "Did the Guild assign you a Guardian?"

Marisa whisked her hand in the air to dismiss his ludicrous question. "Of course not." Caught off guard, she paused. "Wait. You know I'm Guild?"

"It's no secret you belong to the Psychic Guild. I'm

aware of their more prominent members." A Cheshire cat smile brightened his face. "Plus, I like to know who I'm getting into bed with."

"Are we getting into bed?" Her left eyebrow vaulted toward her hairline, and his irresistible smile spread another swathe of fire over her skin.

"If I had my way. Alas, it's up to you."

"Appears I have much to ponder."

He drew back in the chair. "Ouch."

"Well, we are talking about uprooting my entire life."

"I'll make it worth your while." He trailed his fingertips across the back of her hand.

Both edgy and excited by his touch, she slipped her hand out from under his and stuck her arm beneath the blanket. "Anyway, the incident with the park lunatic was random." *And then some.* "The Guild didn't assign McAllister as my Guardian. Lily Falbrooke and her Guardian are just overprotective." Oddly nervous discussing Guild matters with him, she changed the subject. "I'm sorry about the depositions."

"They've been postponed. The defendants are finally willing to talk settlement."

"I thought Edison didn't want to settle. They have uncontroverted evidence on their side."

He scooted the bedside chair closer and steepled his hands. "We recently discovered documents the defendants are required to disclose might give a leg up to our competitors if this goes to litigation. We'd rather settle to keep those documents from the public eye."

Or shed light on activity Edison doesn't want to publicize? A thread of unease teased her stomach, instigating a round of hungry rumbling. A noise by the door chased the rumbles. Ric hulked up the doorway, and her insides did a little joyful jig.

He carried a bouquet of red roses, the color for love.

No, he didn't go there, did he? Maybe they only had red in the hospital gift shop. The men glared at one another, like two WWE contestants bouncing against the cage ropes—Delaney versus McAllister. Her mystified hormones couldn't catch a clue if she dribbled diamonds on them.

A nurse excused her way past Ric, carrying her breakfast tray. Avoiding the simmering pair of men sucking up too much space, she concentrated on feeding her bellyaching stomach. Both Ric and Kenny reached for the plate cover and nearly knocked over the unopened juice box.

"Gentlemen, please give me a little space here," the nurse said.

Eyeing each other critically, the hovering pair of testosterone backed into the far corner and grumbled introductions to each other.

The nurse checked her vitals. "The doctor's making his rounds, and if all is well, he'll release you this morning." The nurse inputted her notes in the computer attached to the wall.

Refusing to wait one more day to dig into her *Twilight Zone*, she was chomping at the bit for the hospital to spring her. Marisa ate half a blueberry muffin and picked at bland scrambled eggs, the crumpled note beckoning against her thigh beneath the blankets. Ric and Kenny's stilted conversation about the weather instigated a round of glee inside her. She loved healthy competition in all aspects of her life. Yet in this case, her head, heart, and hormones placed its bets on Ric. The McAllister charm Lily kept alluding to had definitely worked its magic on her.

"Yesterday, I heard you'd left the law firm earlier. Why were you still in the area?" Ric asked, not even hinting at a tease.

"My accountant's in the same building. Two birds, one

stone," Kenny replied, his suave voice unfazed by Ric's stern interrogation.

The nurse left the room, and the testosterone brigade shouldered their way to her bedside. Before she blinked, Lily's familiar stride and clacking heels echoed in the hallway. Thank the psychic deities for her wing woman.

"Oh." Wearing a green, long-sleeved sheath that accentuated her red hair and every curve, Lily drew back in the doorway. "You have visitors already."

"They were just leaving." Marisa gave the men an encouraging wink. "Thank you, gentlemen, for the flowers and thinking of me. Kenny, please call me after the settlement meeting. Let me know how it went and if I can help."

"Of course," he replied. "May I visit?"

Ric made a grumbling click in his throat. *Did he just growl at Kenny? Rein in your misplaced jealousy, dude.* Nothing going on here for either man, Marisa's brain lied to her body.

"Maybe tomorrow," Lily replied for her. "Marisa needs quiet recovery time. I'm sure you understand. Bye, Ric." She winked. "See you later." The not-so-subtle wink proved Ric would be included in her day's adventure at some later point. *Yay, me.* Excitement swirled in her chest. *Shut up, happy hormones. Find another host body.*

Marisa silenced her mouth with a piece of muffin before it took a spin at her best friend.

CRSO

Silent, Ric marched side-by-side with Delaney to the parking lot. They barked hasty goodbyes, and Delaney drove off in his gazillion-dollar luxury car. Something about the man bugged him to death, well, beyond the hard-on he had for Marisa. And he didn't like the way

Marisa's head felt around Delaney, as if the asshole himself severed Ric's strange connection.

He climbed into his SUV, angrily jammed on his baseball cap and sunglasses. "Why do you care? She's nothing to you except an assignment."

Regardless, he Googled Delaney's name and sat back to cram on everything Kenneth Delaney and Edison WebWorx. Anything or anyone in Marisa's life was now on tap for full investigation. Once he hit home, he'd use his Guild privileges and drill into the secure sites for a complete profile on the dude. He scrolled through the useless search engine hits. Single, never married, no rug rats, a top dog on the corporate heap, loaded as all get out. The bastard was as clean as a whistle.

"Come on, give up something." After another couple minutes, he shut down his browser, picked up a drumstick, and tapped out a solo on his center console.

Lily exited the hospital and speed walked to the parking lot. She discreetly waved, knowing he'd be there in stealth mode. A few moments later, she drove her Mustang to the pickup zone, and a nurse rolled Marisa out in the requisite wheelchair. Marisa wore black leggings and a black sweater. The clothing fit her voluptuous body like second skin. His heart fluttered in its cage, like an eagle preparing to soar with its mate above the highest mountains. *Man, I need to dial down the crazy.*

Marisa slid into the front passenger seat of the sports car. Part of him wished she were sliding into his SUV next to him. And it wasn't his Guardian role making the wish. The other part wanted nothing to do with the queen of darkness, the queen of his darkness. Something unfathomable plagued her, marred her core. When she'd connected to his clairvoyance, her ebony fringes pressed upon his brain, and it scared the living daylights out of him. Not only did she display darkness from her exterior, but it wafted off her in waves. Did no one else sense it? He'd noticed a marked change in her the moment he stepped into her hospital room when Delaney butted in his way. Like Delaney had stolen part of her mind, burrowed in its place and oozed oily evil across her skull, seducing the darkness... seducing Marisa. *Creepy-ass stuff.*

Driving at a discreet distance, he followed Lily's car. Something was messed up in Dodge, and he planned to explode Marisa's darkness into smithereens. Did his plan mean seducing the darkness himself? Seducing Marisa, the one woman he dreaded *and* craved above all? He feared the tar might drag him into whatever pit it languished in. He feared light might never penetrate her darkness. Did seducing Marisa mean using his psychic powers for evil intent, a direct violation of his personal code?

Marisa's psychic makeup changed after she'd bonked her head. Before, she automatically nudged his walls, pushed on a stuck door, and waltzed right in. When he blocked out her intrusions, a niggling bug remained implanted in his head. The bug had permanently disappeared after the shooting, leaving him bereft in a wholly uninviting way.

"Padded cell for one," he groused to the ether. "Who is Marisa Meadows? Who's playing her like a well-strung guitar?"

He refused to let her harm Lily, his brother, his entire family, or the Guild at large. Only one way to find out what beat Marisa's drum. He planned to seduce the darkness even if it flayed him alive. Only problem was, if she sucked in his heart, he didn't know if he'd survive.

CHAPTER FOURTEEN

Marisa sipped heavily doctored caramel coffee, ambrosia to her tongue, reminding her of Ric. *Gah. I got bonked with a stupid rock in the park.* "Go back to work." She swished her hand at Lily in the doorway of Lily's kitchen. "Geez, you'd think Wesley shot me the way you're helicoptering."

"Aren't you glad I dragged you to that self-defense class? Pretty badass of you. But kind of stupid."

Marisa tightened her lips in a straight line. "Really? Should I have just gone along with him?" And discovered where the Cabal was hiding?

"The cops had it under control." Lily practically chewed the frost off her lipstick. "Didn't they?"

"I did too. I wanted to take the asshole down myself." She scanned the room. "Speaking of, did the cops return my gun?"

"Jake has it. I didn't know you were packing. Did you start because of those evil vibes?" Lily tossed her purse on the table, a sure sign she planned to hang longer.

Take a hike, Lily. LEAVE. Marisa wished she possessed the ability to coerce. She had things to do alone and a wadded piece of paper to read. "Women living alone need protection. I got it a while ago."

"You never told me. In fact, if I remember, you didn't

want *me* getting a gun."

"Because you can't handle one."

Lily tossed a balled-up napkin at her. It skimmed her arm and landed on the granite counter. "What's going on up here?" Lily tapped her temple.

Black holes of nothing. Marisa drew her spine straight against the counter edge. "What do you mean?"

"You're playing the evasive game."

Painting on a poker face, she relaxed a smidge. "Just on edge with everything going on." She blew on her coffee, sipped more liquid fuel. "Another cup and you won't be able to stop the Triple-M train."

Lily stepped closer. "Don't make me break out my flying monkeys." She twined her index finger around a lock of Marisa's hair and tugged it playfully.

If anyone knew one wit about losing psychic powers, Lily was the one. She'd lived over ten years absent hers and only recently recovered her double whammy clairvoyance and telekinesis.

"How out of whack are you?"

Raising her eyes, Marisa honed in on Lily's gorgeous hair, blanketing her shoulders in a shiny auburn tide, ceiling lights glinting on fiery red streaks. "My telepathy didn't return to the roost." The lack of mind reading left her supremely vulnerable, just when she'd vowed to use her unique talents to figure out why she'd turned into a bad-luck minion. And the susceptibility... she had the strangest feeling her mind was no longer hers to control, like another psychic with the ability of coercion could have a field day in her current state.

"You're still blocked?" Lily hugged Marisa, not a normal day-to-day thing except when they hadn't seen each other in a while. She needed a sympathetic friend to hold onto before she crumbled into a field of snow and ashes.

"Oh, hon." Lily held her tight.

Marisa sniffed before she totally compromised her cool composure. "It's never happened to me. How did it feel for you?"

"Let's sit." They ambled into Lily's deceased father's former inner sanctum with his stamp on every nook and cranny. Lily had left the dark furniture and multiple stained-glass lamps in the homey office. All her father's books packed the floor to ceiling bookcases to the left of the scarred, well-loved desk.

They sat on the supple leather sofa facing the desk, and Marisa spread an earth-toned afghan over their laps. "You haven't changed a thing," Marisa said.

Lily plucked at a loose yarn on the afghan. "If I change one thing, it'll be like Dad never existed."

"Not true." Marisa knocked her fist to her heart. "He'll always live in your heart."

"I know, but in here, it's like he's really *here*." A flush worked up her neck and jaw. "I talk to him sometimes."

Marisa squeezed Lily's hand, preventing her from unraveling the afghan, one of many family heirlooms in every room, crocheted by Lily's maternal grandmother. She smiled. "Does he talk back?"

Lily chuckled. "When I've done something stupid."

"That's the devil on your shoulder giving you an earful."

"Exactly. My father." Lily fisted her shamrock pendant. "Don't turn on my waterworks. Let's get to the nitty-gritty." She kicked off her pumps. "First of all, what's up with you and Ric?" She bumped her shoulder into Marisa's upper arm. "Getting friendly with the help?"

"Help? Last I heard he's not my Guardian." The unread note still burned a hole in her pocket. Would she ever get alone time to read it? At the rate she was going, the zombie apocalypse didn't sound too far off. "Hey, I thought you needed to get to work."

She grinned. "I know the owner. But Ric—"

"No buts, missy. Nothing going on. He stalked me at the park."

"Ha! That's what I accused Jake of doing when I returned for Dad's funeral."

"So it's a stalker-to-lover thing between you two? Stockholm syndrome, anyone."

"You're just a barrel of LOLs." Lily turned her back against the sofa arm and pulled her legs up on the seat cushion. "Anyway, about our psychic abilities, I lost mine due to PTSD, not physical trauma. It blocked me until I came to terms with my identity and my family history. Much different than what you're dealing with."

Getting comfortable, Marisa crossed her legs on the sofa, her muscles tightening from lack of exercise. "Did your head feel hollow, like you'd lost your identity? Plus, I feel like it's gone forever."

"No, I didn't feel like I possessed any psychic abilities to miss. For the most part, I felt normal, except part of me knew I wasn't who I was meant to be. I didn't feel like I fit into the world I lived."

"You do now?"

"Every bit of me. I'm where I belong. I may not be the best clairvoyant or telekinetic on the planet, but I'm kicking ass. Name taking will come later."

"Does your clairvoyance project onto others like Ric's abilities?"

"Not that I know of. Do you think *you* drew Ric into your head?"

Marisa shook her head so violently her brain cells revolted and blew embers throughout her hollowness. She stretched out the kinks in her neck before they attacked her aching head. "No way, no how. Those visions came from drummer boy."

"You sure?"

Marisa scrubbed her hands on her yoga pants, back and forth, fighting the denials ready to trip forth. "I don't know. I'm not right. Not just the concussion and the loss of my abilities."

"Acceptance is the first step."

"This isn't AA."

"We're a club of two, and it took me a long time to figure out why I was blocked."

"I'm *not* mentally blocked. This is different." Blocked was calling her loss mildly. The shooter had blasted her telepathy out, leaving death and decay. Marisa rose off the sofa and paced the room. "Don't take this the wrong way, but aren't you supposed to be at work?"

Lily's head swung toward the antique wood and brass clock on the credenza behind the desk, a twin of the one in Jake's office. "Oh crap." She bounded off the sofa and snagged her tiny purse the size of Marisa's wallet. "I've got a meeting in an hour. I need to prep. New client."

"You getting a lot of new business?"

"Surprisingly, yes. Dad's demise hasn't impacted the business. On that note—"

Marisa held up a forestalling hand. "I'll think about it. Delaney did make an enticing offer."

"More than one?"

"One what?"

"Geez, Mar. That concussion sure did a number on you." Lily flicked a finger at her shoulder. "Did Delany make more than one offer to *you?*"

An unnatural red haze plunged over Marisa's chest. "Maybe. I don't know. He's got me twisting in the wind. Plus, he's a client. I don't do clients."

"At least he's not Guild." Lily winked. "Or Ric McAllister. Regardless, I need you whether or not we land his business."

Marisa lobbed a pillow at Lily. "Stop or I'll leave and never return to San Jose."

Lily sauntered out the door, her hair flouncing in red ribbons down her back. "Liar, liar, pants on fire." She backed up. "Seriously, you sure you're okay alone? Later, we can test your telepathy with Jake. Or with Juliana Falbrooke. She's a master telepath, figure-outer."

"Sounds awesome… with Jake later. I'm not up to meeting anyone else yet. Go. I'll chill, eat bonbons, and watch who's-your-daddy, I'm-doing-your-sister talk shows all afternoon." Marisa waited for Lily to leave before she squeezed out a glob of sanitizer and killed the real and mythical germs on her hands.

Gingerly, she smoothed the crumpled paper on the desk. The typewritten note contained neither identifying marks nor signature.

Follow my instructions to the T. Deviate from them and you'll wind up like your mother in that special secret facility in Tucson. Everyone you know and love might end up like her. Or you all might end up like your sister.

I hope you get my drift. Stay tuned for my next communication.

Air lodged in her throat, and her rumbling heart battled the clog preparing to suffocate her. She folded the note and stuck it in her wallet. The words struck her, buckled her knees onto the Oriental rug covering the hardwood floor. No one was supposed to know where her mother lived under an assumed name. After Marisa's older sister committed suicide, her mother's descent into a psychotic madness accelerated during a very public serial-murder case she was assisting the police with in San Diego. When she failed to prevent two more murders, the case made national headlines, outing her to the world.

The case destroyed her ability to maintain a steady relationship with anyone, let alone any man. No one wanted a cuckoo mind reader tagging along in his life, a woman who held no ability to block others or to resist reading any open mind. A fate that scared Marisa to death, or had until she'd killed her gift yesterday. Maybe her lack of telepathy might be a good thing in the love department. *No, no. Don't be an acorn short of an oak tree.* She'd rather die than live without her telepathy.

Drained, she leveraged off the floor, grabbed her phone, and hit speed dial number one, the private number of her mother's nurse.

The phone rang three times before Jillian answered. "Hi, Marisa."

"Hey, Jill. Is my mom okay?" She pressed the phone to her ear to hold it steady.

"Yes, why?" On guard, Jillian's chirpy tone lowered an octave.

Marisa concocted a fast lie. "I had a weird dream she'd left the facility during the night."

"Are you kidding? She'd miss us too much. She's having the time of her life here. In fact, she's sitting in front of me with a group of her friends kicking their butts in canasta. She'd love to hear from you."

Relief snipped a frazzled knot in her neck. "No, don't disturb her fun. You know how sad she gets when she talks to me."

"No prob. When do you think you'll make your next trip here?"

"I'm in San Jose on a case. I'm not sure." Marisa refused to risk drawing her mysterious stalker to her mom. Maybe the psycho didn't really know where her mother lived. Denial taunted her. "Don't tell her I called. She'll just fret." Only half relieved, Marisa hung up, leaving Jillian instructions to keep a closer eye on her mom.

After typing a to-do list on her cell, Marisa hefted her purse and called for a rideshare car. Time to get a rental car. Time to visit the scene of the fire and exact her own breed of justice. A puppet master was setting her up for an epic fall, and she'd be damned if she planned to sit by and watch them destroy her or people she loved.

CHAPTER FIFTEEN

Marisa shut the door on her silver rental sedan and stepped into a cool fall breeze. She didn't know what to expect at the fire scene and was unpleasantly stunned to locate it too near Lily's house in the San Jose foothills, and so near the Guild compound. A swarm of bees buzzed her belly, baiting her paranoia buttons.

Propped against the car, she ran a news search about the fire on her phone, read the one mention alluding to a link to the Guild. The Guild wasn't a secret club, but they would never out the couple in an ongoing case, especially with increasing Cabal threats.

The charred remains of the partially standing house tempted her closer. Fires and their aftermath didn't bother her. Dying people did. She ducked under the canary caution tape, glad mature trees and vegetation on the half-acre hillside lot hid the yard from neighbors and the street.

Anything to shed light on why Ric experienced the vision might help her understand her own deal. She didn't buy the randomness, and her intuition warned her it all rolled into one big bitchfest. The blood-red flowers begged to return to their familiar mental landscape. The field remained brown and desolate, bone-dry fissures in the dirt dying for a drop of nourishment from the tapped-out waterfall.

Singed bushes and trees close to the left side of the house mimicked her lonely, bleak cerebral landscape. The two-story house's right side remained unscathed, like her outward appearance hiding the truth within. The burnt bedroom sat at the top left rear corner, a skeleton of half-blackened walls. Studying the scorched remains, she tried to recall subtle details she might've missed from Ric's vision. Had he projected everything?

Fingers virtually crossed, she dodged singed boards, embers, and scattered glass on the ground toward an intact rear door. The patio accommodated a round fire pit and a rock-lined koi pond nestled along the perimeter. Passing by them, she slipped on garden gloves she'd scrounged from Lily's garage and twisted the knob. Locked. "Well, of course." She hiked to the other end of the patio where two sets of glass doors opened onto the wooded backyard. Both sliders were locked.

Leaving on the gloves, she wandered to the pond, tinkling water erupting out of a center spout. She sat on the edge and watched the orange and white fish swim unfettered among the water lilies and grasses in the murky water. A black koi swam close, the sun casting her shadow over the fish. It floated in place, its mouth gaping open. Seven orange and white fish circled Blackie, bobbing around him as if he were king. They waited and watched her. Had anyone fed them since the fire? A beige plastic storage bench sat off to her left, revealing a container of dried fish food, a net and other pond, and gardening paraphernalia. After reading the directions on the container of food, she poured the requisite amount on her palm, doubled it, and returned to the pond's sunny side.

Sunlight glinted off a silver bracelet caught on a thick lily stem near her right hand. Intrigued, she dislodged the bracelet, fisted it, and then sprinkled in the crunchy bits. The koi devoured the dried food like hungry zombies. The short chain's allure earned her full attention. The fine sterling held two silver Guild logo charms, each the size of a quarter, the logo's Celtic heart and trinity knot as familiar as her hand. Stunned beyond belief, she wiped the charm bracelet on her jeans. It hadn't been in the water long enough to tarnish, maybe only a few days.

"Marisa?" The familiar voice flung her out of her disbelief. She shoved the bracelet and gloves in her jacket pocket and spun to confront the source of interruption.

"Kenny, what are you doing here? Are you following me?" She only half kidded as she searched for his car.

His rich laugh skated up her spine in a mixed wash of temperatures. "I live at the end of the *cul-de-sac*, saw a car parked in front. Curiosity got the better of me due to the fire. It's the first car I've seen here other than emergency personnel and news vans. Did you know the couple?"

Kenny looked good enough to eat in his black tailored suit, eggplant tie hanging askew, a lock of his impeccable hair hanging over his brow in a boyishly charming manner, ready to confront the end of a short workday. Marisa held her fingers to her purse, hindering them from smoothing the lock of hair into place and drilling into his thick chestnut waves. His dark hair reminded her of Ric's much shorter cut, the hair color she liked most on a man. The resemblances to the two ended there. Just the thought of Ric's sexy, slow smile underneath the bill of his baseball cap renewed a hormone frenzy and caressed her in her most intimate areas.

Shaken and stirred, she mentally kicked her devilish sidekick off her shoulder and said, "Lily lives nearby. I took a drive to clear my head. I read about the fire in the paper and was curious." More like read about it from Ric the town crier. "Did you know them? How long have you lived in this neighborhood?"

Kenny's fingers feathered her hand, a bare breeze on her skin. He didn't say anything, as if he was memorizing every spec of her face. The intense invasiveness sent ants trucking across her scalp, and yet Marisa wanted more, wanted to please him and allow him to please her in ways that included stripping off all their clothes. Insanity must have shot her with a double whammy overnight. *Someone's definitely peeing in my cup.*

"Unfortunately, my busy work schedule has kept me from getting acquainted with my neighbors in the five years I've lived here." His gaze zipped over her shoulder in the direction of Lily's house. "I didn't know Lily lived nearby. Coincidence?" His wide, even-toothed smile almost melted her, until she realized his words didn't mesh. Or was paranoia her new best friend since she'd become a victim of malicious and nefarious activity? He took another step closer until the tips of their shoes met. "Why are you really here, Marisa Mae Meadows?" he asked, lethally enticing.

As if coerced, she blurted out, "Honestly, I didn't read about the fire in the paper. I sort of had a nightmare about it."

He canted his head to the side. "You're clairvoyant? Or did you telepathically read it from someone else?"

Almost ready to blurt out Ric's name, she forcibly locked down his identity. She refused to implicate him. "No. Possibly read it."

"Did the perpetrator slurp you into his mind? I heard that happened recently to a Guild member." He gently toed her flats. "What's her name? Julie—"

"Juliana. A homegrown psychic during the kidnapping of her fiancé's niece."

He snapped his fingers. "Right. I've heard of

criminals projecting their crimes upon telepaths or clairvoyants. Did the same happen to you?"

"Possibly," she lied, confused and wondering why she'd given up the goods. "You know a lot about psychics."

Kenny walked his fingers across the back of her hand, intimately driving beneath her jacket cuff. "I have a healthy fascination regarding extrasensory perception. I thoroughly conduct my research before I engage in business with anyone. Your background is no secret."

"Only business?" she kidded coyly, before mentally slapping herself silly. Coy held no meaning in her personal dictionary.

Easing closer, he put himself and his mouth in strike distance. "Business, pleasure, in all things I do." He drew her against his very hard chest.

Marisa's palm landed on his muscular pectoral to hold him at bay. She hadn't experienced a healthy flirtation in a long dry spell. Six months? Far too long. *He's a client*, cried the wing-flapping angel on one shoulder. *Go for it*, shouted the pitchfork-stabbing devil on the other.

"Kenny," she said, "I'm not sure—" Birds chirped from her purse, followed by a familiar melodic sound. Saved by the bell. "I'm sorry. I need to check my texts."

He didn't release her. "By all means. I'm not going anywhere."

She pried her phone out of her purse between their bodies and checked her message. Anonymous. Squinting, she shielded the screen from him and the sun.

> *Don't return to the Falbrooke house. Don't respond to or contact Lily Falbrooke, the McAllisters, or the Guild for the night. Let's see how well you follow directions & keep your friends intact. Stay safe, precious.*

Her skin crept in waves of goosebumps. Did this

mystery asshole plan to hurt Lily overnight? Was he really testing her?

Another text:

Don't do it. Put the phone away. Turn it off.
You follow directions, your friends and
mother stay safe.

Blanching, she stealthily hunted for the lens following her every twitch. Nothing but flora and fauna met her anxious search.

"Bad news?"

Marisa punched her phone off and dropped it in her purse as if rancid. Freaking out inside, she stepped away from him, and he freed her hand. "Just a pang in my head."

"Why didn't you say you were in pain? Let's go to my place. Are you okay to follow in your car?"

She waved off his concern given the perfect opportunity to decompress and assess. "I'd love to visit your place."

Pleasure suffused him, leaving her with no doubts about her decision. Worried Lily would be going crazy and sending the star fleet after her soon, she gnawed on her bottom lip. She'd find a way to get a message to Lily.

After a short drive to the end of the street, they arrived in the circular driveway of Kenny's multi-level Mediterranean-villa-style house. A humongous three-tiered fountain tinkled in the center of the lawn, the hypnotic splashing drowning her unease. Kenny opened the right double front door with its wrought iron overlay, and she entered a gleaming marble foyer of whites and blacks.

"You have impeccable taste," she announced, capturing the ambiance, driving another wedge of unease six-feet under. The luxurious home exuded a sterile peacefulness, unlike Lily's family home's death and grief layering the normally homey atmosphere.

"Thank you. The house was originally built for the CEO of a failed startup, and he was forced to sell it before taking residence." He took her hand and guided her to the living room in front. "A decorator updated and furnished it to suit the house's style."

"Tons of space for one man." She stroked the floral jacquard sofa. "I could get used to a man who has no beef with floral patterns."

"I hope to fill the house with a family one day. The decorator assured me this style appealed to the female species."

"Please tell me you have black leather somewhere."

"Every home must have a man cave. I'll take you to my playroom."

"Your whole house can be a man cave."

He stopped short in the wide hallway. "What if I don't want it to be?" His fingers drifted to her hand again, and she almost flinched from the familiarity. "Like I said, I have the dream to marry and start a family." He kissed her mouth, his lips firm and soft, inviting, and so wholly ill-advised.

Marisa nearly choked on her spit and shoved away. "I'm sorry if I've led you on, but I don't mingle business with pleasure."

"I do." With a wink, he led her toward the rear of the house. They entered a family room carrying forth the grays, blacks, and whites. Leather furniture, the darkest walnut occasional tables, a red-felt pool table, and a bevy of old-fashioned slot machines sat next to two humongous flat screens with an array of gaming consoles between them. An expansive wall of windows and a French door opened to a garden oasis surrounded by a thick garden of privacy bushes and trees.

"Gamer?"

"It allows me to cut loose after a tough day in the office. Do you game?"

"No. I represent a game company and picked up the lingo and tricks of the trade." Marisa fingered the spotless consoles, stopping on one shaped like a pyramid.

"I've invested in a game company. Our console is unique; however, our game will also work on other manufacturers' consoles, phones, tablets. Everyone will be hooked." He used a remote to turn on the pyramid console and the screen on her left flickered on. "Our inaugural game is a huge hit with our testers. We're currently preparing to bring it to the market. Sit. I'll show you."

Marisa got comfy on a plush, leather gamer chair, and Kenny sat beside her on the sofa, adroitly maneuvering the controller from one screen to another until a dark wasteland of death and destruction, similar to the dystopian games currently on the market, filled the screen. The graphics were flawless, the 3-D landscape so real, a little something dipped in her stomach.

"What's so special about your game?"

"It'll be a game changer." He chuckled at his lame play on words. "Seriously, we expect it to explode upon the gaming world and beyond. We're already working on versions two and three. Need to stay one foot ahead of our competition. The field is fairly competitive."

"Yeah, war games seem dime a dozen." Despite the impressive graphics, Marisa wasn't enthralled by the cityscapes and bleak landscapes scrolling past.

"This isn't just a war game." Kenny picked up a pair of virtual reality goggles and handed them to her. "Put these on. There's a speaker on each side only the user can hear from."

Marisa slipped the lightweight goggles on, and they adhered to her head as if custom made for her. Birds in singsong and the wind's whistle pervaded the room. A brilliant verdant jungle landscape rolled to a dazzling waterfall on the screens. The splash of water sprinkling in a pond far below it in diamond water drops sent her slouching comfortably into her seat, which acclimated to the perfect temperature for her body. The goggles and the chair became part of her, as if they shot tranquil drugs into her muscles in an indescribable alteration of all her senses.

Kenny smiled. "You feel it?"

"Oh. My. This is incredible. Are all VR setups like this?"

"No. We've perfected the electronics to work with your brain waves, to connect to your five senses. The VR works with or without the monitors."

"Wow." A parade of pitchfork-stabbing minions set course for her stomach.

A man backed out of the jungle on the screen, wearing nothing, his tanned, muscular backside and delectable, firm ass facing her. His dark, wavy hair fluttered in the breeze drifting through the jungle, chilling her very real passion. He was as real as Kenny sitting so sinfully close. Her girly parts began a little anticipatory jig. *Holy witch balls.* Marisa had never been keen on watching porn as it did zilch for her desire. She'd rather treat her senses to the real thing, and she had no end of willing partners whenever she wanted. However, the wanting didn't come often enough. "Trade secret, I presume?"

"Perceptive as usual."

The man on the screen slowly turned. His muscular biceps created an excited stirring in her breasts. She thrummed with pleasure at the majesty of his godlike naked form. His erection sprang out of dark curls, pulsing with his own excitement. Heat wafted off his too near body.

Kenny Delaney.

Mesmerizing orbs pierced her, and she drizzled into them like a fine mist on a mountain lake. No landing met her, only a freefall in the dark cavern of his eyes. His mind connected with hers, probed every nook and cranny, learned everything about her from her earliest memories to her goals and even long-forgotten memories. He sprinkled the barren wasteland of her telepathic mind with words, commands, lifeblood. The eerie evil tailgating her became an indelible part of her being, killing her ability to resist.

Light snuffed out, Marisa slumped against the chair and buried her five senses in the jungle and the darkness compelling her, beguiling and seductive. She immersed her all in the man who ignited fireworks in her welcoming insides.

CHAPTER SIXTEEN

A sprawling, gnarled oak surrounded by cedars on the perimeter of Delaney's property provided Ric the perfect spying roost.

"What are you up to, Marisa?" The lenses of his binoculars steamed up. A thin thread of jealousy wiggled its way inside his angry heat. "Head trauma my ass."

His phone vibrated. He dropped the binoculars on his neck cord and answered. "Yeah." He glanced at the caller I.D. "Sorry, Lil, what's up?"

"I've been trying to call Marisa. Where is she?"

"At Delaney's house. Did you know he lives between your place and the Guild compound?"

"Had no clue. What's she doing there? She's supposed to be resting."

"You tell me. She's your friend." Not wanting to fret the flower child further, he chose not to divulge Marisa's visit to the burnt remains of their shared nightmare.

"She hates sitting around. Maybe she's hammering out settlement terms, or decided to take him up on his offer."

Another thread of jealousy twined around the first one and he began to slide off his perch on a lower branch of the ancient oak. "What offer?"

"Take him and his company on as a client if she

relocates here and joins my firm." Smugness laced her words.

He jumped off the branch to the ground, now only able to see the roofline through the trees from his position on a slope.

"Hey, did you hear what I said?"

"Yeah."

"Keep an eye on her."

"I'm doing my job." Sighing, he leaned a shoulder against the oak trunk. "I'll report in later." He clicked off, intrigued by Delaney's offer and especially by the idea that Marisa may move to San Jose. Maybe he had a shot with her. He scratched his head, gouging sense into his testosterone-addled brain cells. *Not the queen of darkness. No way, no how.* Not if she's hooking up with Mr. Rich and Mysterious Delaney.

Ric had found nothing on his internet witch hunt to incriminate Delaney in nefarious activities. The man was as clean as a whistle rolling off the assembly line. Philanthropic, esteemed CFO with a Harvard MBA and a couple Ph.Ds. Two older brothers and their parents owned and operated a Las Vegas hotel and casino.

Ric climbed aboard his bird roost again. The moment his ass bumped the branch, an intense vision hit him. He braced himself against the tree trunk to prevent a topple to the ground

Delaney strutted into a spacious reception area of a gleaming office tower. The earth-toned tiles, veined marble walls, and the glass art display of old world inspired replica artifacts gave away the building's identity—the building housing Falbrooke & Associates. Delaney evaded three groups of people in the waiting area before exiting through the doorway to the stairwell.

He climbed the steps two at a time, exited onto the third floor, and then took the elevator up to the fifteenth

floor. In the empty hallway, he straightened his tie and sidled to a door marked "San Jose Accountancy."

The small reception room was empty and he bypassed the uncluttered desk.

A tall swarthy man of Italian descent, sporting a bulbous nose and curly, salt-and-pepper hair met him in the hallway.

The Italian bro-smacked Delaney between his shoulder blades. "You bear good news I hope."

"She's the one."

A wicked grin drew the Italian's face into comical land, displaying a crooked set of snow-white teeth. "Game on." His rotund stomach and beefy jowls jiggled.

"She'll be mine soon." Delaney sat in a chrome and pleather client chair in front of a desk piled high with files, coffee cups of varying degrees of emptiness, two laptops, and a keyboard connected to a tower.

"You mean ours."

Delaney flicked his hand in annoyance. "What's mine is yours, ours."

"Completely?"

"A few more compulsions and there's no turning back. Minor compulsions have been working for months now at level one. There's no stopping us."

"Excellent." The Italian slapped his hand down on his shoulder, and Delaney flinched under the weight. "We knew you had it in you to accomplish this task. Get this broad under our thumb and others will follow. She's all yours to command. Unless you can't do the job."

"Maybe not the ones you want to follow." Delaney shrugged the man's hand off. "And don't threaten me."

"Touché." The man returned to his seat behind the desk. The chair creaked under his weight. "They aren't the only fish in the sea."

"No, but they're the sharks among minnows."

"Point taken." The man tapped sausage fingers on one of his keyboards. *"One at a time."* The screen seemed to preoccupy him for a moment. *"I sent you the latest field test. We're testing a couple new subjects. Working out new bugs."*

"Anything I need to worry about? The code's nearly perfect as-is."

"Nothing's perfect." The man closed the laptop. *"Test subject ninety-five used a bug in the code to break out of her level three compulsion."*

Delaney sat up straighter, tugged on his constricting tie. *"It's the third time with her."*

"Exactly. She's too big a threat."

"It may not be a bug." Sweat wet his nape.

"It's not." The man landed a pointed look on him. *"She'll be eliminated tonight."*

"No." Delaney rose, braced his palms flat on the desk between two toppling files of printed code and budget projections. *"She's too good. I can fix this."*

"Too late. The order's been given from up high. I've already found a replacement."

"It brings too much attention to us."

The Italian bellowed out a gleeful chortle. *"No. It lands all the attention on them. Not us. We're clean. Now take a hike."*

After a two-fingered salute, Delaney escaped down the stairwell to avoid foot traffic. He tapped in a number on his phone, and tones and blips met his ears. He followed with another sequence of numbers and spelled the name *Marisa Meadows,* test subject number 100.

Shock jolted Ric into an unceremonious heap onto the rocky ground. This time he was unable to prevent the tumble and literally fell out of his clairvoyant vision. Crackling oak leaves smashed into his cheek and a branch jabbed his right thigh. Twilight descended and golden light seeped from the large windows of the shuttered house. The darkness surrounding Marisa clung to him, smothering the glow of landscape lights flickering on around the lawn and driveway.

Massaging his thigh, he sat on his rear. He clanked his palm against his head as if to stabilize the loose marbles. "Were Delaney and the Italian man Cabal members? Were they playing games with Guild psychics? Or was Delaney involved in a gaming company?" Ric drummed his fingers on his knee, missing his drumsticks to diffuse his nervousness and help stir up his sluggish brain. It always took too long to return to full function after a clairvoyant episode. He paid the price each time in the currency of headaches sucking his entire body dry.

Ric pushed off the ground, slapped the leaves and dirt off his jeans. Hiding in the shadows of deepening indigo dusk in the woody fringe, he worked his way closer to the house. Fortunately, Delaney liked privacy. The woods also hid a twelve-foot-high solid fence surrounding the entire property. One he'd expend too much energy scaling. *Damn mysterious vision.* At least one thing was crystal— Marisa needed real Guardian protection now.

"Not me stalking her like the paparazzi," he grumbled to a maple tree dangling brown leaves clinging to summer long past.

The front door opened, spilling a swathe of light along with Marisa onto the porch. Another half-dozen coach lights lit up the front yard and circular driveway, small amber puddles defining the perimeter of the property.

He peeked around the maple's thick girth. Marisa's long straight hair was disheveled, strands floating up around her ears. Had Delaney drilled his fingers into her hair? Marisa straightened her jacket as if the bastard had placed his hands on her breasts and rumpled her clothing.

Shitshitshit. Soon he'd need a reboot to fix his

jealousy-rattled mind. *Get your shit together.* Everything in him wanted to go to her, to show her she didn't need Delaney, not as a client or anything more. As much as he feared her, he wanted her to the depths of his soul. The moment she'd first stepped onto the Guild compound patio, he sensed she was the fire starter... and so much more. He'd even kept one other vision to himself. Marisa had come to him in the dark of night, not a stitch of clothing on, alluring and beckoning, awakening him from a deep sleep. Smiling, she climbed onto his bed, placed his hands on her hips, and straddled him. He'd awoken afterward so hard and crazed for her, he had to take a cold shower to boot her out of his head, had to scrub his body three times to get the feel of her off his skin. It wasn't enough.

Delaney tailed her to the driveway and opened the door of the car Ric had spied her snagging at the rental agency. They shook hands, and he kissed her cheek.

Ric vowed next time—if there was a next time—she showed up here, he'd bring his long-rang listening device. He raced to the bottom of the hill to his SUV hidden in trees off the roadside. Breathing heavily, he reached his rope ladder and climbed to the other side of the fence. The visions zapped his energy, doubled their toll on him since the first fire revelation. He racked his brain to recall another time he suffered from such a long recovery, but came up with the short stick. A psychic shrink might be able to dig through the morass upstairs. Later.

Tires crunching on the tarmac kicked his rear into gear. By the time Marisa's silver sedan drove through the open gate, he was behind the wheel with his engine running. He flicked off his headlights and gave her plenty of space ahead to avoid suspicion. She cruised down the hill and turned right. Not left toward Lily's house.

"Ah, Marisa. Now what're you up to?" Ric followed at

a discreet distance. He passed a few cars driving the opposite direction, and another car tailed him as they entered the more traveled main road. The road led to the Guild compound and also to a couple Guild director residences. How many members lived in the foothills so near the compound? What did it mean, other than Guild members were rolling in dough? Certainly didn't apply to Guardians. He and Liam shared a house with his black lab, Barney, due to the high cost of Silicon Valley living. Jake rented the loft above Lily's family home while he saved to buy his own place. The trio couldn't scratch up enough dough to buy a house together in the ritzy foothills.

At the compound gate, Marisa punched in her passcode and drove through. He turned down the side road leading to the rear gate to avoid detection. Only the Protectorate, Guild directors, and a few high-ranking Guild members had access to the back gate.

Once he cleared security, he zoomed up the hill and parked in the small back lot. Ric slid his card in the reader at the walkway gate and dashed toward the house. Landscape lights lit up the gardens and patio, and his brother Liam met him at the side access door to the kitchen.

"Dude, you're on door duty?"

Liam scowled. "Shut it. I get these crap-ass jobs while you get to chase after hot wenches." He kinked his head toward the left. "Marty at the front said Marisa went down the hall toward the offices."

"Anyone still around?"

"This place is emptier than the police station next to a donut shop after six."

"You keep scowling and your face will lock in place." Ric shot through the kitchen.

"Call me if you need backup," Liam shouted after

him.

"You're on." Ric knew his brother salivated to return to Guardian work after getting the shaft from a high-ranking psychic who'd set him up for a fall. Liam was serving the last couple months of his sentence. Aside from owning a securities business, being a Guild Guardian pretty much ruled the McAllister blood going back generations.

Ric jogged past the security station in the foyer, and Marty shot his thumb toward the hallway leading to the first-floor offices and conference rooms. Administration offices packed the first floor and the second level housed the directors' offices and primo bedroom suites for muckety-mucks and visitors.

A door at the end of the hallway clicked shut. Ric peeked through the sidelight window into the main administrative office. One overhead light blinked on inside and Marisa rifled through desk drawers. She flipped through a file cabinet and shot photos on her cell phone of the contents. Once she finished the cabinet, she snapped photos of the office, and continued taking photos as she exited. She took a shot of the hallway and tried to open the other doors, but they were all locked. Ric knew for a fact she had no access to anything but a bedroom on the second floor, if she chose to use it.

From his hidden position behind a trio of indoor trees, he watched her enter a conference room and her photo album continued to fill. He scuttled after her, hiding behind fake plants and furniture as she snapped photos of the entire downstairs, avoiding Marty in the foyer. The public areas contained nothing interesting to scope out, and she didn't stop to investigate. By the time she worked her way to the back patio, his gut seethed. Blatantly, as if he owned the place and wanted her to know it, he stood in front of the French doors in plain view and watched her shoot pictures of the backyard.

Bewildered beyond belief, Ric stepped onto the patio, slammed the door shut. Marisa acted as if she hadn't heard a thing. Her index finger flew on the phone before she returned it to her purse. Suddenly, she swayed as if an earthquake rolled beneath the ground. He lunged toward her and caught her in his arms, scooping her up. Her head lolled on his arm, and he hugged her tight to his chest.

"Marisa..." He exhaled her name, her slight weight forcing him down on a cushioned bench. "What the hell?"

She was out colder than a hibernating bear in Greenland. His heart pinged his ribcage. He gathered her close and carried her up to her assigned room in the visitor wing. Since unofficially appointed her Guardian, he'd already been granted room access. He laid her gently on the king-sized bed. Her purse hit the floor and he toed it out of the way.

He shoved the bedcovers aside, and then stripped off her jacket and shoes. To stop himself from stripping her bare, he locked his arms to his sides. *Goddamn, she's gorgeous.* Beautiful, mysterious, seductive, and darker than any psychic he'd ever met, darker than the mantle of lustrous hair fanning the pillow.

"Where does your darkness stem from, Marisa? Do you even know?"

A tear slipped out of her right eye and threatened to dribble into her hair until he caught it on his thumb. "Baby, what's going on with you?" He licked his thumb and tasted the salt of her sadness and pain.

She whimpered, and the sound nearly broke him. Without another thought, he kicked off his boots and jacket and spooned her, protecting her body from her demons. He wished he possessed the ability to protect her mind from the evil trailing her. Until they figured out what new hell plagued her, he remained at a loss. It gutted him. The feelings he held for her snowed him under. Never had he felt such an intense attraction to a woman who mystified him to no end, someone who harbored danger and evil, whether she invited it or not. The hazards of the dark side of her mind bullied them both. It threatened to break her if the connection they shared strengthened. Plus, she could easily destroy him, leading to his failure as a Guardian at the least. No McAllister had ever failed his Guardian duties. With her, the concern was excruciatingly real.

His phone buzzed in his back pocket, and he read the text from Lily asking about them.

At compound for the night. She's safe. C U in morning. He texted back.

You both have explaining to do.

Chill. Tomorrow.

Marisa snuggled her perfect ass into his crotch, and his instant erection drove between her butt cheeks. Still asleep, she settled his hand on her flat stomach, narrowly missing her left breast.

Did she know she snuggled with him? Did she hope it was him? Or Delaney?

"Cold," she mumbled. "Closer." Her teeth chattered.

Throwing caution to the manufactured breeze in the room, he wrapped his entire body around her, his hard planes a safe haven for her sinfully soft curves. Her summery floral scent shrouded him, and he breathed deep as if to memorize every tiny nuance about her. As he twined both arms around her, she turned and pressed her mouth to his chest. The softness of her body against his awakened his every sense. One of her hands slipped between them and touched down on his zipper, then pressed against an erection to beat all erections. A tangle of pleasure and pain forced out a groan, and he battled the need to unbutton his jeans and free his dick. Did the little witch know how her touch enchanted him?

A serene sleep claimed her while he remained aware of her every breath warming his skin. Afraid to move for the next two hours, he dozed on and off until her arm slid off him.

"McAllister? Where are we?"

He hid a yawn. "Your room at the compound." She stiffened against him as if his response surprised her. "How'd you know it was me?" he replied.

"The hint of cardamom in your cologne." She pressed her nose to his chest.

"Yet you stayed."

"You were warm, snuggly." Her hand pressed against his erection again. "And so very hard. Just the way I like my men."

Her words seared a painfully pleasurable path straight to his groin. "Am I your man?"

She laughed a sultry, heavenly sound he wanted to listen to every day and every night. "You could be for a while," she said in a teasing lilt, "if you tell me why we're in bed together."

"Have you changed your tune toward me?"

"I march to the beat of my head." Marisa nonchalantly removed her hand from torturing him and rubbed her head. "At the moment, it's going to town on a Zeppelin drum solo."

"I'm sorry." Ric skimmed a kiss across her cheek. "What can I do? Is it really Zeppelin?" *Dayam, I wish she were rubbing on me instead of her head.*

"John Bonham in the flesh. Or maybe it's Tommy Lee from Motley Crew."

"I'm impressed. You know your drummers." A thrill shot up Ric's spine.

"Sue me, I like music. Give me old metal or give me

death. Right now, I'll take death." She pressed her palms to her eyes. "Alex Van Halen just joined the crew."

"That's it." Reluctantly he disentangled from her and drew the covers up to her chin. "I'm getting you some drugs."

Her lips kicked up in the cutest smile, erasing everything evil about her. A smile for him only. He wished. "I'll take one of everything, please," she replied. "Then get your fine ass back in this bed. I'm still cold."

"Well, hell." He jetted to the door. "Coming right up on both accounts."

He gained access to the first-floor infirmary with his keycard. Elizabeth, the Guild healer, made sure all Guardians had access to an over-the-counter medicine cabinet for anything from headaches to toenail fungus. He grabbed two bottles of water and a handful of soft caramels from the candy dish.

He reentered Marisa's room, and she appeared so alluring, young, and peaceful sprawled on the bed. Her velvety skin invited him to touch her. Wiped of her trademarked deep red color, her plump lips beckoned. And her scent. Goddamn, he could die just smelling her summer meadow breeze all day long.

"What took you so long?" She squinted at him through one eye. "A person could die of... many things in the time you took."

"Such as?" He flicked the top off the bottle of pain relievers and unscrewed a bottle of water. She lifted up on her elbows, her tongue slipping slow and provocative between her lips.

The pain of too tight pants nearly unhinged him. Focusing on her health and not her teasing tongue, he set two pills on her palm, and she popped them with a few sips of water.

"Hand me one of those caramels. How'd you know

they were my favorite?"

"Because they're my favorite too."

"Really." She stretched out the word and gobbled up the caramel. Pure bliss shot another arrow to his groin. When she threw aside the covers and patted the empty space beside her, the arrow exploded in a blistering bang, and he slipped onto the bed. Without waiting for another invite, he drew her into his arms and halfway on top of him.

She mashed her right breast against his chest. "I thought you didn't like me."

"I thought you hated Guardians."

"Hate's a strong word. You have your place in our regime. Just not stalking me."

Ric winced, battled against tipping his hand. "I don't dislike you."

"You don't trust me."

"I trust you enough to hold you in my arms, to lie in the same bed with you."

"Keep your enemies closer, blah, blah, blah." Her soft fingertips danced a slow tango on his bare arm. A long slow shiver sliced him in two.

"You don't even know me, yet apparently you trust me enough to hold you," he croaked out, the pain of his pulsing erection doing an epic number on him.

"I'm cold." The pink tip of her tongue shot out, and she licked her upper lip.

A groan escaped him. "Yeah. That's it. Me too."

She stifled a giggle. "So you're a drummer?" she asked.

"Was in a rock band in high school and college. Now the drums gather dust in the garage. I don't have time for them anymore."

"What did you major in? Guardians 101?"

Affection assailed his chuckle. Her questions gave

him hope that she was truly interested in him. "Criminal justice."

The lightest press of her hand on his chest rocketed his heart into orbit. "Makes sense for your business."

Before he comprehended where the indescribable moment was leading, Marisa straddled him, placed his hands on her hips, and pressed her soft lips against his.

CHAPTER SEVENTEEN

An intense craving for Ric decimated Marisa's will. Screw the Guild Girl Code. She wanted him like she wanted her sanity intact. She tasted caramel on his mouth and parted her lips to taste more of him. He skimmed his hands up her sides, cupped her neck, not allowing her to break contact, his hands slightly rough on her skin. Straddling him, she avoided his hard-as-sin erection. If she felt him again through his jeans, she'd unzip his pants and free the iron rod, but she wasn't ready to dust off the cobwebs. Guardians weren't supposed to get involved with their charges. Since he hadn't been assigned to her, all the sex they wanted sat on the table of need and want. Yet walking away afterwards might endanger her heart. Sex was better left served alone in the wake of her turmoil where Ric McAllister was concerned. Or none at all.

Blue eyes hooded, radiating lust, Ric groaned and his mouth parted. He took her mouth, hot and fiercely, as if he was dying of thirst. Hot exhilarating electricity flooded her body. Their kiss deepened, and his tongue probed her lips, parting them to plunder her mouth. He stole no more and jerked his head to the side, breaking contact. Panting, she drooped against him and a frustrated sigh escaped her. His dizzying kisses drove every bad thing out of her except him. He'd handed her a forever type of kiss. And she didn't do forever.

"You're no fun," she said, both hating and loving the moment.

"What are you doing, Marisa?" he demanded, grooves of frustration marring his strong forehead.

"What's wrong with just a kiss?" *Idiot! Go poke your mind's eye out.*

"I don't do casual. I don't—"

Her spine grew rigid, and she rolled off him. "You don't what?"

"Nothing." Pillow pressed over his crotch, he sat up, his back against the headboard. "You need to tell me what the deal is."

"Just a kiss. Nothing more." Glowering at him, she crossed her legs yoga style, deciding she needed a yoga session or two to balance the whack out of her system, to quiet the lies spewing out of her mouth.

"Don't play games. That's not what I'm talking about."

She slicked on a light coat of lip gloss, making a decision she hoped she'd not regret. "First, will you call Lily and Jake and make sure they're okay? Don't tell them why you're asking." She stretched across him and snatched her purse. "I need your help, if I can trust your discretion."

"I'm here, in your bed, aren't I? Why do you think Jake and Lily are in trouble?" She handed him the menacing note. As he read the cryptic message, his skin blanched. "Where did you get this?" He drew his phone out and tapped in a text, waited for a response. "They're cool at the house."

While she told him about the note, she unlocked her phone. The texts had vanished. Shocked, she scrolled and scrolled, finger stabbing her screen. She didn't recall deleting the texts. "They're gone." She repeated the gist of the messages. "I called my mom to make sure she's okay. I'm uneasy. No one knows where my mom lives. She's in her facility under an assumed identity."

"In Arizona, right?"

She punched her fists in the air above her head. "Does everyone freaking know?"

He held up a hand to forestall her rant. "Lily mentioned it in the context of your background, nothing more."

"Then you probably know why my mother's holed up there, why I only *do* casual," she said through gritted teeth. She wasn't angry with Lily. In fact, if she got closer to Ric for the purpose of helping solve her shitstorm, then she was glad he knew about her mother. Glad he comprehended her inability to survive a long-term relationship.

Ric dug his hands in his pockets. "I won't betray your trust. It's in your secure Guild file. She's not the first psychic who's needed mental help. Our friend Juliana Westwood and Lily both met in a similar New York facility when they were eighteen."

A new round of anger flushed up Marisa's neck. "Why do you have access to my Guild file? You're not my Guardian."

"You need a Guardian."

"No, thanks."

"Really, Marisa?" He stabbed the note resting on the comforter with his index finger. "You don't think you need protection?"

Renewed need for Ric and the idea of the safety he provided sprouted within her, overriding her sense of independence. "Not at the risk of my mother, Lily, all of you. Whoever's terrorizing me seems to know a boatload about me. I can't jeopardize you. Hell, I'm already jeopardizing you."

"You're asking for my help now. What's the difference?"

"I'm asking you to keep this under your belt and not blast it out onto social media." She ran her fingers over the patterned lines in the jacquard comforter, an inch from Ric's fist.

"I won't make it obvious I'm your Guardian." He unfurled his hand, his fingertips touching hers.

"Are you implying the Protectorate has assigned you to me?" She snuggled her fingers firmly beneath his hand, already knowing the answer, no longer feeling the energy to battle him. Her life was spiraling in a way she'd never experienced. If she didn't stop the freefall, she'd end up catatonic in a bed adjacent to her mother, or in a hole in the ground next to her older sister.

"Yes." Ric's lips were so enticing, his eyes beseeching her acceptance—verbal and otherwise. "Let me protect you." He smiled mischievously, then sobered. "I mean let me help you. We'll solve this together. I'll stay in the background to shelter your mother and everyone. I'm good at what I do. When all is done, we're done, you return to San Diego, stay here, whatever."

"What if it's never done?" Confusion took a nasty spin over her, leaving her jittery. "What if the Cabal's toying with me?"

He tugged her onto his lap, her back against his muscular chest. His arms folded beneath her breasts, and she hugged them close, loving the steel beneath his soft tan skin.

"We'll do this together. You'll get your normal back. Meanwhile, if we can take down the Cabal, then I'd say we'd scored a major payday, maybe even a pot of gold at the end of the tunnel. Now are you willing to tell me everything?"

"You mean pot of gold at the end of the rainbow?" Marisa nestled her head on his shoulder. Damn it, he felt so freaking good wrapped around her. She'd never had a Guardian, never needed one. Never knew what one felt like. "Do you always sleep in the same bed and hold your charges like this? You don't do casual, remember? So what's *this* about?"

"One question at a time." He kissed the top of her head.

"Answer."

"No and no." His arms tightened.

She sucked in her stomach. "And?"

"I want you." His breath seared her scalp.

"Why? You know who and what I am. I don't hide behind a façade to please men. There's no long term with me."

"What if I'm the one who can change your thinking, your feelings? Did you ever anticipate such an alteration in your short-timer spin on life? What if *I'm* your long term?"

Marisa sat for the longest time, absorbing his words, her warring desire and morals. "My head hurts. Just lie with me for a while, okay?"

"I'll take what I can get."

"You're crazy, you know that? And don't say you're crazy for me."

He stretched out on the bed, holding her tight against him, his touch so gentle, it weakened her resolve. Shock zipped through Marisa, a strange and powerful sense of safety and vulnerability from being in Ric's arms.

"Not half as crazy as you," he murmured.

"Acceptance is the first step. I accept the moniker." More than ever from the moment she'd landed in San Jose and became the fall gal for a boatload of nefarious activity.

"And do you accept me as your Guardian?"

"I won't be guarded." An anchor weighed her eyelids down as drowsiness conquered her surprise. Falling asleep in a near stranger's arms never topped her list of relationship etiquette. How had she missed this plunge into a sea of bliss her entire dating life?

"You will."

"Do I have a choice?"

"You always have a choice." He nipped her earlobe playfully, sending a new round of tingles across her breasts. "You also have the choice of another Guardian." He tensed against her as if waiting for the wrong answer.

She linked her fingers in his over his abs and fell asleep.

∽

Marisa pushed out of his arms, and Ric reluctantly released her. "Do you need anything?" he asked half asleep. Without responding, she fell back asleep. The loss of her exquisite touch and her luscious body against him left him hollow. How had he fallen so hard for this complicated mystery woman? For all he knew, she was a Cabal member directed to destroy the Guild. Or out to destroy him from the inside out.

Twilight had turned into a glittering star-studded night, and he lay there, debating whether to spoon her again or give her space. Stomach growling, he ate the handful of caramels he'd dumped on the nightstand. He didn't want to leave her to scrounge up a late dinner in the kitchen. Minutes ticked by and midnight hit. Just when he decided to chuck caution to the wind and blanket her with his body, she tossed and flailed her arms and legs as if someone was attacking her.

"Marisa?" The faint aroma of her baby powder lotion

feathered his skin.

No response. She rolled to the opposite side of the bed, swung out a leg, and hovered for a few seconds on the edge before she shoved off. Without a glance at him or the bed, she slipped on her running shoes, and left the bedroom, the door thudding against the wall.

"Where are you going?"

Silence.

Gun in his hand, Ric crept behind her, his stocking feet soundless on the floor. Maybe she was hungry. Marisa hopped down the back staircase. Motion activated nightlights glowed on as she entered the empty kitchen. She took an apple out of a bowl on the stainless counter, bit into it, then tossed the apple into the trash.

Battling with the need to interrupt her, he halted in the doorway. Never awaken a sleepwalker, resounded in his thoughts. Instead, he turned the video on his phone, recording her every move. *Proof is in the pie.*

She opened the door leading to the side yard where the trash bins were stored and strolled toward the twelve-foot-high back gate. Propping it open with her foot, she dug her hand into her right pants pocket, stared into the darkness for a moment as if contemplating her next action.

Marisa stuck a small landscape rock in the gate opening to prevent it from locking. He sprinted to the gate, sure to leave the rock in place, because, damn it, he'd forgotten his keycard and he didn't want to use voice activation. Not good.

The darkness and the woodsy foliage cloaked her, and he hid in the shadows, remaining close to the perimeter fence. They walked twenty feet until Marisa spun in a circle and rested her hip against a landscape boulder rising up to her butt. She stroked her hand over the rock and dangled it in the space between the trio of boulders.

Mesmerized, Ric wished the moon shone to illuminate her. Even without nearby lights spotlighting her, she had an ethereal beauty stemming from nature, as if she was one with the night, or belonged to the darkness dancing within her.

He left the shadows to announce his presence, to determine if she was sleepwalking. A sudden intense longing rolled over him, and he wanted his lips on hers, wanted her to remember them in this moment. Too dark to determine a flicker of recognition, she stared right through him as if he were a spirt of the night.

Allowing her dream state to guide her, she sat next to the boulders, stretched out her legs to lie flat on the ground facing the star-spangled sky. A thrill shot through his body. The truth of his magnified feelings for her clanged through him like alarm bells. He recorded every second and fixated on her dreamy, otherworldly beauty.

"McAllister?" A perimeter guard, Lucas Saldivar evidenced by his slight Spanish accent, crunched through the woody debris covering the ground.

"Shhh." He spun on his heels, headed Lucas off track. "Yeah, man. Just escorting Ms. Meadows for a walk. She's restless, needed air."

Saldivar holstered his gun. "What's she doing lying on the ground?"

"Communing with nature." Ric wished his words held a semblance of truth. "Some yoga BS."

"I've never seen my sister do this kind of yoga and she's hardcore."

"Must be a San Diego thing." Ric winked. "Go on about your rounds. I'll secure the gate behind us."

"Sure thing. Hey, see you on poker night." Lucas's footsteps faded into the silent night. Not even an owl hooted or a rodent scampered through the underbrush.

Ric hated the idea other hidden guards may be

witnessing Marisa's luminous beauty under a panorama of glimmering stars. He propped himself against the tallest boulder and waited ten minutes. Marisa didn't budge a muscle the entire time. Finally, he scooped her into his arms. Her eyes remained closed the entire way back to her room. Gently, he laid her on the bed, and her eyes flickered open.

"Ric?" Her voice was raspy from the autumn night. "Why'd you leave the bed?"

Confusion set up another aisle in his shop of oddities. He didn't know what to say.

"Why are my clothes cold?" She glared at him. "Are you one of those cover hogs?"

"You don't remember?" he asked cautiously.

"Did I throw the covers off and kick you out?" She wiped her hands on the comforter as if she realized what she'd done.

"You went into the woods."

She scoffed. "Yeah, right. You're dreaming, Guardian guy. Next you'll tell me I set that house on fire again."

"It's true. You're wearing your shoes. I have video." He waved his phone.

Marisa snatched the phone from him, scratching him with her plain, short fingernails in her panic.

The video rolled and alarm blossomed on her face. At the end, her mouth hung open. "I don't sleepwalk."

"Were you awake?"

She wobbled her head. "I don't remember anything after we fell asleep. Not even a dream or one of your freaky prophecies." She dropped her face in her hands. "What's going on with me? Do you think it's the concussion?"

Ric scrubbed the nape of his neck. "Start at the beginning of today after you left Lily's house." He was dying to fill in the gaps after an emergency security breach called him and Liam to a job, leaving her unguarded for a couple hours. Dying to know what she'd been up to with Delaney for more reasons than he cared to admit.

Cotton candy pink slashed her cheeks, and Marisa leaned against the headboard. "I wanted to see evidence. Thought I might get a vibe at the burnt house." She tapped her temple, and then pulled something out of her pocket. "Only thing I found was a silver Psychic Guild charm bracelet in the koi pond." She handed the bracelet to him, started to retract it, flicked her hand to relinquish it.

"The couple weren't Guild."

Eyes downcast, she elevated her fingers off her thigh, let them fall. "Maybe it's a setup. Whatever. The cops missed it."

Without asking additional questions about the charms, he handed the bracelet back to her and she cupped it in her fist. If a Guild member were involved, there'd be hell to pay. If the Cabal set them up, he wanted to know who the bracelet belonged to, who the Cabal may be manipulating to do their dirty work.

"Why did you go to Delaney's house?" He asked the question searing a hole in his well of curiosity.

"He saw my rental car. Then I got the text telling me not to go home. He offered, I accepted. I figured it was a good time to talk about the offer he made."

"Is that all you talked about?" His shoulders knotted in anticipation of bad news.

Contemplating, she raked her fingers through her hair from scalp to the tips. "Ric, what's wrong with me? I remember touring his house. We didn't talk about representation. Then I was standing in his driveway and drove here. Next thing, I'm waking up in bed with you curled around me."

She innocently batted sultry eyelashes at him. He wanted to keep her safe within the sanctuary of his body and never let anyone else touch or hurt her ever again.

He weaved their fingers together, and her soft slender fingers seemed to become a part of him. "Do you recall snapping photos around the compound?"

"Right. Get real." She grabbed her phone off the nightstand, scrolled through screen after screen, then handed him the phone. "There's nothing here. Nothing in trash or email either. Nothing on my cloud."

Stunned, Ric swiped through her phone, not like he didn't believe her, but he was stumped.

"You ransacked the offices and shot photos of files."

Groaning, Marisa collapsed onto the bed. "I'm screwed, right? Someone's messing with my head. Someone stole my DNA out of my purse at the airport. I don't know how they're doing it. I don't even—" She cupped her mouth as if afraid to reveal another truth.

"You said you weren't missing anything." Stiff-limbed, Ric began pacing the room. "What else aren't you telling me?" The tendons in his neck throbbed painfully.

"I didn't notice my lipstick and glob of gum missing until Lily gave me a replacement handbag." She seemed to gauge him for a moment. "What aren't *you* telling me?"

"I had a vision of Delaney in Lily's office tower." Her eyes bugged out. To her mounting agitation, he relayed the images.

Marisa hopped off the bed and stomped around the room behind him. "I'm a freaking test subject? How?" She thumped her knuckles on the wall.

"Are you sure you can't remember anything that happened at his house?"

"My head's so screwed up, we probably did the nasty, and I don't remember it."

Ric's lips curled up. "Believe me, when *we* get down to

business, I can guarantee you'll never forget it. I can guarantee I'll be doing more than *doing the nasty* with you."

"*When?*" She quirked an eyebrow. "You're pretty sure of yourself, aren't you?"

He cupped her cheek and pressed the barest breeze of a kiss on her mouth. "One thousand percent." He nipped her lobe and trailed tiny kisses down her neck to her shoulder. He knew she wanted his mouth on hers evidenced by the hum in her throat spurring him on.

Marisa plastered herself against him. "Ric. This isn't the time. *We* aren't in this time together. And I don't do Guardians." Her soft, curvaceous body glued to his said otherwise.

"So you've said. Yet here we are." His hands landed in the small of her back, and he lost himself in her lust-swirled eyes again. "Our time will come. Count on it."

"Proven by a vision?"

"No vision needed. I'm going by gut."

"As long as it's not your heart." She slipped out of his loose embrace, the loss of her warm body a blast of wintry reality. "I'm being set up or targeted. We need to focus."

Ric kept his distance, trying to hide the incessant and infernal bulge in his pants. "Do you think Delaney's Cabal? Have you tried to read him?"

"Really. Do you think if he's Cabal, he'd leave his mind flayed open for one of the best telepaths on planet Earth to raze it?"

"You've tried to read him?"

Marisa growled out in frustration. "No! He's a client. I don't go there."

"But he requested your assistance on his case. Didn't he think you'd use your telepathy in the depositions to his corporation's advantage? He's offering you and Lily a lucrative contract to get you to San Jose. Why? I mean, I know you're a good lawyer, but things seem a little too neat in my playbook."

She caved in on herself, slunk onto the bed. "I agree. Everything going on with me points to the Cabal, except for one thing. Who the hell can drill into my head and coerce me, make me lose time and memories? Not even the best Guild psychics are all that."

"We don't know who the Cabal has recruited. We think they're targeting non-Guild psychics now."

"Who? The Guild has tabs on all the known psychics worldwide, whether they've joined or not."

"Not if someone has hidden their abilities."

"And just happened to stumble upon the Cabal for shits and giggles." Laughter with a biting edge erupted out of her.

Ric sat beside her, took her hand in his, unable to cease touching her since she'd quit resisting. "We need to drill into Delaney's head, Test Subject Number 100."

She shuddered. "Don't call me that. I can't afford the bad karma."

A telltale glow inside Ric's head formed, foggy and staggering. His eyes rolled back, and he listed against Marisa's shoulder.

"Ric!" She propped him up. "What's going on?"

He opened his mouth, but no words rolled out on his silent cry. Flames immersed his mind and he sought refuge inside Marisa's head, open and waiting for him, unable to block him out even if she tried. The utter desolation slayed him, and he tried to scramble out as fast as he dove in. Something curious and evil caught him and towed him down into emptiness. He slumped backward on the bed, submerged by a deep cavern of nothingness with no escape hatch.

CHAPTER EIGHTEEN

"Ric!" Marisa gently slapped his cheek. "Oh, hell in a handbasket." She surged back as if he carried the plague. "McAllister, come on, wake up." She seized a bottle off the nightstand and sprinkled water on his face.

A sharp pain sliced her skull and Ric groaned in pain. She'd almost forgotten her concussion. Yet this pain was different. The machete carved up her brain and her cry of pain echoed Ric's.

Slumping onto the bed, she waited for transference of Ric's images to her head. Machete chopping away, she curled against him as he lay on his back, moaning, eyeballs scrolling behind his lids. Not one frame of his vision hit her. The emptiness inside chided her, sneered at Ric's inability to intrude on a path he had no problem previously traveling. Breathing in deep of his enticing cologne mixed with the hibiscus scent warmer across the room, she let the myriad scents appease the machete demons.

After fifteen minutes, her pain subsided and she leveraged up on her elbows to stare down at a conked-out Guardian. *My Guardian.* A strange exhilaration oozed over her frigid trepidation before reality smacked her upside the head.

Lethargic, she lifted Ric's phone off the nightstand

and called Lily's house. "Screw my instructions not to contact anyone. They can't be tapping every phone in the world." The line rang three times before Jake picked up. "Jake, it's Marisa."

"What's wrong?"

"Funny how you go straight to wrong." Her sarcasm refused to be caged.

"Nothing's right with you. What's wrong with my brother?" He nearly shouted into the speaker.

Not surprised by his insinuation, she told him what happened. "He won't wake up."

"He doesn't pass out. What did you do to him?"

"Nothing." She banged her fist against the bedpost, willing Jake's smug face ingrained in the wood. "I'm calling you, aren't I? I'm in my room at the compound. Do you want me to call nine-one-one?"

Jake spoke to Lily in the background. "No. I'll call Elizabeth, the Guild healer. I'll be right there."

"Don't hang up." The words spewed out. "Don't leave Lily alone."

"Son of a bitch. You've got to be kidding me."

"The Cabal's still out there. I won't allow you to jeopardize her."

"Don't mess with me, Marisa. You better come clean when we get there." The line clicked off.

Marisa brushed the hair off Ric's damp forehead. He'd settled, his face serene, but his eyeballs kept his lids undulating as if in REM sleep. "Ric? Can you hear me?" She tried her telepathy. *"Come on, handsome. Wake up and I'll break the Code and go on a date with you."* Nothing. Not a sign he'd heard, not as if she expected it since Ric wasn't telepathic. Not even a sign her telepathy worked.

She pressed her lips to his, meeting firm coldness, tasting a hint of caramel. She clasped his hand on his flat abdomen, his cool fingers lifeless. Before she skidded off the rails, she double-checked his pulse, a finger to his neck, her ear against his heart. Both beat steady, and a ripple of relief untied one of a million knots twisting her muscles into pretzels.

A keycard clicked in the door and it swung inward, revealing Lily with Jake so close behind her, they appeared attached.

Jake hurried to the bed, checked his brother's vitals. "Elizabeth's on her way. How long has he been out?"

"Going on an hour. He knocked me out at the beginning, and I could barely bat an eyelash from the pain, coupled with my concussion, which I'm sure made it worse."

Jake frowned. "He's never connected with anyone, until you."

"Not even a strong telepath?" She slipped her hands in her pockets to stop them from adopting a life of their own. *A strong telepath with dead telepathy.* Had Ric linked to her dead mind? What if he didn't awaken? Didn't the same happen to Juliana Westwood with a kidnapper during an abduction case and with Jake recently? *No. No. No.* That was two telepaths connected together. Ric's not a telepath. And, well, her abilities had flown the way of the latest space shuttle. "We didn't connect this time."

"Do you have your telepathy?" Lily asked in her ear.

"No," Marisa whispered sharply.

The door clicked again, and Guild healer and part-time office manager at Lily's law firm barreled in. *Incestuous Guild.* Elizabeth greeted them with a quick nod. She'd met Elizabeth at Michael Falbrooke's funeral and found her competent in empathic healing. With a simple tweak of Marisa's neck, Elizabeth had reduced her migraine to nothing.

They gathered around Elizabeth as she listened to Ric's heartbeat. Marisa plumped a pillow beneath his head. She caressed his forehead, trying to smooth out the grooves that didn't belong on his handsome face.

"Touch him again, Marisa," Elizabeth said.

Elizabeth pressed the stethoscope to Ric's bare chest beneath his T-shirt. Marisa feathered her fingers down his cheek and rested her hand on his shoulder.

"He's responding to your touch."

"In what way?" Jake demanded. "Does she need to back off?"

"Jake," Lily admonished. "It's not like she did this on purpose."

"Maybe not intentionally." He clenched Lily's shoulders from behind her, hauling her against him as if to protect her from Malevolent Marisa.

"His heartbeat accelerated when she touched him. It's a positive sign." Elizabeth conducted vital checks. When she finished, she turned to the waiting crew. "Good news, he's not in a coma. Bad news, his mind might have been compromised. We won't know until he awakens."

"What do you mean compromised?" Jake advanced on Elizabeth, his fists clenched at his sides. His long dark hair flowed off his face like raven wings. For a moment, he looked like he was preparing to launch himself in flight to peck out her eyes.

Elizabeth held up a forestalling hand. "He's dreaming or having a nightmare. I can't tell. Might be a clairvoyant episode."

"Is he stuck in someone's head?" Lily laced her arms under her breasts, edged closer to Marisa as if to protect her from Jake's mutinous demeanor.

"That's my fear," Elizabeth replied. "Let's get him to the infirmary. I want to do a brain scan. Doc Wildwood's on standby."

"Languishing in someone's head could destroy him." Jake's voice broke. "Tell me what happened, Marisa? You said you blacked out. Were you drilling into him, breaking down his blocks? Is that what you do? Is that how you win your court cases?"

Lily hugged him. "Marisa would never intentionally harm him."

Tears pooled, exhibiting a vulnerability Marisa never revealed to the outside world. If she caused this condition in Ric, she didn't know what she'd do. Commit herself to Arizona? She refused to hold back. Jake deserved to know. "My telepathy's gone. The concussion destroyed it."

Elizabeth jack-knifed upright. "Why didn't you tell me?"

"There's nothing you can do," Marisa retorted. "Am I supposed to report everything to the Guild?"

"Jake, get a wheelchair." Elizabeth waved him off. "We'll discuss further in the infirmary. I want Doc to do a full workup on Marisa too."

Silent and somber, they all trooped to the Guild infirmary on the first floor, using the elevator for Ric strapped into the wheelchair. The infirmary rooms were much fancier than the boring hospital. Although the rooms weren't as opulent as the compound guest rooms, they mimicked the bedrooms of an expensive private institution. Everything about the compound reminded Marisa how much money the Guild raked in from their legit businesses using psychics for legal purposes, publishing, and media. How different was their business from what the Cabal wanted psychics to do?

Once Dr. Wildwood began his examination and tests, Elizabeth herded Marisa into a separate room and examined her.

"No telepathy at all?" Elizabeth peeled off her gloves.

"Dead."

"I have a mix of herbs which aid in psychic abilities. Do you want to try some in a tea?"

Marisa steered clear of the known psychic herbs. Too many side effects, too many memories of her mother using them to either rid her of her telepathy or her demons. She'd held Mom's hair out of the toilet way too many times as a teenager. "Side effects?"

"Possible dizziness, nausea, body aches if they don't work. Basic flu-like symptoms."

"What happens if they work?"

"Your telepathy will return temporarily, which will prove your gift is only being impeded by your concussion."

"Foolproof?"

"Nothing's foolproof when it comes to the mind."

Marisa ran her hand under the sanitizer dispenser on the wall and worked the gel into her skin. "If Ric and I are tethered, will it reveal him or his vision? Will it affect him?"

"You might see him in your mind. You might view what he's seeing, if anything. It shouldn't hurt him any more than you already might be hurting him." Despite the implied threat, Elizabeth rested against the counter, clearly pleased at the questions Marisa was asking. "You know a lot about the herbs."

"I know a telepath who used them."

"Good or bad?"

"All bad." The locked glass cabinet of drugs to the right of Elizabeth captured her attention. Maybe she could reach Ric, shift him back to his mind to awaken him. "Let's do it."

They reconvened in Ric's larger room. Proximity to him was necessary to determine if they shared a link.

The doctor hadn't discovered any reason why Ric passed out, and his scan confirmed normal brain functions. "I'm not too worried yet. It's not unusual for clairvoyants to pass out for hours on end. It's one way to keep their minds intact."

"Ric doesn't zone out. What if he's connected—" Jake started.

"It's a concern, and I want to keep my eye on him overnight."

Jake fiddled with Ric's drumsticks on the counter, as if he wanted to jab them in Marisa's eye sockets. The sticks clinking together annoyed Marisa, and she wanted Ric tapping his drum solos against his thighs. "He was A-OK until he met Marisa."

"Not totally." Lily stood on her toes and kissed him, trying to appease him. "Remember how he projected on me when you were kidnapped?"

Lily's closeness to Jake and her empathy made Marisa uncomfortable. A private moment between lovers she had a sudden wish for herself, touching Ric with loving fingers and feeling his adoring touch all over her.

"He revealed the previous occurrence during the post mortem," Dr. Wildwood said. "Possible natural progression of abilities. Doesn't happen to all clairvoyants or telepaths, but it's not out of the realm of possibilities. Some psychics bury their true potential, and it emerges in dribs and drabs throughout their lifetime, especially when confronted with trauma. Might explain today's phenomenon."

"Let's find out if he's linked to me." Despite Jake's black glower, Marisa propped her hip against the bed, refraining from touching Ric. Jake might stick the drumsticks down her throat if she touched his brother. She matched his glower with her own darkest one. "No matter what you think, I didn't do this on purpose."

"Are you sure about this?" Lily tapped Marisa's arm.

"Can I have a moment alone with Ric?" Marisa addressed her question to big, bad brother Jake.

He said nothing for a long moment, and then tromped out of the room. The room cleared and Marisa waited for the door to click shut.

She held Ric's hand to her cheek. "Are you trapped in me? Is my emptiness holding you hostage?" She kissed his palm, inhaling the faint scent of caramel. "I'm so sorry. Wake up, will you?"

The ventilation hiss drowned the room with emptiness. Ric stirred in his sleep, mumbled unintelligible words, and jerked his hand out of hers, balling his fist on his stomach. Did she have the ability to bring him back to the living?

Marisa bent over him, skimming her breasts against his arm, and gloved his fist in her hand. She kissed his cold mouth. His lips softened, parted, and she slipped the tip of her tongue between them. He relaxed his fist, flipped his hand around, and slid his fingers between hers. And yet he still didn't wake up. At least not his body. But his mouth awakened and warmed under her pressure, almost returning her kiss in his sleep. It awakened something deep inside her core, a forever dormant sensation, a devotion she'd never felt for another.

She cupped his jaw, slid her mouth to his ear. "I'll be here for you when you wake up if you still want me." Did casual still exist in her vocabulary? Could she leave him and return to her lonely San Diego existence? Everything about her life revolved around loss and longing. She was sick to death of losing out. Could she take the chance now and see where Ric and her longing led her? If only he knew how much she wanted him, how much she wanted to belong to a man she wouldn't drive to the bowels of Earth.

Shock riddled her. She should fear the man who signified much of what she'd dismissed for an eternity.

But he'd tossed her lifelong convictions out with her telepathy and turned her insides into a hormone-spitting machine. She'd downloaded more to him in one night than she'd ever spilled to a living soul.

The door opened and Jake rescued his brother from the evil psychic. She refused to let go of Ric's hand, didn't want her moment to end on the bottom of a teacup.

"Let's do this before you kill my brother," Jake groused without much passion.

"Remember, *he* connected to me." She gave him the palm to check his dark, sullen rant. "I'll do everything I can to return him to you. Why do you think I'm going under dangerous hallucinogenic herbs? Certainly not for shits and giggles. I don't know what you have against me, but I'm freaking tired of your 'tude."

"The minute you barged into our lives, everything hit the crapper." He propped his shoulder against the doorjamb, arms crossed. "Ric, Karma."

"And *me*." She thumped her chest. "The crap is all wrapped around me with a freaking pink bow. Would I do all that to myself? For what gain?"

"For the Cabal."

Marisa simmered inside, a hot vibrating roll from her neck to her toes. "Wow. You really think I'm Cabal? Does Lily think the same?"

"No." Lily squeezed past Jake in the doorway. "We think maybe the Cabal has a subconscious hold on you." Lily backed into the protective hulk of her Guardian, as if to avoid Marisa's demonic wrath.

"Okay. I get it." Marisa let go of Ric's hand before her death grip broke a bone or two. "Then we're on the same page."

Lily gasped. "It's true?"

"I don't know." Marisa trailed her index finger over Ric's strong arm, and for once in her life didn't feel like she needed her antibacterial gel. "Ric and I were tossing conspiracy theories around earlier." She refrained from booting Kenny under the bus. She didn't want the Guild to go after him when she hadn't proven his involvement. Plus, she figured she could finagle information out of him on her own without the Guild dogs chasing him. If he got an inkling he was a target, he'd clam up or worse. They could be sitting on the first major clue regarding Cabal identities and whereabouts. She refused to jeopardize it by blabbing to the Guild world and risking a leak.

Elizabeth barreled past Jake as if she owned the building and her herbal arsenal. "Sit in the chair." Marisa remained on the bed. "You may get sick," Elizabeth warned.

"Fine, give me a bucket." She rounded on Jake. "You can play guard dog all you want to keep me from hurting your brother."

Jake side kicked the doorjamb. "Fine. We do it your way. I want answers now."

"Again, same page."

Marisa sat in the bedside chair and Elizabeth handed her a steaming pale-green concoction. "Drink it all. I've sweetened it with honey to help disguise the taste."

Marisa crinkled her nose at the dung-heap smell. She recognized rowan. "Rowan for aiding psychic powers. What else?"

"Trade secret. Nothing will hurt you. It'll help you see clearly."

Marisa sipped the tea, cringed. "Tastes like dirt."

"When was the last time you tasted dirt?" Lily tried to defray the palpable tension smothering the air. Jake slid another chair in for her, and he hulked up the doorway again. Preventing Marisa from escaping?

"First and only time." Marisa gulped the tea, handed the cup to Elizabeth, and waited a moment as the warmth leaked into her heaving stomach. "What now? Whoa." Wooziness seized her, and she began to figuratively float off the chair. "Is this supposed to happen?"

"What?" Lily's hand turned into a dragon claw piercing her shoulder.

"I'm... falling... into Ric's mind." Marisa began sliding off the chair. Jake sprang forward and caught her in his arms before her butt kissed the floor.

CHAPTER NINETEEN

The last Marisa remembered was Jake dumping her gently on the bed. She rolled onto her side facing Ric, her hand over his heart.

"Marisa?" Ric's voice invaded her head. *"Where are you?"*

"I'm here." A black cavern swallowed her words.

"It's dark. Empty. You shouldn't be here," he said.

"Ric? Is it really you?" Marisa's brow crinkled. Her mind butted against another foreign entity. Ric? She had no way of knowing for certain. *Why can't he read me? Oh, check, he's not telepathic.*

The moment she questioned herself, Ric's thoughts rushed her in a traffic jam of epic proportions. She mentally high-fived herself for the return of her telepathy. She singled out a coherent thought, but the scene in his mind sped her off down the two-lane highway. Not again!

The slender woman with the long black ponytail headed through a gate to the backyard. Darkness and clouds hid her, not even the moon offered her up. She exuded a confidence in her trepidation, as if she knew exactly what to do, but worried about taking her first step and adding it to the layers of misdeeds on her rap sheet.

An element of excitement rolled off her. Not her

excitement. Nothing about her seemed to belong to her. A puppet dangling from marionette strings. A puppet he wanted to awaken, take into his arms, and protect from the insanity encapsulating her. It was evident then the evil lurking within her didn't belong to her, wasn't her.

Another presence hid in the shadows, an invisible being forcing Marisa's actions, stealing her free will.

"Marisa, baby. It's you," Ric said.

With a loose backpack strapped on, she slipped through the rear door of the dead silent house, careful not to bang the walls.

"Stop, Marisa!" Ric shouted. "Don't go in there."

Two of them lay, a man and woman, backs to each other on the bed.

"No!" Anguish shredded Ric's intestines. He clawed the air as she escaped his reach. "Wake up, Marisa Meadows! Don't do this."

Ric tried to run after her, but his feet were rooted to the landscape of her mind. He caved in on himself, lost and imprisoned in the inky abyss with no outlet, no ability to reach Marisa and stop her or the person who held her in thrall. Incapable of ending the scene or halting Marisa, he once again watched the gruesome images unfold from starting the fire until she confronted the man in the vehicle.

The tie binding her mind stretched another notch, allowing emotions to spill into her brain. Remorse. Terror. Horror. A strange satisfaction. A smug arrogance.

"Look. At. Me," the man in the car said, his features no longer a cloudy haze.

Slowly, she rotated her head. Smoke filtered into her mouth, though the air was clear in the vehicle. She gagged on the thickening cloud. The stench of charred flesh undid her.

"Why?" she asked.

"You know why. You're the one I want."

"I'm not all here." She tapped her skull. *"I won't be useful to you."*

"Wait until you are all there." He kissed her hard. She clasped his shoulders and returned his kiss. *"You are everything to me,"* Kenny said.

Rage detonated in Ric, and he flailed his arms, trying to break through the intangible bars imprisoning him.

Suffering Ric's swat to her side, Marisa's eyelids fluttered open and remained glued on his ghostly visage. Jake pinned Ric's arms to the bed, and Liam held his legs down. Deep anguish bracketing his mouth, he remained out of it. Caramel tinged with his sexy musk brought her back to him.

"What happened?" Lily asked. "Is your telepathy still there? Did you connect with Ric?"

Elizabeth handed Marisa a glass of cloudy water, then helped her sit up. "Salt water will clear the herbal residue."

Marisa slugged down the salty water. She'd drink anything to rid her being of the toxins and fire, to purge the evil clinging like a starving eel.

"It was me," she croaked out, her throat hoarse from the salt, or maybe intangible smoke.

"What?"

"The fire. I set the house on fire."

"The couple in the bed?" Jake's voice plunged low, lethal. "That means you connected to Ric. His mind's still intact."

Ric settled into a peaceful slumber. If you could call whatever mode he remained in slumber. Or peaceful.

Marisa pumped antibacterial gel onto her hand from the bottle on the bedside table. After slathering on a dollop, she said, "He's still there. He tried to reach out to me, and I was unable to talk to him. I think my being out of it triggered another vision. I don't freaking know. I can't read anyone. For the length of the vision, I had my telepathy. It's gone again." She scratched her nose, the faint scent of alcohol permeating her senses, sobering her. "Was I coerced or hypnotized? Did I set the house on fire by sleepwalking? Why is Ric witnessing me there? How is he transmitting his vision to me?"

"Elizabeth?" Lily tentatively said. "Is Doc Wildwood still around?"

"Better question, why is Ric having a clairvoyant vision of the past?" Liam's voice boomed in the room, causing Marisa's pulse to lurch.

Liam's hair was the same dark chestnut color of Jake and Ric's, but a little longer than Ric's, not as long as Jake's rock star locks. A softness missing from Ric's angular face lent him a boyish appeal. They shared the same eye color, same blade nose, same fan-frigging-tastic McAllister buff body.

"Are you saying Ric only has foresight?" Fingers crossed, she hexed herself against the pending answer.

"Damn straight." Liam thumped his tablet on the counter.

"Maybe his clairvoyance is changing," Lily tossed out.

Elizabeth toyed with her ubiquitous strand of pearls. "Ric could be repeating the same vision if he's linked to a person involved in the event."

Jake towered over Marisa like a volcano about to erupt, ending the dance of movement among the players in the room. On wobbly legs, she stood and stepped into the corner. "No freaking way. Get it through your thick McAllister skulls. I didn't consciously set a house on fire. I didn't kill those people. Do you sincerely believe I'm such a monster? Do you believe I've misled Lily for all the years we've known one another?"

"There's something unresolved in his mind about the

event, about you," Jake said gently. "No, I don't believe you did it consciously. I think Ric's tied to whatever evil is tailing you up the west coast. Okay? Truce?" He extended a hand. Marisa hesitated to take it, but she needed allies. She needed the McAllisters on her side. And she craved Ric McAllister like a drug. She yearned for the indescribable sanctuary of his body, the fun and joy she believed possible with him. It excited her beyond reason when it should drive her screaming to the far reaches of the galaxy.

She took his firm hand, and they shook on it. "Truce."

Lily chuckled behind Jake. "Can we all hug it out?"

"Let's not get all wild and crazy," Liam grumbled, scrutinizing the screen on his tablet.

The group separated, and like obeying a silent command, they all spun toward Ric... and met his round, stricken blue eyes.

CHAPTER TWENTY

A jackhammer went to town in Ric's skull. It did nothing to drill away the memories of the darkness twisting him up, the evil encapsulating Marisa, or the weird visions of her. It also left behind a strange unrelated vision dumping Marisa in the direct path of a gunman in broad daylight. He peered at her through his splayed fingers. Hollows formed beneath her eyes, painting her beautiful pale face with fatigue. Her hair lay loose like an inky mantle cloaking her shoulders, strands hanging down to her breasts.

Ignoring his inevitable headache, he surged forward and cupped her exquisite face between his hands. Unable to stop himself, he kissed her, one hand pressing her head to him, the other digging into the round softness of her butt, hauling her closer. Her arms laced tight around his neck as if she never wanted to let him go. Her lips tasted salty, and he drove his tongue between them as she made way for him. He wanted his kiss to burn to ash the demons hitching a ride on her back. What he'd witnessed was nothing short of devil work taking her for a spin on a one-way ticket. Her darkness had seduced him, spiraled him into a black void open to suggestion for the right commands. Apparently, he didn't possess the right combination to unlock her mind to his commands.

"Um… get a room," Lily said, raising an embarrassing red flag. "I take it you're okay, Ric."

Marisa whimpered, and he reluctantly released her. "You're not leaving my side," he ordered.

"Good to see you too, little brother." Jake's somber, sarcastic timbre slung reality back into Ric's face.

"How long was I out?" he asked.

"Couple hours," Liam replied. "'Bout time you woke up. You scared us to death."

"Scared myself too."

"Are you all there?" Petite Elizabeth's voice rose from behind his hulking brothers.

Ric laid his cheek against Marisa's silky cheek. "I think so."

"Then tell us what happened before I shake it out of you." Liam stalked around the confined space, his agitation tangible in the frigid air-conditioned room. "We didn't know what to do."

Marisa's entire body quaked against him. "Is it me? Did I do this? I'm so sorry."

"Shhh." He kissed her again, a quick, soft peck on her luscious lips, bare of her trademark color. "You didn't do this."

"Can we discuss or do you two need a room?" Ric appreciated Lily's teasing banter to defray the apprehension suffocating the room.

"What happened to you?" Ric tightened his arms around Marisa.

"You first."

At Jake's suggestion, Elizabeth scurried off for water and a bottle of whiskey. Ric cuddled Marisa between his legs, her back against his chest while he rested against the padded headboard. She leaned her head on his shoulder and clutched his legs as if seeking his strength. He had never, in his entire life, wanted a woman as much as he wanted Marisa, even knowing what he knew and suspected about her. He let her fruity shampoo and the baby powder scent of her lotion saturate his soul. He vowed to decimate the menacing power play going on inside her if it was the last task he accomplished alive.

After a large swig from a half tumbler of whiskey, Ric began his frightening story. He hated divulging Marisa's problems to outsiders, but he trusted his family in the room above anyone.

"I told them about the fire dream, how you—we—saw me setting the fire." Marisa's voice cracked on a sob.

"I don't normally have repeat visions once the event occurs, but I've never linked to another psychic. It's totally messed me up," Ric said. Marisa balled her hand on his knee, and he gloved it, stretching her fingers out of her tormented fist. "I'm not blaming you. It is what it is. Someone's latched onto your telepathy."

"But I've lost my telepathy," she said bitterly.

"It's still there in a dark corner," Ric replied. "I think whoever's controlling you, lured me in when I passed out. All I saw was a dark hole of nothing."

"Well, that explains a lot." Lily kidded again to keep it real.

Marisa toed Lily's arm. "Funny. Laugh a minute. Seriously, Ric, you were calling me, but you couldn't hear my replies."

"I didn't hear you since I'm not telepathic. I was lost in a bleak landscape. Some foreign, evil thing flitted along the edges. It wanted to command you, and it was waiting for me to take a hike. That's when I knew it wasn't you. It wasn't only taunting and hurting your psychic ability, but mine too. Like it wanted to own us. Worst part is, it feels like it already owns you, is *you*." Marisa's spine tensed, and he stiffened, the softness of her breasts cushioning his hands beneath them.

Jake scratched his jaw. "This is something heavy going down. Marisa, you said you'd been feeling this evil for a few months. Do you recall what event precipitated your first indication?"

She stroked her hand down Ric's leg. "Couple months ago, I was powerwalking along the running path outside my office building in San Diego, and I tripped on an uneven sidewalk. I started to fall, but someone caught me from behind. Next thing I knew, I was sitting on a nearby bench a few minutes later. The strangest sense of *déjà vu* crept all over me, and I thought I imagined it. I lost my ability to erect my telepathic walls for the rest of the day."

"You never told me that." The skin around Lily's eyes pinched tight. "You told me you just started to feel weird one day."

"I didn't want to confess what a klutz I am."

"Yeah, you do like to pretend you're perfect." Lily winked.

"Anything else?" Ric asked. "Did you lose time or your ability to erect your walls again? Did it happen at the airport?"

"She never loses her ability," Lily said emphatically. Marisa wiped her hands over and over on her pant legs. "Wait. It happened again?" she nearly shouted. "Why haven't you told me any of this? Geez, Mar, I thought I was your ride or die."

"You *are*, Lily. Don't sweat the small stuff."

"This isn't small stuff." Liam knocked his fist on the wall. "You're supposed to report changes in your psychic makeup to the Guild."

"How do you know I didn't?"

"Because it's not in your records," he lashed back, his blue eyes tossing tiny switchblades at her.

Irritation vibrated Marisa's back against Ric. "Who gave you permission to read my file?"

"Take it easy." Liam held up a hand to preempt her rant. Ric shook his head at his brother, tried to get him to shut up. Too late. "I'm your second. Guardians are supposed to know everything about their psychics."

Marisa lunged out of Ric's embrace and turned on her knees. "Are you freaking kidding me?" Her eyes blazed; red-fire highlights lit her dark hair under the fluorescent lights. She was a goddess personified, and he desperately wanted her in his arms again to soothe her annoyance. "You were already assigned as my Guardian? I thought Liam was on the bench for another couple months. When did all this happen?"

It's not like she hadn't already accepted his guardianship. "Two days ago," he replied, not bothering with the pretenses, unable to drag his gaze off her fiery beauty. Strange flutters plagued his chest whenever she was near, and she hit all his senses at once in ways that teased his heart, his soul, and least not his groin. "I've been following you. Liam was granted preliminary clearance only as backup. Keep your friends close and look before you leap." Marisa blinked rapidly at his botched attempt at humor.

"Enough already." Jake rattled a tray of medical supplies. "You know the rules, Marisa. Accept the Guardian detail or leave the Guild. Take your pick."

"If I leave the Guild, you'll never take down the Cabal. I know enough to be lethal to both them and the Guild," she blasted back. "Ric knows it too."

"Whoa, what?" Jake swung on Ric. "What aren't you two telling me?"

"Shut the door, take a seat, and zip it," she ordered. Once everyone grumbled their way into a seat, she sat cross-legged on the foot of the bed, keeping her distance from Ric.

"My second lost time incident happened the day

Kenneth Delaney met my boss in San Diego, a few weeks after the walking incident. I was supposed to pop in and meet him. But I'd lost my charm bracelet. It belonged to my sister." She dug into her front pants pocket and withdrew the silver bracelet. "I found it in the koi pond behind the burnt house yesterday." She dangled the silver chain with the two identical Guild logo charms.

CHAPTER TWENTY-ONE

After detonating her verbal bombshell, Marisa faced the firing squad and exposed everything. She'd already blacked out in a major way and was beyond scared. What if it happened again and she did something, oh, like burn a house down and kill people? "I think Delaney works for the Cabal, and he's luring me inside, setting me up. And turning me into his personal henchwoman."

Once the show-and-tell session ended, they spent hours into the early morning devising a plan to expose Delaney, using Marisa as bait. Ric hated the idea. Marisa wanted to eviscerate the evil surrounding her. If it meant taking down Cabal members, two birds, one stone. It might hand the Guild its first true clue into elusive Cabal membership. The Cabal had gotten sloppy with Delaney and the park incident. Their sloppiness just became the Guild's gain.

By three in the morning, Marisa was curled on the bed, spent and ready to crash. Lily had already fallen asleep in the chair, her feet propped on the bed. The three McAllister brothers were still going strong, brainstorming and dismissing plan after plan.

Yawning, Elizabeth popped in and shooed everyone out of Ric's room. "Time enough after sleep to exact your vengeance."

"I don't like this plan." Ric's hair stood up in unruly tufts. Marisa wanted to sift and smooth those silky strands as well as calm him.

"You don't have to like it." She smothered a yawn. "I'm doing it. You aren't my keeper."

"I *am* your Guardian. You said so. I heard you." Ric smiled, bringing spots of pink to his wan face.

"Yes, *master*." She fake sneered and stretched out on her back. "I hereby accept you as my Guardian, in front of witnesses, until such time as you no longer prove useful."

Liam snorted and Jake thumped Ric on the back. "Welcome to the world of Guild women, bro," Jake said. "Welcome to my world."

"It's not my first Guardian rodeo." Ric's face reddened, so freaking cute.

"Not of this caliber psychic. Or woman." Jake stood and gathered his belongings.

"Rodeo?" Marisa wanded her hand down her front. "There won't be any riding this."

"Maybe not tonight." Ric's limbs practically gelled onto the bed, proving his exhaustion.

"Lily and Marisa are in a class by themselves. Along with Juliana Westwood. The power of three could kill us if we let them," Liam tossed in, a slight Southern inflection missing from Ric mimicked Jake's pitch.

"Why, Liam McAllister, is that a compliment?" Sleepily, Marisa quirked an eyebrow. "After Jake's compliment? How lucky can a girl get?"

"Compliment, criticism. Take it any way you please," Ric joked.

His exhaustion bogged down the room and dissolved another slice of Marisa's heart. She'd caused the brewing storm. Not that he expected her to make it up to him, she planned to, somehow. Her limitations reared up and propelled her off the bed into a listless stance.

"I'll sleep in my room upstairs," she declared.

"Not without Ric," Liam announced. "Or me, if Elizabeth confines him here."

"Nope. I'm going with you." Ric gained a surge of energy, jostled his brother away from Marisa, and gave Elizabeth an awkward triumphant high five.

Elizabeth waggled her fingers. "Fine. Don't call me when you crash. I'm going home."

Marisa dug her fingers in her neck. "What if my mind drags Ric in again?"

"Since you're both exhausted, there's little likelihood of it happening again tonight. No guarantee, though," Elizabeth explained. "Wildwood said the worst is over for now. But he thinks this most recent event has much to do with the hole in your abilities since you've already forged a connection. Yet, if you come into contact with whoever did this, all bets are off."

"We shouldn't take the chance." Marisa clamped onto Ric's arm. "I won't be the one who kills your mind."

"You heard her. The worst is over," he said wistfully.

The raw lust in his eyes buried Marisa's doubts. Could she capitulate to what he wanted? For once in her life, was there a pot of McAllister gold at the end of the rainbow? Will either of them live long enough to find out? Too many *what-ifs* dinged her. "Whatever. You know the hazards of my evil mind."

Ric grinned and an unexpected thrill jolted through Marisa. The shock of Jake and Liam's unobjectionable silence chased her thrill with another. Everyone scattered to get a few hours of sleep before dawn's arrival carted the start of a Cabal takedown.

Ric followed close on her heels to her suite upstairs, touched her arm just outside the door. "Wait here." Pausing, she rolled her eyes, affording him the benefit of her disdainful doubt. He drew his gun, checked the room, closet, and private bathroom. "All clear."

"Did you expect Cabal members to jump you from the bathtub?" She toed her sneakers off, stripped her sweater, and tossed it on the padded window seat.

"I never expected Cabal members to jump me from your skull." He holstered his gun, slipped his shoulder harness off, and set it on the nightstand.

Lightning danced in her blood. "Do all Guardians share their client's beds?"

"Nope. But this drummer plays to the beat of his own drum." Slowly and seductively, he advanced on her, his finger tapping a silent solo on his hip. He trailed his fingers across her cheek and into her hair. "I've wanted to touch your hair since forever. Feels as silky as I imagined."

"Ric." She backed out of arm's reach. No way, no how. Ric was everything she'd ever wanted and oh so unattainable. And he knew everything about her, who she was, who she was designed to be, and he hadn't freaked out yet. "No touching. Just sleep." He peeked at her shyly, toying with the hem of his T-shirt. "Don't you dare take it off." *Strip it, please!*

His lips spread in a teasing grin. "So you admit you're attracted to me?" He kicked his boots into a heap.

"Sorry, buster, but it's against Guardian rules to get involved with your charges. Taking your shirt off is—" *Going to get you involved.* She bit off the damning words. *Stick to your guns. No involvement.* "You take the bed. I'll take the chairs."

"The hell you will." Ric tossed his drumsticks on the bed. "I'll let you play with my sticks if you share the bed with me." His hand brushed over the distinctive bulge in his pants. "Or at least one of them."

"I suppose you toss your lame come-on line to all your groupies."

He narrowed the distance between them. "Just the ones named Marisa Meadows."

She buzzed with the insane need to stroke her hands all over his bare skin, to kill her inhibitions. Not even her fatigue dampened her craving for this god among men. What a huge difference a day made in her hormone cache.

He inclined his head toward her, his lips a hairsbreadth from hers. "I'm sorry I can't protect your mind, but I *can* and I *will* protect your body. Will you let me?"

"Who will protect my heart? Who will protect yours when I walk?"

"I have no plans to let you walk." His breath fanned warm air on her skin, carrying the faint scent of whiskey.

"You say that today. I'm merely a conquest." She wrung her hands to keep from running them under his shirt and over his sinful abs.

"I told you I don't do casual. I'm breaking rules that could get me kicked out of the Guild. For *you*. If you really feel that way, then I'll back off, but I know you don't. I know you're feeling something going on between us. Deny it. *Deny it.*"

Annoyance bristled through her. "Did you pluck that from my empty head?"

"Nope." He nuzzled her neck. "I feel the same, for you. It's insane, I get it." His lips pulsed against her neck with each word. "But it's worth seeing where these mutual feelings take us. *You're* worth it." His lips did indescribable things to her earlobe.

She stretched her neck, giving him more access to her inflamed skin. "What if it takes us to a six-foot hole in the ground?"

"Then we dive into a six-foot hole together." He sucked her earlobe between his lips, and a groan escaped her. "I'm willing to risk my life and everything I know for you."

"It's your Guardian job." Sarcasm drizzled from her tone.

His mouth locked onto her neck, and he kissed his way up her jaw toward her mouth. "Nope. I, Ric McAllister—a single, dying man here—am willing to risk it all, for you." He took her hand and placed it over his crotch.

"Oh, I get it." She pressed his erection, applying just the right amount of pressure by the catch in his throat. "You just want to hit it and quit it. Been there, done that. It's my motto. Cool. It's all you'll get from me. Glad you straightened it out." Insanity hung in her family tree after all. Why let it wither and die with her sister and mother? *Come and get me, white jacket and padded cell.*

Ric growled fiercely. "Give me a break. Give me a chance."

Marisa stood so close to him, his unexpected touch caused a shiver to work up from her toes to her chest. One night wouldn't break her, but one night might not be enough. She wanted to scream and rant at life's injustices, at the gift that destroyed her sister and her mother's lives once love entered the picture. Not that Ric was talking about love. But the way he spoke and felt led her to believe love waited in the end zone. Casual was all she knew, to keep her sane, to keep her on the top side of Earth. No man ever offered her what Ric offered. No other man ever fully appreciated the scope of her abilities or how those abilities destroyed her family.

"It won't happen to you. I won't let it," he said as if he was telepathic. "I swear, Marisa."

"Then you really are promising to protect my mind." She held no punches. "As well as my body?"

"Body, mind, heart, and soul."

"Only God can do that."

"Then let me be your god," he whispered low, lethal.

"Now you're being blasphemous." She melted against his muscular body, a small part of her accepting what he presented as she plastered herself against his length.

"It sounded good." He grinned. "Where will it get me?"

She wound her arms around his neck. "Shut up and kiss me."

He sobered, folded her in his sinful embrace. "I'm only human, not God. But I swear to the best of my abilities—"

"Kiss me, damn it." Her mouth met his, and she dissolved in the scent and hardness of his body devouring her. After a brief, sensual kiss, full of passion and acceptance, she put a whisker of distance between them. "You may sleep in my bed, fully clothed, wrapped around me. I offer you nothing more."

"You're on. I'll take it." He scooped her in his arms, carried her to the bed, and laughing, they fell onto the rumpled covers. Arms linked around his neck with her breasts mashed to his chest, she pressed tiny kisses along his neck and up his jaw, day-old bristles scratching her skin. "Hey, you're cheating. Kissing's not part of the deal," Ric said, with no resistance.

Marisa kicked her head back, drowning in his blue-lagoon eyes. "I'm testing you."

"You little sneak." He tickled her lower abdomen, her most ticklish spot, and she yelped, trying to shake his hands off her, merely spurring him on.

She shrieked. "Stop, Ric. That's not fair."

"Payback for teasing me." He stifled a yawn.

If they didn't snatch a few hours' sleep, they'd join the walking dead tomorrow.

"For real, I need to crash. You too." Exhaustion mired her down. The intense lure of Ric's body wasn't enough to keep her awake, not after the double whammy to her system. Their connection strained her already stressed telepathy. Eyelids drooping, she rolled onto her side, giving him her backside. He didn't wait for an invite to spoon his body to hers, and she didn't stop him from snaking his arm across her hip to hug her closer. Without skipping a beat, her heart thrummed in sync with his against her back, and she welcomed his presence in her bed, even if all they did was cuddle and sleep. It's all she wanted, right? She clenched his hand to her stomach, linking their fingers, shutting down her pesky doubts. Everything felt so right in the moment.

His lips nuzzled her neck again. "I'm happy with us like this."

"Umm. Me too," she said groggily, snuggling her butt closer to him, letting sleep claim her razed mind. He didn't take advantage, but the tangible force of his desire consumed her all the same.

"For now," he said against her neck before he planted another trail of steaming kisses across her shoulders, and into her heart.

CR&SO

Marisa awakened after eight and maneuvered out from under Ric's arm without waking him. She dreaded sleeping longer in such close proximity and risk linking to him again. She knew he wasn't already in her head because a wasteland still existed in her old noggin. No telepathy, no transferred visions, and no Ric.

Her few hours of sleep went a long way toward rejuvenation. She stretched her arms and the kinks out of her shoulders. Her bleary gaze drank Ric in, glad he wasn't in her San Diego bed, or she'd feel compelled to kick him out of both bed and townhouse. Mornings were sacred, and she never let sleepovers interfere. Not that she had many sleepovers, or slept with a lot of men. She really didn't like leading men to believe sleeping over meant another step toward a steady relationship. Easier not to do sleepovers rather than explain her need to remain unfettered. She never led them on, and it made it easy to leave as emotions changed. After all, she knew instinctively when fun and sex began to lean toward romance and love.

Strangely, adding another notch on her belt of weird stuff, she liked Ric sleeping over, disregarding his job to guard her. *Ugh.* She never believed she'd need Guardian protection.

Striding toward the bathroom, she stripped off her blouse. To her surprise, unopened lotions and cosmetics nestled in a basket on the bathroom vanity. A few casual clothes hung in the closet, tags still on them, in her size and color. Lily must have set it up.

"Girl, you rock." Marisa smoothed her fingers over a black cashmere sweater.

By the time she finished her shower, primped, and donned the sweater and a pair of skintight black pants, her empty stomach rumbled. And the strong scent of coffee filtered under the door.

"Now that's what I'm talking about." She left the bathroom. Standing barefoot in front of a small table and two chairs, Ric fussed over a breakfast tray and a pink rose in a bud vase. "I could kiss you."

He grinned slyly. "I wish you would."

"Actually, I was talking to the coffee carafe."

"Ouch."

She took the empty cup he offered and let him pour steaming, heavenly coffee in it, leaving her to doctor it up with her favorite caramel creamer.

Rising on her toes, she kissed him on the cheek. "That'll hold you."

He fake pouted. "For like two seconds."

A sudden chill attacked her insides as the crazy plan they'd concocted in the early morning hours caved in on her. She took fortifying sips of coffee and grabbed a blueberry bagel off the tray. "Have you seen my purse?"

"Hunting for these? They rolled onto the floor last night." Ric handed her the small bottle of blood sugar pills. "Diabetic?"

"Borderline and hypoglycemic."

"I made a strawberry yogurt protein smoothie for you."

Her mouth hung open. "How'd you know that's my favorite breakfast?"

He fiddled with the rose in the vase. "I asked Lily."

"Aren't you special?" Her excuse generator was spitting out duds. Ric was too good to be true.

"I'm trying. Is it working?"

She downed a pill with a slug of coffee. "Keep it up. I'll let you know." No man ever cared enough about her diet to ask what she liked let alone make it for her. The smoothie was scrumptious. She licked the foam off her lips, relishing the thick fruity drink. "You made this?"

"Sure. Fresh strawberries too."

"It's definitely working."

With an arrogant gleam in his eyes, he laughed. "Good because there's more where that came from."

"Don't get cocky, Guardian. We have a job to do." Marisa snatched up her purse, trying to ignore the buzz of Ric all around her, the hum of her hormones sparking to jubilant life. And the thrill of tiny naysayers freaking out her head and her heart.

Her cell chirped a new text. She bit down on her lip. With a healthy dose of trepidation, she read the message.

"U did passably well obeying my instructions. Dump the Guardian and leave the Guild compound."

She showed the text to Ric. "Different number than

Delaney's."

"Probably a burner. Could be anyone."

"Not if he was instructed to get me in line."

"That presumes Delaney *is* Cabal and he's working from several angles." Ric stroked her hand, and she wanted to flip it around and press her palm to his.

"It's the angle we're addressing. We take down Delaney and hopefully more crumble with him." Just as she began to slip her phone in her purse, it chirped again.

Another message from the unknown number, this time with a photo which turned the steaming coffee in Marisa's gut to ice.

The phone slipped from her fingers and Ric caught it before it hit the floor.

The photo depicted her mother sitting in a lawn chair on the patio of her institute, dated yesterday. The message read, *"Don't forget. We know."*

CHAPTER TWENTY-TWO

Ric handed Marisa the phone and guided her to the bed. A haze obscured her surroundings. She sat and stared at the phone in her hand. After a long foggy moment, an unnamed compulsion forced her to delete two texts and a photo.

"I promise no one will hurt a hair on your mother's head," Ric said as he texted Liam.

The fog dissipated and confusion replaced it. She squared her shoulders. "What? What are you talking about?" Her short fingernails dug into the flesh of his forearm.

"The text and photo," he replied as if talking to a child.

Rattled, she swiped her screen to reveal nothing, the blank moment of time wreaking havoc on her memories and driving her batty.

Pressing her fingers to her temples, she said, "I lost a moment, didn't I?"

He hugged her close. "I won't let you lose another."

She desperately wanted to place her faith in him, but this *thing* latched onto her ridiculed his efforts and battled her unnamed feelings for this man who'd become her unwitting lodestone.

An hour later, Ric and Marisa arrived at Lily's law

office. Jake waited in the main conference room. The morning sun glittered through the windows, showcasing the dry, golden foothills holding onto summer's end, as desolate as Marisa's mind.

"Delaney arrives at eleven," Marisa said. She'd already texted him to meet her there. The texts glared at her, not lost to the ravages of time like the threatening ones before them.

"Hit it, Ric." Jake cut his hand through the air in the direction of the door. "I don't want him thinking Marisa's being guarded."

"I don't like leaving her unguarded."

Jake opened his suit jacket to reveal a gun in his shoulder harness. "You don't think I can guard her *and* Lily?"

Marisa splayed her hand flat over Ric's heart. "You have to remain incognito. If the Cabal gets wind I'm being guarded, they'll beef up their efforts and go after you, and my mother."

"We've assigned a Guardian to your mother," Jake replied. "He's already in position posing as a health-aid worker. He won't leave her side."

Only a smidge of relief skated up Marisa's spine. "Thank you, Jake."

"What about the other text you received this morning?" Ric asked.

She'd deflected the same question in the car, but her moment of reckoning was upon her. "Same threat."

"Let me see." Jake held his hand out.

"I deleted it." Without a twitch, she took the hit from his dark, impaling expression.

"Why would you delete evidence?" Jake dragged a hand over his hair, catching his fingers in the leather band holding it in a ponytail.

"*I* didn't." She thumped her fist on the glass table.

"Don't you get it? Someone's in my freaking head."

"So you say."

Ric turned on his brother. "This is our big break. Don't go Benedict Arnold now."

The door slid open, and Lily joined the fray. "Everyone to your respective corners. We went over the plan a zillion times."

"It'll fail if Marisa keeps dumping evidence." Jake yanked out a chair and engulfed it as he sat down.

"Not like we have choices. You already checked my phone and records. There's nothing you can do about it, except take my phone away." Ric rolled out a chair for her. "Thank you."

"I'll be next door." The smolder he bestowed on her left a spark igniting in her breasts. "Don't let the world go to shit in a handcart while you've ghosted me."

"Wouldn't dream of leaving you out of my clusterfuck." Avoiding the table, she wrung her hands on her lap, gave Ric a crooked smile as he exited stage left.

Dawn carried in a loaded coffee tray. Lily passed out mugs, poured coffee, deliberately set an empty cup near the chair next to Jake. "Are we ready?"

"Does it matter?" Marisa white-knuckled the table. "Either way, we need to know if he's coercing me."

"I'm sorry." Lily sat beside her across from the empty chair.

"It is what it is."

The intercom buzzed and Dawn's voice brought a new round of anxiety to the room. "Mr. Delaney's here." A chain reaction of ants chomped a path up Marisa's spine.

Although she preferred Ric to grumpy Jake, Jake's presence nearly offered the same safe haven she felt with Ric by her side. Jake had the ability to read Delaney, whereas the head conk had hosed her gift, all part of their grand scheme. That is, if Delaney didn't shutter himself from Jake's intrusion. A big if. If he was Cabal, he'd understand the psychic talent filling the room and would be on guard. Jake also possessed the ability to sense mental walls, hence his double duty. Unfortunately, he possessed no ability to breach those walls the way Marisa did.

The door opened. Marisa forced a smile and rounded the table to greet Kenny with a handshake and a half hug. "I'm glad you had time to meet with us this morning."

He shook Jake's hand and then Lily's, gripping her hand a little longer than necessary. An explosion of crimson up Jake's neck nearly flung him into an apoplectic fit.

"McAllister, I didn't know you were joining us." Kenny took the designated chair next to Jake. Lily poured him a cup of coffee, and he smiled appreciatively, waving off the cream and sugar. "Heaven in a cup."

"Lily and I discuss all our prospective new, larger clients. Plus, adding Marisa as an associate is a firm matter." Jake adjusted his black suit jacket, ran his finger along the collar of his charcoal dress shirt. He was as black from head to toe as the insidious darkness inside Marisa. She wanted the ink stain gone so bad, she almost contemplated dousing her soul with bleach. One sip at a time. If only it worked and wouldn't kill her.

"No offense meant." He lowered his chin condescendingly. "I wasn't aware you were involved in the law aspect of the business."

"Is that a problem?" Marisa asked. "Jake has a law degree and is a full partner."

Kenny clunked his mug on the table. "No problem. However, I choose who handles my legal affairs, and I pay handsomely for it. I'm choosing Marisa. Are you in or not?" His unwavering gaze pinned her face, and she didn't flinch a muscle, despite her internal cringing.

Lily pushed a blank legal pad toward Kenny. "Let's get started then. Give us a retainer number that represents the list you emailed me earlier. Then we'll let you know if we accept your offer."

He beamed at Marisa. "Does this mean you'll move to San Jose and join the firm?"

Marisa tapped her index fingernail on the table. "Is it worth my while?"

Kenny pulled the pad closer, picked up the fancy silver and marble pen. "By all means. I wouldn't have made the offer if I wasn't prepared to propose a lucrative deal for you and the firm. Between my personal legal needs, my various business and corporate needs, and," he glanced at Jake, "my security needs, you'll be happy with the business I bring."

Lily's dark brows drew inward into unibrow territory, almost sending Marisa into a giggle fit to sidetrack her nervous energy. "I don't mean to offend, but how much legal aid do you need? Are you in trouble? We don't handle criminal law."

"No criminal trouble. As you read on my preliminary list, I'm involved in many business matters. I need good contracts lawyers like you and Marisa. My various business endeavors don't have in-house legal teams." He wrote a retainer number on the notepad and slid it between Lily and Marisa. "Oh, by the way, we settled the case today. Marisa's off the hook for the depositions."

Lily hummed, quickly recovered. Marisa held her own, willing the stunning number to disappear. *Is he asking the firm to handle Cabal business too?* The retainer held enough bite to pay all their salaries for a year or more.

Kenny stood, cupped the mug. "I'll wait in the hall while you discuss."

"No need," Lily said, nearly choking on her visible excitement. "I've formally extended an offer to Marisa to join the firm."

Marisa and Lily had already decided if the number met their needs not to bother negotiating. They didn't want to drive him away and risk losing the potential link to the Cabal. The number staggered. No negotiation necessary.

"I accept the offer to join the firm. As long as you don't need me on an immediate case, I'll need a short window to return to San Diego to handle my affairs."

"Magnificent." Kenny shook hands with the trio, holding onto Marisa's hand at the end.

"You can rest assured you'll be well represented," Jake replied. "Lily and Marisa make a formidable legal team."

"I'm well aware of their abilities," he said as if dismissing anything Jake proffered. "I'd like to celebrate our partnership. Would you all join me at my house for a dinner my personal chef will prepare tomorrow night? I'll show you the technology I'm working on."

"Your confidence is inspiring." A slash of a smile hid Marisa's disdain.

A Cheshire cat grin upped her smile. "I usually get what I want."

"Sorry," Jake said. "Lily and I have plans elsewhere. We'll take a raincheck, though."

Hell to the no. Marisa bit the inside of her cheek. "Sounds wonderful. Seven good for you?"

"Perfect. I'd like to show you new features in my software."

Software? A game console from his gaming company acquisition formed in her memory, vanished into the abyss. *Why can't I remember my previous visit?* Had he caused the hole in her memories?

Marisa showed Kenny out, and they reconvened in the conference room. Jake wrapped Delaney's mug in a plastic bag to check for prints against the prints on Marisa's purse. Ric zipped into the room and attached himself to Marisa like a limpet.

"You okay?" His troubled and adoring eyes slurped her into his sphere of being again.

"A little creeped out." She poured sanitizer on her hands.

"Why? Did he try to dig into your mind?"

"No." Jake slid the notepad closer. "He has no telepathy. But he does know how to build walls. I hit dead ends."

"Not all founding and original Cabal members possessed psychic abilities. It's why they're building their ranks from Guild members," Marisa said. "He creeps me out now that we're on to him."

"We may be on to nothing." Lily lowered their expectations. "We're speculating."

"With all the psychics the Cabal's drafted, surely they have enough recruiters combing the valley. Like idiot Wesley in the park," Ric said.

"Which means Delaney's not a recruiter. He may be a founding member." Jake freed his long, thick hair and tossed the band on the table. "I can't see them using green recruits to hunt down gifted psychics like Marisa. Plus, he has the connections, the money, the looks, and bullshit to target and get his hands on her, without being a psychic."

"I'll be damned if he gets his hands on her." Ric curled his fist on Marisa's shoulder. "Over my dead body."

"No, not over your dead body, little bro," Jake ordered. "We play this by the book we wrote this morning. Marisa joins him for dinner, wired for audio. You'll watch from as close as you can safely get. Then we reassess the outcome."

"I don't like the idea of Marisa being wired." Lily clutched her shamrock pendant as if it bestowed the world's luck on them. "What if she falls into a time lapse again, he tries to seduce her and takes her blouse off. Won't he see the wire?"

Ric groaned. "I won't let it get that far. Wired means wireless these days. He'll never find the device."

Plopping onto the padded desk chair, Marisa rubbed the new ache plaguing her temples. "If he touches me, I'll blow two holes in his balls. I'm taking my gun."

Lily slid the legal pad to Marisa. "Just make sure he's our Cabal target, partner. Don't go blowing off the balls of our newest client if he's on the up and up."

"Believe me, the man's guilty of something," Ric retorted. "Remember, I saw him at the fire scene. He's Cabal. I'll bet my dog on it."

"You keep seeing me in the vision too. According to you, I'm the one guilty of murder," Marisa said sterner than she intended.

"Not if I have anything to say about it." Ric spun her chair to face him. "The police have no evidence pointing to you."

Marisa dangled her Celtic Guild bracelet from her wrist. "I have the evidence right here."

"The chain and bigger charm belonged to my sister. I added my charm to it after she died. Now we know it was stolen from me in San Diego."

"Speaking of." Lily engaged the intercom and asked Dawn to send Karma McAllister in.

The young college student with dark blonde hair entered the conference room, her face grave, sweeping a sympathetic glance over Marisa. She had already sent Marisa a "Thank You" note and bouquet of fall flowers for Marisa's rescue in the park. Though Karma was Ric and Jake's cousin, her petite nose and hazel eyes leaning more toward gold than green and her winter skin were all her own. Not a freckle marred her face, her eyes ancient and soul-filled, sorrowful as if she already knew too much tragedy in her short life. Maybe she did with her touch telepathy.

Karma sat and faced Marisa. "I read objects with a history. I don't read futures," she explained. "I usually read an object well touched by someone, not that I don't get impressions off briefer touches. There's just more to read with a span of touch, like an old keepsake." She slid the notepad squarely in front of her, her mouth forming an *O*. "This dude's seriously loaded." She blinked rapidly. "Sorry. Distracted. Marisa, are you okay if I divulge what I learn to everyone in the room?"

"I hold no secrets." Except the ones she'd hidden from her consciousness. Marisa unhooked her bracelet and skimmed it across the table to Karma.

The room grew so quiet they could hear a bee buzz. Visually, Karma studied the sterling silver charms and chain. Using a pair of tweezers, she picked it up and studied both sides of each charm. Eyes shut, she sat stiff and silent, not touching, not speaking, just absorbing the whisper of the charms. She picked up the chain between thumb and forefinger, slid her thumb over a few links. With her other hand, she picked up the pen Delaney used. She dropped the pen so fast, it rolled off the table and clinked onto the tiles.

Marisa reached to pick it up, stopped by Ric's hand grasping her wrist. "Don't touch it," he admonished.

An unmistakable sorrow overshadowed the young woman's ancient wisdom. "I'm so sorry. I didn't realize this belonged to your sister."

"My mother gave it to Celeste after she joined the Guild. She never took it off. The smaller charm is mine."

"She took it off when she was with the man who held

the pen."

A prickly and tense silence shadowed Karma's words.

Stunned, Marisa leapt up, air in short supply. "What did you say?"

"He touched the bracelet. His imprint matches the imprint he left on the pen."

"Did Delaney steal the bracelet from Marisa in San Diego?" Ric's fingers tightened painfully around her wrist. They hadn't yet keyed Karma in on his name or anything about him.

Karma tweaked a rubber band around her wrist, let it slap her skin. "The man who touched both the bracelet and pen *knew* Celeste. He used to take the bracelet off her. Told her not to wear it around him. He was the last man—person—Celeste spoke to."

"The reason Celeste killed herself." A haze descended over Marisa, and she wrenched her wrist out of Ric's clasp. Air clotted in her throat as her heart prepared to shatter once again.

CHAPTER TWENTY-THREE

Marisa clawed through the tar clogging her throat and barked at Karma, "This is a sick and cruel joke."

Eyes wide, Karma scooted her chair back, distancing herself from the table. "Just because I usually get paid to do this—"

"What?" Jake and Ric simultaneously shouted as they rounded on Karma like bulldogs.

"You're not supposed to be playing tricks any longer." Jake kicked at the chair beside him.

"You promised," Ric said through gritted teeth. "Your revenge games are what got you into trouble with that SOB in the park two days ago, not to mention the other times."

Karma didn't bat an eyelash as if she expected the outburst from her overly protective caveman cousins. Ignoring them, she said to Marisa, "As I was saying before my fake bodyguards interjected their so not useful opinions, I never lie about my readings. I have nothing to gain. Especially if I'm gonna start working for you." She directed her encouraging smile at Lily.

"You already got the paralegal internship." Lily touched her fingertips to Marisa's arm. Lily had entered Marisa's life four years ago and helped her pick up the pieces of her shattered world after Celeste had killed herself, and her current presence silenced the internal naysayers.

"I'm sorry, Karma. Please continue. I want to know everything," Marisa pleaded and sat rigidly in her chair, on guard for another jolt to her system.

Nodding, Karma closed her eyes again, clutching the bracelet in her tiny fist. "You were best friends. You looked like twins, although Celeste was three years older. She's been gone almost five years now. She always said you were the family star, called you Maristar."

Marisa choked down a sob, hiccupped. She wanted to crumple into herself in a way she hadn't done since Celeste had passed away. Once she'd adopted an iron spine, she refused to allow anyone to hurt her like others had hurt her sister and mother. Ric's fingers sifted into the hair at the nape of her neck, leaving goosebumps traversing her shoulders. He remained by her side, never wavering, lending his quiet, stoic support. She refused to let him suffer from her eventual mental slippages or as she followed in the footsteps of her mother and sister.

Kenneth "Kenny" Delaney, oh, how she'd make him suffer. He was a dead man walking.

"When did she meet Kenny? How long were they together?" Had her sister lied?

"I can't tell when she met him exactly. Appears to be spring, full blossoms on the trees. In San Diego, if it's like San Jose, could be as early as February."

"She first talked about a new man in her life in March."

"Your sister professed her love as they hiked a mountain trail in the fall. Trees are orange and gold."

"At Thanksgiving time, she told Mom and me she'd fallen in love and wanted us to meet him. She didn't divulge his name. He kept finding excuses. It bothered her. Soon after, she withdrew from us. When I confronted her, she confessed he was married, same old cliché, trying to leave his clingy wife, kept filling Celeste with empty promises. So desperate for a husband, she believed every one of them."

"Delaney's never been married," Ric interjected. "I ran a full background on him, and there's no mention of a wife, no marriage license."

"Then he lied. Or she lied. Everything about the man is a lie. We can't believe anything now." Inside, she was fragmenting into a million pieces of glass to be ground into sand. She'd never felt the urge to kill anything except ants and spiders, but if Kenny were in the room, she'd gouge his eyes out first, then slit his throat from ear to ear. "This is personal. It may not be Cabal related after all." She didn't know how her tone remained so wintry and calculating. "I'll do anything and everything in my arsenal to take this bastard down before he hurts anyone else." Steady, she rose, wriggled Ric's hand off her shoulder. He clouded her clarity, and she needed distance from him now... and forever.

"You're not going off half-cocked." Ric spread his legs in a defensive stance. "This changes everything."

"Hell, no," she nearly spat out. "We stick to the plan. I'll get his confession before I die. Then I'll treat the earthworms to a nice tasty dinner after I gut him." Her fingers crimped as she gripped the back of her chair to keep her knees from buckling or flaunting weakness to Ric.

"We'll make adjustments and add Liam to security backup at Delaney's. It can work," Jake said, for the first time exhibiting commiseration instead of his usual defiance and half-assed hatred.

Ric tapped a drum solo on the tabletop. "I don't like this. Not now. It's too personal."

Marisa rounded on him. "You don't have to like it.

And you're right. It is personal now." She beat her fist on her chest over her heart. "To me. To my family. He destroyed us, and he's not walking away scot-free. He will not destroy *me*." She covered her mouth, stifling the sob rising up her throat amid the grinding glass.

Ric opened and shut his mouth, seemingly unable to dredge up a coherent word, until he finally uttered, "Anything else, Karma?"

Karma scraped her blunt-tipped fingernails on her wrist, plucked at the leather bands entwined in silver bangles. "There is. It's epic, knowing what I know now."

"I need to know everything, please." Marisa refrained from reaching across the table and touching Karma, knowing how sensitive touch-telepaths were, especially when using their gifts.

"I gleaned one last impression. He offered Celeste two choices. She agonized over them, until she made her decision." Pausing, she twirled the beads on her bands. The agony of Celeste's choices was written all over Karma's mottled face.

"Spit it out. All of it," Marisa said frostily while her heart disintegrated into the Sahara sand.

"Choice number one: join him and leave the Guild. I don't know what he meant." Her shoulders slumped. "Choice number two: remain in the Guild and lose her sister and mother." A tear fell from Karma's right eye, mirroring the tear dripping from Marisa's left eye. "She took choice number three. Clear as day. She refused to allow him to manipulate her further or to hurt you and your mother. She believed her choice was enough to save you both."

Ramrod straight, with stiff and sure steps, Marisa shuffled out of the room. Ric's booted footsteps rang out behind her, and she didn't wait for him, didn't hold the door open.

"Ric, let her go. This is what she needs." Lily's voice drifted away as the door shut with a muted click.

Marisa entered Lily's office, locked the door, and slid down the smooth panel to the floor. She tucked her knees to her chest and buried her face in them. A familiar cold numbness swept over her in a tide, washing away the emotions she needed to preserve her stability. Her breath hitched, and for a moment, she didn't think she'd ever breathe again. Air soon flowed, meeting her lungs' demands and her decision to live long enough to destroy Delaney.

The idea that he'd targeted her family left vague unanswered questions. Why? Because they were three strong and unattached women? Three strong psychics? Did Kenny or his family know her family? Did his actions have anything to do with her father who'd left his family, driven off by the pressure of both his daughters winding up like their mother? He was a mere mortal, as Marisa liked to call him, with no psychic ability. He eventually grew to hate Corinne Meadows and her telepathy. He drove Corinne to flee San Jose, needing distance from him and his role in the Guild. If her parents had stayed together, her father likely would have grown to abhor his two powerful daughters. As a cop and an oxymoronic professional thief, he had too much to hide leading two contradictory lives. Had her father mixed it up with the Cabal? So many what-ifs, she didn't know if she'd ever find answers in the clue jar. The questions stuffed too much space where her telepathic powers needed to inhabit.

She knocked her fist on the floor. "Do I have to brain myself for my telepathy to return to the roost? I need my abilities to destroy Delaney." Even though Jake didn't have the ability to drill past Delaney's walls, didn't mean his walls were impenetrable. Everyone possessed cracks in their foundations. Walls were meant to crumble. She'd decimated the best.

Twenty minutes of absorbing the day's nightmare later, she stood, stretched out her cramped legs, vowing to return to her ritualistic yoga sessions before her body betrayed her.

"Marisa," Ric said softly from the hallway.

She rolled her shoulders, loosening the tight knots, and then opened the door.

Tentatively, Ric walked in, shut the door behind him. He'd never witness the true extent of her emotions behind her false chilly façade. Screw the consequences, but she wanted to feel his arms around her, silent and comforting.

He started to reach for her, clenched his thigh instead, as if unsure of her reaction. Another step closer and she fisted his polo shirt. Then without a word, he embraced her. The steady rhythmic beat of his heart thawed her.

"Marisa—"

She planted a finger over his lips. "Don't say a word. Just hold me for a minute, and then I need to go."

He kissed the top of her head in response. She breathed in his familiar cardamom as if she wanted to imprint the last man she'd ever get close to upon her senses. After she annihilated Delaney, Ric would run for the hills to escape her. Acceptance was a familiar anchor in her middle. Nothing changed in her mission, except the stakes. It couldn't get any more personal, and she refused to allow Ric McAllister, or any other man, to throw a wrench in her path of revenge.

"Where do you need to go?" Ric cupped her face. "I'm not leaving your side."

"I need alone time to remember the last weeks of my sister's life, to see if I can piece it all together."

"Okay. Lily's house?"

She nodded. "Sure." Just being in his presence talked her out of her real destination. Odd as it sounded, she needed to drive to the coast to the nearest lighthouse. Designed to guide ships into and away from shore, she'd always experienced an affinity toward the guiding lights along the California coast. The close proximity to one always calmed her, helped her see clearly, even when the sea churned and roiled. The turbulence granted her wisdom. She needed the illumination, hoped to shed light on her mind and give her clarity to remember the end of her sister's life five years ago.

Ric took her hand in his, his fingers strong and safe. Deception ruled her and a small twine of guilt threaded through her chest.

As if she were being watched, the moment she picked up her purse from Lily's desk, she received a text message. The soothing low-toned melody accompanied the text chirp notification. Shielding the phone from Ric, she read the message.

"Dump the Guardian. A car's waiting at the rear entrance to the building. Get inside and the driver will give you further instructions. Don't divulge your plans. Erase this message. Give your phone to the car driver."

A photo of her sister in her open casket at the funeral flashed onto her screen. Fog crammed her head, and she stabbed the delete button on both the text and the photo. The hazy cloud partially evaporated.

"Another warning text?"

Part of her returned to the present, the other part focused on her instructions. "An update from my boss." The lie rolled off her tongue like a snowball in an avalanche.

"You'll need to tell him about relocating."

"Will I?" She avoided Ric's outstretched hand. "Not if Delaney's dead."

Ric's face turned hard and flinty. "You're still joining the firm, right?"

She shrugged. "The only thing I want to do is destroy that asshole. Then who knows. I can't make plans for my future. Maybe he'll kill me first." Pushing away from him, she swallowed her anger and strode to the door.

"No one will hurt you." Ric's footsteps stomped the tiles behind her quick steps. "Not on my watch."

"Don't make promises you can't keep." She deliberately baited and angered him in the guise of driving him away. In the end, he'd thank her for saving himself from her.

"I keep all my promises. Don't do this, Marisa. I know you're upset and angry. I'm trying to help you." They strode down the outer hallway toward the elevator.

A heatwave of guilt swooped over her, and she hated herself. "I know, Ric. I get it. I just can't."

"Can't what?" His hands spanned her hips from behind as she jabbed the elevator button.

"Shoot, hold up. I forgot my files. Wait for me here."

"I'll go with you."

"I don't need a babysitter. You can see me enter the office from here." She bolted, slowed her roll so as not to arouse his suspicions, and entered the door to the firm offices. The reception room sat empty, and she headed toward the emergency exit leading to the stairwell. A billion steps later in her short heels, she exited the rear lobby. The car driver flagged her down, and within seconds, they drove toward the center of downtown. Hoping against hope, she tried to read him, anything to help her figure out her life, but she hit a very silent brick wall.

He handed her a new cell phone with no identifying labels. She didn't recognize technology's latest and greatest. "Turn it on," he instructed. "Give me your phone."

By rote, she handed him her phone, and he pocketed it. The moment she turned on the new device, another text chimed the sounds she'd grown accustomed to, a soothing melody. A thicker layer of fog descended upon her as she read the text:

"Driver will drop you off at the downtown branch of Coastal California Bank. He'll give you a key and instructions to open a safety deposit box and will wait for you in the parking lot. You're to put the package you retrieve in the secure briefcase on the backseat floor."

Confused, she honed in on the aluminum briefcase on the floorboard. She was screwed six ways to Sunday if she failed her assignment. It was all that mattered. Nothing more. Concentrating on her impending task, her stray thoughts slipping to the wayside, she gripped the phone as if afraid to lose it.

Ten minutes later, the driver dropped her off in front of a small branch bank, with an envelope in hand and a soft-sided briefcase strapped around her like a cross-body purse. The moment the car drove away, she had the strange sensation of someone watching her. She didn't notice anyone taking any special interest in her. Before she entered the bank lobby, she opened the envelope and slipped the key onto her palm, read the instructions on the small notepaper. *Safety deposit box. Check. Snag everything in the box. Check. Ignore everyone around you. Got it.*

Entering the bank, she memorized the box number and instructions and slipped the notepaper and envelope in the briefcase. The security guard greeted her, and she nodded, walking to the far side of the teller counter where a sign indicated Safety Deposit Box. The fish bowl feeling evaporated under the guise of her instructions.

"Hello," she greeted the clerk, set her driver's license

on the counter. "I'd like to access my box. Number seventy-four, twelve."

The clerk retrieved the signature card and compared it with her driver's license. "You haven't been here in over five years, Ms. Meadows." The clerk had her sign the card on the line below her two other signatures.

Marisa started penning the "M" on her first name, held the pen steady, and studied the two signatures above hers. Puzzlement reigned. Nothing made sense.

"Ms. Meadows, is there a problem?" the clerk asked.

"I'm sorry, no. I was just thinking about the last time I was here," she lied. She'd never stepped foot in the bank. *Why am I here? Who did the box belong to? Who forged my signature?* Regardless of the nagging questions, she signed the card. A new band of fog vaporized the questions.

As the clerk led her to the vault, her instructions revolved to the forefront of her memory, and she mentally repeated them over and over. She held the key so tight in her fist, it dug into the flesh of her hand. Walls of cement-gray safety deposit boxes of various sizes filled the vault from floor to ceiling.

The clerk fit her key in the midsized box labeled 7412, and Marisa followed suit. Then the clerk pulled the box out and guided Marisa to an alcove with four partitioned counters. "Buzz me when you're done." The woman pointed out the button on the wall.

The box in front of Marisa riveted her attention. Lifting the lid, she recalled her instructions mandated she not inspect the contents, just dump everything in the soft-sided briefcase. Once her gaze pierced a ragged journal, fascination caused her pulse to whoosh in her ears. She touched the black cloth cover of the two-inch thick journal, opened it to reveal page after page of handwritten names and private information about each person, including addresses, family trees, and psychic abilities. Stunned and fighting her internal battles, she snagged her phone. She hovered her finger over the camera icon. *Stop! Don't do it. It's not in your instructions.* Something unnamed forced her to snap photos of the box, the vault, the journal and several pages.

A melodic tenor followed a text message:

"STOP taking photos! Read the instructions again. Now. Strike one."

Four calming tones followed the first three and forbade the insanity from running amok in her mind. She read the instructions again, followed them to a T, dumping the journal in the briefcase, ensuring she'd emptied the box. After buzzing in the clerk, she exited the vault, and the moment she entered the bank lobby, the sensation of being followed clobbered her again. Her spine tensed to the point of pain.

Strike one. What did it mean? Her memory latched onto the soothing melody, and she focused on it to ignore her surroundings, to complete her task. Outside, she rounded the corner of the building and speed walked into the parking lot. So intent on following her instructions, she didn't hear footsteps behind her until the barrel of a gun lodged between her shoulder blades, and someone prodded her behind a tall hedge of photinias, their red tips joining the autumn bloom season.

A frisson of panic demolished the repetitive litany. The only thing that mattered was escaping whoever stabbed a gun in her back.

"Don't turn around," a gruff voice demanded. "Just hand it over."

"Hand what over?" Fingers jittery and uncertain, she clutched her purse. *Return to the car in the parking lot after you leave the bank building.* The instruction battled with an urge to break free and flee.

"Don't make me ask again. Hand over the briefcase. Now!" Pain lanced her spine as he jabbed the gun against her back.

Gun. Gun. A new litany played itself out. *In purse.* The words vanished. There was no telling what would happen if she lost whatever treasure she possessed before she fulfilled her task. *Purse. Return to the car. Put the contents of leather briefcase in the metal briefcase and spin the combination lock.* It seemed like a millennium passed as war waged in her skull. Perspiration formed on her nape and her blood sugar levels took a nosedive.

"Lady, what the hell's wrong with you? You have a death wish?"

The words sliced through Marisa. "Okay. Okay. Let me untangle the strap," she said, unsure where the words stemmed from. She withdrew a small handgun from her purse. An entity within her suddenly forced her physical motions to dominate her muddled thoughts.

Hand on the strap crossing her torso as if she planned to take the briefcase off, she spun around and slammed her knee into the man's crotch, estimating his height dead-on. As he bellowed and bent double, she whacked the side of her handgun on the back of his neck to incapacitate him. The gun thumped against skin and bones and reverberated up her arm as the man hit the ground. Hand and wrist aching, she scurried out of arm's reach. Still not a soul in sight, she darted out from behind the hedge. The screech of wheels and a blur of black nearly ran her over. Hand against the fender of the car, she caught her balance.

The front passenger window rolled down. "Get in the back," the quasi-familiar driver yelled, his dark glasses and beanie shielding his identity.

Three tones dinged on her phone and something inside her broke, relaxed. She climbed into the back seat and slammed the door. The driver zoomed out of the parking lot before she caught her breath. The melody dinged again, and she pulled out the crumpled paper with her instructions. Following them, she finished her chore, turning the three combination dials and ramming the aluminum briefcase back onto the floorboard.

Ten minutes later, the driver booted her out in front of a dim, hole-in-the-wall bar downtown and sped off. As instructed, she sat in a booth in the near-deserted bar and ordered a beer. Half the ceiling lights had burnt out, lending little reflection off the wood-paneled walls of the Irish pub. Only two other small booths were occupied by older men losing themselves in drink.

Marisa took a pull on the beer bottle, puckered her lips at the taste, but took another long draw, praying it chased away the fog, which descended upon her the moment she received the first text. Or send her to oblivion if she downed a few more of the strong microbrews. She loathed beer in any form and the taste alone might speed her descent.

She waited five minutes. Her phone dinged an incoming text. *"Strike one."*

Marisa stared at the message until it vanished. She'd lost time again. Pain lanced her right hand and wrist. What had she done? How did she get to the bar? Where was Ric? The last thing she remembered was standing outside Lily's office with him.

Exhaustion anchored her, and she slunk into the crackling pleather seat. She scrutinized the strange phone and called for a rideshare car. She couldn't confront Lily or Ric. If she didn't get a grip on her personal version of hell, she'd be dead along with her mother, Lily, and all the McAllisters, if the assholes directing her every movement had their way.

CHAPTER TWENTY-FOUR

Annoyance twitched Ric's shoulder muscles into tight knots as he raced to his vehicle. A witness had spied Marisa speeding off in a black sedan. "What are you up to, wench?" The weird and frightening vision he had of her entering a bank and facing a gunman when she exited refused to abate. He called and texted her ten times, and she didn't answer. Was she under coercion? Off getting killed?

Ric followed the direction the car took, but he was two bucks short and a fiver late, sliding in and out of traffic, getting blasted by ear-piercing horns, barely avoiding several patrol cars. He wished he'd been able to install a tracking app on her phone, one way Guardians kept track of their charges in crucial situations. And Marisa sat in a sketchy situation with some asshole hypnotizing her, the worst quandary. Nothing else explained her blackouts. Either a strong psychic coerced her or someone was hypnotizing her.

After checking a half-dozen downtown banks to no avail, he drove to Lily's house, found it empty, then drove past the scorched house and Delaney's place. No sign of her. Last stop, the compound. Each place on the map seemed too well connected in the San Jose foothills, too coincidental, something he wanted to investigate. Later.

When he approached the rear gate, he tore apart his SUV hunting for his keycard. He must've left it in Marisa's room last night. He used his fingerprint, stated his credentials and password to the intercom, and the gate slid open. Marisa's rental car sat where she'd left it the day before.

As he entered the building, he greeted a few Guild members and Guardians before spotting Liam reading on his tablet.

"You see Marisa?"

"Just stormed through here. Said you abandoned her at Lily's office. What's up? Do I need to shadow you?"

"Are you serious? Why would I jeopardize her? I think she blacked out again. She dumped me and took off on her own."

"You do need a shadow. For both your sakes. I'm so freaking bored, I'm dying."

"You need to keep your hands clean and run our business full time. Don't jeopardize your Guardian status. Next infraction and you'll get the boot for good."

"Not exactly what everyone was thinking last night." Liam poked his brother in the shoulder. "I'm part of this case."

"As my backup." Ric massaged his shoulder. "I don't need you shadowing me. If the Guild gets wind, you're screwed. It's risky due to our plan."

"Really? Then where's your client?" Liam stormed off, lugging his ever-present tablet under his arm, his footsteps thumping down the hallway.

Despite including Liam in their plans, neither Jake nor Ric wanted him to meet trouble face forward after all the months he'd spent in Guardian jail. Two more months and he goes into Guild parole, able to take on assignments once again. Resurrection of the McAllister Musketeers. "Stubborn ass." Ric hopped the stairs two at a time and sprinted to Marisa's room.

Lacking his keycard, he punched in his code, pressed his thumb to the bio reader. The door hissed open and closed behind him with a definitive click. Darkness met him, the light-blocking blinds drawn.

Marisa lay on top of the covers, barely making a dimple in the king-sized bed. Her black hair fanned out around her in silky ribbons. For once, she hadn't straightened her hair, and it resembled inky waves against the hunter green and gold pillowcases. Sacred womanly items spilled out of her purse on the floor beside her shoes at the foot of the bed as if she'd dumped and crashed. She still wore the slacks and sweater she'd left the compound in earlier that morning, accentuating every luscious curve of her body. Ric grew hard just being in her presence, wishing she lay in his bed waiting for him.

"Marisa?" he said softly. "It's me." She moaned, mumbled incoherent words. "You know, Ric, the Guardian you ditched earlier."

Her eyes fluttered open. "Ric?"

"Expecting someone else?"

Eyelashes blinking up a storm, she propped up on her elbows. "Where am I?"

He flicked on the bedside light. "At the compound. What do you remember?"

She drooped back onto the bed. "I was with you in Lily's office, and then I bumped into Liam downstairs asking about you." She let out a deep groan. "Oh, no. What did I do?"

He perched on the bed and toyed with her long hair, sliding the silky strands between thumb and forefinger. "You received a text and ditched me at the elevator. A witness saw you get into a black car with a driver. I called and texted."

"I got another text." She wriggled off the other side of

the bed, deliberately putting distance between them.

Ire shot through him at both her action and response. "Why didn't you tell me?"

"I was instructed to dump you." She massaged her right hand as if it pained her.

He slanted his head, not quite believing her. "You remember that detail, but nothing more until you got here?"

"Am I supposed to put my mother's life in peril to stroke your Guardian ego?" she snapped. "These people know what they're doing and doing a spectacular job."

Tension stiffened his biceps, and he stood in a combative stance. "I can help you."

"There're holes in their instructions, or they're not sticking. It's all I remember." She flung up her arms. "You don't get it. They tell me what to do. I do it whether I recall it or not."

"If they tell you to drive your car off the Golden Gate Bridge, you gonna do it?" He curled his fists at his sides.

"Screw you, McAllister." She clambered up on the bed and got in his face. Annoyance carried spots of color to her usually porcelain cheeks. A surge of heat kindled in Ric's groin. "They can make me do it. Don't you get it? No choice here. Despite the small holes, I can't fight them when I'm under their control."

"I can. You know it. You got the text, you remember that much. You should've shown it to me. I can shadow you and witness your actions, stop you if you're walking into trouble."

"Are you kidding me?" She knocked her fist into his shoulder—the same one Liam just thumped. "You'd jeopardize all of us if they'd made you."

Again, Ric gently probed his pained shoulder. "How can we solve this if you don't trust me to keep you safe?"

"I don't care what they do to me as long as they leave

what's left of my family, Lily... others alone."

"I care!" Ric bent forward to force his words upon her. "I fucking care." He advanced, his legs hitting the bed. "I care enough not to let *anyone* hurt you or your mother."

Marisa bared her pearly whites. "We do this my way or the highway. I refuse to depend on anyone, any man. Any McAllister. Everything changed today. We don't even know if there's a connection between Delaney and the Cabal, or whoever's mind-fucked me."

"Which means we could be up against three independent foes."

"Exactly. I'll chase one. You chase the others." She flung back her hair, and it cascaded over her shoulders in a black tide of silk. "I'm done here. I have things to do."

His groin tightened in his constraining jeans. "You're not going anywhere." His knee hit the mattress between her spread legs. She inched backward. He inched forward, both knees now on the bed.

"Hit your post at the door, Guardian. Do your job." Her tone turned husky, and another flush worked up her neck. "When I leave, I'm leaving alone."

"The hell you will. That's not in our plan."

Marisa lunged off the bed, and he anticipated her move, scrambling with her. They squared off nose to nose. Her short panting breaths fanned his face, her meadow-fresh perfume filling his senses with her hot fury. He wanted to slip his tongue between her lips and kiss her until she accepted his protection, his desire, and his need for her.

"Back off, Guardian." Not one muscle balked in her body.

He needed her like air to live, like sunlight to illuminate the dark crevices inside him. He wanted to shine his own light on her darkness and drive it to the far reaches of the galaxy. Unable to stand not touching her a second longer, he crushed his lips to hers and his arms gathered her close. He'd kill to have all of her that night. Simply holding her didn't come close enough to sate him.

As she braced herself against his chest, her tongue tangoed tentatively with his, and her little whimpers spurred him on. He fisted his hand in her hair and caught the airy little moan that escaped her into his mouth. Again she feebly pushed him, yet her mouth and her tongue ruled her actions, and they were definitely not pushing him away. Returning his kiss and then some, she took him beyond his limits with a silent passion killing his ability to do anything except kiss her back. His tongue leisurely explored the inside of her mouth, teasing and tasting as hers mimicked the motions.

With a moan, she broke free and panted. "You don't want me. I told you I don't do casual."

"I do want you." He released her hair, and his hands drifted to the small of her back. "I'll change your mind about casual."

"Really? You think you're better than all the others who've tried? Ego, meet Ric McAllister."

He knew she lashed out in order to discourage him. Unfortunately for her, her words incited an impetuous conga line in his gut, dancing straight toward the hardest erection ever. If he didn't appease his hunger soon, he'd go stark raving bonkers. He left his fate in her hands. Her breasts heaved in annoyance, and she still hadn't budged, granting him a healthy serving of hope.

"I am better, by a million degrees of awesomeness," he said. Marisa flung to the side and off the bed. He wheeled on her. "Tell me to go then."

"Go, McAllister."

"My—*our*—kiss affected you. You know it."

"Of course it did. I'm not immune to your... negligible charms. A kiss is a kiss. Bye, McAllister." She paced to the door, opened it, and waited for him to depart.

Remaining by the bed, he challenged her, his erection straining against the front of his jeans. Ric undid the button of his pants and the ripping zipper sound cast a hungry flush to her cheeks. The tip of her tongue flicked her bottom lip, and he imagined it flicking the tip of his cock, intensifying the sensations flooding him. Still he didn't move, waiting for her to come to him. Going to her wasn't even a question. If she didn't come willingly, he'd do what she asked and walk. Until tomorrow.

"It's all yours for the taking."

Eyes sparkling, she shut the door and tromped over to him, stopping within arm's reach. Lust overshadowed her anger, and she probably fought her longing to reach for him, clenching her thighs to keep her hands from taking what they wanted. "Despite your magnificently long and thick appendage, I don't want it. Get out."

Another burst of irritation swamped him. His dick pulsed, seeming to increase the heaving of her perfect breasts straining against her blouse.

Before he could blink again, her fingernails bit into the flesh of his upper arms and the softness of her body pressed against him. The edge of his control slipped.

Her lips feathered across his cheek. "Is this what you want? What you really want? You gonna walk when all is said and done? Will you be able to walk?" Marisa pressed the hard length of him into her middle, as if surrendering to her body's infidelity, unable to destroy his carnal cravings tipping him toward the threshold of madness.

He breezed a kiss over her cheek, then claimed her mouth in a blistering kiss, serving to silence any objections she might declare. Her lips parted for him, her tongue curling around his in a fierce duel, and he ground himself against her, frantically trying to salvage his sanity. Just in case she really, really didn't want him.

He'd die if she teased and taunted and let him go. Her kiss devastated him, making his chest ache with an intensity he refused to ignore.

Nails no longer biting into his skin, instead she wound her arms around his neck, her hands fisting his hair, sending hot bristles poking his scalp. Never breaking their lip-lock, gazes glued to the other, he hoisted her up, his hands kneading her so perfect ass, and she twined her legs around his waist.

She tore her mouth off his. "Take me hard and fast before I lose it, Guardian. No bed though."

Ric didn't need a further invitation. Locking his mouth onto hers in another demanding kiss, he backed them into the chair. He managed to get his pants down before his ass hit the seat. Without breaking their kiss, they managed to slide her pants down and slip a condom on him. Later, he'd make love to her. But this crazy, angry sex turned all his buttons on. If he didn't bury himself inside her wet heat now, he didn't think he'd make it.

Heaving up, she positioned herself over him, and her lustful eyes never unlocked from his. When her hand fisted the base of his erection, he bucked up, begging to enter her. Without warning, she lowered herself over him, and he pushed into her like a length of velvet-encased iron coming home. Molten, flaming, and his mouth latched onto her neck to stifle his bellow. Marisa ground her hips down on him fully, so damn tight and hot, holding him steady. She froze, her teasing tongue flicking across her lips enticingly.

Groaning, he twisted beneath her to encourage her to resume her seduction. Not that he didn't love her tight heat wrapped around him. "Marisa! Baby, don't tease me like this. I need to feel you move on me."

She tangled her fingers in his hair and brought him

closer. Her gaze on his face was like a kiss of sunlight on an icy winter day. "This is what you wanted. It's my way. Or no way."

A glacial slap of reality hit him, and he stiffened. "Is this what *you* want?"

"I'm here. I own you right here, right now."

His shaft pulsed in her tight sheath, and excruciating sensations of ecstasy ripped him apart. "Then fucking take me," he ground out. He reached under her blouse and cupped the most exquisite breasts—not too big, not too small; they fit his hands to perfection—to prolong her sweet torture. "God, you're so beautiful," he said, his eyes glazing over. "You make me feel things... you floor me. Every bit of you."

Rising up, she allowed him to withdraw before she impaled herself on him again, then again, erotic, mind blowing. Harsh gasps of arousal erupted out of her before he captured her mouth with his again, his tongue mimicking the motions of her riding him. Her thighs tightened around his legs, and she stilled, her whole body tensing. The relentless assault on his mouth never surrendered. He couldn't get enough of her, didn't ever want her to withdraw the agonizing waves of her rapture beating down the doors to his own. She ground herself harder, granting no mercy, riding him until she unraveled in spasms around his hard length.

Without pulling out, he lifted her off the chair, ripping his mouth from hers and barely made it to the bed. Beneath him, she whimpered and dragged his face back to hers, her fingers clawing at his head to hold his mouth on hers. Concentrating on the hot spikes of sensation piercing him, he plunged to the hilt inside her, once twice, and his own release shattered him, killed his ability to think of anything but the demon woman in his arms. Exactly where she belonged.

CHAPTER TWENTY-FIVE

They lay knotted in each other. The very caress of Ric's
fingers on Marisa's skin launched fireworks in her body,
striking every nerve ending. Sex before Ric felt like poorly
written chapters of her life, cheap thrills lacking any real
substance. Maybe there was something to dating a
Guardian or a McAllister. Or Ric. *Definitely Ric.* At least
until he bailed. She could guard her heart temporarily,
right? Friends with benefits? *Right. Who are you kidding?*
Ric was already seeping into all her senses. She'd need a
gun to blast him out.

Ric's mouth latched onto her neck, his gasping breath
hot and moist against her sizzling flesh. He kissed her
hairline near her ear, his mouth lingering on that
sensitive spot that riled up a new round of desire. Now
that she'd sampled him, she needed the whole enchilada.
She'd never experienced angry sex before. If it always felt
like a bomb of lust detonating in every cell of her body,
she'd have it every day.

"Damn, what'd it take, thirty seconds?" Ric's gravelly
voice interrupted her short-circuit.

His carefree laughter left her knees weak. "Maybe
two minutes." She smoothed out the double-dose of chaos
she'd created in his short hair.

"Sorry," he said in her ear. "But it was the hottest two

minutes of sex ever." He lifted up a smidge to peer down into her face, and her fingers fell onto his shoulders. "Are you still mad?"

"Yes." She smiled despite herself.

"Then I'm game for a second round."

He grinned so freaking gorgeously, she wanted to melt into the blue pools of his eyes and swim off to a deserted island together where nothing could harm them. *He's a Guardian*, the angel shouted on one shoulder. *Screw that, he's hot as hell. Screw him again*, the devil shouted over the tiny harangue on her other side.

"Haha. You're a laugh a minute." She shifted, and they both rolled onto their sides, facing one another. Ric hauled the comforter over them. "I meant what I said. Guardian and psychic with benefits. That's all."

A vein in his neck pulsed. "Whatever." He skipped his fingers up her arm to her neck where they danced another passionate tango.

She wanted him touching every inch of her... wanted him to leave before he destroyed her heart, before she destroyed *his* mind *and* heart.

He dipped his index finger into the V of her blouse, traced the upper swell of her breasts, leaving a trail of igniting lust. Halting his seduction, she held his hand before his touch torched the remainder of her willpower.

Numb and accompanied by Ric's groaning, she left the bed, kicking her pants off as she entered the bathroom to prepare for her dinner with Delaney. The mirror reflected the aftermath of hot sex in the flush of her cheeks and her plump lips. She patted cold water on the stubble burn on her neck, her fingers lingering to hold onto Ric forever.

Once she'd showered and left the sanctuary of her steaming bathroom dressed only in a robe, carrying a bottle of blood-red nail polish, she rejoined Ric. Watching her peruse the clothes hanging in the closet, he sat in the chair, fully clothed. A sexy, black dress Lily delivered earlier hung inside the open closet.

"I smell you all over me," he said. "All over this chair."

"I can give you my bottle of perfume if it'll help."

"Not what I mean." He kicked his left ankle over his right knee.

"What now?"

"Tell me what happened today."

"I really, *really* don't remember." She lifted her purse off the floor and hunted for her phone, instead found a phone she didn't recognize. Her eyes narrowed. "This isn't mine."

Ric jumped up and snatched the cell from her, punched on the screen. "No password. It's non-branded. Where'd you get it?"

"Beats me." She clutched his arm between them to temper her sudden heebie-jeebies. Pain shot through her wrist and a sudden cloud formed in her head. She didn't belong there. Didn't belong in bed with Ric. Didn't belong in the Guild. Didn't belong to any life she knew. A better way, a better life existed around the bend. She only had to take it and embrace it. The freakish thoughts collided, and she waggled them and the hovering fog off.

"What does 'strike one' mean?"

She studied the screen over his arm. "What? They let me leave a message?"

"Look at the time. After you left the offices. You think the driver gave it to you and took your phone?"

"Possibly." She rested her head on his shoulder, her palms on his chest. As much as she wanted separation, she needed him more than ever to solve the tempest her life careened into in a measly few days. "I'm scared. I've never blacked out for such a long period. I think my lack of telepathy has made me more susceptible." Silent, Ric froze and his hard chest seemed to cave in. The phone dropped on the rug between their feet. "Ric?"

He began to slither from her arms. With all her strength, she maneuvered him to the bed where they both fell onto their backs, legs dangling over the side. His eyes rolled up into his head, and he left the here and now.

"Ric? Can you hear me?" She didn't know if it was possible or wise to wake a clairvoyant out of a trance.

No response. She swung his legs onto the bed and stretched him out. Just as she was about to call Jake, a piercing pain stabbed her skull and she crumpled to the floor.

"No, no, no." She wrapped her arms around herself, fighting Ric's hold. "Not again. Ric, don't do this to me." *Don't do this to Ric.*

He fell into her black hollow, and his mental images flooded her like a tsunami, filling her emptiness.

Marisa sat on a dark leather sofa, wine glass in hand, ankles crossed. The wine as red as her fingernails flushed her face, roasted her body. He sat beside her. Unable to see his face, her anticipation didn't need an introduction. She was exactly where she desired to be.

"Come here." She set her wine glass on the coffee table next to the empty bottle and crooked her finger. "I'm ready to take this to the next level. I think we deserve to test us out."

"You agree all that other business doesn't matter?"

"Of course. Despite my previous hang-ups about mixing business and pleasure, and other matters, we only have one life. Why not make it worthwhile and meaningful. In all the ways."

Noise crackled in Ric's head, brain synapses broke apart and extended feelers throughout the darkness, and hit a well-developed and well-oiled barrier. The noise disappeared as fast as it hit and lapsed into a reigning silence.

He buried his face in her neck, one hand combing her hair, the other gently cupping her left breast. He left a searing path of kisses across her neck, continuing to the low neckline of her blouse.

"You taste heavenly." His lips traveled her prickly flesh.

Her anticipation evolved into a strange and confusing tide. The mystical fence she sat on wobbled. The sensations he created were too right.

Too wrong.

He skimmed his hand up her thigh, closed in on intimate territory, igniting heat between her legs.

"Don't stop," she panted out.

"No. No," the angel shrieked, fracturing the silence. Was the devil on one shoulder stabbing the angel? As her arousal grew, her bewilderment magnified. They began battling. One half of her demanded she stop before the point of no return. The other half demanded she give in to temptation and abandon her current life to earn her ultimate rewards.

Static splintered her head. To stop the intrusion, she stuffed the warring factions into a crevice and focused on a well-timed seduction, and a world of choices and promises.

His mouth left her skin, and his fingers stopped their dance on her flesh. "Marisa, I'll give you the world. Will you take it with me?"

Not a moment's hesitation. "Yes."

Perplexed, she blinked rapidly, and then a small smile played on her lips. "Let's take this to your bedroom, Kenny. Let's seal our deal the proper way."

A voice shouted. She screamed back. Chaos ensued as the voices battled for dominance until they dissipated into another void.

Silence. No static. No voices. Nothing. Just the lilting music.

Then a fiery sword severed the link, cut right through one mind, then the other linked to her.

Whimpering and head hammering, Marisa blinked open her bleary eyes. She'd rolled into a fetal position beside the bed to protect herself from harm. The inside of her skull broiled as if someone had ripped out her brain, spilling molten lava behind. Ric's vision and her role in it slowly emerged and shock seized her cramped limbs. Did Delaney have the ability to coerce her alter ego to have sex with him? No way did she intend to take this ruse to his bedroom. *Holy crazy train.*

For a moment, clarity seemed a long way off until a rustling on the bed slammed her back to reality. Her elbow throbbed, and she massaged it as she gained her footing. Pain contorting his face, Ric thrashed on the bed, murmured her name, throwing in an occasional "no" and "don't."

"Ric, can you hear me?" She kissed him, her lips lingering on his, hoping to instill her presence, memorizing the soft, firmness of his lips, possibly for the last time. If she slept with Delaney, Ric would hate her. Maybe doing the deed solved her problem.

Cement hardened her heart for what was about to happen to them. Although there really wasn't a "them," she could potentially have a life with Ric if her telepathy never returned. Something she now feared and coveted more than ever.

Marisa lay beside him, slid under his arm, and positioned it around her. "Come back to me. Let me know you're still here."

She finagled Ric's phone out of his pocket and punched in Lily's number.

When Lily answered, she told her everything. "Just

get the equipment set up in your suite here. The plan's still on the table." She hung up.

Jake and Lily planned to conduct monitored surveillance of Delaney's home from the compound, while Liam kept his eye on Ric near Delaney's house. If Ric awakened. If not, she'd cancel her date.

By the time she clicked off, Ric's breathing leveled. Marisa laid their joined hands on his abdomen.

"Ric? Can you hear me?"

His eyes flicked open, and the first reaction spanning them was accusatory, not relief, not the lustful joy she'd witnessed whenever he gazed at her. "Did you see my vision?"

She squeezed his fingers. He wrenched his hand out of hers and sat up, his back against the headboard.

"I saw." No sense in telling him he'd knocked her out. His angry jealous thoughts struck her like a bolt of lightning. No telepathy needed.

"You can't do this."

Marisa hissed air out between her teeth. "This is our way in."

"And let him screw you?" Ric slung off the bed, stomped to the door, spun to face her. He wobbled as he recovered his equilibrium.

"I won't sleep with him," she said emphatically.

"What if he hypnotizes you? We can't take the chance." Silence fell like an ice storm. No answer would appease him. He looped his arm around the bedpost for support. "Something happened at the end. It wasn't my usual slide out of the vision. Something severed it."

Alarm radiated up her torso. "What do you mean?"

"A dark presence oozed evil. A serrated knife sliced and diced my mind."

More convinced than ever they didn't belong together, the threat to his mind and her heart refused to quit nagging her. She reached for him, and he shrank back. She dropped her hand, sucking up the unexplained pain still lingering in her wrist. "Are you okay?"

"I'll live. I've got a bad feeling about tonight. I think we need to can this plan."

"Do you think I cut you off?" How linked were they? Was she truly the evil darkness everyone believed?

A bang in the hallway alerted them to Jake and Lily lugging up their equipment. "Jake will have me on audio. You'll rush in if anything goes awry."

Ric's silence was too telling. He didn't trust her. Hell, she didn't trust herself under the influence of Delaney's control. If Delaney was the culprit, that is. They could all be barking up the idiot tree if Delaney turned out to be merely a businessman trying to wine, dine, and bang her.

The door pushed open, and Jake hustled in, Lily on his tail. Relief remade his handsome face when he spied his brother standing, propped against the bedpost.

"You come out okay?" Jake's gaze traveled over Marisa, bounced back to Ric.

Ric regaled his brother and Lily with the high points of what he'd envisioned. "Tonight's too risky for Marisa."

"It's her choice. Everything's in place," Jake replied.

"What triggered the vision?" Lily plucked an edge of the comforter over the rumpled bed.

Marisa flushed. "Me. What else? I need to get ready."

Jake and Lily left Marisa to finish dressing. Ric hung behind with her, despite Jake's insistence to go over the plan one more time.

He approached her in front of the bathroom mirror as she applied her lipstick. "If you do this and something happens to you, I don't know what I'll do."

"If I don't do this and something happens, I don't know what *I'll* do." She met his distressed gaze in the mirror. He stepped forward until his chest pressed against her back and his hands skimmed her hips.

"*We* may not come out unscathed." He buried his nose in her straightened hair, mussing it up.

There is no "we." The idea battled the part of her wanting him like heroin to an addict. Ric was not cut out for her life. She'd stay in San Diego if it meant saving him from her. "How do I escape the darkness when it's inside me?"

"Let me drive it out of you, let me be your light," Ric said huskily. She opened her mouth to speak, and he stuck his index finger across her lips. "Don't say a word," he said. She swore he must have developed telepathy. "This isn't casual. I think I'm falling in love with you."

By the time the night ended, he may regret his words. He may fall in hate with her.

She may loathe herself... if she lived long enough.

CHAPTER TWENTY-SIX

Marisa compelled herself to deny Ric's words, a seriously impossible feat. She'd heard the same from other men, for purposes of sex, arm candy, a free lawyer, a telepath to do his dirty work. None of those user sentiments rang true, until Ric McAllister expressed them, and mimicked her own feelings. *Think. He only said he "thinks" he's falling in love. You still have time to escape. Intact may be another story.*

Her mind whirled until she stepped out of her rental car in front of Delaney's house, her spike heels striking the driveway with definitive clicks. She straightened the slinky sleeveless dress beneath her black lacy shrug. The hidden listening device under her watch face weighed nothing on her wrist, yet it anchored her actions.

McAllister Security & Investigations owned and deployed the techiest surveillance equipment. Liam monitored the receiver to the wireless audio from a safe distance, which fed the information by satellite to Jake's computer. The equipment lent her a small protective barrier and only a bit more intrusiveness than she cared to admit.

The front door swung open, and Delaney smiled at her. Impeccable as always, he wore a casual long-sleeved dress shirt and black slacks. She stifled a sneeze when his musky cologne infiltrated her senses and booted out Ric's familiar scent.

"Right on time."

He bound his arms around her in a friendly embrace. His cool lips skimmed her cheek, and she forced down a flinch.

"Good to see you again, Kenny." She eased out of his personal bubble and set her purse on the marble console table. "I'm sorry Lily and Jake had other plans."

"I'm not." He trailed his fingers softly down her sleeve, dipped beneath the hem. "Is this tiny coat part of your outfit?" He tweaked her sleeve. "Or shall I hang it up for you?"

"Part of the outfit. Later," she winked, "I might be inclined to *shrug* it off."

"And more?" He traded a teasing wink.

"Now you're being greedy."

"A man can hope and dream, can't he?"

Her shoulder grazed his arm as she strode farther into his house, her blood-red stilettos clicking on his stone floor, every tap ratcheting up her unease.

"Would you like a drink? I have champagne on ice."

"Sounds perfect."

He led her to the family room where his home theater occupied a major chunk of real estate. The screens and pyramid console on the gaming table rang familiar bells. Had he shown her the game during her first visit? *Wait, he said he did. Why can't I remember?*

Myriad white candles interspersed the room and lent the otherwise dark space a romantic vibe Marisa might appreciate in another home, with another man... with a particular Guardian. He'd also scattered bouquets of mixed flowers around the room, and the floral scent mingled with the spicy Italian sauces riding the air.

She spun on her heels and accepted the bubbling flute

he offered. "Beautiful room, and whatever your chef has prepared smells exquisite."

"How do you know I didn't prepare it?" His eyes twinkled, and one might forgive the evil languishing behind the sparkle. Almost.

"Do you treat all your business associates or your wives the same way?" Her eyebrows arched in amusement.

"Ouch. Wives?"

"Not even one? I can't imagine you haven't at least visited wedded bliss once."

He pressed forward and said, "I haven't met the perfect counterpart yet."

Brushing her left breast against his chest, she suppressed a shudder. Intimacy and arousal promised to lead him down the path of full disclosure encouraged by innuendo and false platitudes. "Any woman come close?"

Pain washed the edge of yearning from his expression. "One. A few years ago."

"I'm sorry. What happened, if you don't mind me asking?"

"In the end, she just wasn't *the* one. She didn't possess what it takes."

"To satisfy you?"

"Among other things," he said. His shoulders slumped and his left arm fell heavily to his side. If Marisa didn't know any better, she'd swear the movement was forced for show. "I don't dwell on the past too much."

Sensing his reluctance to divulge more, she asked, "How long did your chef spend concocting those splendid smells?"

"Are you reading my mind?" He clinked the rim of his flute against hers, a tinkling song only the best crystal sang.

"I suspect your mind is as blocked as a cement cell. I

don't make a habit of intruding where I'm not invited." She clicked her tongue in her cheek. "You already mentioned your chef would whip up a gourmet meal." She chanced the question burning a hole in her since she'd met him. "Speaking of, do you possess psychic abilities?"

He squinted at her as if she'd asked an uncomfortable truth. "No, of course not. I'm leaving that aspect of our business relationship to you."

"Are you saying you expect me to use my telepathy on business dealings? Is that the reason you hired the firm?"

"An opportunity may present itself where telepathy might come in handy. I hired you and the firm for your various expertise and recommendations. Certainly Guild psychics provide a certain, shall we say, offense in business dealings and negotiations. However, I'll never expect it of you, Lily, or Jake."

Except when you command me or my bestie, Evil Eddie? "Do you find it helpful when your opponents know you're in bed with the Guild?"

"Now you're catching on. Even if I don't use your abilities, just hinting at your skills will get me what I want much easier."

"Surely your opponents will suspect the illegalities involved in using psychic talents for fraud, advantages, and certain other purposes." *If you believe I'm telekinetic, raise your hand and I'll sell you swampland in Florida.* In her capacity as Guild attorney, the Guild required her to use her telepathy in certain dealings. Never illegal, but it created one reason why her moral compass had cracked. Maybe she ought to leave the Guild and wash her hands of them.

"The beauty of it. The mere knowledge keeps adversaries on the up and up. You don't use your talents without permission, and we all stay legal." He took her hand in his warm dry clasp. "Come. I'll show you a new level in my VR game. My new business has captured my greatest focus. I'll expect you to draft a lot of contracts to license out the technology and bring other partners onboard. A ton of royalty fees and other perks are a huge component of the end game."

The events of her recent visit remained elusive. He'd shown her the game, put the headset on, and then a void. *Did he drug me? Or connect with my emptiness and toss my memories into a darker cavern? Right. Like it's even possible. Get a grip.* "Is this the same game you showed me last time?" Fruitlessly, she probed him. Very few people possessed such intense blocks circling their thoughts. Normally, she had the ability to dip into any tiny fracture and glom onto words here and there. Not all made sense in those cases, yet she enjoyed the ability to pick apart a tiny seed and grow it into a burgeoning field. Without her telepathy, he remained blocked in all ways.

"Exactly. We've added functionality improvements, new levels, and background lands. In-house beta testing is nearing completion, and we're ready to take it to the next level."

Putting distance between them, she sat at the far end of the black leather sofa, the gaming console and a pair of VR goggles on the coffee table. Two gaming chairs bracketed the sofa and a memory of sitting on one filtered in. "External beta testing?"

"We've handpicked a test group under a nondisclosure agreement, and we're ready to roll it out."

"Do all games go through different levels of beta testing?"

"This is more than a game. It's a way of life. So we're employing multiple levels of testing on various test groups."

The game! Oh. My. God. Does the game connect to a psychic's brain? Was it manipulating her via the text messages? No... she'd blacked out before she'd tried the game. Did she dare try it again? Did she dare not? The weight of her watch became unbearable. The moment something significant occurred to alert Jake on the audio end, he'd send Ric in so fast, it'd make Delaney's head spin off into his virtual reality lands. *Keep it cool. Play Delaney's multifaceted games.*

"Would you rather eat first, then have our fun?" He picked up the remote control to the game console.

"If dinner will keep, let's indulge in our fantasies first."

"Fantasies are only as good as real life allows. I think you'll find more than real life here."

Delaney spoke as if he knew she didn't remember their first VR indulgence. Thorns skittered across her breasts. What kind of game erased one's memory? Or had he hypnotized her before she put on the goggles and tripped into the land of his fantasies? *Ick. Excuse me while I hurl.*

The screen flickered on and depicted a 3-D rendering of Delaney's property and house in exquisite detail. "It's extraordinary, so lifelike." She examined the fine details, down to the stained glass dragonfly window above the front door.

Delaney nudged the VR goggles against her thigh. "If you think it's good now, put the goggles on. It'll blow your mind."

"You don't need to spin it on me. I'm not a gamer."

"Darling, it's an epic way of life." Careful not to catch her hair on the bands, he settled the goggles over her head.

The moment audio kicked in, a distinctive tone permeated her ears, like second nature. The vista riveted her, and she became one with the woman in the game. She *became* the woman.

Standing in front of an infinity pool with an outdoor kitchen behind her, she drew in the perfume of the lush tropical trees, hibiscus, and other tropical flowers surrounding her in verdant glory. Magical, freeing, and decadent. A song streamed into her senses, infiltrated her entire body, and Kenny strode along a sandy pathway leading to a beach beyond the trees. A lighthouse stood stalwart and tall in the distance, too early for the beacon to shine. The sun sprinkled golden highlights in his hair, glistened on his summer skin, his strong limbs, and granite abdomen. An arrow of dark hair led to the waistband of his swim trunks. Soft music played, the beautiful notes beguiling, and the soothing plucks on the harp created a buoyant tranquility.

Drinks in hand and wearing a billowing sheer cover-up, Marisa approached Kenny and handed one to him. Before he took it, he kissed her, soft and aroused. When she draped an arm around his neck and he held her tight to his naked chest, his kiss possessed her, became demanding, and she succumbed, parting her lips, granting him entrance. Their tongues dueled, then explored languidly.

Gasping for air, he broke free, his eyes hooded. Now only a snip of a black bikini top separated them. He untied the back strings and let the twin patches fall to the ground. The sun warmed her bare breasts, taunted her nipples, and his focus hardened them into bullets.

"You're exquisite," he whispered over the beguiling music.

"You're not so bad yourself."

"Do you want me? Here, now?" He kept her at arm's length, only touching her with eyes infused with deep longing.

Although, her hands begged to skim every inch of his muscular body, she maintained the distance he created.

"What do you think? I'm not running."

"Do you accept me? Will you follow my every command?"

"Is that how you like to play?"

"Always. In everything."

He took her hand and placed it on his lower abdomen, just above the waistband of his shorts. Something sizzled in her mind as fire deluged her most intimate parts. She slid her hand lower, traced his erection through the thin material. He inclined forward, his dark hair tickling her breast and he flicked his tongue over one erect nipple, then the other until she gasped.

"Show me how much you want me," he whispered. "And that's as far as we go today. I want you comfortable with me on your terms before we take the next step."

"Is that a command?" A soft tease edged her words.

He chuckled. "Yes, if you want it to be."

The landscape evolved and a three-sided cabana open to the ocean surrounded them. Soft flowing fabric walls wafted in the balmy sea breeze. A round bed took up the lion's share of space, surrounded by potted palms and exotic flowers perfuming the outdoor room with their spicy scents. Dozens of candles flickered, and food and champagne covered a table set for two.

A hot breeze sifted through her skull, replacing her pockets of darkness with sputtering light. Marisa shook her head to dislodge the prickly sensation.

As she stroked Kenny's erection through his swim trunks, she worked kisses up his neck. When her mouth met his, she said, "I want you. Here, now." The moment the words rolled out, a sharp dagger sliced her skull and she whimpered. The pain disappeared as quickly as it arrived. *What did I just say?* She jerked back as if he'd burned her and gripped her thigh.

"What's wrong?" He combed his hand into her hair

and cupped the side of her head. The lilting melody filled every crevice of her body, the familiar notes tinkled, calming her. The song spun to the beginning and began a new scintillating aria encouraging her to sway in his arms.

"Nothing. Everything's just right." She blinked rapidly. "Tell me what *you* want." A note in the song escalated higher and higher and suddenly plunged.

"Marisa Meadows, will you let me guide you through the life you were meant to live? Will you let me lead you in love? Will you let me rule your mind? I promise to give you everything you've ever coveted, and everything I have is yours. We'll make a perfect and powerful mark on the world together." The sweet melody traversed her mind, whipped a burst of heat down her body, quickly chased by a strange cold front.

She melted against him. "Of course. Yes," she said in a rush as the song's crescendo crashed. "You are all I've ever wanted." Finally, she found the one man to tame her doubts and fears. The one man whose mind was a blank refuge, containing an impenetrable shield from her darkness, from her guilty intrusions. They meshed so well. Did he embody the same darkness?

Lightning struck the acceptance clouding her, striking her with a sudden languidness. Unable to stand, she sagged against him and he lifted her into his arms. He laid her on the pillowy bed, his arms bracing her.

"Marisa? Are you all right?"

Perplexing words rolled off her tongue. "Just the excitement of tonight." The strange moment passed as quickly as it hit. Trembling, she teased her fingertips down his arms, twined her legs around his legs, and pressed herself against his softening erection until he became steel again. "I want you so bad, it overwhelmed me." She laughed a laugh she didn't feel.

Doubts battered her and flickers of light kept winking on and off. A tempest of voices inundated her. *Whose voices?* The hyperawareness of her telepathy exonerated her pain. When the light winked out, every sound and thought evaporated, except of the here and now. The idea of Kenny and making love to him, the desire rolling off him consumed her. His perfection. Their heaven. She'd be crazy not to give in to this man and the life he promised, embodying the deepest desires she believed she'd never allow to the surface.

She fell into his kiss with a hunger that sent her riding a wave of silver and gold to paradise. A weird buzzing scored her brain and voices fought for control on one tarnished wave of silver. The chiseled handsome face framed with dark hair and ocean-blue eyes of a beloved man she had trouble placing revolved to the forefront. The image disappeared as quickly as it arrived. Two voices remained, battling one another, ripping her mind apart, discarding bits of silver and gold on her path.

Suddenly, Kenny jolted back and peered over her shoulder to the white sandy beach beyond their private paradise. "Stay here," he demanded. Softer, he said, "I need to take care of something."

Unsettled, she nodded. The barest shadow of a man wafted away on an air current in her mind's eye. Was it the strangely familiar man? Did she know him?

"Marisa! Wake up, baby! Can you hear me?" The voice grew louder, splintering the darkness encompassing her mind. *"Come on. Wake up. Take off the VR goggles."* Static hissed and expanded in her mind, flashes of light and ink smothering the beach scene. Electricity arced across her internal midnight landscape. Thunder boomed and smashed the darkness, allowing the light to sliver every crevice. The excruciating pain forced out a sob.

"Marisa, it's Ric. Take off the goggles."

For the first time in days, Marisa heard the telepathic voice of another, and she wasn't tethered to a clairvoyant vision.

CHAPTER TWENTY-SEVEN

The second Ric recognized Marisa switching mental channels he knew for certain Delaney was brainwashing her somehow. Their link left him reeling, like the devil had ripped out a piece of his soul, leaving a gaping hole in his chest. Using a VR game to brainwash was insane, evil, and downright brilliant.

Jake had tuned Ric's earpiece to the audio feeding his computer from the listening device in Marisa's watch. Ric hated the words spewing out of her mouth and wanted to destroy Delaney. He knocked his fist into the tree branch, suffered the jagged pain.

The strange melody inside the house triggered red warning flags. The electronic harp kept repeating and he counted patterns among the notes. "The hell?" Then he heard it, the familiar three tones, and then four. The notes played on Marisa's phone, including her new phone. The same melody triggered her text messages.

"Son of a bitch." He whipped his binoculars up. Marisa and the asshole still sat on the sofa immersed in the game. Delaney mesmerized her through the music and his VR scenes. Why target Marisa and her sister? For the Cabal or personal revenge against her family?

The couple depicting Marisa and Delaney on the monitor panned into a backyard oasis. A white sand beach and an aquamarine ocean set the backdrop. The scene appeared so lifelike in near 4-D quality. Too real. Was the same scene playing out through the VR goggles?

When the Delaney character untied Marisa's bikini top, Ric nearly fell off his perch in the camphor tree's thick evergreen limbs. Banging his fist against a branch, he battled every killing urge not to race into the house and play whack-a-mole on Delaney's head.

"It's not real. It's fake." His hand fisted around his gun. Marisa wasn't about to have sex with Delaney. Or was she? What if the game led to reality? Was she even cognizant of reality?

Ric spoke to her, although he knew her telepathy had taken a hike, and he'd not hear her respond. *"Wake up, baby. Marisa!"* His words traveled to the stark flatlands of her mind. *"Can you hear me?"* The darkness splintered, like a sharp glint of light dicing it apart. It towed him into the new fragments. *"Come on. Wake up. Take off the VR goggles."* Fissures opened wider, the crackling deafened. Darkness exploded, and her screams destroyed his heart. *"Marisa, it's Ric. Take off the goggles,"* he yelled until his mind seized up.

Swords of light carved up his brain, and he fell into a pool of darkness. In slow motion, he hovered on the surface before gravity towed him under. He tied his mind to a strong current and let it pull him in. The stormy void seized him, and he lost his tenuous connection.

He slammed the ground, his head banging the base of the tree. Pain zipped down his spine, and the jolt knocked the air from his lungs. Panic stopped his heart until his training took over and he let his body relax.

The darkness expanded and his heartbeat slowed, thunk... thunk, until it barely beat. One tiny glow remained, and he mentally reached for it, tried to hold onto reality. He held no life left to speak one word, verbally or nonverbally.

The pinprick dissolved into the black, and he winked out.

CRBO

Delaney disappeared around the cabana, and the waves crashing on the beach competed with the mental voice demanding she take off the goggles. What goggles? Whose voice? How did she get to the beach? Had she decided to take a trip to Santa Cruz to tour the lighthouse and find clarity? She racked her memory for a clue, but all clues remained secure in the jar.

Another lightning bolt struck her and broke apart the morass submerging her. Thoughts rushed in like a tidal wave toward the shore of her consciousness. The darkness burst, dinging her skull in excruciating pain. Through her screams, she heard Ric call to her.

Static replaced him, and her mind fell silent, as if someone severed his link to her soul.

"Ric? Can you hear me?" She gripped her head to stop the pain from obliterating her, and her hands smacked the goggles. *What the what?* Then it hit her. Delaney wanted her to check out his new VR game, and that was the last she remembered.

Marisa ripped off the goggles along with strands of hair, and she overheard Delaney on the phone in a nearby room. The monitor froze on the cabana sitting on the pristine white beach, foam-tipped waves in mid curl edging the aquamarine ocean.

"It's strike two," Delaney whisper-shouted. She strained to hear him. "This wasn't supposed to happen. He can screw with her susceptibility if it happens again." He paused as if to listen. "She wasn't ready in San Diego, too strong. I don't know what shifted the tide, but she's ready now. We're so close I can taste it. Just take care of the situation on both fronts."

His words held meaning she was hard pressed to figure out in her current muddled state. Soft music sifted in and she focused on the serenity. The sheer cabana curtains fluttered in the breeze, candles flickering a soft yellow glow amid the purple-gray dusk on the screen. The melody skipped and stopped, then started over again. It turned loud, invasive and she fruitlessly covered her ears to block out the confusing dirge. The song of evil flipped on the switch of her memories.

The last half hour of the VR scene inundated her consciousness. The harp music gentled and she dropped her hands. The three notes triggered her actions, killed her guard and her inhibitions. It had encouraged her to tease and seduce the Delaney caricature, until the figurative lightning struck her.

Her telepathy saturated her head. Welcome relief wafted in and left an airy defensive sensation she'd missed. The field of blood-red flowers waving in a breeze, the unbridled waterfall raining into the grotto, and lush rainforest hills replaced the beach scene. Ric had entered the VR landscape via her mind in their odd connective way, unlocking the prison doors to her telepathy.

When Delaney spotted him in his weirdly linked VR way, their battle of wills triggered her blockage to shatter the prison doors. In doing so, it also wiped out Ric. *Oh, God! Is he okay?*

"No. No." She leapt up and scanned the room for her purse, recalling she'd left it in the foyer. Small favors her memory returned as well as her telepathy and she'd bounced out of her hypnotic trance.

Pocketing his phone, Delaney entered the room. The haunting melody started from the top note and became a subtle song following her, stemming from tiny speakers embedded in the ceiling. He stopped before her, and she fought the mesmerizing music. Since her telepathy had now returned, the music became easier to resist. Playing Delaney's game, she forced a blank mask and her tense body to relax.

"Sit, love," he said. She obeyed like a complacent child. "Will you let me lead you tonight?"

Was he testing her? The three distinctive notes in the song ascended, and she played along. "Of course, as we agreed. In everything."

He grinned. "Good. Good. Shall we eat dinner? We can commence our little party upstairs whenever you're ready tonight, tomorrow, or some other time. Or we can go back to the game. Your choice." He flicked his hand at the game console.

"Definitely dinner." She trailed her fingers down his abs and rested them on his waistband. "I'm feeling a little faint. Must be hungry."

"I'm sorry. You need to take your pill, for you blood sugar, right?"

"Yes. I need to take my pill." How did he know? She'd never told him, not even at the airport.

He drew her into his arms as if he thought she'd wilt to the floor any moment. *As if.* She refused to give him such command of her body again, not in reality and not in his sinister games.

"You did well with our game."

She loathed his musky scent and stifled a gag. "I did well in our new life," she mimicked a thought stemming from him. Since her abilities had returned, and he believed her under his compulsion, his walls descended and she oozed unobtrusively in his mind. "How did you know about my pills?"

"I blew it. Celeste mentioned they both had the same blood sugar condition." The thought hit her. "You told me

the first time we entered the VR landscape. Even in the game, you were cognizant of your condition. Just goes to prove how much willpower you retain in the game."

Goes to prove what a freaking liar you are. Unable to stop herself, Marisa cringed, nearly died on the spot at his unspoken comments. Truth stared her down. Delaney had indeed caused her sister to commit suicide by drug overdose. The arms of a murderer tightened around her.

Composing her boiling insides and internal thoughts, she forced a flat monotone. "Yes. I remember. May I get my pill from my purse?"

He brushed a kiss across her lips. "Of course. Then join me in the kitchen."

Nearly cringing from his touch, she wondered how long she planned to maintain the charade. *Won't he see through my ineptitude? How am I supposed to act? Am I supposed to have* any *free will? Shitshow, welcome to my life.*

He led her to the foyer and left her to return to the kitchen.

She dove for her purse. When she opened the clutch, her pulse jumped. Nestled inside sat her gun. *The charade ended now.* She looked down her skimpy dress, realized she had nowhere to hide the weapon. A plan gelled.

"I've changed my mind. Let's get back into the VR and finish what we started," Marisa said for Jake and Ric's benefit. With a sudden burning desire to destroy Delaney without the McAllister brigade knowing more about her personal life, she slipped off her watch. She buried it in the bowl of fake sunflowers and mums on the credenza, kicked off her heels, and left in search of the kitchen.

CHAPTER TWENTY-EIGHT

Serving utensils clinked on pots and pans, an everyday life kind of sound almost tripping her up. Before Marisa rounded the corner of the hallway opening into the kitchen, she set her purse on the floor against the wall, the gun in her right hand. She jammed the weird phone—her failsafe—into the top of her bra, and then flicked the safety off the small handgun. The crap just hit the fan in her book.

Delaney whistled a tune matching the melody wafting from the house speakers. Marisa waltzed into his view, the gun targeting his heart.

"Why did you do it?" she asked cool and level, contradicting her inner turmoil.

A pot clanked onto the marble counter and Delaney raised his arms. "What's going on, darling?"

"Don't *darling* me." She probed his mind but his barriers sprang up. "Did you think your crap-ass hypnotism or mesmerism seriously worked on me?"

"It did."

She tightened her grip on the gun and approached the wide center island separating them. "For two seconds."

"Don't be so sure."

"Why are you targeting my family?"

"Do you mean Celeste?"

"You know what I mean." Her arms already bogged down with the weight of the gun and her predicament. The bastard wouldn't survive the night even if she wrecked every muscle in her body.

"I loved her." He leaned forward and let the counter take his weight. "Life didn't agree with her. You saw what happened."

"Liar. Why. Are. You. Targeting. My. Family?"

His too-long hesitation jacked up her suspicions. "I'm not targeting your family. I simply love beautiful and strong telepathic women," he said.

Her paranoia skyrocketed. "Why? So you can bend us to your will? Play your mind jerks on us? Bully us if we don't do your bidding?" She searched for pinpricks in his mental walls again.

His telling, evil smile displayed the barest hint of his straight snowy teeth. "Think what you want." He lowered his arms an inch. "How did you know? I know for a fact Celeste never told you my real name. *She* didn't know it."

"Get bent." Celeste never told her a name. As best friends, they used to share everything, until Delaney entered Celeste's life and she withdrew into a cocoon of loneliness. "You told her you were married. Why?"

"She told you she was dating a married man? Great ingenuity, if somewhat clichéd."

"What happened between you?" she asked as if spitting glass shards. "Why did you break up?"

"Because she wasn't the beautiful Meadows sister I coveted." Marisa almost lost her balance, and struggled to maintain a steady aim. "Nor the smart or strong one. Weakness did her in. She was more in love with me than proved healthy. Her obsession ruined her telepathy. She became fanatical about learning to erect two-way walls in her head, all to prove she was stronger than the telepaths in your family who let their talents destroy their happiness. In the end, her obsessions destroyed *her*."

Disgust and fury churned acid in her intestines. He continued spewing out the story she desperately needed to hear, for better or for worse.

"Although I loved her, she killed my love with her inadequacy in the end." His arms drooped. "May I put my arms down?"

"Spread them, palms flat on the counter." She waved the gun at a bare spot clear of utensils on the expansive countertop. "There. Make one move and you're a dead man." Studying her, he flattened his palms on the gray veined white marble. "So you dumped Celeste for me?"

"I broke it off with Celeste before you fully hit my radar. Your sister told me you had the better ability to break down mental walls, much better than her abilities. I waited and bided my time."

Nothing seemed sacred where Delaney was concerned, and her hatred elevated to rocket-launching levels, itching her finger on the trigger. "Did you coerce private information out of her?"

"Celeste gave herself freely to me. In *all* ways."

Too much truth existed in his words. Celeste had been the weaker sister, the one who'd do anything to possess the perfect man and hold him in her life. Marisa remained silent for a long moment and decided she didn't have much to lose by busting a vein. "Did you give her a choice? Offer her an olive branch?"

His lips quirked up at the corners, but his smile didn't extend to his dead flat eyes. "You know a lot more than she let on."

"We're psychics, asshole. Do the math."

"And so am I." His trademark evil smile flashed to a calculating grin.

His admission gave her pause. Nothing in his mental

makeup offered any indication of ESP ability. She'd dipped into the heads of too many psychics to recognize the signs. Did he have grand illusions his VR game handed him psychic gifts? "Liar. You're a two-bit wannabe relying on stupid games to manipulate people who have real psychic talent."

"Ah. I knew you'd figure it out. You're too smart for your own good. Don't worry. I've factored all contingencies into this *game* we're playing. One level at a time."

The crawl of ants up her spine marched into an icy tundra of pinpricks. She'd barely suffered from his mesmerism in her missing moments before she lost her telepathy. Did he still possess the ability to hypnotize or mesmerize her now? Would she suffer longer blocks of missing time where her "alter ego" took her body for a spin to who knows where? More walls erected in her head, strengthening the existing thin shield. She tuned out the melody playing in a loop through the house speakers. She hadn't heard the three tones in a while. Deliberate? Was he waiting for the perfect moment? Or did her normal mind tune them out? *It's been delightful, but I have to lobotomize myself now.*

"What choices did you offer her?" She needed to hear the words trip from his mouth, needed to know if he was Cabal or personally targeting her family. So far, nothing he'd said proved dirt. No matter what, she'd get a confession out of him before the McAllisters descended. *Ric. Oh shoot.* Was he pissed at her for ditching the watch? Was he preparing to storm the house? Had he survived his mental intrusion? Her gun-toting arm wavered. Delaney honed in on the dipping weapon, and she strengthened her fatigued arms. "Choices. Cough them up."

"I offered her the choice to be with me my way, or take the highway. She had trouble deciding between the fork in the road, and instead took her only other option."

She snorted in disgust. "Nice guy. Ever heard of compromise? So what's *your* way?"

"Come now, you're not that dense."

"Exactly. Don't underestimate me. I have my arsenal."

"Ric McAllister? Guild Guardians?" He drummed the counter, parodying Ric and his drumsticks. "I wouldn't count on your Guardian to rescue you anytime soon."

"He's not my Guardian." She deflected, hoping to reroute Delaney off Ric's trail. The likelihood of Ric being intact diminished into a thimble of nothing. The slight connection she'd felt the moment he'd shared his first clairvoyant vision with her had evaporated when she escaped the VR game and her senses bonked her back to reality. Amid the tossing and turning in her belly, her blood sugar plummeted and perspiration dotted the nape of her neck.

"Lover, Guardian, who cares. He's out of the picture."

Jitters rocked her as his implications sank in. "Where do we go from here?"

"I'll offer you the same options I handed Celeste. I hope you're intelligent and strong enough to take the right path to more joy and freedom, and more power than you'll ever experience on your own."

"Right." She stretched out the word. "As if I have a choice."

He fluttered his fingers on the counter. "Try me. I'm not a dictator. I have much to offer and not just financially. In time, you'll even grow to love me. We've enjoyed a pretty good start, agreed? Great chemistry between us. I only see it growing."

"Are you insane? You're blackmailing me. You're freaking assaulting me with your plan to manipulate me through your stupid games and hypnotism."

"Ah, now, Marisa, don't think like that. I can introduce you to worlds you've only dreamed about."

Absorbing his delusions, she took a long moment to think, faking him into believing she legitimately was considering his options. In phony contrition, she asked, "If I go along with you, you'll treat me like the queen I deserve, let me use my telepathy without compunction, legal, illegal, and any way I choose?"

His fingers quit dancing on the counter as he considered her response. "You have such untapped talent. I was hoping to persuade you into using it for the greater good. I can protect you in ways no one can."

"How?" She lowered the gun a smidge.

"First we'll get married. The people behind me will revere you. You're one of the strongest of your kind."

"What people behind you?" Playing dumb and contrite didn't come easy, and she forced curiosity to remake her expression. "The Cabal?" she asked in an awed whisper.

"Bingo. Did you think otherwise? I had a feeling you steered clear of Guild Guardians until recently because you had your *issues*. When you asked to be removed from the Guild legal team years ago, you earned another mark in your favor. When Celeste told me how the Guild destroyed your family, I knew you'd remained among them for possible revenge. What better way to get revenge than by joining the Cabal?"

Marisa blinked rapidly, ready to go loony tunes on him. How dare he presume? How dare Celeste tell him about their family? Marisa wanted to drip into a puddle and wallow in her grief, but the moment was too perfect, too explosive, too revealing. Too much grounded in reality during a turbulent period of her life, when she'd wanted to abandon the Guild and leave everything to do with ESP behind. She'd literally wanted to cut off her head to rid it of her gift, and the internal and external voices. The

Guild wanted to use her more and more on cases to break down other people's walls. It went against her morals, and she'd fought the Guild tooth and nail.

As it turned out, in good conscience, she couldn't leave them and merely suffered the occasional hit to her morals. They were too ingrained in her family and her life, and she could fight the injustices better from inside. Was a Guild implosion imminent? Was their fragmenting the reason the Cabal had risen so strong over the last few years? Had they waited and watched from inside the Guild? Watched people like her and Celeste who'd teetered on the edge?

"Why all the subterfuge to get me to join the Cabal? Why didn't you just ask?"

"It's not so simple. I needed assurances, to know your capabilities, if your loyalties were rooted or easily transplanted. You came to San Jose and into the fold of your best friend, who is the new Guild darling, I might add. I needed to ensure you'd leave the Guild at the opportune time."

"Did you start coercing me in San Diego?"

"Coerce is a strong word."

"You know what I mean."

"You were somewhat resistant or confounded by mental suggestions. I stepped it up a notch once you arrived here."

"What did I do in San Diego under manipulation?" Anxious, she chewed on her bottom lip.

"Nothing. You blacked out a few times. I ensured your safety."

"Did you make me listen in on people?"

"Not yet." He shrugged. "Was I wrong to think you ultimately wanted to join the Cabal?"

"How did my prints get on the cigarette lighter in my purse?"

"I pressed your fingers to it during one of your blackouts, and dropped it in your bag when I rescued it from the thief at the airport."

"The thief you hired as a ruse to save a damsel in distress?" Her tone dripped contempt.

"You are a celebration of womanhood. The perfect package."

A burst of his perspiration weaved the raw scent of his ego into her nose. "You stole my sister's bracelet. Why?"

He barked out a surprised laugh. "You are more perfect than I imagined. Beauty, power, and brains. I planned to return it to you, but I got sloppy and lost it. It served its purpose for our touch telepaths to drill into your memories."

"You threatened me in the hospital with the pillow and the note, right?"

He lifted a hand, let it thump to the counter. "Another test. Didn't you ever wonder why hospital security or the police never followed the leads?"

"Well, it wasn't as if I had nothing going on to distract me from the bucket loads of crap you've dumped on me."

"All for your own good, steps leading to your transformation, the note, the texts, the suggestions."

Marisa took another long moment to ponder the proper answer to hand him a lethal dose of hope. Once upon a time, she might have aligned with people in the Cabal and gone against the Guild for boatloads of hurt a particular Guardian had unloaded on her mother and family, the man otherwise known as her sperm donor. A dark family secret her mother pretended never existed in life, let alone within the Guild, the entity that promised to protect and harbor psychics under Guardian care. Did her subconscious still embrace those feelings of Guild betrayal? Did it make her more susceptible to Delaney and the Cabal's mental machinations? They'd royally screwed her family. The events formed the biggest reason why she'd joined the Guild legal team, not for revenge, but to dig deeper into the scandal. As time crawled by, she'd discovered the Guild wasn't entirely to blame. They owned their faults, and the pros outweighed the cons. Although her loyalty to the Guild remained unwavering, her indecision still haunted her. Those reasons led to adoption of her Guild Girl Code.

Ric McAllister's desire for her was unforeseen collateral damage. The temptation and stakes were too high with Ric—for him. She'd never survive if she lost him. Life without him already promised to engulf her in darkness. Right back where she'd started.

Tired and squeamish, her arms wobbled. Time spun backwards. She ought to bang Delaney down for screwing with her. Mow him down for contributing to Celeste's suicide and her mother's mental decline. Gun him down for spewing the twisted truth. Kick his ass because he knew more about her than anyone had a right to know.

"Why did you want me to join the Falbrooke law firm if you didn't want me in the Guild?"

He flicked his hand again. "I want the Cabal and Guild working in synergy."

"Wesley? He was recruiting for the Cabal, and you recognized him in the park, right?"

"He was on the short list of new hires. We would've skipped over him once we completed our due diligence. We don't want drug addicts mucking up our business. He almost exposed one of our satellite offices, and he wasn't supposed to approach any Guild members."

A bead of sweat dripped between her breasts. "Did you truly think I'd betray my best friend and divulge Guild secrets to you?"

"The Guild is sinking fast. I hoped to sway Lily and

the McAllisters over to our side."

"Your side is riddled with fraud, danger, illegal activity, everything the Guild is not."

"Not true. You know as well as I the Guild is anything but pristine, legal, or ethical."

She faltered a step. The sketchiness he claimed pervaded the Guild always bothered her, and even helped her on certain cases. "We don't kill, bully, or blackmail people." Resignation filled her voice; lies filled her words. Was the Guild no better than the Cabal?

"Are you so sure? I've seen enough illegal activity enacted by Guardians that puts the Cabal's activities to shame." His voice lowered to a stage whisper. "And my deceased father worked with your father as Guardians."

Shock struck Marisa, and she nearly dropped the gun. Thrusting out mental feelers, she found a small fissure in his mind. Sympathy carried the truth of his words. Leveling her tiring arm, she tromped down her revulsion and hatred to concentrate.

"Yes, I know everything about your family. *Everything.* Probably more than you, if the stories passed on are true. We'll compare notes. I'll leave it up to you to believe them. Know this though, your entire mother's family, including Celeste, wanted to escape the Guild. Your maternal grandfather's greatest wish was to establish a new order separate from the shysters sitting on the top rungs of Guild management. Your grandfather first called for the Cabal's establishment once he realized the Guild refused to change for the better. Unfortunately, he died during the Cabal's inception before his dream reached fruition. With his own agenda to rule the Cabal his way, your father talked your mother into staying in the Guild, convinced her that her father's ideas were pipe dreams."

Her father had irreparably broken her mother,

leaving her vulnerable. He'd destroyed Marisa's family, everything she cared about. How could she ever think about a normal life with Ric, another Guild Guardian? Or believe he could ignore her telepathic abilities and what it cost her, and might cost them. She may as well kiss the heavenly slice of Ric McAllister pie goodbye.

A monster awoke and unfurled its wings in the pit of her stomach, and Marisa's world imploded. Her arms dragged down, her knees watered. Perspiration popped over her breasts and up to her hairline as her blood sugar levels nosedived. Stars flickered in her eyes, and she wilted onto the cool floor tiles.

CHAPTER TWENTY-NINE

Groggy, Ric forced his leaden eyes open. Pain lanced his back, and he lay curled up on a firm surface in pitch black. He didn't remember cement under the camphor tree. Hell, he hardly remembered falling from the dumb tree, but his aching body proved it.

The final wisps of a clairvoyant nightmare slipped away, leaving him steamrolled. He strained to recall the details until sick fragments filtered back.

Marisa and Delaney were about to do the nasty in a beach cabana. Delaney had offered her the choice and it seemed like she'd chosen the dark side. Had he lost her to that asshole's manipulations so easily? Ric's muddled mind refused to surrender to clarity. The absolute darkness surrounding him didn't help matters.

Grumbling blue curses, he sat up and whacked his head on steel. "What the hell?" He banged the surface above him, realized he lay in the trunk of a parked car, not beneath the tree on Delaney's grounds. *Shitballs.* Their plan had definitely taken a turn for the worse.

The last thing Ric remembered, Marisa lost herself in the VR game with Delaney and his hard-on. She'd booted Ric into her black depths, and he watched the game unfold, until Delaney noticed his shadow in the landscape and tore after his mystical persona. Then his head ignited real time, and he felt himself airborne as he toppled from the tree. He hit the ground in a jarring heap and blacked out.

"Freak-ass stuff." How had Delaney noticed him? Was his VR game so technologically advanced, it bonded to Marisa and transmitted her images, thoughts, and emotions to Delaney. *Did my mental connection to Marisa screw them both?*

"It's the stupid game and weird repetitive song playing in a triggered sequence." Fortunately, the hypnotic harp music had no impact on him. He'd never heard of an electronic form of mesmerism all tied up with the tones on her phone, the text messages, and the VR game.

How else did Delaney see me in the VR scene? The man and his minions were freaking brilliant. If the Cabal hid this technology in their back pocket, they'd doom the Guild, maybe even the world if it worked on other psychics or even ordinary people.

"Like your telepathic brother Jake." Ric's intestines tied into knots. He patted down the trunk, searching for the child safety catch. What happened to Liam, his backup? Ric may be the only coherent one to rescue all of them from their idiotic plan.

Other than a grease-reeking rag, Ric found nothing to aid his escape. Hopeful, he patted his pockets for his knife and found it missing, as well as his phone and wallet. They'd even stolen the microscopic listening device from his ear. He picked at the trunk lock, traced his fingers along the seams to no avail. He tried to kick out the trunk lid, but its strength resembled steel from older cars.

Heaving out a breath, he froze and listened for telltale sounds from outside his coffin. Nothing, as if he lay in a deep, dark hole in a cemetery.

"Let me out!" he shouted.

Silence responded.

"Hello! Anyone out there?"

More silence.

"Son of a bitch." He scratched his jaw. *"Yo, Jakeman, you listening to me?"* He issued the mental question, hoping Delaney's people hadn't moved him too far from Jake's telepathy range.

Again, resounding silence served to whip up his dread. Not like he read minds, he hoped for a sign of sorts, any inkling. *"Jake? Marisa? Anyone?"* Only Jake and Marisa possessed telepathy, and Marisa's abilities were shot.

"Wait a hot minute?" A memory overwhelmed him. Marisa's mind had exploded in the VR, tossing him into oblivion. "Huh. Did she break her mental barriers?" Too many questions bombarded him. Confidence overrode the lot. Marisa's telepathy had definitely made a roaring comeback. She just might find a way out of this mess if she broke past Delaney's mesmerism. The idea was sketchy at best, but served to keep him from going cuckoo.

"Delaney must've dug his hooks into her before she came to San Jose, according to the tiny blackouts she experienced in San Diego." The conk on her head and losing her telepathy must've made her more susceptible. The text messages. Strike one. Strike two. Definitely Delaney stood behind it all. Behind what, though? The Cabal? Revenge against her family?

"Anyone, if you're listening, I'm stuck in the trunk of a car. No light, no sound, no unusual smells, nothing." He mentally repeated the mantra a few times. *"Jake, go after Marisa. She's a sitting duck in Delaney's headlights."*

Ric kicked the trunk lock again, but his prone position limited his stretch. "Damn it." On his fifth kick, a clawed dagger pierced his skull. "Marisa?" The familiar dark field smothered his light. The images hit him strong and violent, spreading fear and jealousy throughout his body.

Kenny held a glass of orange juice to her mouth. "Are you okay? You passed out. When was the last time you ate?"

Marisa drank half the juice. "I skipped lunch. Not such a great idea, huh?"

"I'm glad you're okay now."

"Where am I?" She struggled to sit.

"In my bed."

A strange sense of determination emanated off her until a melancholy capitulation conquered it. Frowning, she rubbed and probed a spot on her upper left arm.

The lilting harp music drove her rampant emotions into a corner. Three high, two low, another single high and low notes triggered a further round of submission. She glanced at Kenny's handsome face. How did I ever doubt him and his ways? *He embodied the perfect life partner, what she'd always wanted. Celeste had thrown him to the dogs. She refused to follow in her sister's footsteps. Weakness held no place in her world.*

"In your bed, exactly where we belong." She walked her fingers up his arm. "I'm sorry about earlier, the gun, the questions. I needed to know what happened between you and Celeste. The Guild confuses me. I just don't know how to get out without incurring their distrust. With my position on the legal team, they'd interpret it as an act of betrayal and possibly espionage."

"Stay with me and I'll forgive you everything." Kenny kissed her cheek, his hands sliding up her arms. He held her in place as he kissed her eyelids, her forehead, before his lips explored her neck.

Her head tipped back, and the erotic sensations his mouth incited on her heated flesh roused a trickle of heat between her legs. His fingers slipped beneath her dress and up her bare thigh, triggering butterflies to party in her lower torso. His fingers slowed their dance, and his mouth found hers again. She clapped her hand on his, forcing him to move on her flesh again. "Don't stop."

He held his hand steady. "As enticing as your invitation sounds, you need to eat first. Then we have a task to accomplish tonight. I want to see where your loyalties truly lie. Are you up for it?"

Marisa floundered, unsure which direction to take in the fork in her mind's road. Part of her understood something was wrong. The other part knew following Kenny's lead was the true way forward. It afforded her every opportunity to set things right in her world, from the moment her Guardian father abandoned his family, to the first moment Marisa decided to leave the Guild to escape all things psychic. Yet, she'd never contemplated joining the Cabal, nor considered the pros of doing so. They could help her exact revenge upon the Guardians who'd sided with the father she'd never really known.

"What are you thinking?" Kenny slipped his hand off her leg and weaved his long, slender fingers in hers. He hauled her into his arms and clicked the small remote pinned to his shirt pocket. "Listen to the music. Let it guide your thoughts."

The music volume increased, and she mentally followed the notes and strums to the three guiding tones, then the new four notes solidifying her allegiance to Kenny.

"What you said earlier about my father. Did the Cabal or Guild kill him? Who did he betray?" She pressed her palm over his heart, feeling the steady rhythm echo up her arm.

"He betrayed your mother and grandfather. Randall convinced your mother the Guild was the only way. He didn't want her in the Cabal."

"She wasn't convinced." Marisa rested her cheek on his dove-gray dress shirt. "Many times throughout my childhood, she wanted to leave the Guild."

"She never mentioned the Cabal, right?"

"Right. She just wanted out. Done with it all."

He sifted her long tousled hair. "Because Randall convinced her to remain in the Guild, told her your grandfather's dreams and goals were idiocy. The Guild was the preeminent organization to sanctify and organize psychics. He never let on that he wanted all the power himself. Randall decided being a Guardian wasn't enough, the rules too strict on what psychics can do within the Guild and the law's boundaries. He wanted to establish the Cabal and lead it, and he wanted her in the Guild to play his stooge. Randall caused your grandfather's accident, took all his plans and allegiances, and established the Cabal his way."

Marisa gasped, kicked back her head to the truth in Kenny's eyes. "How do you know all this?"

"Shocked? We've documented the Cabal's progression and membership from day one."

"But it's skewed. You're killing off Guild psychics."

"Only the ones who threaten our ways."

"It's not what the Guild believes." The three and four notes kept triggering Marisa to battle against an alien hovering in her darkest recesses.

"What does the Guild believe?"

"That you kill any psychic who refuses to join your ranks."

"Usually only Guild members."

Another tiny gasp chased Marisa's first one. "You admit it."

"It's certainly not a secret, no different than the Guild destroying our members. The Guild's been subtly trying to dismantle us from day one. You just don't hear about it.

Work with me, Marisa. Together, we can merge the Cabal and Guild in harmony. We're all on the same page. It's what your grandfather and your mother both wanted. Not the way your father—and my father to some extent—went about it. Not the way we are now. You and I can change both groups for the better. We just need to cull certain Guild members who don't fit the new regime. We need new blood." He reached around his back and placed a thick, clothbound journal in front of her. *"This belonged to your grandfather. It's loaded with information on psychic families around the world. There are thousands upon thousands of psychics we can tap to form our new ranks."*

She tentatively touched her fingers to the scarred cloth cover of the journal. A glimpse into it forced memory snippets to surface. "I got this out of a safety deposit box for you."

"Yes. Is that all you remember?" Gauging her, he nodded slowly.

"A man tried to take it from me in the parking lot."

"Correct. One of my men guarding you. He went rogue. I've dealt with him."

Marisa swallowed hard. "Does that happen often?"

"No. He got greedy. It was his third strike."

A long beat of silence changed the conversation's focus.

Marisa wrapped her mind around the concept of a stronger Guild packed with an untapped population, and had a tough time deciphering his words. "The Cabal founders and original members aren't psychic. You're not."

"Are you so sure?"

"What are you hiding from me?" She rose up and kissed him until he chuckled against her mouth.

"As much as I want this, we need to go or we'll both be booted out of the Cabal."

She pouted. "You're assuming I'm in."

"As far as I'm concerned—and I hold significant

weight—you are *in.*"

"*You didn't answer my question. What are you hiding from me?*"

He deposited a chaste kiss on her forehead. "*I'm not psychic. That's why you and I fit so well together. There's a need for expertise from non-psychics, but most Cabal members are psychic now.*"

"*Former Guild members?*"

"*And others who held no allegiance to either group.*"

"*Then why are you a Cabal member?*"

"*Power, money, fame, and fortune. It's all there for a technologist like me.*"

She emitted a stilted laugh. "*An offer you couldn't refuse?*"

"*Exactly.*" *He took her hand.* "*Let's go. The sooner we return, the sooner we jumpstart our new life together.*"

She edged closer, mashing her breasts against his chest. "*I'm all yours now.*"

"*But will you be all mine later?*"

Without a second's hesitation, she replied, "*In any way you want me.*"

"*I* will *have you in all ways.*"

Electricity slashed Ric's mind, jolted him awake. He groaned, not so much from the excruciating pain, but from the knowledge he'd learned, and from the hypnotic spell imprisoning Marisa. It was no longer easy to tell when they were connected or if he was having a clairvoyant vision. The sensations eerily merged into one big clusterfuck.

Again, he tried to sit up and bashed his head against the trunk lid. "Son of a steel bitch!" He probed the growing lump near the one he'd earned earlier. "That went over like a lead brick." The darkness didn't reply.

His heart sank into a pond of acid. His feelings for Marisa were fiercer than ever. Was he strong enough to protect her mind as a Guardian or as her lover or even husband? *Husband?* They hadn't even gone on a first date, and he already had them married. *Ten pounds of stupid.*

After all was said and done, would the real Marisa even be intact? Or had the darkness always been there, ready for the right man to take it for a spin. Obviously, Ric wasn't the right man to spread his light within her inky landscape. Failure strolled the line of his options. Maybe Marisa had Cabal written all over her from birth.

No. Hell no. I refuse to believe it. Delaney can't have her. I'll be damned if I let him get his slimy paws on her in any way.

"I need to stop this one way or another." Ric kicked the trunk lock, shouting to the ether.

A crowbar cracking the outside of the trunk lid split another excruciating crack in his skull.

CHAPTER THIRTY

Both dressed in black head to toe, Marisa and Kenny sat in a nondescript black sedan outside the Guild compound. Darkness hid them in undulating shadows from the dim landscape lights reflecting off the trees. A wispy cloud cover obscured the stars. The moon shone on another part of the world, and it wouldn't bear witness to their activities. Kenny handed her a tiny earpiece and watched intensely as she inserted it in her left ear. He gently combed locks of her hair over her ear, his fingers skimming her cheek. Tromping down a flinch, Marisa pressed her face against his fingers, giving him what he wanted, fighting the unreasonable doubts plaguing her. *Why did everything about this night feel so wrong? Why does being with Kenny feel both right and wrong?*

"What's this for?"

"For you to receive my guidance and words of encouragement."

She rubbed her fingers on her leggings. "Aren't you going with me?"

"Better I remain here, less suspicious. They won't think it unusual for your presence since you have entry credentials."

"I don't have my keycard."

"You know what to do." He stuck her cell into her

hand.

In a moment of lucidity, she asked, "Did you start the fire at the other house? Why them?"

"She failed the final test. She knew too much."

She pocketed the phone. "Is that what's going on here?" Marisa bit her bottom lip, chomping on her pesky doubts.

"Don't worry about the reasons."

The lulling music drowned out their conversation. Kenny kissed her, and the scent of brandy on his tongue drove off her residual confusion. With a mega dose of confidence, she exited the car and slung on her backpack.

The music became one with the night, a chorus to a cricket to her left, an aria shooing away a rodent in the rustling brush to her right. She carefully darted through the dark woods until she approached the clearing at the rear parking lot. In full sight of outdoor cameras, she approached the three boulders near the back gate. Dim lights deposited golden pools on her black sneakers. No matter, she had every right to be there.

Memories from the other night flitted through her mind. Leaning her hip against the lowest boulder, she retrieved her lipstick from her pocket and reapplied it, lost her balance and rolled the tube in the crevice between the three landscape rocks. "Oh, shoot. Not good," she said loud enough to wake the dead. She shone her phone's flashlight app down into the crevice and discovered Ric's badge lodged where she'd dropped it the other night. "Bingo," she murmured, following *his* commands.

Her receptiveness to him now ruled her mind and body. However, her soul remained in the gray, and she battled it tooth and nail to choose a side. The vulnerability made sense when nothing else in her life had. It obeyed the beautiful music hypnotizing her into a Zen-like vessel. The decision she'd made to leave the

Guild after fighting her internal struggles for years felt so right. Kenny Delaney waited for her at the end of her rainbow, like a pot of gold, luck, and love. With the Cabal. The place she finally figured out had been calling to every cell of her being her entire life. Why had it taken twenty-eight years? Why had her mother never encouraged her to travel where her heart led her? Damn her father for turning the Cabal into an evil, corrupt organization. Now she had the ability to right his wrongs.

Niggling doubts crisscrossed her back in slimy ooze. Why did her mother hide family history from her? Shame? Escape from the memories or the troubles of her mind? No matter. She refused to let her qualms deter her from her orders, or else she'd disappoint Kenny and endanger her loyalties.

A nippy breeze feathered over her, carrying the scent of cleansing pine, wafting charcoal-dark clouds over the mansion. Approaching the gate, Marisa secured the band on her ponytail.

The midnight darkness surrounded her. Although she knew exactly what to do, she worried about taking her first step and adding it to her growing hoard of misdeeds. They played havoc with her heart, even as an alien element of excitement rolled off her. Stumbling to a standstill on the patio, she realized nothing about her belonged to her, not her thoughts, not her actions, not her at all. *What am I doing?* Perspiration broke out on the back of her neck and nausea bloomed.

The relaxing music elevated in her ear, dissolved her momentary weakness. The autumn winds of change dried the perspiration on her neck and booted her bafflement out. She used Ric's keycard and slipped through the back door of the dead-silent house. In quiet sneakers, she tiptoed down the hallway, up the staircase, and to the back corner room. The closed door to the suite beckoned, and she slipped inside the room.

Two bodies lay on the king-sized bed, indistinguishable lumps dead to the world asleep beneath the covers. Going about her tasks, she listened to the music, kept her ear tuned to pending commands, refused to let her doubts and thoughts interfere, refused to let the alien part of her berate her actions.

She struck the first flame, set it to a stream of accelerant near the door, and watched it catch. A tiny spark at first, growing into a devouring amber flash. The amber and crimson flames fed on the liquid fuel and danced up a foot. The fire spread across the hardwood floor and licked the rug at the foot of the bed. Unaware, the couple slumbered on. She lit another stream of lighter fluid on the other side of the door, ensuring the fire slithered to the window. Death became the only escape, as well as her ultimate test and ticket to the life she craved.

Finalizing her tasks, she stuffed her tools into her backpack and froze, struck by another deceptive doubt. *Stop it! Failure isn't an option. There's no strike three.* She refused to confront the consequences of failure. She fought her qualms, stomped them into the dusty crevices of her brain. Blocking her mind from the impending screams of torture, she fled the room down the dark hallway, barely wondering why there were no guards roaming about.

All clear, she trotted out of the house the way she'd entered. A light spritz of rain wet her skin, drowned the seed of triumph blossoming inside her. Would the rain ruin her if the couple lived? Failure meant death. Maybe she deserved death.

Death would kill her turmoil and the insidious voices.

The foothold of fear loosened as she approached the car waiting at the end of the greenbelt behind the house. The earpiece slipped halfway out, its tiny weight now tangible, its presence epically confusing. She pulled it all the way out and tossed it into the woods. Plumes of air ballooned from her mouth, the house's heat expelling from her body. Bands imprisoning her mind loosened another notch as she climbed into the passenger seat. Absent the constant music winding through her nerve receptors, another band loosened.

"Go." She glanced over her shoulder. The lack of flames shooting toward the night sky ballooned her anxiety. *Did someone put out the fire? Did they escape?* The battle of good versus evil whipped inside her gut, and she didn't know what side she sat on.

Why? What did I do? Marisa Meadows slowly slipped back into the body impersonating her alter ego. The imposter had one foot out the door. Without the music confusing her, Marisa regained a bit of her sensibilities even as the night's events snowed her. She choked down bile, gripped the door handle, ready to flee. *Holy hell on high. What did Delaney force me to do?* She kneaded her turbulent forehead, hoping to make sense of right versus wrong. Cabal versus Guild.

"We'll go when I say," Kenny said, his features cloudy. "You hit the right room?"

The skin on her back stung with apprehension. Still not sure who she was, she gave the only answer she knew. "Yes. I know where her suite is." She fisted her hand, her nails digging into her palms. Still no flames. No sirens, no lights. Nothing.

"Were they there as expected?"

Her mind tangled. Were *who* where?

"Marisa?"

An electrical arc blasted her mind, and she cried out at the loss of something vital and relevant to everything within her, her morals, her light, and her soul.

Kenny shoved her hair behind her ear. "Where's your

earpiece?"

Earpiece? She cringed inward, fighting the pain consuming her, searching for clarity, for the one who kept her sane. Her lodestone. Confused, she didn't recognize anything about Kenny except his façade of evil. Nothing about him offered any indication he anchored her to reality. She hunted for a clue to no avail. "I must have lost it in the woods."

Kenny pressed a button on the tiny remote and her cell rang. The familiar notes and sequence tricked her, connected her to him. She relaxed. Pain subsiding, her pulse normalized. The vulnerable side in her head won the battle against the dominant one. The black oozed toward the gray. She belonged to Kenny and his darkness. Before she could get the phone out of her pocket, it quieted.

The house behind them remained dark; no sirens chased the flames. The silence in and outside the vehicle jitterbugged down her spine as if tangible. Flames had surrounded the bodies in the bed. She'd made sure of it before securing the door. What had gone wrong? The scene was exactly as she'd foreseen several times before. *Wait! What? When did I foresee my actions?* She wasn't clairvoyant. *God, what is wrong with me?*

Wanting to scrape out her brain, she booted her bewilderment to the wayside and said, "Everything went according to plan. They told me they'd be there tonight and they were. Lily Falbrooke and Jake McAllister will die tonight. Their deaths will start the Guild's implosion. They won't know who to trust any longer." The words sounded strange, and she couldn't reconcile them with fact or fiction. She'd followed her instructions to the T. Anything beyond left a gaping hole in her head and her dead heart. The music took her for a spin into the new world of her making, and she went in kicking and screaming for the light.

CHAPTER THIRTY-ONE

The trunk lid creaked. The moment it opened wide, Ric scrambled out, fists ready to fly, and staggered against the car as his cramped legs betrayed him.

"Whoa, bro, don't kill yourself." Liam's gruffness was happiness to his ears.

"It's about time." He rounded on his brother. "What took you so long?" Scattered and dusty machine parts and old vehicles appeared abandoned in the musty warehouse. Grime coated the windows high up on the steel walls. "What happened? Where are we?"

"One question at a time." Liam steadied Ric, handed him water and two pain relievers, standard fare after a clairvoyant event. His brothers knew him too well.

Ric downed the tablets and drank the entire bottle of water. "Thanks." He tossed the empty bottle in a rusted truck bed.

"Delaney's men found you conked out under the tree."

"Yeah, got lost in Marisa's head again. Kicked me into oblivion."

Liam knocked his fist into the old beater car's rear fender. "She's bad for you. This can't happen again. There's no telling if you'll ever roll out of her head, sane or at all. You got lucky again."

"Too late. I've already fallen for her." Teaming

endorphins went to work, and he stretched out his legs, began a gimpy gait toward the warehouse door. "Let's hit it. She's in trouble."

Inside the warehouse door, two of Delaney's men lay crumpled on the dusty, grease-stained cement, wrists and ankles duct taped. Tape held wadded rags in their mouths, noses carefully left uncovered.

Liam padlocked the door from the dark outside, a faint streetlight granting a slant of illumination on the steel siding. "Good thing we're all wearing trackers."

"Then what took so long?" He only half kidded.

"Screw you." Liam fake punched Ric's upper arm. "Like I could waltz up here and ask them to let me in? Had to strike at the right time."

Ric climbed into Liam's car, waited for his brother to get rolling. He recognized the light industrial-retail area near the base of the west San Jose foothills. "At least we're not far."

"She's not at Delaney's," Liam said tentatively as if waiting for an imminent explosion.

"She set the compound on fire?" Ric seethed inside. How was he supposed to compete with Delaney and his forced coercion of Marisa? Did free will or freedom exist in her any longer? "Damn it. This plan was bad news from the get go."

"At least you saw enough from your foresight to recognize *she* planned to set the compound on fire."

"To kill Jake and Lily. I've never experienced a prophecy go so backassward. I've always identified the people to varying degrees. Eventually." Hammers flailed in his head, and he wondered if Delaney's men knocked him around before trussing him up.

"You identified her well enough."

The visions after the first house fire finally made sense. He'd never experienced a vision of a past event, which led him to believe the event had yet to occur. The house fire with the other two people was a bizarre coincidence, or a well-planned ruse by the Cabal. "What else did Jake catch off audio?"

"We still have no proof Delaney's working for the Cabal or if he targeted her for personal reasons. She removed her watch. Jake didn't realize it until too late. I was already on your trail."

"Which left her vulnerable." Ric drummed his fingers on the dash. "There's no telling what he's done to her."

"Bro, she set the compound on fire. As far as she knows, if she's still under Delaney's control, she *killed* Jake and Lily." He did air quotes. "Are you getting it? It's why we didn't tell her we knew what *she* was planning. Her mind's shot. We may have lost her to Delaney, the Cabal, who knows? She's too volatile, too vulnerable."

A distress so intense burned through Ric, it consumed him, almost demolished the darkness Marisa's mind left behind. And he needed that darkness to feel his connection to her. He counted to ten, forced his insides to quit poking him. Didn't matter if she'd turned all dark and evil, he'd find a way to bring her back. To him. No other choice existed. He was falling in love with her, knew it the moment they first meshed their minds.

"It is the Cabal." Ric explained the gist of his last vision to his brother, leaving out the parts where Marisa touched Delaney and let Delaney touch her. He may have truly lost her to that psycho Cabal BS and Mr. Perfect Delaney.

"A Cabal and Guild merge?" Liam's jaw dropped. "No way it'll ever happen."

"If the Cabal's screwing with psychic abilities, and if they get Marisa on their side, there's no telling how far they'll advance. Look at how many people they've already recruited. She's one of the strongest telepaths. If they can overpower her, how easy will it be for them to control others? How many more are under this virtual reality spell? The Guild's suffering while the Cabal's dominating. Whether we like it or not, a merge is already happening."

Liam sped his car toward the highway, passing the main street to the Guild compound.

"Where are you going?"

Liam grinned and tossed his phone to Ric. "I planted multiple trackers on both her car and Delaney's. They're in his car traveling west on Highway 17."

"Toward the coast?" Ric watched the two red dots moving along the blue twisty line of highway.

"Toward the ocean, bro. The *ocean*."

The significance hit Ric. Telepaths either hated or loved being on the beach. The booming waves gutted their voices. It either soothed them or left them frazzled and incapable of using their psychic gifts. The thundering surf would kill any connection he and Marisa shared.

"Why not just take her to Cabal headquarters? What's he hoping to gain by wasting time at the beach?"

"Maybe the Cabal headquarters *are* along the coast. Maybe they don't have headquarters and are scattered around the world." The highway began to climb, the thick woods on either side of the road another shroud of darkness encapsulating his world. Liam cut in and out of traffic to drive around the slowpokes.

"Or he's leading us there."

"Don't think so. He found one of my three trackers and shit-canned it."

"Where are Jake and Lily?" Ric asked, clearing the dregs of his incapacitation from his mind.

"Safe at the compound. A team hid in Lily's closet to douse the fire after Marisa barred the door. Everyone's on high alert. The compound's overflowing with Guardians. Delaney's house is on expanded watch."

"Yet, we're heading into the viper's nest alone." Ric's confidence waned with the magnitude of impending doom. If Marisa played her cards right or Delaney maintained his control over her, she'd remain safe with him. If she faltered or he saw through her ruse... *No, no, don't go there.*

"If we send too many after him, it may jeopardize Marisa. There's a Guardian unit on standby in Santa Cruz if we need backup."

"We don't know where he's taking her." Ric followed the two blips on the screen. "Should've rescued her after we lost audio." Their plan had gone to the birds of hell after he fell out of the freaking tree.

"By the time Jake lost audio, you'd already been trussed up like a pig and hauled away. You're first priority."

"No," Ric said adamantly. "Marisa's first priority. Number one Guardian rule."

"You know what I mean. This wasn't a sanctioned Guild takedown. We're working under the radar. If the Guild had gotten wind of this beforehand, she'd probably be dead, no longer any use to Delaney or the Cabal with too much Guild interference. This is exactly where we want her. Alone with Delaney. No Cabal, no Guild to screw us up or jeopardize more of our members."

"I doubt Delaney plans to endanger the Cabal in open warfare and expose them. They work on stealth."

"Exactly how we retaliate. Stealth mode. Guardian rule number what-the-hell-ever."

The red blips on the GPS turned off Highway 17. "Take the 1 north exit."

In thick, tense silence, they drove to the more secluded 4 Mile Beach north of the Santa Cruz city limits. A few cars were still parked in the lot, and the sign indicated the beach closed at sunset. How often did rangers patrol? Why was Delaney risking exposure?

The harbor lighthouse emerged in the distance, its beacon a swath of light cutting across the darkening sea. The sun had set, leaving a gray-purple edge to the ends of the world on the Pacific's watery surface. A tall rock formation vaulted out of the water near the beach like a silent, dark beacon.

"What's he up to?" Ric asked, not expecting an answer. The waves booming on shore clouded his concentration.

Liam parked between two SUVs opposite Delaney's late-model BMW. "Beats me."

Ric checked Liam's spare gun, stuck it in the back of his waistband. "Follow my lead. Don't do anything to jeopardize Marisa."

Before Liam opened the door, he asked, "Bro, are you okay?"

"It doesn't matter. She's all that matters."

Liam clicked open the door and hopped out. "If your head's screwed up or you get lost in her, it's gonna matter. I'm not taking the hit from Jake or the Guild if you don't walk from this unscathed. Are. You. Okay?"

"I'm fine. I'm not asking you to." Ric joined his brother at the front bumper, both hidden between the two hulking SUVs. A temperate wind blew in off the water, not cool enough to assuage Ric's fiery fear. "Free will's working here." He motioned Liam forward, and side by side, they jogged down the sandy path leading to the beach. The tang of salt and brine cleansed his palette of emotions, fueled his nerves, and sparked a surge of endorphins in his blood.

CHAPTER THIRTY-TWO

The song of the waves rushing in and rolling out quieted Ric's mind. He visited the beach often and never truly noticed how it comforted him, and he didn't even possess telepathy. Maybe he imagined the weightless and freeing sensation and the tug into Marisa's darkness he craved.

"What's wrong?" Liam set a heavy hand on Ric's arm, stopping him.

"The waves quiet my head."

"Quiet what?"

"Everything."

"Are you having a clairvoyant vision?"

"No."

"You're not telepathic."

"No shit, Sherlock. I think I've reconnected to Marisa here." Ric followed the larger and small sets of bare footsteps over the damp sand he believed belonged to Delaney and Marisa.

Liam clenched Ric's arm, jerking him to a stop. "Then we're calling in support before we confront them. It's too risky for you, too risky for her."

"So you care about her now?"

"I never said I didn't. I care about what makes you happy. If it's Marisa, then I'm happy for you, happy for her. She's a cool chick when she's not trying to murder you."

"We don't have time. It's fine. Something broke in her earlier tonight, which booted me out. I think she got her telepathy back."

"Doesn't matter. You connected before she lost her mind."

"I remained in control those times. When she lost her telepathy, I lost myself in her, lost my control." The ocean tempers the link.

"Why risk yourself?" Liam dug his shoe in the sand. "You're as stubborn as Jake. I can't believe I'm the only voice of reason among the three Musketeers."

"No. You're just shell-shocked and chickenshit," Ric kidded, tried to set his brother at ease. "Let's hit it. Time's not spinning backward."

"I have a right to my chickenshitness. I'm done risking my life for manipulators and frauds."

"So I'm a manipulator and a fraud now?" The sea breeze carried Ric's chuckle toward the myriad lights of Santa Cruz popping on across the bay. Any other night, he'd appreciate the multihued glow of lights brightening the Boardwalk off in the distance.

They approached a low, rocky outcropping. The wind wafted Marisa's elated, lilting voice to Ric.

Ric and Liam hid behind the rocks and peered through the crevices at a secluded cove bordered by rock formations creating a windbreak on three sides. Tiki torches fenced the small semi-circle around a blazing fire. Amber and crimson flames danced toward the sky, twining and twisting around one another like a mating ritual. *Not a good sign.* Candles and flowers decorating a picnic table surrounded baskets of food and champagne on ice. Classical music hovered in the air until the wind stole it away. Ric recognized Chopin, instinctively knew it wasn't geared to hypnotize Marisa, but to set the romantic, celebratory ambiance. Delaney and Marisa danced in the sand, laughing and talking, stealing an occasional kiss from one another, almost a recreation of his VR game.

Lead balls plummeted in Ric's gut, and his heart nearly imploded inside the coffin remaking his ribcage. He took one step forward before Liam locked his arms around him, forcing him back behind the rocks.

"What's your plan?" Liam blasted him. "We wait. I've called for backup."

Backup might work, but he refused to wait and jeopardize losing more of Marisa. His pride knew when not to get himself killed. Not at Marisa's expense, though. "I'm gonna waltz in there and take back what's mine." The heat of Ric's anger vibrated up the length of his spine, thumbing its nose at the mist-laden wind.

"She doesn't appear like she's yours." Liam jerked on Ric's wrists. "She's under his spell, or in league with him and the Cabal. We can't risk crashing their little tea party or her screwing with you if the ocean hasn't killed her telepathy. If he's truly Cabal, then we're probably already being watched."

"Then where are his minions?" Ric wrenched out of Liam's hands. "I say we go in guns blazing, ask questions later."

"You'll kill her for sure then, dumbass." Liam flicked his finger at Ric's ear. "Think, man. You're better than this. You didn't get this far in the Guild thinking with your stupidass heart or your dick."

Ric caved in on himself and a strong gust of moist autumn wind knocked sense into him. He raised his face to a span of stars in a pocket of the overcast sky as somber as his mood. "Because I've never cared about anyone like I do Marisa."

"All the more reason to go slow and careful."

Ric held up a capitulating palm. "I'll join their little party on my own, no guns, no antagonism. But I'm not waiting for backup." He touched his gun in his waistband, his trusty backup if his mouth failed to convince Marisa to leave Delaney.

Just as he straightened his jacket, both Liam and Ric's phones vibrated. He read the text from Jake, saw the backup photo. *"Marisa's mother's safe in Guardian hands."* The photos depicted a beautiful older version of Marisa surrounded by four Guardians. Two Cabal cavemen dressed as orderlies were hog-tied to chairs.

Liam heaved out a long, low sigh of defeat. "I've got your back. Don't make any sudden moves to trigger him."

"Don't fret. Once Marisa sees me, she'll regain her senses, or tip her hand if she's playing him."

"Regardless, keep your guard up. She's not all she seems. I'll text you when backup arrives."

With one desperate thought, Ric hiked around the boulders separating him from the woman he was in freefall for. And the asshole who'd taken what belonged to him. A few long seconds elapsed before Delaney and Marisa spied Ric entering the cove. Thick clouds rolled in and smothered the budding starlight, a perfect backdrop for his takedown.

The heavenly sight of Marisa nearly undid him. Her hair framed her ethereal face, a vibrant and beautiful contrast he'd never tire of. The connection existing between them snapped, not even a fine thread remained behind. Knowing how effective the ocean was in blocking telepathy, he still stretched his mind to recover the link. *No dice. Nothing but a pounding arc of pain.*

"Marisa? Do you recognize me? Are you still there?" He'd never hear her answer since he didn't possess telepathy, but he wanted her to know who he was. *"Remember me telling you I was falling in love with you? I*

was wrong. I have fallen *in love with you. I know it's a crazy kind of insta-love. But it's true. I feel the rightness of us in my gut."*

Delaney and Marisa stopped dancing, and Delaney snaked his arm possessively around her waist. She entwined her arms around his torso as if she belonged to him and wanted Ric to know.

Hell to the no. He tried not to let her actions bother him, didn't need the distraction, but *dayam.* He wanted her arms holding him. And he hated the loathing and disgust painting her face as she pinned her glower on him.

"Are you stalking me, McAllister?" she asked with no small amount of animosity. "What do you want?"

"McAllister." Delaney nodded in greeting. "I heard you'd escaped your confinement. Didn't think you'd find us, though. Kudos on your ingenuity."

"Well, I do own a securities company. I'm not without my means."

"I did factor in that knowledge and scanned my car for GPS." He kissed Marisa's temple. "Guess you have a GPS implanted on Marisa."

"You guessed wrong." Ric flicked his hand as if flicking away a pesky fly. *Scan my ass.* He found one rinky-dink bug, but not the high-tech ones impenetrable to low-grade scanners. "Let's dispense with the BS."

"He dared not plant a tracker on me without my knowledge," Marisa replied. "Besides, I already ditched the watch with the listening device."

"Touché." Delaney grinned. "What's it going to be, McAllister?"

Over the thundering crash of waves on the sand, a scuffle mounted behind the rocks, and angst for his brother pummeled his confidence.

"Marisa, you're coming with me."

"The hell I am."

"You'll never get away with this, Delaney." Ric exhibited a cool detachment, contradicting his skittish concern. "You may have her brainwashed now, but it'll never last. Remember strike one, strike two?" Stifling his need to gloat, he tipped his head to the side.

"She won't hit strike three. She passed her final test here at the beach. Her transformation is complete." Delaney waved an arm wide to encompass the endless ocean. "*Pacific.*" He pronounced the keyword distinctively. "You hear the music over the ocean, darling?"

"Sure do. It's always on, a break from the myriad voices." Her smile gloated, her prideful poise killing a bit inside Ric.

"Can you hear Ric's thoughts?" Delaney asked her.

"Not a one. Thankfully." The distaste in her tone took Ric down another notch. "Guild Guardians are so one-dimensional in their thinking. It's tiring."

"You've drugged her," Ric blasted back. "There's no way your little mesmerism stunt is so thorough or permanent."

"Don't be so sure. I have two Ph.Ds in engineering and biological sciences. I know what I'm doing." His egomaniacal grin hit Ric's disgust buttons.

Thin bands of fog rolled in, a fine mist dragging down the night air, wetting his face. The drizzle didn't seem to bother the couple still draped in each other's arms. He hated the scene with all his being. He loathed the fact that Delaney may be right. What did he know about mesmerism, engineering, and computer software games? He had one job to protect her, and he'd failed so miserably, he may as well quit the Protectorate before the Guild stripped him bare.

"We're connected," Ric insinuated, stalling while his brain cells returned to full-time work.

"Whoever heard of a clairvoyant attached to a telepath?" Delaney chuckled. "Even if you were, you're not any longer." He grinned his evil Frankenstein grin.

"You saw me in your VR landscape, right?" Ric tried to trip up Delaney.

"Didn't that prove the effectiveness of my methods?"

"How many people you playing this way?"

"I'm sure you'd love to know."

"What will the Cabal do without you?" Ric taunted.

Delaney clucked his tongue. "Who said I'm going anywhere? Who said I was part of, what did you call it, the Cabal?"

"Don't play me, man. I told you we're connected."

Marisa finally dropped a crumb into the conversation. "We're no more linked than you and Kenny." She ghosted him, and it shattered him, caused him to falter on the uneven sand.

Ric abhorred the truth of her words, the disgust marring her beautiful face, the golden spark of indignation reflected from the fire in her dark eyes. *Marisa, baby. Remember me. Remember I'm here for you, remember the Guild. I'm your Guardian,*" he mentally shouted. Steadier now, he took two steps closer to them, hoping Marisa saw him better in the circle of tiki torches flickering yellow life toward the roiling clouds. "We were connected until Delany turned your brain into his personal playground. It's all fake, Marisa. He's manipulating you, hypnotizing you, making you believe lies about your life and family."

"Screw off, McAllister. You have no clue." The sparks in her eyes shot fireworks straight into his heart. "We're not connected, never have been, never will. I've always been meant to be with Kenny. You were just a pesky gnat refusing to bug off."

The fireworks detonated. "You'll never belong to

Delaney or the Cabal. You're too strong for them, too smart." Ric's pitch lowered. "First strike, you lost your telepathy. Bet you didn't know it, Delaney. She lost her telepathy when that psycho in the park knocked her into the bench." Delaney sputtered in surprise, quickly recovered. "Second strike, her telepathy returned when she was connected to me in your stupidass VR game earlier tonight."

"Ah, yes, I knew something had gone wrong. No matter. Never will be a strike three."

"Strike three, the fire she set at the Guild compound didn't kill Jake McAllister and Lily Falbrooke." Ric moved another piece on the chessboard and sauntered closer to the pair. They'd separated, no longer in each other's arms. Independence worked for him.

Delaney chortled. "Too bad. However, it wasn't my sole intent to kill them. They'll find themselves in a six-foot hole in the ground soon enough if they don't join the Cabal. Happy now, I've admitted my allegiance to them?"

"The intent was to gauge how far I'd take my loyalty to the Cabal." Marisa spoke slowly to emphasis her hurtful words. "Haven't you figured it out yet, *Guardian?*"

Another bolt of killing lightning struck him. With the disdain and loathing projecting off her, he feared she wasn't faking it. Everything told him she'd succumbed to Delaney's machinations, Cabal to the core. Maybe she'd played him and his family for fools from day one. She'd infiltrated the Guild with a horrible perfection. How many others mirrored her moves? Shit was slamming the fan and splattering all over him.

Liam's doorbell ringtone dinged his phone. Ric blew out a relieved sigh assured his brother survived whatever scuffle had ensued behind the boulders. The text meant the cavalry had arrived.

He took another couple steps closer, withdrew his

gun, and leveled it on the bastard. "Let her go, and I might let you live."

In an equally sudden move, Delaney jerked a gun out of his rear waistband and aimed it at Ric. "If you kill me or take her, you'll destroy her mind. And her mother won't live to see another day. Besides, I'm not keeping her here, am I, darling?"

"I'm free to do as I please." She sneered at Ric again. "And I don't please to do you. Run along, little Guardian. Go back to your man cave." Nothing about her indicated she was faking it.

Behind him, footsteps slogged through the sand. Delaney fired his gun in tandem with another bang of gunfire from behind Ric. The cracks obliterated the booming surf for a long second. A bullet hit Delaney's left thigh. Screaming bloody murder, he sank to the sand on his right side. Marisa lunged for the gun dangling from Delaney's hand. Ric dove across the sand toward her, stopping a few yards away, the smoldering fire pit between them. Smoke blew into his face, and he swatted at it, his eyes stinging.

"Show him how your transformation is complete, Marisa," Delaney said through gritted teeth. "Pacific."

The gun wavered in her hand and indecision etched her face. *"Don't do it, Marisa,"* he thought. *"I, Ric McAllister, want you. I love you. Not Delaney."* He wanted to beat his fist against his chest like a caveman, drop to his knees, and profess his undying love for her. Not like it mattered. Maybe he really was too late. His lunch almost made a reappearance, and he swallowed hard.

Delaney kicked out his right leg to throw Ric off balance. The man lost his strength, and he only tripped Ric up for a split second. He balanced, leveled his gun against Delaney's head.

"Third strike, asshole." Ric gritted his teeth. "I win.

She's mine."

"Don't shoot him, Ric. I got him," Liam ordered. "Take care of Marisa."

As Ric straightened to his full height, another gunshot boomed in his ears. White-hot pain blasted his right shoulder. A scream rent the dark spaces, and his mind fractured. Shouts rang out, sparks burst from the fire pit. Gun dropping from his hand, his knees hit the cold sand. The explosion shot tiny missiles from corner to corner in his skull. Multiple images flickered in his mind, but nothing made sense. "Marisa," he said. "Am I in your head?" Had he spoken aloud?

"You just don't get it, do you, McAllister?" Marisa's broken voice resounded from somewhere. In his head or outside? Or did he dream her.

Delaney scrambled for another gun from a pack behind him. Arm wobbly, he aimed past Ric and fired.

Ric steeled himself for another gunshot. Another two cracks splintered the drizzly night, and Delaney collapsed forward onto the sand. *Hope you choke and die.* Ric tried to laugh through the tempest raging in his mind. A flurry of people descended upon the scene.

Another implosion turned the crumbling pieces of his mind into dust, and he fell forward, a faceplant in the sand. Marisa's crumpled form blasted his every active nerve. She writhed on the sand as if in excruciating pain. *Why won't she look at me? Why can't she hear me? Why can't I hear anything? Had the last gunshot hit her?*

Her eyes opened, bored into him. He attempted to reach for her, but Liam kept trying to flip him over on his back. The cold, stony hatred she aimed at him stopped his heart dead, the final implosion.

A clairvoyant vision struck him in the most ill-timed moment of his life: he walked away from her and everything he'd ever wanted. It decimated the remainder of his heart and soul, and his world spun out from under him.

The boom of a double wave slammed the shore and seized his troubled attention, granting him a second of clarity. It meant he was alive. For how long? The tide ebbed and stole his last thoughts, leaving darkness and emptiness in its foamy wake.

CHAPTER THIRTY-THREE

Twenty-four hours after Ric hit the beach, literally a face slam onto the sand, he found himself lying in the Guild infirmary, same bed as his previous stint. Residual drugs created a euphoric effect, popping in his blood. Numbness captured the stark landscape of his mind, but he recognized a gunshot to his shoulder and his right arm strapped to his chest proved it.

Darkness shrouded the room, and not a whisper of light seeped through the shuttered blinds. Unlike his first rodeo in the infirmary, no one hovered in the room. No Marisa.

Marisa. Had someone shot her? Was she alive? He mentally searched, hoping a knotted thread tethered them, and hit a dead end. The pieces of his mind had knitted back together and liberated him from whatever darkness she'd succumbed too. After the events on the coast, he didn't know how to feel about her. She'd shot him. Marisa Meadows had aimed to kill him. The anxiety snaking in his torn gut found no room for anger. Delaney had destroyed her completely. Thank the lucky stars of hell for her lousy aim.

He pressed the call button on the bed. The infirmary nurse hurried into the room, calling behind her.

"Mr. McAllister, you're awake," the matronly red-haired nurse said as if she'd just won the gold star for keen observation. "How many fingers am I holding up? What's your full name?"

"Four fingers and a thumb, Richard McAllister. I'm fine. My head's screwed on right where it belongs." He thrust the covers off and swung out a leg. Fatigue and pain slayed further efforts to move. "How long have I been under?"

"Twenty-four hours, give or take."

"Where do you think you're going?" Jake stomped into the room and assisted the nurse with the covers. "Please get the doctor."

Ric settled back onto the bed, held his head with his left hand. "Is she alive?"

"She's in a coma."

"Who shot her?" He tried to decipher the showdown on the beach through his fuzzy memories.

"No one shot her. When *she* shot you, she went down. We guessed you two connected at the moment of impact."

"We did." He wasn't ready to talk about it. "Is Liam okay? Lily?"

Jake slid a chair closer. "He's fine. No harm done. Delaney's shot blew wild. Lily's fine."

Relief loosened a knot in his good shoulder, no such luck on the other one. "Who shot Delaney?"

"Local cops, after he attempted to shoot Liam."

He needed to see Marisa like he needed the blood coursing in his veins, needed to understand what happened. "Is she here? Or at the hospital?"

"She's here under guard." Jake scrutinized him, raked him with his death ray glare. "The hospital can't do anything for her."

Her nearness cast a cool calm over his internal fire. "I need to see her." Ric didn't attempt to get up, not if he wanted to set up another shop of horrors inside his body.

Pain management failed against the fire blazing in his right shoulder.

"There's nothing you can do for her."

"Maybe I can help her wake up." Ric's shrug tumbled into a heap of fire-tipped needles dancing down his right arm.

"Then what? She's gone, bro," Jake said gently, tapping his ear, his meaning implicit.

"We don't know for sure. Doc can't diagnose until she wakes up!" Ric scrubbed his scalp with both hands, feeling sand grit in his hair. Man, he needed a shower bad.

Jake held up a pacifying hand. "You're right. Maybe they'll let you visit her tomorrow when you're better. I don't want you near her when she awakens. There's no telling what she'll do to you."

"Delaney messed her up bad."

"The crux of the matter. We don't know how effective or deep his brainwashing went. He said his transformation was complete. We can only assume his hypnotism is semi-permanent without him calling the shots. Who else was working with him? Is she under the mind control of another? We don't know shit."

"Did Liam fill you in?"

"Except what happened to you. Care to share?"

For the longest moment, Ric considered lying by omission, not telling Jake how Marisa vacuumed him into her minefield. This last time, he'd survived the less absolute darkness and avoided the train wreck. The worst damage she'd inflicted on him happened during the period she'd lost her telepathy. Beforehand, the harmless times they'd connected left no lasting effects on each other, except for the memories. Something they'd both have to get used to... that is if he didn't leave her for good as his latest vision portrayed. Or if she really was broken. Or if she really hated him. However, he needed to figure out why she'd turned dark again when he was certain she possessed her telepathy and should've been able to fight Delaney's mesmerism better. He needed the experts to figure it out if he hoped to have a chance with her. *Am I messed up or what?* She'd shot him, hated him, wanted him dead, and he only wanted to hold her, caress her silky skin, breathe in her exotic scent, and never let her go, never let anyone harm her mind, body, and soul again.

After his internal battle, he broke his silence and told his brother everything from the moment she'd towed him into her head while perched on Delaney's tree, until he'd woken up moments ago. "If it ain't broke, don't confuse me," he said.

"Or don't fix it? If you can't convince them, confuse them?" Jake smirked at Ric's thin attempt at humor. "How's the old noggin now?"

"Fine. I didn't even have visions or weird stuff happening while conked out. She shot me, I went down, I woke up. End of story." The image of walking away from her wasn't weird in the true sense, but he couldn't fathom walking away from her for good. *Why would I allow myself to abandon her? Not happening.*

"Tell me about the Cabal," Ric suggested, bored out of his gourd. "Did we at least make inroads?"

"With the intel you just dumped on me, it'll help, if true."

"Only Corinne Meadows, Marisa's mom, can make the call. She's okay, right?"

"Yeah. We detained the Cabal guards posing as orderlies. She's under full Guild protection now." Jake leaned back in his chair and crossed his arms for the long haul. "Niles got wind of Liam's role in this takedown and his suspension's been extended another three months. He's not allowed inside the compound."

Ric growled and fisted his hand. "That's bull."

Jake held up his hand. "It's the official ruling. Unofficially, Liam's taking undercover lead on the Cabal case. They won't see him coming. We have enough information to investigate their recruitment efforts and how they're manipulating psychics."

"He's been chomping at the bit to take lead on something big. At least we're not starting from scratch."

"He's already scoured Delaney's house, found papers leading to his businesses and the VR company," Jake explained. "With the cops' help, we tracked the fake accountancy firm and apprehended the principals. We got a boatload of evidence, photos Marisa snapped of the compound, her phone, and the software they used to divert everything on her phone to a cloud server. Detective MacKenzie's taking lead since he's now the Guild's official liaison to the San Jose police." Jake scrubbed his hands together. "We're so close to scoring a Cabal coup, I can taste it."

"What about the journal from the safety deposit box?"

"Yep. Got it. Psychic roll call from every corner of the world. Thousands of people the Guild's never heard of. Enough psychics to rule the world, or cause significant chaos."

"Who else may have their hands on copies?"

"No telling. We've beefed up security at the compound where we'll keep the list locked up. Guardians are on high alert."

Ric blew out a breath. "Delaney did us a huge favor."

"He got cocky, sloppy. Probably why they work independently. It keeps the other members safe when plans go sideways."

"Not the sharpest bulb in the shed." Ric grinned, loving the black looks Jake tossed him at his screwed-up metaphors. "One down, how many more to go?"

Jake's demeanor went stony. "Too many. Delaney was top of the Cabal food chain, same as the Italian dude. He's still at large. We know they're recruiting big time. It's enough to go after them hard."

"Do you think what he said about the Cabal origins and the Guild imploding is true?"

"We need to talk to Mrs. Meadows and then speak to the founding Guilders. I've got a gut feeling it's all true. Niles and the Protectorate have handled inside infractions for years. He told me last night not to involve anyone *inside* the Guild except him. Everything we learn goes through him alone. He's the only one I trust now."

"Not me?" Ric nudged his foot at Jake's thigh.

Jake frowned. "Nope. Not while you're hooked to evil incarnate. We don't know whose ear she's bent in the Cabal, no matter if Delaney's dead. She may've been in their pocket all along."

Ric shook his head. "Lily would've known. They're best friends." He willed his heart to stop torturing his chest.

"Don't know." He patted Ric's leg. "Sorry, bro. She got under your skin, huh?"

Unable to form another coherent sentence, Ric sobered and succumbed to his fatigue. "I need to sleep, 'kay? We'll yak later."

Jake departed the dark room. A new drip of drugs drove a fine line over his pain. Marisa needed to spill it all before anything made sense. If she woke up. And she may very well be enemy number one. *His stupid dick and his heart can't argue with black-and-white proof.*

More drugs followed their leader, and he fell into a soundless sleep, a welcome darkness he didn't fight.

CRSO

The next morning, the lure to the room down the hall refused to abate. Ric sat up in bed, given the okay earlier to walk the halls to regain his strength. The gunshot wasn't life threatening, and he'd gain full use of his arm. The Guild resident nurse left with his half-eaten breakfast after helping him dress in clean sweatpants and his favorite black Metallica T-shirt. His brothers were on their new Cabal-mission-critical errands, although no new evidence emerged since he and Jake had conferred yesterday.

The solitude weighed on him when Marisa lay so very near. The Guild Council placed her under house arrest and refused to allow her in any other wing of the compound, not that she'd awoken from her coma. They refrained from deciding her fate until she suffered a full-blown Guild tribunal.

He held his arm close, his sling taut to prevent him from using his arm. Shuffling down the near-deserted hallway, he peeked into the two doors of the empty rooms he passed. One Guardian flanked the third door.

"Hey, Ric." Rafael had visited him before he'd taken up his post earlier.

"Niles said I could go in. Might help her wake up." No lie. Niles and the doctor had given permission before breakfast.

"You're on the list." Rafael scanned his card in the reader and opened the door. "Holler if you need me."

The door clicked shut behind Ric, and he closed the blinds on the door's small window. He wanted privacy. Rafael got it. The whole Protectorate knew he had a thing for their newest enemy. Who was he kidding? The *thing* was called love, no matter that she'd tried to kill him. The Marisa Meadows at Delaney's house and on the beach wasn't the Marisa Meadows he'd fallen for. She wasn't the one he'd made hot love to on an afternoon that had left an indelible imprint on his memories. The faint scent of her perfume overrode the antiseptic infirmary odor and fired a flare of arousal to his groin.

He rolled the padded guest chair close to the bed and sat, happy to take the load off his wobbly legs. Skin über pale, her shiny hair fanned her face and shoulders on the pillow like a black veil. Her left hand lay on her stomach. He touched a finger to her wrist and her warmth belied her cold, corpse pallor. REM cycles moved her eyeballs behind her lids, and he wished he were in her head. She lay so gorgeous and pure he ached for her.

"Marisa? It's the Guardian you love to hate," he kidded. Who knew how much truth laced his words? "Baby, come on, wake up. We need you to set things right with the Guild." *I need you to set things right with me.* He kissed her palm, his lips lingering a moment on her skin as he inhaled, missing her baby powder scent. "I need you. Remember I said I was falling in love with you. I totally lied. I *am* in love with you."

He'd spoken those words once before, and he'd say them again and again. Hell, he didn't think he'd truly love another after feeling the joy and happiness Marisa created in all his senses. "I know it wasn't you on the beach or at Delaney's house in his VR game. Everything will be okay if you just wake up. We'll start fresh, go on a date, see where it takes us. But I refuse to allow two minutes of hot sex to last me a lifetime. I need way more. All of you. Forever more."

Nothing changed. She didn't twitch, didn't respond, didn't show any sign she recognized he held her hand or tried to connect to her. A beautiful shell he wanted to reel into his arms and protect from the evil in the world. Or drive the evil out of her and the world, if it was his last task on Earth.

A soft knock on the door preceded Elizabeth's entry

into the dim room. "Nothing yet?"

He knuckled the wetness from his eye. "How much longer can she remain like this?"

Elizabeth squeezed his shoulder. "We don't know. Honey, I'm so sorry. She may not be the same when she awakens."

"I know." He sniffed and squeezed Marisa's hand. "I won't judge you. Just wake up so we can discover how amazing we can be together." He kissed her jaw, her stillness chasing the goosebumps on his arms. "If you don't wake up, we'll never know what a beautiful life we can share, the drummers beating to our tune, the hot, sexy music we'll make. I love you, Marisa Meadows. If you don't hear anything else, hear that. I love you." Then he felt it, an infinitesimal movement of her fingers in his. A tear slipped from her left eye and into the hair at her temple. He caught the droplet on his finger, and gently kissed her again.

"She squeezed my fingers."

"A good sign. It's possible she heard you."

They waited another five minutes, but Marisa remained the beautiful zombie.

"It's time for you to rest. Jake and Lily will be here in a couple hours to take you home."

"I'm not leaving her. She needs me nearby."

"Not as much as you need to rest your arm and return to normal."

Ric wheeled on her, thumped his chest. "*She* is my life, my new normal." But he'd failed her, failed in his Guardian duties to protect her, to protect one of his charges for the first time in his life. Normal may never be in his reality.

Elizabeth's compassionate mask crumbled. "I hope so for your sake."

After slogging to his solitary room, he fell into a fitful

sleep, dreaming of a beautiful, ethereal light erasing the darkness shrouding him.

Later in the afternoon, he memorized every feature of Marisa's face before Jake and Lily carted him to their house, to baby him while his arm healed. In reality, he knew they guarded him from visiting Marisa, hoping it might prevent him from falling deeper.

Too late. He was in freefall.

CHAPTER THIRTY-FOUR

Nightmares and dreams collided. Unable to parse fact from fiction, Marisa blocked every intrusion behind a flimsy wall. She buried herself in welcome darkness, and the quelling music played for an eternity until her mind rallied against the repetition and revolted one time too many. The full-scale war thrust her into consciousness for the second time that day.

The first time she'd awoken from a weeklong coma, she was unable to talk or form a coherent thought. At first, she barely remembered her name. Alien thoughts and voices, nightmares, and dreams spun in her head. The doctor injected another drug in her IV to remand her to comaland. Apparently, she wasn't ready to live again.

Everything that'd occurred before her coma crashed back, forcing her awake the second time. She'd thrown up bile in the bed pan until dry heaves settled in and she plunged back into her drug-induced sleep.

Upon her third awakening, the fading incessant harp music kicked her out of a drugged sleep. She asked the nurse to turn a rock station on the radio to kill the sickening harp chords begging her to gouge drumsticks in her ears.

The fourth time she'd awakened, the melodic music ceased altogether. Silence swallowed the internal monologue, and reality hit her over the head. It had taken a few hours after awakening this last time to determine the nightmares dogging her were real. Ten days ago, the dark side had called a challenge and won.

Worst nightmare of all—she'd shot to kill the man she wanted more than life.

It tortured her, how easily she'd succumbed to the darkness, how easily a hacker manipulated her. Once she believed she was the strongest of her family to fight the trappings of strong telepathy. In truth, she was no better than her sister or her mother, three sad peas in a pod unable to deal with life and telepathy in harmony. She'd spent her life building her walls, and Delaney had torn them down in one second and stomped them into roadkill. Back to square one, she battled herself and the voices, having to forcefully prevent herself from drilling into every open mind around her. They ought to just lock her up in this infirmary room, no light, no happiness, no one to crack open and read. No more guilt. Definitely no access to a gun.

During her less than lucid moments, the doctor refused to allow anyone in her guarded room other than infirmary personnel and Lily. On the down low, Ric had spent hours in her room day in and day out. Even in her coma, she'd sensed his presence in the very air she breathed. He held her hand, talked about anything and everything, most of which she didn't understand. The sound of his voice brought her baffling joy. *He* returned her to the living.

The lack of Guild members bombarding her once she'd fully awakened suited her fragile coherent state. For the first time, she'd regained a small semblance of her old self. The rest of her had been remade into an alien being, different than the puppet, alien all the same. Now she needed to confront her friends, the Guild Council, and Ric.

God, Ric. She refused to press the call button, feared tackling her life's next chapter and the horror and guilt filling every chink of her broken being.

The door opened a crack with an angle of light, and Lily peeked in for one of her umpteenth checks. When she saw Marisa's eyes latch onto hers and the small smile Marisa attempted, she quickly shot into the room and shut the door.

"Are you awake? For real?" Lily traced the tubes sticking in Marisa's hand as if she feared touching evil.

"No and no." Throat dry, she barely heard her ragged first coherent words, other than screaming at the nurse to turn the stereo on to obliterate the harp music slaying her. Her attempt at a wink caused her eyes to water and eyelids to flutter.

"Oh, my." Lily hugged her, careful of the tubes. Even if part of her was dying to sink into her best friend's embrace, shame, guilt, and a slew of other unnamed emotions flooded the other part. The pitchfork-stabbing devil and wing-flapping angel certainly hadn't declared a truce.

Noticing her glacial demeanor, Lily drew back. "Do you... um... which—"

"You've never been one to stumble on your thoughts," Marisa croaked out. Lily handed her a cup, and she gratefully drank a few sips of tepid water. "Are you asking which Marisa am I?"

Tears gathered in Lily's eyes. "Yeah. Sorry, yeah. We've spent the last ten days wondering if we'd lost you."

"Does it matter? I'm a lost cause no matter who I am." Marisa couldn't halt her own waterworks. "Now you've got me crying."

Lily chuckled and handed her a tissue. "Seriously, are you okay? Do you remember what happened? Should I call the doctor?"

Marisa held up her hand, forcing Lily to stop the inquisition. "Don't call the doc. I remember everything. I have no clue if I'm okay or not." She snaked out her hand and gripped Lily's wrist. "I screwed up bad." Remorse and sorrow jarred her empty soul. "Delaney destroyed me. He—" Unable to continue she let the sobs roll up her chest.

Lily sat on the bed and hugged Marisa again. This time, Marisa held onto Lily as if she never wanted to let go. "No. He didn't destroy you. You're here, and that motherfucker's dead. You're alive. You're coming back to us." They clutched one another for the longest time until Marisa coughed up her last sob.

"Do you want to rest?" Lily asked.

Marisa examined the calendar on the wall with the red Xs on each day of her mental incarceration. "I've suffered ten days of rest. I don't want to sleep anymore. I want to live. How much trouble will greet me when I step out of this bed and jump-start my life?"

"Same old. You'll face a Guild tribunal. Thanks to you, a bunch of info has already come to light, so I don't think it'll be too bad." She tugged on her pendant, scratched her neck as if afraid to carry on. "Maybe a suspension, small chance of expulsion. Do you want to tell me what happened?"

Powerless to hide from her thoughts one second longer, Marisa told Lily everything from the moment she'd strolled into Delaney's home, until the final scene on the beach in Santa Cruz. "I was fine until my blood sugar levels kicked my ass and I passed out. It was weird. I never get that bad like at the airport. It's as if he'd drugged me all along." She shrugged. "Maybe he did slip something into my drink. When I awoke, he had me in thrall again. I fought it, but couldn't get past it again."

Lily gripped Marisa's arm. "That asshole implanted a

device in your arm. It worked with his mesmerism."

Nausea blooming anew, Marisa picked at the bandage on her upper left arm and continued. "When my bullet hit Ric." She choked up and searched for the puke pail. Lily handed her the cup of water and she drained it. "When I shot him, our minds linked. He was screaming, trying to help me. And I shot him. I shot him." She buried her face in her hands.

"He's okay, Mar. We all understand you weren't *you*. He understands. Do you know he's spent every waking hour holding your hand, talking to you? The Guild got wind yesterday and banished him from the compound. They believed he was detrimental to your recovery even though Niles and the doctor approved his visits."

"I sensed him. Even when he wasn't here, he was in my head. Sort of. Or maybe I conjured him up." She tossed up her arms. "I can't read anything."

"You couldn't have conjured up a more perfect specimen of man."

Marisa stopped herself from sticking her tongue out at Lily. "Anyway, the bullet's impact on Ric connected to me, and I passed out." Exhaustion anchored her limbs after the long conversation. "Can we finish this later? I think I'll take you up on your offer of rest."

Lily hopped off the bed. "You bet. I'll tell the nurse and doctor you're awake *awake*. They'll want to run tests."

"Lovely." Marisa yawned. "Can't freaking wait. Oh, Lily? Can you tell them I don't want to see Ric? Please, please keep him out of here." She drifted off to sleep, thoughts of Ric's blue eyes taunting her, deriding her actions, his loathing palpable. He'd found the place inside her no one else ever had. The place she'd kept well hidden. But he'd easily battered down her barriers with his clairvoyant visions. Because she'd let him, maybe wanted him to shine his light on her darkness.

That was then, and this is now. The transferred vision of him walking away from her for good quaked through one side of her and loosened the knotty shoulder on the other side. Walking away solved part of her problem. Losing him for good, killed her hopes and dreams, stomped her heart into dry desolate particles of nothing.

CR&SO

Sitting in a comfy armchair in front of the window overlooking the woods, Marisa stared at a squirrel on the edge of the patio, its cheeks bulging, preparing for a lonely winter. Marisa held the speakerphone near her mouth, the scent of antibacterial gel strong in her nose. She couldn't stop slathering it on, as if she wanted to obliterate every trace of Delaney from her mind and skin. "Mom, it's Marisa."

"Sweetheart! Oh, goodness, they told me what happened. Are you okay?" Her mother's smoky voice centered Marisa.

"I'll be okay. I'm on the mend. The question is, are you okay? I heard less than savory men were playing orderlies."

"Oh, they were perfect gentlemen. That is, until they were exposed for frauds, and the Guild grounded them to mush." Silence met the end of the phone. "I wish I could be there for you."

"I know. I'm still coming to see you," Marisa said.

"Not until you're well *and* well protected."

Protected. By another Guild Guardian? "Mom, about Dad and Granddad. Lunatic Delaney told me things. Things I didn't know. Lies, truth, who knows? I found something I think belonged to Granddad."

"Tell me," her mother demanded.

Marisa read off her smartphone note application everything she'd learned from Delaney. A mountain slid down her arms with every sentence. In the end, she held her breath waiting for her mother to acknowledge the lies.

"It's true," Mom said. "Yet not as bad as Mr. Delaney suggested."

Marisa expelled an angry breath. "Yet you never deigned to tell me? All this time I've been in the Guild, wanted to leave it so many times for reasons I didn't understand. Because I come from black blood from both Dad and Granddad." Disgust fired her insides.

"No, sweetheart. It's a little skewed, that's all. Your grandfather was a good man. My father thought it a grand idea to expand the Guild, to recruit psychics and not follow the Guild's usual ways of letting psychics come to them of their own volition. He wanted to leverage their resources, advertise and hire out psychics for legal purposes, give them ways to make money off their God-given talents and provide ways for the Guild to sustain their nonprofit status." Her mother paused, coughed. "When Derek caught wind, he hounded my father to proceed with the expansion. But he wanted to use the new recruits for illegal purposes for his own selfish gain. Granddad caught wind of your father's real purpose, and they had an altercation that caused Granddad to have a heart attack."

"So it's true, Dad caused Granddad's death." Marisa's fist curled into a tight ball.

"Yes. That nasty bitch karma returned for your father a year after he established an arm of the Guild with former members who weren't so ingrained in the organization."

"You never told me this story. You said Dad was killed in a car accident on a Guardian assignment."

"True. He'd already left us, but he was still tied to the Protectorate guarding another psychic. He was on the outs for his abandonment of us, and he knew it. The Guild doesn't take abandonment well. But he was well ensconced in this new group by then, the Cabal, as we know it now. Once he died, the group broke ties with the Guild and took Derek's ideas and goals to the next level."

"And here we are, battling them for supremacy."

"I'm sorry you got caught in the crossfire. I tried to bury your father's indiscretions. There was no need for you to know what an awful man he became. Bad enough you knew he'd abandoned us."

His desertion formed her resistance to Guardians and relationships in general, more than enough to screw her up. Now this? "I hate that I'm a daughter of the Guild and the Cabal. The Guild's accusing me of working with them. They think Delaney too easily swayed me due to alleged ties to the Cabal."

"The Guild will implode if they don't get a handle on the Cabal, especially when good people like you are targeted with their high-tech ways. The Cabal's hammer is swift and mighty. Its roots are strong. They need to be severed sooner rather than later."

"I know, Mom." Anger swirled in her chest. "I found a journal, a directory of psychics. Where did it come from?"

Her mother clucked her tongue. "The list. Oh, hell. I haven't seen it in years."

"When did you last see it?"

"Six years ago. I put it in a safety deposit box." Her mother's voice lowered as if covering up an awkward truth. "No one was supposed to get their hands on it, but I just couldn't talk myself into destroying it. It took years for Granddad to compile it, and your father wanted it more than life."

"But the box was in my name, with my signature,"

Marisa accused.

"I'm sorry. I used your ID, and you know how much we look alike." Her voice broke on a sob. "Honey, I'm so sorry. I thought out of anyone in the family, you'd know what to do with it."

"Then how'd Delaney get the key?" Marisa scratched her jaw.

"I lost the key not long before Celeste—"

Marisa banged the phone against her head. "He coerced her into giving it to him, but he needed me to access the box."

"I should've burned it. Torch it, Marisa. No good will come of it." Insistence strengthened her mother's voice.

"It's up to the Guild now," Marisa explained. "Everything's up to the Guild. *Everything*."

After making plans for Marisa to visit the moment Nurse Ratchet sprung her from the infirmary, they hung up. She needed a break from her life, to breathe less Cabal-polluted air. Then she was going home to San Diego to shift her life back to an even keel.

CHAPTER THIRTY-FIVE

Five days later, after avoiding Ric the entire time as if he carried a heart-demolishing curse, Marisa faced him across the conference table at her Guild tribunal. He was like a waft of fresh air, and she wanted to inhale him into her soul and never expel him. The anticipation softening his handsome face tempted her, and she forcibly had to resist his lure and concentrate on the inquisition.

The doctor pronounced her clear of most traces of Delaney's mental machinations the day before. She was still crushed to learn that not only had Delaney inserted a device in her arm, it also released drugs to relax her and an unknown substance they believed worked with his hypnotizing efforts. Tests were still under way. With the drugs and music largely out of her system, she had regained a new semblance of her old self. Yet nothing promised ever to be the same again. Not even the gunshot had blasted Ric out of her system like she'd once believed possible.

She peeked up at him, surreptitiously studying her phone on the table before he caught her and she glanced away. A new pain flared up around her heart.

The brightly lit room overlooked the back patio and the woods beyond. It was the patio where she'd met Ric the first time. Such a bad start to their so-called relationship. Such a horrible ending too. Wanting to creep into the woods to join the chittering squirrels and flitting blue jays in peace and harmony, she shifted her focus off the ill-fated patio back to her execution.

Ric sat next to Niles Nevin, the Protectorate Director, who maintained he'd assigned Ric to shadow her before Ric's official Guardian assignment. Marisa didn't hold it against him. She appreciated his job and challenges, had met Niles over multiple occasions. He was a straight shooter, stand-up guy.

After all the evidence lay on the table so to speak, the Guild president asked her, "Do you wish to leave the Guild?"

Marisa contemplated her desires and future, consulted her pros and cons list on her note app. "I'd like to take a sabbatical if I'm granted the right to remain. I understand if you want to revoke my position as Guild lawyer or expel me entirely. Regardless, I'd like to help undo my father's division of the Guild. I want to help create a powerful organization again." She held her head high, met Ric's tentative smile. He'd already given his testimony and hadn't thrown her under the bus, a good thing, she supposed. Not like it mattered. Her remorse already kicked the crap out of her and continued to do so every minute. "I'd like to know what you plan to do with the book of names."

"Do you wish to have it back?" Niles steepled his fingers under his chin.

"No. I don't want it used for ill, though."

"It may help the Guild fight the Cabal," the president replied curtly. "It remains under Guild protection until such time as it proves useless to us."

"Or dangerous." Ric groaned.

"Or dangerous," Niles reiterated. "It's time for us to render our verdict, ladies and gentlemen."

The Guild tribunal, made up of the top seven Guild members, conferred on the other side of the large conference room next to a credenza covered with a water, coffee, and tea service. Silent and with one eye on Ric, she tapped in her notes of the meeting.

"Can we talk afterward?" Ric asked, his jaw ticking, ready to battle her reply. "Can I take you out to dinner?"

His voice launched a traitorous shimmer of delight to her toes. "We can talk on the patio," she replied. No way, no how did she plan to go on a date with him. Delaney had shot her defenses to hades specifically concerning men, and one man in particular.

The council members returned to the table, and Niles, the council secretary, read the verdict. "The Guild grants you a sabbatical of up to six months. You may return to your regular Guild duties in twelve weeks at a minimum, at which time you'll serve probation for a year. We believe the pros outweigh the cons with your continued Guild membership. Ric McAllister will remain your Guardian since we believe you're still under Cabal threats." Marisa gasped. Ric smiled. *He knew! Is this his version of hell or tough love?* "Further, if we find you colluding with the Cabal, criminal charges may be assessed pursuant to the fullest extent of Guild and public law. Do you understand and accept our pronouncement?"

Marisa coughed. "I understand. However, I don't need a Guardian, and I reject Ric McAllister." Ric chuckled, and she wanted to snatch him bald-headed.

"It's a condition of your sentence. Do you wish another Guardian?" the president asked, his baldpate gleaming under the fluorescent lights. Marisa unconsciously tried to read him, any mind for that matter, and met their forced walls. It wasn't unexpected. They knew how to protect themselves.

Ric stood as if to force his hulking shadow upon them.

"I'll guard her. It's my duty. I signed up for *her*."

Signed up for her? *Fat chance.* She knew full well she'd never shake him even if she chose another Guardian. As she scraped the blood-red nail polish off her thumbnail, a sigh escaped. "Fine. I accept him. Temporarily." *You will never be the boss of me, McGuardian McAllister.*

"This matter is concluded." The council members rose on cue, and Ric rushed around the table to usher them out. As the last to leave, he held the door open for her.

Brushing past him and avoiding dangerous contact, Marisa charged down the hall. His thumping footsteps chased her to the patio. She drew in a draft of pine-scented air and sidled to the patio's edge separating the grounds from the woods. If only she possessed the ability to shape-shift into a snake and slither off into the shadowy forest.

When she spun on Ric, she nearly melted at the aching love and desire written across every feature of his face. She steeled herself against what almost happened between them, invited in the autumn air to dampen his heat seeping into her. She'd finally found a possible soul-deep love to last forever. But her forever ended on the short stick and it would kill Ric's forever.

As she spoke, she made herself into an iceberg, cold, distant, and formidable. "You're not my keeper."

"I'm starving. Can we talk over dinner?" He jammed his baseball cap on, shadowing the upper half of his face. "I'm not ready to throw in the night and give up the towel."

She blinked slowly. "I'm *probably* very busy." His mouth became an unreadable slit and her word hemorrhage continued. "For the record, I never ever contemplated joining the Cabal. When I informed the Guild I was confused regarding my membership and wanted to leave several times, it was because of what happened to my family and how my father treated my mother and his abandonment. Not because I wanted to exact revenge. I need the Guild like family."

"I know, babe." Ric ran his fingers down her wrist, and the resulting tingles chased up her arm. She backed up a step. "Are you confused now?"

She emphatically shook her head. "Not after hearing the truth about my father. Not after what Delaney did to me. I want to bury the Cabal."

"Good." He took a step closer. "It's what I want to hear."

"You believe me? Or did you have a vision?"

"Of course I believe you. Why do you doubt me?"

She snickered, forcing down the emotions threatening to burst her fake icy demeanor. "Well, I did try to kill you."

"Hey, when one door shuts, the tough get going."

"You do like to mix up your sayings, don't you?" She gave him a wonky smile she almost felt inside.

The walls in his head collapsed, and she instantly snapped up his fragmented thoughts. She'd lost all ability to cease reading minds until she rebuilt her own defenses. Desire and love boiled in his thoughts, scorching her resolve.

Eyes welling, she fisted her hand around her purse strap. "Why do you still want me, Ric?"

"Because I love you."

Tears tracked down her face, and she fingered them away, hating her vulnerability when she wanted to slide past her angsty moment and escape before she did something regrettable. "For two seconds I dreamed of a life with you. I'll never forgive myself for what I did. I'm so very sorry. Small words, but I don't know what else to offer you. There's no life for us. I'm returning to San

Diego. I need to fix *me* before I drag anyone else into my shitstorm. I need to get my head on straight. I'm not dragging you down or having you blame me every time I read or misinterpret you."

Ric shuffled his feet, drummed his fingers on his thigh. "Please don't go. None of this was your fault. I don't blame you, and I forgive you. Lily still wants you to join the firm. She needs to hire another attorney regardless of Delaney's lost business." He paused his word vomit for a moment to catch his breath. "We'll work through it all. We can solve the telepathy issue. Other couples manage to work through it. Jake and Lily are working it out." He took a step forward, and his fervent heat enveloped her. "Damn it, Marisa, I won't leave you. Ever. I'm not Delaney. I'm not your bastard father. McAllister men don't walk from the women they love."

Tenderly, she cupped his face and kissed him, her lips cool on his warm, soft mouth. They just touched lips to lips, and she imprinted his senses on her memory. He tried to deepen the kiss and embrace her, but she stepped back, unable to control herself if he touched her another second longer. "It will never work between us." She grazed past him and headed toward the door. "Goodbye, Ric," she whispered.

"I'm still your Guardian." He followed close on her heels.

By the time she reached her rental car, her blurry eyes obscured her sight. She fumbled her car door, and he tried to take her in his arms again.

"Go," she yelled. "I can't do this with you. *Ever.*"

"Don't say that." The horrible hurt eviscerating his face nearly undid her. "You get a free pass tonight. No guard. No me. Tomorrow's a new day." He wheeled around and strode away and a claw squeezed her chest. His shoulders slouched, his tread slow, hesitant. But he never glanced back, not even when he drove past her still sitting in her car and dying inside. Deep loneliness flowered in her core, her hurt and despair so profound, her body spasmed in a soul-wracking sob. His vision of walking away from her just came true.

Numb, she drove in the direction of Lily's house. She pulled off the road below Lily's driveway and texted her. "I need time alone. I'll see you later." An uncomfortable silence met her. She kept the radio off, not willing to risk hearing one note of the freakish music Delaney used to condition her. Eons would pass before music offered her any joy again.

Glorious autumn red, orange, and gold among the evergreen firs, pines, and the occasional redwoods colored the hills. She stopped at a year-round fruit stand near the small town of Saratoga just outside the San Jose area, bought a fruit salad and water, and moseyed into the half-full campground next door. She found an empty picnic table and enjoyed her snack, watched the sun drop from the tree tops until it dappled the woods in pink and coral as dusk settled. Camp lights flickered on, extending the light until night snuffed the sun out for another day, hopefully a better tomorrow.

Too much mental stuff kept jamming up her thoughts and memories. The only thing making sense was Ric McAllister, and loving him. Not loving him refused to entertain one iota of space in her emotions. For the millionth time, she pushed him out, and he popped right back like an irksome zombie. What kind of boring, sad, and lonely life did San Diego promise?

Purple dusk chased the last of daylight. A few people ogled her since she hadn't budged from her seat at the lonely picnic table in a long while. She ignored their curiosity. A lifetime of loneliness rooted her. Seedlings of doubt sprouted, some died a not so tragic death, and others flourished in her meadow of dancing red flowers.

Marisa tried to muffle the monologue berating her weaknesses up one side and down the other, until sense sank in and the new seedlings dominated. Letting go of her past and insecurities had no room in the garden. She had a home and people she loved in San Jose. She had a man who accepted her flaws and faults, who promised not to let them drive him away. Nothing else mattered. Marisa trusted her new reality, trusted in Ric, if he still wanted her. He was worth changing her life for.

Not a doubt remained. Happiness surged and popped in her blood.

"I let weakness overcome me. I will not let my history define me. Nope. No way, no how." With determined steps, she returned to her car, and drove out of the dark woods, down a couple hills, and up another to Lily's house, glowing with light, a beacon to her diminishing darkness.

When she set one foot onto Lily's porch, she dialed her number two on speed dial. She waited a moment, listened to it ring twice, until he answered, solidifying her decision.

A frozen tundra attacked her body and her words rushed out. "I need you. I need my Guardian."

"Are you okay? Where are you?" Ric's voice escalated in alarm. "I'm on my way."

The front door opened and he stood there, like a ray of sunshine on a cold winter's landscape, his good arm in his jacket, the other sleeve hanging loose. A haggard pallor had remade his face from his earlier joy. The scent of beer wafted off him, but he hadn't drowned all his sorrows yet by the clarity in his eyes. Before she uttered a word, he wrapped his good arm around her and hauled her tight against his hard and welcome body. She breathed him in, her ear pressed to the rapid thump of his heartbeat.

Fire gutted the freeze holding her prisoner. "You're like air to a dying woman. You're my air, my life. I know it now. I'm no longer drowning because of you." Her purse fell to the slate porch, and she wound her arms around his torso, pressed tight to him, afraid to release him. "I can't ever do casual with you. You drove the casual out of me."

The last of his tension drained from him, and his joy buzzed down his length. "Now that's what I'm talking about."

"Will you come with me somewhere?"

"I'll follow you anywhere, even into a walking dead horde." He flicked off his baseball cap and mussed his hair, his smile so radiant, her knees almost liquefied.

"Well, I guess you have to, you *are* my Guardian."

"Yo, Jakeman," he shouted over his shoulder, a buoyancy in his tone Marisa had never heard. "I'm lawyering up. Going out with Marisa."

"Ah, hell. Don't let her take her gun," Jake shouted back. "What is it with psychics shooting their Guardians lately?"

"Take care of her. I need my best friend." Lily stood behind them on the porch. "I need both of you."

Ric couldn't stop touching Marisa as they walked to her car. He held the driver's side door open for her and then hopped into the passenger seat.

Somber, yet feeling so light and free inside, she faced him. His devastating grin made her believe everything she'd decided was so right and perfect. She scarcely believed she hadn't ever allowed herself such joy. "I warned you not to get involved with me. You still have time to escape."

"Too late." Leaning over the center console, he kissed her hard, a kiss full of passion and happiness. "I take my challenges seriously." His mouth landed on hers again, and she met him with a deep hunger, breathed him in all her senses.

Ric's walls crashed. The force of his feelings careened into her, a storm catapulting her into his turbulent epicenter. When he released her mouth, she knew her life raft capsized into his sea of desire. They broke apart, and Marisa settled into the driver's seat, soaked in bliss.

She drove toward the highway. "He... Delaney, broke me," she admitted.

Ric slid his thumb over her palm. "We'll fit the pieces back, together." His voice caught as he held his breath, waiting for her to say the words she knew he wanted to hear. She just needed him to understand first.

"Okay. Thank you for shining your light on my darkness and ending it." She maneuvered the car into the fast lane and accelerated out of a curve. "I can't have you in my crazy life without you being all in."

He pressed a kiss on her palm. "We can tackle your cray-cray life together. Babe, I'm not going anywhere, and I'll never let anyone hurt you again."

"Promise." She sounded small and vulnerable.

"On my dying breath."

"Then let's not let you get shot again," she kidded, finally letting the last of her pent-up doubts float off into the dark woods bordering the highway. Clouds converged overhead and flashes of lightning lit up the sky over the Pacific.

"Sounds like a plan. Give me your gun." He laughed, and she giggled, a mingled sound of optimistic cheer. "I wanted to confess something. I had a prophecy of you at the bank. I saw everything before it happened, but it was in bits and pieces. I'm sorry I wasn't there for you when that man attacked."

"Don't be sorry. Please, Ric. The time for sorry is past." She gripped his hand. "Tell me about it. I don't have all the pieces." She ticked her finger against her skull and then listened without comment as he relayed his vision. Whether or not it all happened as he saw it didn't matter any longer, but it helped fill in some missing pieces.

"By the way, where're you taking me?" he asked.

"Santa Cruz."

Ric tensed against the seat. "Are you sure you want to return to the scene?"

"The beach is my solitude, the ocean my balm. I need to climb back onto the horse, or I'll hate my sanctuary forever. It's my escape from my head."

"If it helps you wake in the morning—"

"Or sleep at night?" She snickered. "You're crazy weird. I love it."

"Crazy for you and your crazy."

They drove through central Santa Cruz, straight toward the ocean until Marisa pulled off onto a different beach south of where her nightmare had ended. Clouds roiled over the balmy night, deserting the beach for an early fall thunderstorm. Again, Ric refused to let go of her hand as they hiked through the sand to the waves curling onto shore in a foamy tide. She peeled off her jacket, exposing her arms to the salty night, letting the breeze sanitize her clean of her torment and turmoil. Careful of his injury, Ric gathered her close. He breathed in deeply several times, expelling air as if he was expelling the last of their nightmare. Waves rumbled in the imminent storm, pounding the shoreline with double and triple curls. A lighthouse loomed off in the distance, its beacon lighting a new path forward across the dark ocean. Strikes of lightning seduced the darkness, stroking the sea's inky surface, flaring out in all directions in an indigo sky, obscuring the swath of light over the dark water.

"How do you feel?" he murmured in her ear, almost

purring his contentment.

They were on an island alone together and nothing else mattered. "Like I'm standing in my sanctuary at the world's edge. A much better world with you gracing it." For the first time in her life, she grasped what people meant by having chemistry with a person. They had it in spades and it changed her life. It felt so right, so perfect.

"I'm glad. Um… will you let me be your haven now?"

"It's definitely a better world in the haven of your arms." She turned, brushed her fingers over his face. "I think I started to love you from the moment your mind touched mine the first time, and you opened your all to me. I didn't know what I was sensing. I want to be part of your dreams forever. I want you in my reality, virtual, real, and in all ways. I can't live each day never knowing or loving you, whether this is only a short romance or a lifetime."

"I'm gambling on forever." Ric groaned and pressed his hardness into her soft curves. "I will never hide anything from you." His mouth met hers, and they kissed, tongues tangoing, the scent of heaven surrounding them. Lack of air parted their mouths. Ric buried his face in her hair, his warm breath fanning her ear. "The greatest darkness can't snuff out the smallest light. Remember that," he said in her ear. "Your light will never diminish, not when you let me be the one to illuminate you."

"A poet and you didn't know it," she teased.

"Oh, I know it all right." His laugh vibrated against her neck.

"Seriously, though. I was afraid to love you. When I woke up and booted out Deranged Marisa and learned I'd almost killed you, almost lost you, I wanted to die. Never seeing you again numbed me, left me in my dark hollow. But I had accepted it. Now I'm more afraid of spending my life without you."

Ric shuddered against her, his tension rolling off his taut body and blowing away on the salty breeze. "I'd have waited forever for you to realize that."

"Can we survive our weird connection? Will you be okay?"

"You know I never had a problem with you reading my mind."

"That's not what I mean, but since you mention it, I don't plan to read your mind unless you give me permission."

"I know what you mean. Doc said the worst is over. When you lost your telepathy, it left your mind in chaos, hunting down any familiar path. Since we connected, I was the most familiar."

"But I'm not all right up there." She jabbed her head. "I need time to rebuild my walls, completely get rid of Delaney's mesmerism—"

He kissed her, ending her stated fears. "Doc's hooked me up with a psychic therapist who's training me to build my mental walls differently to prevent your intrusion again."

She smiled wide. "So you hoped you'd get the chance to use your new skills."

"Not hoped. *Knew.*"

His happy laughter sparked another spurt of hunger through her, and she jiggled in his arms to dampen it. Later she'd show him how much she trusted and wanted him.

"Well then, since were on the same page and you're my Guardian and on medical leave, do you have a couple weeks to spare?"

His arm muscles stiffened. "For what reason?" The fear she planned to stay in San Diego shouted from his mind like the bright beacon on the lighthouse. "If you can't live in San Jose, after your family history—"

She shushed him with a finger over his mouth and then wound her arms around his neck. "Don't get all riled up. I want you to go with me to visit my mom. You two need to meet. Plus, I have to pack and rent out my townhouse. I have a new job and new life to start."

The tension flowed down his steely arms. "With me?"

Strands of her hair fluttered freely in the wind and her laugh chased the breeze. "I'll say it again in case you didn't get the picture. You're not getting rid of me so easily."

Flinching and not caring about his gunshot wound, he embraced her tighter. "Good. Because I've fallen in love with you, and I don't think I'll ever fall out. Even if you shoot me again."

"Funny. Haha."

"Can we start your—our—new life tonight? I need to see you in my bed. I want to make love with you, not two seconds of hot-as-hell sex." His eyes smoldered, and she loved the words tripping out of his mouth. "Whoa, you're moving in with me, and you haven't even seen my place or met my dog."

She let out a surprised but happy giggle, inciting another surge of hot and happy hormones tightening her lower region. "Slow down there, drummer boy. My plan is to live in Lily's master bedroom since she's practically living with Jake in the loft."

"I have a master bedroom." He pouted, cupped her face with one hand.

"It's a bit soon living together, don't you think? You don't really know me. You don't even know my favorite color."

"Black."

"No, silly. Red."

"Blood red?"

"You guessed it." She pressed into his fingers cupping

her face. "And you don't even know my favorite food."

"Everything I do know about you feels right. *You* feel right in my life. *We* make sense together." Ric kissed her, a light brush across her lips.

"Did a clairvoyant vision tell you so?"

"My gut, my head, my heart." He nuzzled her neck, his skin scratchy against hers.

"Tell me what else you know." A tiny sigh escaped her. "Then I'll tell you what I know about the kind, funny, loyal Guardian who lights me up inside."

"I know how you like me to touch you here." He dipped his fingers down the V of her blouse, and his thumb caressed her nipple. She groaned and a tiny thrill zinged across her nape. "I know how you like me to kiss you here." He pressed a light kiss on her neck above her shoulder, trailed kisses up to her earlobe, and sucked it into her mouth.

She moaned, craned her neck to give him free access, and he kissed her hairline near her ear, in that one sensitive spot she loved. "Where else?"

His lips moved over her lips again. "Oh, I'll find out. We have forever to learn about each other. Starting now." He tongued apart her lips, and she fell into the light of his mind, the joy in his heart and the happiness in his soul, mirroring everything she felt. She buried one hand in his hair, pressed the other to his bare back, needing skin-to-skin contact like she needed water to quench her thirst. Their gentle kiss turned deep, leaving no walls to hide behind, no darkness to lose their way. His thoughts, feelings, and emotions lay on a silver platter for her taking. They crashed into her mind in an array of pureness, joining her desire until she couldn't tell which sensations belonged to her or which belonged to him. Their kiss spun them into a sky of frothy clouds until a trio of lightning flashes decimated her darkness for good.

DID YOU ENJOY
SEDUCING DARKNESS?

If you have a few moments, I'd love for you to leave a review for *SEDUCING DARKNESS* at your favorite online retailer or review site. Your review is greatly appreciated!

To stay up to date on Erin Richards' latest happenings, including new releases, sales, special announcements, exclusive excerpts, and giveaways, subscribe to her newsletter at: **www.erinrichards.com/connect.htm**

Catch the Psychic Justice Series from the beginning with *CHASING SHADOWS*.

ABOUT THE AUTHOR

After lamenting the lack of young adult books to read, award-winning and *USA Today* best-selling author, Erin Richards, wrote her first novel at the age of eighteen hoping to shift the tide. But the only tide she shifted was moving from high school to college. Then everyday life took its toll on her writerly dreams until she couldn't ignore the writing bug any longer. By then, she had immersed herself in reading adult fantasy and romance novels. Writing suspenseful paranormal and fantasy romance was a no brainer and she went on to publish two adult romance novels and hasn't stopped since. But her muse wanted to give that YA writing gig another chance, and Erin finally realized her lifelong dream of publishing a YA novel with the debut of *Vigilante Nights*.

Erin lives in California. In her spare time, she enjoys reading (of course!) and re-landscaping her backyard, even though she hates digging holes...unless she's burying fictional bodies! She also confesses to a fascination with American muscle cars...and reality TV shows!

Please visit Erin Richards online at:
www.erinrichards.com